# THE SIREN'S STING

Miranda Darling began her career as a fashion model in Paris and London, then went on to read English and Modern Languages at Oxford University. She travelled widely to countries such as Russia, Azerbaijan, Croatia, Namibia and Indonesia before returning to Australia to complete a Masters in Strategic Studies and Defence. She analysed new security threats for a think tank, where she published widely in newspapers and journals. She retains an interest in international intrigue and now writes full time.

# THE
# SIREN'S
# STING

# MIRANDA
# DARLING

*For Michelle*
*love*
*Miranda*
*x*

**ALLEN&UNWIN**

First published in 2011

Copyright © Miranda Darling 2011

Allen & Unwin
Sydney, Melbourne, Auckland, London

83 Alexander Street
Crows Nest NSW 2065
Australia
Phone:    (61 2) 8425 0100
Fax:        (61 2) 9906 2218
Email:     info@allenandunwin.com
Web:       www.allenandunwin.com

Cataloguing-in-Publication details are available
from the National Library of Australia
www.trove.nla.gov.au

ISBN 978 1 74175 920 4

Internal design by gogoGinko
Set in 11/16.5 pt Berkeley by Post Pre-press Group, Australia
Printed and bound in Australia by The SOS Print + Media Group

9 8 7 6 5 4 3 2

MIX
Paper from
responsible sources
FSC® C011217

The paper in this book is FSC certified.
FSC promotes environmentally responsible,
socially beneficial and economically viable
management of the world's forests.

*In loving memory of my grandmother, Margaret*

*No one among us can complain about his death, for whoever joined our ranks put on the shirt of Nessus. A man's moral worth is established only at the point where he is ready to give up his life in defence of his convictions.*

—Major-General Henning von Tresckow, condemned to death as one of the main conspirators in the 20 July plot to assassinate Adolf Hitler in 1944

*Some things are necessary evils, some things are more evil than necessary.*

—John le Carré

## PROLOGUE

A lithe woman with a gait like a panther kissed the Greek on the mouth and leapt into the waiting Riva speedboat.

She turned and looked back up to the dock. 'I'll see you in Monaco, darling.'

Her lover lifted a hand. 'You won't forget your promise, will you—between here and the yacht club?'

The woman laughed, revealing slightly pointed teeth. 'It's for life, darling. Even I could hardly forget a thing like that.' She covered her extraordinary kaleidoscope eyes with dark glasses and tied a Pucci scarf patterned in turquoise and coral around her hair. Then she gunned the engine and the beautiful wooden boat purred to life. 'Are you sure you won't come with me now?' she called back over her shoulder.

Passers-by stared at the couple: the handsome older woman in her silk scarf, the younger lover with his jet hair, his black glasses and tanned, rugged profile.

The young man smiled, tilted his head. 'I'll bring the yacht around this evening, *kukla*. There's no rush. We have the rest of our lives to be together.' He knelt and cast off the mooring ropes. The woman edged the Riva carefully between the other boats. Her skill at handling the boat was obvious, even in such a simple manoeuvre.

She motored slowly into the Bay of St Tropez, then, raising her slender hand in a final, elegant salute to the man watching on the pier, she opened up the throttle.

The explosion shattered the calm of the bay as the Riva was engulfed in a fireball. Somewhere on the dock a woman screamed, then there was only silence as a plume of black smoke shot into the sky, and the smell of petrol and ash filled the air. The wreckage of the boat, still aflame, began to sink slowly into the shining water, and the young lover on the pier, to his knees. He rested his forehead on the jetty and closed his eyes, shutting out the horror on the water.

Over the last of the flames, mystically undamaged, floated the Pucci scarf. It danced in the currents of hot air, hanging over the carnage like a silken eulogy to the smashed body below. It twirled and writhed there a moment, drawing the attention of the watchers on the dock, before it too succumbed to the violence of gravity and sank gently into the sea.

# 1

In the Crisis Response room at Hazard HQ, London, every soul was shattered with adrenaline and exhaustion. All eyes were on a large radar screen. The green blips indicated ships currently transiting the Gulf of Aden, off Somalia, a stretch of water more commonly known as Pirate Alley. Updates from the International Piracy Reporting Centre in Kuala Lumpur flashed across another, smaller screen:

> *0539 UTC: Posn: 13:51.7N–051:05.1E: Gulf of Aden.*
> *Pirates armed with RPG and automatic guns chased and opened fire on a chemical tanker underway. The master sent a distress message requesting help. Skiffs came very close to the tanker and pirates placed a ladder on the vessel's side to board. Due to evasive manoeuvres pirates failed to board the vessel. A military aircraft arrived at location and circled the tanker.*

'Not one of ours,' said Messinger abruptly, and turned his eyes back to the radar screen. The room's focus was on one large dot in particular; it was being shadowed by three much smaller dots moving at high speed.

'I don't like the look of those skiffs,' muttered Betterman. 'The *Atalanta* is going at fourteen knots—should be fast enough . . .'

'It could be fishermen chasing tuna,' suggested young Boyd.

David Rice, head of Hazard, massaged a grizzled temple. He was a bear of a man, ex-SAS, handsome with his iron-grey hair, unflappable. But the strain was showing, even on him. He knew only too well that it was not fishermen chasing tuna. The radio crackled to life. It was tuned to Channel 16, the international distress channel.

'This is Captain Mukkhanda of the *Atalanta*. We have three speedboats alongside. They have sent a message to stop.' The captain's voice was hesitant; everyone in the room could sense his fear.

The distress call was picked up by a nearby British naval frigate, the HMS *Stormont*, doing manoeuvres in the Gulf.

'Can you keep the craft astern?' came the response.

In the Crisis Response room, the Hazard crew could see the small dots gaining ground.

'They are still approaching at high speed. We can try. There is a possible mother ship. Port side.'

Everyone watched as the three blips formed a line and kept gaining.

There was a moment of silence, then the frigate: '*Alalanta*, this is Foxtrot 19. Increase speed to your maximum and start manoeuvring heavily to port and starboard. Immediately.'

Suddenly, over the radio, there was the tearing sound of an explosion, then another, accompanied by the *ack-ack* of automatic gunfire.

'This is *Atalanta*. The bridge is hit. The skiffs are alongside now, repeating their request to stop.'

Another explosion tore through the transmitter, then radio silence . . . The voice of the frigate asking the captain to respond. Nothing. The *Atalanta* had stopped broadcasting.

On the screen, the ship slowed visibly then suddenly veered left, heading for the coast of Somalia and the pirate town of Ely.

'That's not a good sign,' whispered Boyd.

Eyes fell away from the screen and a pall descended on the room. The incident report flashed up on the smaller screen, just in case anyone in the room had any doubts about what had just happened.

*1223 UTC: Posn: 04:59S–043:52E: 415NM south of Mogadishu, Somalia.*

*Pirates armed with machine guns and RPG attacked and fired upon a general cargo ship underway. The vessel enforced all effective counter-piracy measures but was unable to prevent hostile boarding. Pirates successfully hijacked the vessel with her 25 crew members and are sailing the vessel towards Somalia. Further information awaited.*

All thoughts turned to the twenty-five crew of the carrier, now prisoners. The chances were they would be held for months— even, god forbid, years—by the pirates. It was a nightmare. Eyes were lowered; and from a windowless room in the heart of London, what could anyone do?

The team was used to kidnappings: it was their job to get the victims back safely, to negotiate ransoms, organise handovers. A large whiteboard on the wall had a list of names running down the left-hand side. These were the unlucky ones currently being held by criminals, terrorists, guerrillas and the like. Other columns charted the location, time and date of the kidnappings, suspected perpetrators and so on. Large maps stuck with pins covered the other walls. Between them, they covered the globe, red and yellow pins clustered in Chechnya, Colombia, Russia, Iraq, Mexico, the

Philippines . . . Now a cluster of white pins was growing rapidly off the coast of Somalia and in the Gulf of Aden. The speed and concentration of the attacks was something else entirely: not a battle but a war.

'Can we get details of any injuries aboard *Atalanta*?' growled Rice. 'Call our negotiators, call the shipping line, call everyone and tell them to stand by for contact from the pirates.' His mouth was tight with tension, his fists clenching and unclenching, and he rocked onto the balls of his feet, a boxer ready for a bout.

Boyd was busy collating satellite pictures of the area, navy reports, reports from other vessels in the area. He sent the information to the captain at the Piracy Reporting Centre and in a moment the update flashed across the screen for all to see:

**All ships transiting waters around Somalia and Gulf of Aden**
*Possible pirate mother ship activity noted:*

*1228Z in position 08:58S–044:02E, approximately 310NM south-east of Dar es Salaam, Tanzania;*

*1608Z near position 08:09S–045:12E, approximately 360NM south-east of Dar es Salaam, Tanzania.*

*These areas will remain high risk for the next 24–48 hours as weather conditions continue to be conducive to small-boat operations. Mariners are warned to avoid transiting these waters if possible. If necessary to transit these waters, mariners are encouraged to use all counter-piracy measures and employ all best management practices.*

*Merchant vessels transiting this area are requested to report any suspicious activity.*

*The description of some of the suspected pirate mother ships are as follows: long, white Russian-made stern trawlers with names* STELLA MARIS *or* ARIDA *or* ATHENA.

The door to the incident room opened and three fresh bodies entered. Their anxious young faces betrayed the fact that they had some idea of what they were walking into—and yet not enough. Rice held up a hand in greeting, waved them in.

'Right all,' he barked, his throat hoarse from canned air and too much coffee, 'these three are junior support, here to relieve the burden and learn the ropes. Use them—that's what they're here for. Their names are Buttrose, Khan and Mellon.' He pointed to the two men and one woman, then addressed the newcomers directly. 'Lightning briefing, boys and girls: we've just had sighting and descriptions of a couple of mother ships. We are circulating these to all the captains transiting the area. Mother ships are large trawlers or tankers used by the pirates to refuel and supply the smaller attack skiffs. The mother ships are often vessels captured in earlier pirate attacks, so they can be trawlers, tankers, you name it. Their use means that the pirates can operate as far out to sea as they want to, in international waters or in remote oceans where target vessels normally consider themselves safe from shore-launched attacks.'

Rice glanced over Boyd's shoulder at the newest updates popping up on the computer screens, then returned to the briefing. 'Pirate activity,' he continued, 'is on the upswing the world over.' He gestured to the massive maps on the walls. 'From the west coast of Africa, through the Middle East, past India and Sri Lanka and deep into Southeast Asia. Pirate gangs make use of topographic particularities such as "chokepoints", narrow passages of water that make large ships vulnerable to assault. The Malacca Strait—' he stabbed at the pins '—is particularly vulnerable because the narrow body of water means ships have to slow down to transit the area. Somalia is now a hotspot due to massive instability on land, as are the waters off Nigeria.'

Rice stopped to take a long drink of water. 'What was once

little more than armed fishermen raiding the odd trawler has become something else entirely: the sea raiders are armed with sophisticated weapons and boats, their attacks are well-coordinated, audacious— and lethal.' His bloodshot eyes met those of each of the three newbies, striking that point home. 'Piracy is becoming very, very big business and Crisis Response is now a war room.' He straightened up. 'Questions?'

There were none.

Still the reports rolled in:

*1333 UTC: Posn: 17:27N–056:42E: 20NM E of Kuriya Muriya Islands, Oman (150NM ExN of Salalah).*
*Pirates attacked and hijacked a refrigerated cargo ship underway and took hostage the 21 crew members. Further report awaited.*

*0825 UTC: Posn: 08:42N–067:00W: 430NM NW of Boosaaso, Somalia.*
*Pirates in skiffs attacked cruise ship* ORIANA *underway. RPG and machine-gun fire reported.*

Rice closed his eyes. It was a minute before he could speak. 'The *Oriana*. Stevie's on that ship.'

# 2

Some four hundred and thirty nautical miles from Boosaaso, Somalia, dawn was breaking across the deck of the *Oriana*. The sky was pink and untroubled; silvery wavelets ran from the prow of the ship and, for those keen enough to be up with the sun, there was the distinct possibility of dolphins. Fortunately for Stevie, her client did not believe in exercise, nor in the hours before noon, and so she was free to attend the Awaken Sunrise yoga sessions each morning.

Stretching her hamstrings in a pose of questionable dignity, Stevie wondered at the vagaries of the job that had landed her aboard a luxury cruise ship, in sole charge of protecting what could be fairly described as a human tornado—ostensibly protecting the tornado's jewels from burglary; in reality, protecting her from herself.

For almost twenty years, Angelina Dracoulis had ruled the operatic stages of the world, all the while claiming to be just thirty years old. Any question of chronological improbability was magicked out of existence by the force of Angelina herself, an energy so powerful that it seemed even time would bend before her.

Angelina was contracted to give nightly performances to the rich, silver-streaked crowd aboard the *Oriana* and was extremely well rewarded for her efforts. As befitted a world-famous soprano, she was terribly dramatic and her current lover, Fernando Zorfanelli, an Italian film producer, had insisted she agree on private security to keep her safe, and his own demon jealousy under control.

Stevie had been voted by her colleagues—traitors all—at Hazard as the operative least likely to irritate, and most likely to understand, the diva. And Angelina was a total diva, no question: enormous cat's-eye sunglasses, red lipstick on a massive, mobile mouth, the curves of a racetrack and, of course, the jewels.

*La diva* was paranoid about her jewels, terrified that they might be stolen, and yet she could not travel without them. She had, with some difficulty, been persuaded to have paste copies made, but could not bear to wear them and travelled with both the real jewels and the fakes. The original pieces were indeed impressive—mostly mementoes from lovers—and Angelina claimed they made her feel adored and wanted.

'And I cannot sing when I feel vulnerable, Stevie, darling. My high notes sound shrill and insecure.'

She spent most of her time stretched on a chaise longue on the sundeck of her luxurious cabin, smoking the odd cigarette through an ebony holder, reading romantic novels, and ordering the handsome young stewards about. Angelina had been instructed to introduce Stevie as her travelling companion—nothing more— to anyone they might meet. It was safer that way. Occasionally she pestered Stevie for gossip on other celebrities she had worked with, but most of the time Stevie was left in peace and there was not much for her to do.

The shipboard security measures were excellent. There were discreet security cameras posted at regular intervals, the staff was trained to handle any contingency, and there were even flare guns (safely behind glass) on every private sundeck of the ship. It was the *Oriana's* maiden voyage and nothing was being left to chance.

It seemed everyone in shipping had learnt a lesson in hubris from the *Titanic*. In any case, as Stevie had reminded an almost-hysterical Angelina several times during one particularly stormy night on board, their route was to take them from the Caribbean to Greece and there was not a jot of cold water between the two destinations. Icebergs were not going to be a problem and she should remove all visions of herself freezing tragically and beautifully on a floating packing crate out of her head.

Despite, or perhaps indeed because of, her dramatics, Angelina was an incredible singer and deserved the reverence she inspired. The voice, she had explained to Stevie late one night over a crème de menthe, was the real mirror to the soul.

'And my soul has suffered as only the soul of a Greek woman can. The pain changed the timbre of my voice forever. That is why it is so much in demand.'

If her soul was the key to her voice, the rest of her secret spell seemed to lie, as far as Stevie could tell, in slurping raw eggs before each performance, in remarkable vocal exercises, and in a tortoise-shell comb that absolutely had to be in its place in the thick black chignon before she would deign to sing.

Angelina was not modest but she was extraordinary. She saw herself as the guardian of a fantastic talent, and Stevie wondered what it would feel like to have a talent like that, to be the best in the world at something, to be so sure of yourself and your destiny. It must indeed be a marvellous thing. Every morning would bring with it certainty and passion and confidence that you were doing exactly the right thing in the right time and place. Stevie would have given a lot for that sort of comfort. Obviously one had to be born under the lucky star, but perhaps it was a matter of nurture as well as nature . . .

Had she neglected a burgeoning talent at a tender age, a skill that might have led her to this golden path of certainty? Had she overlooked something? Arms stretching out of their sockets, head still inverted, Stevie could not think of a single thing. She was neither musical, nor artistic, nor could she run very fast; she was far too self-contained for the stage and ball sports were anathema to her; her cooking was simple and edible but hardly something she could call a talent.

Focusing on the positives—this was a yoga class after all—she listed the things she could do well: fence, shoot, ride, disappear. All in all, not a very promising list for a small, birdlike girl with big ideas.

A small boat on the horizon caught her attention and distracted her from these somewhat unhelpful musings. The Gulf was full of small wooden skiffs, manned by fishermen out hunting the fast-moving tuna schools. But this one was very far from land. She knew that the skiffs were also used by people smugglers taking desperate Somali refugees to the promise of a relatively better world—and it was indeed relative—in Yemen. The smugglers were ruthless, and they had reason to be: in Yemen, people smugglers could still be crucified; if the wrong coastguard approached, they were likely to dump their cargo of souls into the sea to save themselves. Stevie shook her head slowly and breathed in through her nose. She had to stop seeing menace and darkness in every situation. It was not a Healthy Outlook.

She could not resist glancing back out at the skiff. Even with her head upside down, Stevie could tell it was going fast, very fast, and that it was moving towards them. The class retreated into the Pose of the Child for the final five minutes of the session. Stevie knelt forward, turned her head and rested her cheek on the deck, her eyes still on the little boat. Another like it appeared and Stevie felt a familiar prickle at the back of her neck. She didn't like the little boats one bit—something felt wrong.

She had long ago made a pact with herself to always listen to her instincts, no matter how absurd they seemed, and so, while the rest of the class rolled up their rubber mats and went down to a papaya breakfast, Stevie remained where she was, feigning meditation, green eyes steady on the horizon.

A third boat had now joined the first two.

No fishing-boat engine could propel the craft forward at that speed. She raced to one of the on-deck telescopes used for sight-seeing and trained the lens.

The boats were fibreglass-hulled Zodiacs—not fishing boats at all—with high-powered engines. In the first, she could make out eight men dressed in combat fatigues. Could they be from the coast-guard? But as far as she knew, Somalia did not have a coastguard, and in any case, they were too far out from land.

Perhaps it was an American or British patrol helping to keep the Bab-el-Mandeb free of drug traffickers and smugglers. The boats sped closer and the prickling on Stevie's neck turned to ice. The men in the other two boats were dressed like locals in a mish-mash of T-shirts with Western logos and traditional headdress, baseball caps and ragged shorts, their dark faces blank of expression. In his arms, each man cradled a sub-machine gun, except for the one at the very front—not more than a boy—who held a rocket-propelled grenade launcher steady at his side.

Stevie leapt up and headed for the bridge. Surely the captain had seen the boats too.

But when she got there the door to the bridge was locked. Stevie hammered on it but no one answered.

The first boat was almost alongside. The man standing at the bow of the first boat raised the RPG to his shoulder and fired directly at the bridge.

There was an explosion like thunder and the deck shook.

*Pirates.*

Stevie's ears were ringing as she ran along the deck. Cabin doors were opening, balcony doors sliding apart, voices rising in confusion. As Stevie sprinted towards Angelina's cabin, she noticed the figure of a man by the lifeboat, standing still and staring out to sea. Stevie recognised him almost at once. Unlike many of the other passengers, who had obviously still been fast asleep at the time of the attack, Socrates Skorpios was immaculate in a pale summer suit and navy tie, his dark hair combed, his tortoiseshell glasses in place. He was watching the pirates. As she passed, she saw him calmly take a cigar from his pocket and light it, eyes still on the sea wolves below. Stevie had a second to marvel at his cool before she turned her mind back to the task at hand. Finding Angelina.

**The captain's voice came over** the intercom, preceded by the usual soft ringing of bells. The voice, steady and firm, told all passengers to stay put in their cabins, to lock their doors and not to venture out for any reason.

There was another explosion, this one muffled by the thick glass and the heavy panelling of the ship's interior. In the breakfast hall, waiters were trying to fold stiff-limbed silver-tips under tables. The room was surprisingly quiet, the waiters calm, the passengers' faces frightened and pliant. Stevie wanted to stop and help, but Angelina would not be handling this well.

After some knocking and reassurance, Angelina opened the door to the cabin. Her eyes and hair were wild with sleep and fright, and she had stuffed her jewels into her brassiere.

'Stevie! For heaven's sake! The cabin boy said *pirates*?!' She dragged Stevie into the cabin, locking the door behind them. Stevie could now see other precious stones spread across the bed behind her, clothes all over the floor. *Where was Sanderson?*

There was another explosion and the ship swung to one side, then the other. Clearly the captain was engaging in evasive manoeuvres, swinging from port to starboard and back, trying to create a huge wash that would swamp the attack vessels. Stevie suspected that the Zodiacs would ride it out with ease.

From the cabin porthole, Stevie could see two high-pressure arcs of white water shooting over the side. The sailors had turned on the powerful fire hoses and were spraying the water down the sides to repel boarding. The attack craft were right alongside the ship now, almost touching it. One man, wearing a balaclava, held a coil of rope with a rappelling hook attached. There was a burst of machine-gun fire.

Water rushed over the porthole and the raiders became the blurry, terrifying figures of nightmares.

Angelina staggered to the window. 'I want to see these pirates!' she demanded. But Stevie refused to let her look. She was frightened enough herself, and Angelina's certain hysteria, Stevie knew from experience, would be hard to handle in a confined space.

Sanderson, Angelina's maid, a staunch British lady of the old school, suddenly appeared from the bathroom holding Angelina's robe. She seemed somewhat dazed.

Action would help keep Angelina calm, Stevie decided. 'Quick, get me all the paste copies of the gems,' she said to Sanderson.

Sanderson hurried to the bed and carefully began to separate the impostors from the real stones. Stevie laid these paste jewels in the empty velvet boxes that lay scattered about.

'We must hide them!' Angelina was pacing the cabin like a caged tigress, her silk negligee falling from her shoulders, her famous hair snaking down her back. She could have been Cleopatra facing the sack of Egypt—one of her most famous roles—and Stevie suspected that a small part of Angelina felt this also and was rising to the occasion.

'If those bandits find them, I'll be ruined—I'll never sing again,' she moaned.

Stevie ducked into the bathroom and came out with boxes of sanitary pads. She emptied the boxes and began stuffing them with Angelina's precious stones.

'What are you doing?!' This did not fit with Angelina's ideas for the staging of the drama at all.

'What is the one thing men—all men, pirates, brigands, play-boys—won't go near?'

Angelina's eyes gleamed. Men were something she knew about, and she knew Stevie was right. She and Sanderson knelt on the floor and began to help. Stevie didn't care about the jewels but she couldn't get through to Angelina while she was still panicking about them. Hiding them would keep her client's mind off the real problem: they were all sitting ducks being stalked by thieves and, quite likely, murderers. Stevie shivered and forced down her fear. She had to maintain her clarity. Her mind raced, looking for a plan—anything.

The bursts of gunfire were getting wilder. The pirates were obviously trying to drive the sailors manning the hoses away from the deck so they could swarm aboard. A fire alarm went off on deck, more shots.

'Leave the jewellery boxes open—strew them about the room,' Stevie told Sanderson. 'It will distract them and hopefully they won't bother looking for more. There are hundreds of cabins. You and Angelina get into the bathroom and lock the door. If there is gunfire, get into the bath. You'll be safer there.'

Stevie opened the timber door to the sundeck and crawled out. The air was thick with smoke and the roaring noise of engines, high-pressure water, sharp shots. Stevie crept to the edge of the deck and saw the three Zodiacs riding the water below. The three drivers, all in black balaclavas despite the heat, steadily and skil-fully kept the attack boats right alongside the cruise ship, poisonous remoras watching for their chance to attach.

The boats carried massive spare tanks of gasoline and Stevie saw one pirate with a hand-held GPS. That explained how they had managed to get so far out to sea. There was probably a mother ship waiting for them just beyond the horizon, bobbing in international waters, beyond law.

There was a long burst of gunfire. One of the pirates, in a Leonardo DiCaprio T-shirt and no older than seventeen, gripped by adrenaline, was spraying bullets about like Rambo and they were ricocheting lethally. Stevie smelt gasoline.

It wouldn't be long before people started dying.

Her heart was calm and her head grew suddenly very clear. She crawled back to the safety of the wall. The distress flare was in its usual spot, behind glass. Stevie smashed the glass with her elbow and took out the gun. Cautiously, she made her way back to the edge and knelt, steadying her shoulder on the railing. The boats were directly below. She knew the flare gun wouldn't be powerful enough to pierce the gasoline tanks—that would take a miracle—but she had to do something. Taking careful aim at the first boat with the boy wild-firing the automatic weapon, she shot the flare gun into the middle of it.

There was a loud bang and a fizz, an arc of hot light, and the flare hit the rubber boat. For a second it lay burning, schitzing red smoke like a failed firework. Then it flared, spewing endless thick red smoke, blinding the drivers, terrifying the spraying boy, who cried out in terror. A crimson thundercloud formed around the boats, all but obscuring them. Stevie heard shouts, then someone fired a grenade. There was a massive explosion somewhere by Stevie's balcony, and a fierce blast of burning air. Stevie fell hard against the doorframe.

Inside, Angelina was screaming, her voice pitch-perfect even in panic; Stevie could hear her, only everything was muffled, as if swaddled in cotton wool. Her face was burning and there was blood on the carpet. She tried to stand, to say something about the possible danger of fire and the need to evacuate the room, but no words came out, or at least she did not hear them if they did. The floor swam a little; Stevie concentrated on stilling the ripples.

Then the chief steward was at the door. There was a blanket over her shoulders, someone holding her head back, the corridor milling with people . . .

Had the pirates taken control of the ship?

Stevie, Angelina and the helpful Sanderson were swept along the hall, Sanderson adjusting a silk robe over Angelina's shoulders as they walked. The ballroom had been transformed into a first-aid station and stewards were busy handing out bottles of water and blankets although no one seemed too interested in either, but rather fired questions at anyone in uniform. There was no sign of armed intruders.

The ship's doctor was attending to the injured (shock and awe; one or two bruises). Stevie caught sight of her face in the enormous dancing mirror and started: blood was trickling into her eye from a cut high on her forehead; her face was milk-white, and the heat from the first explosion had singed both her eyebrows to little orange bristles. She looked a lot worse than she felt, if only she could clear her ears . . .

Someone took Stevie by the arm and pulled her towards the doctor. She grabbed the poor man by the arm and shouted, 'Pirates?' The venerable doctor shook his head and mouthed the word, 'Gone.' A wave of relief washed through Stevie. He examined her face and ears then reached for a pen and paper. He wrote out his diagnosis in a cramped biro scrawl: the cut was quite deep and would have to be stiched; there was no permanent damage to the eardrum. Stevie's hearing should gradually return. She was sat on a chair, her cut dabbed with alcohol and injected with a painkiller. Then she felt the familiar, slightly sickening, tug of the needle and thread in her skin. She focused on the captain, who was now stand-ing on the band stage with a microphone.

Stevie couldn't hear what he was saying but his face was grave and resolute. She tried to lip-read without much success; the assem-bled passengers clapped vigorously then something was said about signals and the Dutch.

*Surely the pirates hadn't been Dutch?*

She turned to Angelina and, although her own ears were the ones with the problem, Stevie found herself gesticulating as she spoke, as if the diva were the aurally challenged one. Ange-lina, having by now rearranged her undergarments and gathered some measure of composure, took a slow breath, parted her lovely lips and began to sing, completely unselfconsciously, at a crystal-shattering pitch. Repeated at such an extraordinary frequency, the captain's message made it through to Stevie.

The ship had been attacked by pirates and had undertaken evasive manoeuvres. These manoeuvres had been successful and the captain wished to thank the sailors for their bravery, especially the person who had fired the flare gun. As a precaution, however, a signal had been sent to a Dutch frigate that was patrolling these waters. Fortunately, the frigate had been relatively nearby at the time of the attack; the pirates off Somalia had the run of something like three million square nautical miles and there was no way an area that size could be successfully patrolled.

Although the damage to the bridge had not crippled it, the owners of the luxury cruise ship were taking no chances and the *Oriana* would dock at Aden, where a thorough damage assessment would be done. Specially chartered planes would evacuate the passengers from there in forty-eight hours' time.

Stevie wondered about the flare gun—something didn't sit quite right. Her attack would certainly have been a useful distraction, but it seemed too little to deter such a professional and well-equipped assault. The captain's evasive manoeuvres, coupled with the aggressive use of the firehoses must have done the trick.

Angelina opened her mouth again. Stevie's hearing was fast returning with the help of the doctor's drops, but Angelina was enjoying her role: 'O-O-O-Oh!' she sang for Stevie. 'The gala dinner planned for the last night on board has been moved forward to tonight. Please see the chief steward for details.'

The unleashing of the magnificent voice had caused a frisson among the passengers and Stevie noticed it had attracted Socrates Skorpios, who was now making his way towards them. He and Angelina had been circling each other since Port Charlotte Amalie; he sat at the front table at every performance and she carefully and infuriatingly ignored him; he sent her vast bouquets of white roses every night (until the on-board florist ran out and he had to make do with pale pink), which she accepted as no more than her due.

What did he remind Stevie of, with his great flat head and low, powerful shoulders . . .? He stopped at their table and smiled, taking Angelina's expectantly raised hand and kissing it elegantly.

'Madame.'

*A great white shark, hunter of mammals and the most dangerous fish in the sea.*

'I trust the events of this morning did not disturb you too much.' He smiled, showing perfect white teeth. 'My private plane will be waiting in Aden. I would be delighted if you and your companion—' his eyes shifted briefly towards Stevie '—would join me on board tomorrow morning. We fly to Turin.'

Angelina raised her chin imperiously and gave him a long, steady stare. Finally she declared, 'Turin will be fine.'

Skorpios gave a small bow and left.

The diva fanned herself. 'The veal is excellent in Turin,' she declared to no one in particular. 'One must have the veal.'

As soon as she could, Stevie escaped to the upper deck and fresh air. A dozen sailors stood to attention, powerful binoculars in hand. Their eyes scanned the horizon. They seemed shaken, as well they might be. Stevie herself felt like she could do with a whisky and some. Yet there was a tension she could not explain but only feel in the men. She followed their gaze and thought she could see something.

'May I look?' she asked the nearest and youngest crewman.

He looked down at the bedraggled and scabbed creature beside him. 'It's just a routine watch, madam. Please go back inside.' His voice was a little strangled, taut. Now Stevie definitely needed those binoculars.

'I fired that flare gun. I think you need to give me a look,' she repeated firmly.

The sailor could not hide his surprise—everyone knew about the flare that had helped drive off the pirates but none of the crew had claimed responsibility yet—and he handed the glasses over. Stevie spent a quick moment adjusting them, then scanned the horizon. .

The ice crackled back into her veins and she almost fell.

Out along the horizon, like a malevolent escort, were the three Zodiacs. They maintained the same speed as the *Oriana*, not coming any closer, not retreating, just riding. The crewman beside her had now dropped all pretence of command and his fear was naked in his voice when he asked, 'What are they doing? Will they come back?'

Stevie lowered the glasses and shook her head. 'It's a message. They're telling us that we got away because they let us.'

It was fortunate for the operators of the *Oriana* that Angelina Dracoulis thrived on drama of all kinds. Rather than frightening her, the incident with the pirates seemed to nourish her, and she prepared for the evening's gala performance with extra enthusiasm. She insisted that both Stevie and Sanderson stay with her in her cabin. Stevie was instructed to lie down on the massive bed and not move.

Several bottles of champagne arrived on a trolley—fortifications, courtesy of Mr Skorpios, the nice young cabin boy had informed them. He too was pressed upon to stay, drawn into the small party, and took to filling and refilling all empty flutes, including his own.

Stevie managed to slip out onto what was left of Angelina's stately deck. Half the rails had been damaged by the grenade explosion. Stevie wrapped her arm around a pole for support and took out her slim phone. There was a missed call already showing—Hazard Limited. No doubt they had already heard of the attack from their sources and wanted a report. She called back on David Rice's direct line.

'Stevie! I've been worried sick. What the hell happened out there?' Rice's voice cracked with concern and Stevie felt a rush of affection for her boss. 'Is anyone hurt?' he asked briskly.

'Everyone is fine.' Stevie was having trouble hearing her

boss—the wind and the cotton wool in her ears weren't helping—
and she was shouting into the phone as a result. 'Angelina is safe
and well.' She told him succinctly about the attack.

Rice was silent for a long moment, then he said, 'I can't seem
to keep you out of trouble—I can't believe this happened. We're in
contact with the Dutch frigate. They've got two Merlin helicopters
shadowing you until you dock in Aden.'

*So are the pirates*, Stevie almost added out loud—but she
didn't want to cause Rice any more concern. The pirates would not
attack again; not this time anyway.

'Zorfanelli is going mad with worry,' Rice was saying. 'Where
is Angelina?'

Stevie glanced over her shoulder. 'Celebrating life with her
maid and the cabin boy and a trolley load of champagne.'

There was a quizzical silence on the line. Stevie smiled as
she imagined his dear face twist with puzzlement. David didn't do
frivolity very well. It wasn't his thing. He was ex-SAS and his shell
of imperturbability seemed impossible to crack. One day . . . She
was sure there was more inside. She remembered the great booming
laughs on her parents' terrace, the way David had danced with her
mother—was it the tango?—and talked for hours with her father.
She wanted to open him up again, be the key to that lock. So far she
had not succeeded and it pained her.

Rice was saying something but her ears were ringing again
and she couldn't make out the rest.

'I'm having trouble hearing you—I'll send a full report to Josie
this afternoon.'

'I said, we'll sort something out in Aden.' Rice was shouting.

'Not to worry,' Stevie assured him. 'Angelina has befriended
a gentleman who wishes to fly us to Turin on his plane: Socrates
Skorpios.'

There was silence. 'A gentleman—not the way I would describe him.' Then, after another pause, 'Zorfanelli will not be happy.'

'I see the problem.' Zorfanelli was paying Hazard; it was Stevie's job to keep the client happy. 'Nevertheless, Skorpios has a plane . . . it's that, or forty-eight hours in Aden. Explain to Zorfanelli that it's an emergency situation. Angelina's nerves might not hold up under too much stress and uncertainty. Zorfanelli is very keen on Angelina Dracoulis' nerves,' she added, remembering their first meeting with the film producer.

'Fine. I'll see you in Turin, then—I'll call when I land.'

'I could book somewhere for dinner,' she suggested tentatively. 'The veal in Turin is very good . . .'

'There won't be time for dinner, Stevie,' he replied curtly, and ended the phone call.

Her fingers hovered for a moment over the number three on her phone, the speed-dial still assigned to Henning. Should she call? Knowing Henning, he would probably turn out to be in the Yemen on some mad, literary treasure hunt and insist on coming down to visit her. She smiled for a moment at the thought of seeing his dear face, then decided there was enough excitement on her plate right now. She needed fewer complications, not more; she would be sensible and concentrate on Angelina. Stevie put the phone away.

**In the great ballroom, the** passengers assembled for the gala dinner, dressed in their finest clothes and jewels. Stevie noticed that a new camaraderie had sprung up between the guests, walls of reserve tumbled down, and the conversation sparkled with laughter. It was an effect she had seen before: the collective brush with death making living all the sweeter.

When Angelina appeared on stage later that evening, there was an intake of breath, a wave of murmurs that broke into enthusiastic applause as she reached the microphone. Dressed in a floor-length gown of red sequins, her hair pinned into a beehive and decorated with shining starfish, she looked like a mermaid dragged from the fantastical deep. Stevie, sitting between Sanderson in her sensible shoes and an older couple from Bath, scanned the room for Skorpios.

She spotted him, alone at his usual table, immaculate in his dinner jacket and tinted glasses. He watched Angelina, his face aglow with desire.

Angelina, too, seemed transformed, her blood aroused by the pirates. There was a suppressed fire in her voice, an intensity to her gestures, that hadn't been there on other nights. She had painted a Coptic eye on each eyelid and when she closed them the effect was eerie; it was as if she never blinked, was always watching, like a sorceress or an oracle. As she sang her last aria, 'Tu che di ciel sei cinta' from *Turandot*, she left the stage and began to wander among the tables—something she had never done before. Angelina headed for Skorpios, alone at his table. There, she sang her death as if it were just for him, as if she were dying for him.

'*You who are girded with ice,*
*vanquished by such fire,*
*you will love him too!*'

She picked up a butter-knife from the table and held it as if she were about to stab herself in the heart. The entire ballroom was enchanted; Skorpios was transfixed.

It seemed that Angelina had netted the great white shark, but Stevie sensed danger. She had a flash of intuition that it would bring her client no good at all. To Stevie's sensitive antennae, Skorpios and his charm exuded menace.

These little bursts of insight had been coming to her quite frequently since her poisoning by taipan venom in St Moritz. She could only put it down to some kind of lingering after-effect, the removal of some block in her mind, or the killing of some part of her rational brain that had made room for this . . . could she call it a gift? It would have been a wonderful boon, if only this perception could be directed and controlled. Unfortunately it usually seemed to attach itself to strangers, or people with whom Stevie had little connection.

# 3

Skorpios' jet cruised smoothly over the Rub' al Khali desert, carrying Angelina and Stevie, Sanderson, Skorpios and a pale man in a suit who introduced himself as Tanner. The interior of the plane was comfortable, elegant, cream and tan to match its owner; a golden scorpion was painted on the tail, and the same motif decorated the china and the linen napkins of the in-flight catering service.

Angelina lay back in her seat, a silk sleeping mask over her eyes, refusing to acknowledge how far from the ground they were. She preferred trains, boats and automobiles. Stevie, on the other hand, stared through the large oval window, mesmerised by the endless sand below, the desolation, the space, the forever-flowing dunes. The Rub' al Khali was probably the largest sand desert on earth; the name meant 'empty quarter' in Arabic, and even the Bedouin only ever traced its perimeter.

High up in Skorpios' upholstered oasis, sipping on fresh blood-orange juice, Stevie thought the desert looked beautiful: the dunes made extraordinary patterns on the earth, and here and there they caught the sun at a particular angle and shone like water. She thought of the explorers who had crossed it in the 1930s and 40s and wondered at the courage it would have taken to head into that emptiness. She, for one, was not that brave. It could possibly be conceded that she had done some brave things in her life, but these deeds had been thrust upon her as the only course of action morally imaginable at the time—not something she had sought and seized with relish. She was not an action woman: she could not run very fast; she favoured ballet slippers over combat boots, never swore, and still suffered from nightmares; she did not enjoy confrontation of any kind. She was reluctant to face risk, and it was a quality that made her very good at her job. Her art lay in her ability to pass unnoticed, to slip in and out of the cracks of life, to be quietly invisible.

The memory that the desert forced forward into Stevie's mind finally broke through her defences. It had been a different desert, one of the sand seas of Algeria, behind the Atlas Mountains . . .

Stevie's eyes filled with tears and she closed them quickly, wishing she had had the foresight to pack a silk sleeping mask like La Dracoulis.

Five years old and her parents were the centre of her tiny universe. Marlise and Lockie, treasure hunters, furnishers of *objets de curiosité* for private collectors all over the world: dukes, tycoons, passionate connoisseurs, heiresses, superstars and aspirants. Often little Stevie was left in the care of her grandmother Didi in Switzerland while her parents went on foraging expeditions to parts exotic; on other, terribly exciting occasions, she went along too.

The high desert sun had made her feel sleepy, sitting in the back of the Algerian jeep. Her mother tossed her a patterned shawl and she snuggled down on the back seat and dozed, enjoying the soft bumping and jolting of the car. Her mother's scream woke her, the jeep screeching to a stop. Stevie flew off the back seat onto the floor. Horses' hooves all around them; shouts; gunshots; the utter stillness of death. Stevie had closed her eyes and curled into a ball, almost too shocked to breathe.

The little girl was eventually found by the French Foreign Legion and sent to live with her grandmother. Rumours circulated—Marlise and Lockie had been mistaken for French spies . . . it was a robbery gone wrong . . . The perpetrators of the shooting were never found.

Stevie's universe folded, crushed by fear and loss and sadness; she didn't speak for half a year.

When she opened her eyes, she saw Sanderson's kind, plain face looking at her. She held out a pair of sunglasses—Angelina's cat's eyes. Stevie hesitated—the glasses were iconic, after all—but then she took them and slipped them on.

'Thank you,' she whispered gratefully. Sanderson simply nodded and turned back to her crossword.

Skorpios was pacing the aisle, a glass of milky ouzo in hand. He found it difficult, Stevie had noticed, to keep still. The man was in perpetual motion. With Angelina resting, and Tanner's well of conversation apparently now dry, he turned to Stevie.

'Look.' His large hand gestured towards her window and Stevie noticed his signet ring, decorated with a scorpion, its tail up, ready to strike. She looked down and saw a forest of steel and glass crystals rising from the sand. 'Dubai. The mirage of the Middle East.' He smiled his shark's smile. 'Have you ever been there?'

Steve shook her head, grateful for the protection of Angelina's sunglasses.

'It is a vile place,' her host continued. 'New pharaohs building modern-day pyramids with slaves from southern Asia. And it will end the same way, with sand blowing in the doors of their pleasure palaces, every glass cube empty, and the bleached skeletons of the slaves who built it poking through the dunes.'

Stevie stared at Skorpios. 'I wouldn't have suspected you were a man of such sentiment, Mr Skorpios,' she said quietly.

'The desert reclaims what it will, eventually. Only the Bedouin, who shift with the sand itself, can last in the desert. It is merely ego to think the laws of nature will change for you.' He turned his gaze back to Stevie and smiled. 'But without ego, nothing truly great would ever be achieved—ego is the audacity to begin a task that everyone else thinks is mad.'

The ouzo was drained from the glass and Skorpios leant against Stevie's headrest. 'There are three forces in the universe: Zim, Zar and Zam: war, women and gold. Kings and countries have always struggled to control these forces with regulations and rules. But for some men, there are no laws; the rules of other men do not interest them, nor do the laws of the universe. Power begins and ends with them.' He clinked the single ice cube left in the glass. 'It is a choice to move beyond God.'

Stevie remembered Skorpios during the pirate attack; truly he had seemed self-possessed and utterly unafraid: a man in control of the universe. She took a small sip of her orange juice. 'And have you made that choice, Mr Skorpios?' she asked as lightly as she could. 'To move beyond God?'

Skorpios stared at her for an uncomfortable moment, then smiled and made a gesture with his hand; it could have meant death, or eternity.

**Turin was asleep by the** time their car pulled up outside the Turin Palace. Stevie ran a hot bath in the huge tub and slid in, closing her eyes and feeling the exhaustion leak out of her into the bathwater. Tomorrow she would see David, and she couldn't wait. He always made her feel safe and comfortable and happy.

The next morning she breakfasted in her room, swaddled in

her bathrobe and enjoying the slightly faded grandeur of the large hotel suite. Like the city itself, there was no fizzle and glitz, only an understated, upholstered comfort that had been there forever. She poured herself a cup of steaming black coffee and pulled the end off a *cornetto*. The pastries looked exactly like croissants, but they were chewier and tasted vaguely of orange water—the taste of breakfast in Italy.

Stevie opened her small suitcase and sighed. The contents were more suitable for the Bahamas via Broadway than a stay in Turin but, when pirates interfere with plans, what can you do? She hung her evening gowns and pastel-coloured Bermuda shorts, neatly lined up her three pairs of shoes. Underwear she arranged in a careful pattern. It was important to be meticulous; any disruption to the order was an infallible way to tell if the room had been searched in one's absence. It was a habit that had served Stevie well in the past and she followed it whenever she unpacked anywhere.

Having booby-trapped her smalls, there was nothing else to do. Angelina would sleep until noon, at the earliest, then had threatened to descend on Turin's opera house, the Teatro Regio, in the afternoon; David Rice had said he would call when he landed at Turin airport. They would make plans then. Stevie drummed her heels on the bed base then picked up the heavy plastic telephone receiver and called her friend Leone Moro, who lived in the hills outside the city. Happily he was at home and sounded delighted to hear from her. He invited her to lunch at the Whist Club.

Dressed in a snakeskin-print silk-jersey wrap dress and delicate leather sandals she went to find a newspaper.

The morning air was still pink and cool, and filled with the smell of coffee and car exhausts and sugar. She picked up *Il Corriere*, *La Nazione* and *La Repubblica* and headed into the covered colonnades that crossed Turin. Modelled on Paris, the boulevards were covered to offer protection from the freezing mountain winters and the scorching sun of summer. The walkways were always dim and cool, the marble floors worn to a grooved and bumped smoothness by the centuries of footfall.

Outside the Caffè Torino in the Piazza San Carlo, a worn brass bull was set flat into the marble floor. As was the custom, Stevie stepped carefully onto its testicles for luck. Then she entered the café and ordered a cappuccino. She only ever drank them in Italy; they just didn't taste the same anywhere else. She began to leaf through the papers.

*Il Corriere* ran the story on the third page, describing a cruise ship attacked by pirates off the coast of Somalia. They mentioned La Dracoulis and a lucky escape, but no details. The other two papers had not picked up the story. Someone was working hard to keep it quiet. And so you would, if you were in the shipping business, Stevie thought to herself.

The planet was seventy per cent water and ninety per cent of the world's goods were transported through it. The pirate attacks were driving up the prices of the goods transiting dangerous waters, driving up insurance premiums, and absorbing the attentions of the navies of several nations, including the Dutch. There was also the personal cost in violence and mental anguish to those directly involved, and their families. It was a problem in Southeast Asia, off the coast of Nigeria, and especially Somalia. It was embarrassing to some that there seemed little to be done about the attack teams of wooden dhows full of Somalians with rocket-propelled grenade launchers and machine guns and rickety wooden ladders. The civilised world had thought it had moved on from Blackbeard and Barbarossa. These attacks were an uncomfortable reminder of the veins of savagery and violence and hunger that ran so close beneath that civilised skin.

Stevie sat up straighter. She was trying to remember to have good posture at all times. Her grandmother Didi believed posture was at the heart of elegance.

The pirates that had attacked the *Oriana* had been far more than hungry fishermen. Their attack vessels had been new Zodiacs with powerful engines and they had been armed with shiny new weapons, many of them protected by body armour; even more telling was their skill: the assault had smacked of special forces training. Pirates were growing more professional, thanks to experience and the fruits of their earlier attacks, but this was something beyond a hand-held GPS and a better engine. This had been expertly planned and executed. The raiders had made a decision to withdraw. Possibly they had not expected the passengers on the cruise ship to fight back. In a way, this unnerved Stevie more than anything; it pointed to strategy. She also knew in her bones that the next attack would be more vicious.

Stevie shuddered. *The next attack.*

People would die. The pirates would have to use extreme violence to reinstil the paralysing fear that was so useful to them in their attacks. Strategic ferocity—all organised crime groups used it. Fear was the great controller. Machiavelli had put it in his advice to princes: is it better to be loved or feared as a prince? he had asked. The answer to his own question had been 'feared'. Stevie wondered whether David Rice would have come to the same conclusion. Hazard had recently moved into maritime security, in response to a growing amount of requests from shipping clients for threat assessments, physical protection, and marine kidnap and ransom policies. The pirates were increasingly becoming David Rice's problem.

Stevie finished her coffee and wandered the city for an hour, heading down to the banks of the river where, even on a sunny summer's day, the banks were shrouded in mist. The heat of the day was beginning to build. Turin was one of the most understated cities in Europe. Despite its beauty and its ancient history—it had been a Roman city—it was not a place for ordinary tourists. Perhaps there were not enough splendid monuments, no recognisable landmarks, no obvious reasons to visit, and very few big hotels.

Dark undercurrents of mystery ran through the town, once the home of Italy's kings. It was an area steeped in witchcraft, prone to deep fog, home to the famous shroud of Turin. Its scale was typically regal, dwarfing the average citizen; even its streetlamps were capped with crowns. Massive statues of pilots and steel workers joined those of kings and knights.

Stevie headed back to the Piazza San Carlo to find Leone waiting. He came towards her in the cool shadows of the arcade, dressed in his pale straw-coloured linen suit, a blue shirt of Oxford cloth and a Panama hat. He smiled the moment he caught sight of her and raised his palms.

'*Cara* . . .' He kissed her on both cheeks then stood back and took a good look at her. 'What happened?!' Leone was looking at the stitches over her eye.

Stevie smiled. 'I bumped into a cupboard door on the cruise ship—it's nothing.'

Leone looked at her critically. 'You haven't changed so much. Maybe a little age, a tiny line of care around your eyes . . .' He traced the edge of her face with a gentle finger. 'But still *la piccola* Stevie.'

Stevie raised her eyebrows in amusement and winced. Her cut stung. Leone was not an ordinary man. His name suited him, with his heavy head, his thick greying curls, his clipped beard; he was tall and magnetic and utterly eccentric. He had not changed at all.

He offered her his arm. 'Let's eat.'

The Whist Club owned a building on the square. Their

rooms were up on the first floor—the *piano nobile*—and included a huge and splendid ballroom with perfectly polished wooden floors and mirrors and chandeliers everywhere. The room was dark and delightfully cool. Stevie felt an urge to spin across it in her flat sandals, an urge she fortunately managed to resist. They moved to the club sitting room, with its gold silk damask-covered walls and furniture, and ordered Crodino. The waiter, very correct and wearing white gloves, brought the bright orange drinks and some salted crackers, then seemed to disappear into the wall. Stevie remarked on it.

'Oh, the Whist Club is full of secret passages and entry ways. And discreet rooms where a gentleman may retire after a heavy lunch and take a nap . . .'

'Or . . .?'

Leone smiled. 'Or.'

Stevie looked over at a tall, handsome man in a dove grey suit—young and slim, with a heavy head of blond curls. She recognised one of the younger members of a major Torinese industrial family. He was having a Campari with a severe-looking bald man, and a very glamorous woman dressed in caramel suede and golden bangles. The sofas were arranged so that the members were visible to each other, but just out of earshot.

Leone noticed Stevie's glance. 'He might be good for you—though a little young perhaps . . .? Unfortunately, his older brother married in the spring.'

Stevie turned back to Leone and smiled. 'I'm not looking for an arranged marriage.'

Leone spread his fingers. 'All marriages are arrangements of one sort or another. Otherwise they would not last.'

'You don't believe in—to use an old-fashioned term—a love match?'

'You are an old-fashioned woman. So like your grandmother.'

'You know I will take that as a compliment,' Stevie replied, sitting up a little straighter.

'And so you should,' said Leone. 'And so you should.'

He leant forward, his elbows on his linen-clad knees. 'But are you very particular?' He made the word sound mysteriously charged with meaning, almost lascivious.

'You mean in general, or in my choice of men?'

Leone made another gesture. *Of course.*

'In some ways, yes, I am. Shouldn't we all be? I'm not particular in terms of, say, a man's profession or what kind of shoes he wears or whether he smokes or not. Even his looks. But there are some things I cannot move beyond.'

Leone prompted, 'Such as?'

'Well, certain character traits, like cowardice or malice or lack of curiosity.'

'Lack of curiosity. That is an important one.' Leone fixed Stevie with a deep stare, holding her eyes for an uncomfortable length of time before she broke away to rest her empty glass on the coffee table.

'What are you curious about, Stevie?' His manner was growing more flirtatious as the conversation grew more personal.

'Why you never married, for one thing.' She flashed him a victorious, teasing smile.

Leone's hand slapped his knee. 'Eh! No one would have me.'

That might have been true if Leone did not possess a beautiful estate outside Turin, a comfortable fortune, and a title to go with it.

'You won't have them, you mean, Leone. Maybe you too are . . . particular?' Stevie raised a provocative eyebrow and winced again. She would have to stop doing that.

'I am too set in my ways to change. A woman—an Italian woman—would demand I change. I cannot betray myself like that.'

'But you think *I* should?'

Leone shrugged gently. 'It is easier for a man to be unmarried than a woman.'

Stevie laughed and gently shook her head. 'I think you are a dinosaur, Leone.'

Leone smiled rather wistfully at Stevie then consulted a pocket watch inlaid with amber. 'I took the liberty of organising the private dining room. I think you will find it charming.'

It was indeed charming: an octagonal room inlaid with wood and painted pale blue. It was decorated on every wall with paintings and mirrors, like a jewelled box.

The waiter held the dishes as Stevie carefully spooned boiled rice, then creamed fish, onto her plate—it seemed Leone's gout was playing up again. Her wine glass was filled with a rather delicious Nebbiolo, from the Piedmontese word for fog, named so because it grew in the mist in the valleys of the Langhe not far away. Her luncheon companion, having briefly discussed the food, was back on the subject of love.

'Sooner or later, in love, the reality comes through the veil of fantasy and people are disappointed. I hate disappointing people. Better not begin with hopes. Managing expectation is the key to happiness.'

Stevie took a small sip of wine. 'Warren Buffett said the same thing once.'

'Who?' Leone's eyes flared with a tiny flame of jealousy.

'Never mind.' She put her glass down. 'You know, you don't have to flirt with me, Leone. You can relax.'

Leone too put down his glass. 'It is good manners to flirt when in the company of a woman,' he said softly.

'I thought that only applied to married ones.'

Leone flashed a smile. 'You are quite right, of course, but it is a hard habit to break.' He helped himelf to more rice and looked up. 'My ex-girlfriend is now the First Lady of France,' he said suddenly.

Stevie waited for him to continue. When he didn't, she asked, 'Do you regret not marrying her?'

Leone exploded with laughter. '*È matta come un cavallo*—she is as mad as a horse.'

**By the afternoon, a warm** rain had begun to fall. The streets glossed over and filled with bustling umbrellas. Stevie, caught without one, hurried to the Piazza della Consolata to meet David Rice. She passed a newsstand on the way and saw the latest copy of *Eva 2000*, a popular weekly gossip magazine that specialised in long-lens photographs of stars on holiday. The cover had a photograph of Skorpios and Angelina—*when had they taken that?*

There was a tiny café—the Caffè al Bicerin—full of dim corners and little tables lit with candles. Stevie, her dress and hair quite damp by now, chose a table away from the window. Rice's training made him nervous of windows.

Moments later, the man himself walked in. He stopped in the doorway and carefully closed his umbrella. Stevie noticed he used the action to cover the glances he threw into the dark corners of the café, left, right, then behind him. He was an operative to the bone and the years would never change that. His customary silver-topped cane was missing and he leant on his sturdy British umbrella.

Despite his limp, there was nothing feeble about Rice; even at fifty he was a force. You could feel it radiating from him, like heat from the sun. Today, however, Stevie's heart twisted with concern when she saw his face. The usual serenity of the broad, beloved forehead was gone; there was a tightness around the eyes and a pallor on the cheeks that she had never seen before. He sat without a word, tired beyond belief.

Stevie would have liked to reach out and take his hand but that was out of the question. She wondered very briefly what would happen if she did . . . David would stiffen, then carefully shift his hand just beyond her reach—perhaps even clear his throat—and pretend the wrong-footed gesture had never been made.

It would be a mortifying rejection that Stevie knew she would never have the courage to risk. David Rice would have to remain what he was and always had been: her boss, a family friend, loved from below, adored from afar, the measure of all men.

When the waiter came to take their order, Rice raised a hand in refusal; Stevie, feeling chill and as clammy as a frog, ordered a *bicerin*. It was the specialty of the café: a small glass filled with hot chocolate, then a layer of hot coffee, and finished with a spoonful of cream. She raked her wet hair back off her forehead and met Rice's eyes. 'Flight alright?' she asked, her question loaded with so many others.

David suddenly smiled. 'I'm sorry.' His eyes warmed. 'How are you, Stevie?' His eyes found her wound. 'What happened?' he asked quietly, the smile gone now.

Stevie touched her forehead gently. 'It's nothing. Probably a splinter from one of the explosions.' She smiled. 'I am otherwise very well, thank you. You got my report on the *Oriana*?'

He nodded once, the tiredness settling back into his face. 'You were very lucky—you all were. The *Zoroaster II*, a tanker carrying chemical waste, was taken the same day not far from where you were attacked. The pirates destroyed the bridge with a rocket-propelled grenade and forced the captain to stop. He was injured quite badly apparently—machete—and the crew are being held to ransom.' Rice rubbed his chin in a gesture of exhaustion. 'It was the fifth attack in those waters this week, if we count the one on the *Oriana*. All the others were successful.'

'Do we know anything about these pirates?' Stevie asked, her eyes still on his face.

'Suposedly they're poor fishermen from the Somali coast looking to make a living in a country that has no functioning government. The piracy problem starts on land: civil war in 1991, fighting between the warlords all over the country, famine. Then the world sent food aid and the warlords stole most of it and sold it on across the border to buy more weapons. Then Operation Restore Hope and the Battle of Mogadishu.'

'When the militants shot down two Black Hawk helicopters with rocket-propelled grenades.'

Rice inclined his head. 'The Americans were leading the operation and they lost nineteen men. The bodies of two of them were dragged through the streets on television. It's not that much better now: a transitional government with virtually no power, backed by Ethiopian troops who, from what I hear, are often part of the problem. Looting, killing, gang rape—no one held accountable . . . And the government wonders why it has no legitimacy in the eyes of the people. The whole country is the worst kind of mess. The only structure that does exist is the clan structure, which often ends up behaving much like the mafia.'

Rice stopped abruptly and turned to stare out the window. In the dying light of the day, his skin was grey. Stevie shifted her gaze; she did not want to see his weakness. It was like seeing him naked.

'Not surprising, then,' she said, 'that the fishermen have turned pirates. It must be hard to see the world's trade pass outside your front door and to be trapped in hell with no way out.'

'Mmm . . .' Rice turned back to Stevie. 'But something tells me there is more to it than that. The attacks are too ambitious, too successful . . . The pirates have moved beyond bamboo ladders and machetes—they're now armed with explosives and automatic weapons, they track their target ships with GPS.'

'So, what are we talking,' she asked quietly, 'in terms of numbers?'

'Two years ago, the numbers were around eight; last year, the number jumped to more than sixty. It's estimated the pirates took around forty million dollars. In the first half of this year, that record has already been smashed. The insurance for cargo ships transiting the Gulf of Aden has gone up ten times. It is not an isolated, nor an insignificant, problem.' He said the last bit as if to himself.

'The pirates who attacked us arrived in brand-new Zodiacs,' Stevie offered, 'with high-powered engines, reserve fuel tanks, the whole lot. They were well coordinated—it takes a bit of practice to move in concert on the high seas—but they looked local, Somali. My impression was that most of these men were trained seamen, even possibly military men; half of them were wearing armour.'

'It's obviously been a lucrative business for the pirates,' Rice confirmed. 'Apparently they're driving brand-new Land Cruisers in Boosaaso, sporting Rolex watches, diamond ear studs, the full bit. They use the profts of the attacks to buy better outboard motors, better weaponry, navigation systems and so forth.'

Stevie nodded. 'That would explain the equipment—but not necessarily the training. Experience, I suppose, but you know what I mean: men who have been in the forces move differently. You can just tell someone with training. The pirates I saw—with the exception of a young Rambo who was just spraying bullets about in a panic—had training.'

Rice said nothing, stared at Stevie for a moment as if making up his mind about something. 'We're in trouble, Stevie.' He looked out towards the street. Black limousines were pulling up outside the church, people were coming out, dressed in the sombre greys and blacks of mourning. 'You know Hazard has started up a maritime security arm in response to the escalation of sea-borne threats in the last few years. It's been rather successful and we've been engaged by a great many of the biggest shipping lines in the world.'

Stevie said nothing. The picture was beginning to form in her head even as he spoke.

'In the last four months, we've suffered nineteen pirate attacks, twelve of them successful.' Stevie's eyes widened. She had not expected the numbers to be so high. No wonder Rice was stressed.

'*Zoroaster II* was also one of ours. Unlucky thirteen. I have two men on board that ship, and one of them is Owen Dovetail.'

'Oh no.' Stevie's hand covered her mouth in dismay. She had worked closely with Owen on many assignments and had a great respect and affection for the taciturn Welshman.

'He was on board as protection—unarmed, of course; the laws don't allow us to be armed. It's a one-sided war out there.' Rice lapsed into silence.

Finally she murmured, 'Are you in contact with him?'

'He's managed to send a few text messages. Apparently, though, they've been locked in the hold so he can't give us any indication of the whereabouts of the ship.' He looked up. 'It doesn't sound good, Stevie. It's almost as if our ships are being targeted on purpose. The number of attacks is too far above the average. That's why Dovetail was on board, and a new guy, Simon Timms, too.'

'Have the pirates contacted anyone yet?'

Rice shook his head. 'The contact will most likely come to us through a middleman in London in the next couple of days. Everyone at Hazard is standing ready. We *will* get Dovetail and Timms back. Trouble is, we have to free the whole crew to get to them.

There are twenty-six different nationalities represented on board and we're dealing with representatives from almost every one of those countries. It's a logistical nightmare. Then, when contact is made, the negotiations customarily drag on for months. The crews of the *Bremen* and the *Asia Pearl* have been held for five and seven months respectively.'

'In terms of Hazard's involvement, how many ships are we talking about here?' Stevie's consternation was growing. The numbers sounded overwhelming.

'We have nine ships, seven with captured crews still held, at various stages of negotiation. That's a total of two hundred and nine seamen, plus Dovetail and Timms. The ships themselves are covered by a war risk policy, which covers acts of terrorism and, increasingly, piracy; we've also been offering a third type of policy of protection and indemnity that covers the crew.' Rice rubbed his chin again. 'We've been able to outsource some of the legal work, but negotiating with the pirates and the insurance companies rests with us.'

Rice didn't need to say it—but he said it anyway. 'Stevie, this could sink us.'

Stevie felt the weight of what Rice was telling her settle on her slim shoulders. 'And the hostages?'

'They're all at risk. We are basically stuck between the pirates and the insurance companies and what they are prepared to pay: Hazard is handling the face-to-face but the insurance companies make the final call. So far, the pirates in Somalia have treated their hostages relatively well—they are, after all, their best asset—but we don't know how long that will go on for. We're doing everything possible. You can imagine what two hundred and eleven hostages are doing to the incident room—and that's not counting all the other kidnap cases we're dealing with all over the world. I've brought in everyone I know, pulled in masses of favours, but it's not enough. We're working thirty-six hours on, eight off.'

Rice didn't have to tell Stevie that he was working hardest of all—his appearance said everything. She had never seen him looking so worn, so vulnerable, so . . . old.

She wished she could un-see it. David Rice and her grandmother Didi were the twin pillars of her world; losing Rice would mean collapse.

Outside, the rain had become a downpour. A small cluster of mourners—the stragglers—appeared at the entrance of the church. They popped large black umbrellas, the blooms of sorrow, and stood waiting, unsure what to do next.

Stevie turned back to her boss. 'Do you want me in London?'

Rice shook his head. 'No. I've put a hold on all new clients until we get a handle on this. I won't need you for some time.' He paused, his eyes on the black and grey shapes outside. 'Why don't you take a holiday?' The words came out heavily.

'I don't—' Stevie began to protest, but Rice dropped a weary hand onto the table.

'Stevie, I don't have the energy. It's an order, not an invitation: take a goddamn holiday.' He rose from the table, and looked down at her. His grey eyes met hers and held them briefly—an apology of sorts?—then he turned and walked out.

Stevie leant back in her chair and pulled out her black Russian cigarettes with the gold tips. She had almost stopped smoking them—she had overdone it a little in Russia—but, every now and then, she still craved the sharp, poisonous bite of the smoke in her lungs. She put one to her lips and lit it with a match; she drew in deeply then exhaled as if deflating, up towards the low ceiling. The exchange had left her feeling hollow and angry and anxious all at the same time. She wanted to help Rice but he didn't need her—didn't want her—and that wounded her. There was no choice but to take off. She stubbed out her half-smoked Sobranie, paid for her drink and went across the road to the church opposite.

The funeral had finished and all the mourners had left. The church had the empty feel of a room once the party is over and all the guests have gone home. Stevie could smell the mix of feminine perfumes, the tang of quality leather and cigarettes, that the visitors had left behind. Huge arrangements of white lilies gave off their own powerful scent and dropped golden pollen onto the waxed timber pews. Underlying it all was the familiar, reassuring smell of beeswax furniture polish, and incense.

She wandered about among the figures of Jesus and Mary Magdalen and St Sebastian full of arrows, nestling in their candlelit alcoves. To the right of the door was a large alcove covered from floor to ceiling with childlike drawings done on paper and stuck to the walls.

Each drawing, she realised as she moved closer, depicted someone in the act of dying: an old man lying in a bed under a grey crayon blanket and surrounded by the figures of his family; a younger-looking man lying under the feet of a horse, crayon blood pouring from his head; a woman in crayon skirts caught under the wheels of a tram; a group of crayon men in army uniform trying to stop a tank on a bridge . . . Hundreds of years' worth of deaths, recorded by loved ones left behind in pencil and crayon, then stuck on the church walls for remembrance.

It was an uncanny idea. The drawings were a reminder of the domesticity of death: it arrived in kitchens, in streets full of shops, in sparse bedrooms; it was happening all around them, to people who drew like children. So many deaths, thought Stevie, were accidental—a careless step, a silly mistake, the premature and unplanned end to a busy life. Life is a fragile and precious thing; we hang by a thread.

That, the cynic in her supposed, was the intention behind the wall: a reminder of our transience and mortality, the kindling of hopes for something to come after—in case we messed this life up.

Her grandmother Didi would say that every day should be cherished, every day was a new beginning, and every day should be mined for pleasures and charm; that was a life well lived. Stevie shook off the gloom that had shrouded her since the meeting with Rice and decided to act: she would head south tomorrow, down to the island of Sardinia, where her grandmother still had an old, whitewashed house by the sea. There, she would soak up the sun and swim and fill herself with serenity.

**Back at the Turin Palace,** Angelina had left a note in Stevie's pigeon-hole commanding her attendance at an impromptu performance at the Teatro Regio. She was to sing her favourite arias for Torino's finest, with dinner and dancing after. Stevie was just slipping back to her room, where she planned to decide in peace how best to refuse the invitation, when the diva herself swept along the corridor in her dark glasses, Zorfanelli on one elbow, Sanderson—carrying Angelina's jewel case—on the other.

'Stevie, my darling, my saviour, my little *oiseau*.' Her voice filled every corner of the marble reception. 'How can I ever repay you for saving my jewels? I've popped you in a box with Fernando and Sanderson for tonight's performance. You will be the guest of honour!'

Stevie forced a huge smile in return as she took the diva gently but firmly by the elbow. 'Really, you are too kind,' she murmured, then went on in even softer tones. 'But I must stress this, Angelina: please never reveal to anyone that I have been anything more than a travelling companion to you, never breathe a word about my background. And if we meet somewhere in the future, the same applies. This is what I ask in return for saving your jewels. Can you do this for me?'

The diva nodded, then caught sight of Stevie's damp hair. 'The performance begins in a couple of hours,' she said in horror. 'You can hardly turn up looking like that.' Then she blew her saviour a kiss and the trio swept through the revolving doors and into a waiting car.

**La Dracoulis was magnificent. It** was as if she knew that everyone in the audience was there for more than her golden voice. There had been rumours crackling like electricity about her incredible survival of a pirate attack off Somalia. No doubt Zorfanelli—his sense of spectacle almost as acute at Angelina's—had played a part in whipping up a sense of danger on the high seas that added a different kind of glamour to the image of La Dracoulis.

Her large, slim hands, wrapped around her shoulders, suggested vulnerability. Stevie noticed her make-up was paler than usual; a bruise showed on her upper arm—something her super-attentive make-up artist would never have overlooked . . . It was all part of the spell she was weaving that night and it was masterful. Turin was captivated.

Skorpios attended. He was seated alone in another box, mesmerised. In his hand he held a single white lily. Stevie recognised in him the same sense of drama. Perhaps it was what drew him and Angelina together. As La Dracoulis sang her final note, she closed her eyes and lowered her head, as if expiring from the effort. The applause was rapturous.

Someone threw a flower onto the stage; a hailstorm of stems followed, green spears flying through the air. They were all lilies. As if by some prearrangement, some extra-sensory understanding, Angelina searched the boxes until she found him. Socrates Skorpios, on his feet now, raised his own flower to his lips. Zorfanelli noticed the exchange and obviously felt the energy flow between them. Sanderson, standing beside Stevie, looked charmed, but the mound of flowers on the stage reminded Stevie of the church, and of the wall of death.

There was a dinner afterwards in an old palazzo, twenty tables around a small dance floor, an orchestra. The entire room was lit with candles, frescoes on the walls glowing in the soft light.

Skorpios was not seated with Angelina but he came over after the first course and complimented her on her performance. Stevie overheard Angelina lament that no one danced the tango anymore, to which Skorpios replied, 'Another lost art, my dear; another tragedy.' His extravagance matched hers in every way.

That night, the orchestra played nothing but tango. Skorpios and La Dracoulis danced every dance. No one at the dinner could talk of anything else but Angelina and Socrates, no one could keep their eyes from the charging, swaying couple. Their chemistry was so powerful it left the room breathless.

At midnight, Stevie rose discreetly and slipped out, leaving Skorpios and Angelina to their dangerous romance. On her way through the marble foyer, she passed Fernando Zorfanelli, a rumpled, broken figure smoking too many cigarettes behind a statue of Vittorio Emanuele.

# 4

Between the vast granite marbles that frame the bays of the Costa Smeralda, a small inflatable speedboat bobbed at anchor. Stevie Duveen lay stretched out along one side, eyes closed under her straw hat, sunbaking. She turned onto her stomach, pressed her cheek against the warm grey rubber and listened to the lap-slap of the wavelets against the fibreglass hull. There was nowhere in the world she would rather be.

A warm, dry breeze blew offshore, bringing with it the rich, oily scent of the cistus, curry bush and rosemary that grew wild all over the island. The faint chatter of voices—bathers gathered on the pebbly beach—drifted over, the crisp trilling of cicadas protesting at the fierceness of the afternoon sun.

Stevie half opened her eyes and gazed out through the lattice of her battered Panama: chinks of emerald green sea, a deeper, navy blue further out, then the white-hot sky above. She thought briefly of the dinner she would prepare when she got in—a fresh *orata* fish, stuffed with wild fennel and baked in paper. She would eat on the roof if the wind didn't pick up, and watch the sun set over the water.

From somewhere in the distance came a faint drone. Stevie squinted up into the sky and saw a tiny plane. She watched it circle slowly. Now the sound of engines—two; no doubt it was holidaymakers looking for a sheltered bathing spot. Stevie hoped they wouldn't anchor too close. Italians were very sociable creatures.

A wash rocked her boat, gently at first then growing stronger until the dinghy tipped violently and Stevie's pocket binoculars, lying by her head, slid into the sea.

Stevie sat up, annoyed at the discourteous boating behaviour, and looked towards the open sea. Two naval patrol ships had rounded the point—sharp noses, flat grey colour, hammerhead sharks—and were now steaming off towards La Maddalena island.

A velvety rumble filled the air, growing quickly louder; over the headland swarmed a mass of helicopters in tight formation, darkening the sky.

In the deep blue water an enormous shadow appeared.

Stevie stood transfixed as it grew bigger, travelling forward, the sea sucking and foaming around it. A moment later, a conning tower broke through the surface and Stevie was staring at the black nightmare of a nuclear submarine.

Of course, she knew they stalked the floor of the Mediterranean. The American naval base on La Maddalena was pitted with submarine caves where the sleek beasts could surface and be serviced in completed privacy. But there was nothing like coming up close. That explained the helicopters and the patrol boats. The plane was likely a spotter.

She stood, the boat bucking under her legs, and faced the sea monster. It was gargantuan. The conning tower was three storeys high and completely smooth, painted black. But, unlike the majestic whales she had seen up close, the submarine was frightening. It had been built for war; it was a stealthy killing machine. Stevie shivered from more than the shadow cast by the giant as it streamed away in a white wake towards the golden horizon.

Stevie tried hard not to believe in omens. She was, after all, an analyst, a risk assessor, trained to cast a cold eye over a situation, quantify the risks a client faced, and then implement steps to counter those dangers. It was a position that, admittedly, occasionally conflicted with her hot little heart—but not omens. They were too distracting. One began to see them everywhere if one started looking. The surfacing of the nuclear submarine in her tranquil bay of emerald green, however, was too big to ignore.

She peered over the edge of the dinghy and spotted the dark shape of the binoculars, perched on a boulder, surrounded by sea urchins, about ten metres down. Stevie took a deep breath and dived, straight and narrow as a pin, into the sea.

The trouble was, she didn't need the submarine to know she was headed for trouble. A call from David Rice had been enough.

'Her husband is a dangerous man, a very dangerous man. Proceed with absolute caution, do you understand?' Rice's voice had been low and in earnest, not a tone he often used. 'No freelancing, no games, take absolutely no risks.'

'Sounds delightful,' she said, then added, 'The scarf arrived, by the way. Unnecessary, but very much appreciated.'

There had been a pause on the other end, then, 'Stevie, if I thought there was any chance of you getting into any sort of bother with Krok I would never send you. I'm only telling you this so that you see you don't cross him. You have a penchant for doing things your way that won't do in this case.'

Rice was referring to her escapades in Russia and the warning hit home. It had been a winter of blood and fear and Stevie was still shaken to her core by the things she had seen.

Rice continued, 'You'll be a guest of Krok's wife—perfectly legitimate and perfectly safe. She's a remarkable woman and I think you will get on.'

The day after Stevie had arrived in Sardinia, a parcel was

delivered to the house by courier—a rare and difficult feat to achieve on the island, where the regular mail service was patchy at best. Inside was a slim orange Hermès box and a note: *Please forgive an old brute who values you more than you know*. It had been signed *D*.

Rice was obviously regretting his rather harsh words at the Caffè al Bicerin in Turin, and any hurt feelings Stevie might have been nursing evaporated. Beyond the gesture, the scarf itself was beautiful: the signs of the zodiac were placed on a white background and edged with brown and gold. It was the sort of gift one might receive from a lover, she thought—only Rice did not intend it that way. Unfortunately. However she did like the idea of being valued more than she knew; the happy possibilities seemed ill-defined and infinite, and if she didn't examine David's motives too closely they might even remain that way.

Stevie stuck the note to the bathroom mirror with a tiny dab of toothpaste.

The day after that he had called her. He needed a personal favour, a tiny job that only Stevie could do, and that had been the end of Stevie's holiday.

Clémence Krok was the third wife of Vaughan Krok, owner of STORM, the world's largest private army. She had known Rice in his gayer days, he had explained, in London. Clémence had been a beauty; she, well . . . he had not needed to explain further. Stevie, irrational and inappropriate hackles of jealousy rising to prick the faint hairs on her neck, had understood perfectly.

She had a distinct premonition of trouble ahead, in one form or another. But David Rice was the only man on earth she could not refuse. Although he had no idea of how she felt, he was the man she admired most in the world and the standard by which, if she were brutally honest, she judged every other man. His dismissal of her in the café had hurt her feelings, mostly because Stevie often wondered if Rice took her seriously. She was regularly attached to assignments that involved soothing the hysterical, reassuring the mad, and babysitting the famous. Her colleagues at Hazard assured her it was because no one else could do those jobs like she could: an ex-SAS captain would have a very different approach to client concerns. Stevie's skills, matched with her unthreatening, unassuming appearance, were a golden combination. But the worm of doubt sometimes whispered in her ear: *He doesn't believe you can do it. He doesn't think you can handle anything serious.*

The discussion in the Bicerin had reawakened the worm that had been sleeping since Russia. Stevie could not have said no, even if she had had a good excuse. One day, she would prove to Rice that she was a force to be reckoned with.

Stevie's face broke through the surface and she breathed a lungful of air, binoculars clutched in her hand.

*Damn the man.*

She wiped the lenses as best she could. The glasses were tiny, deceptively powerful— 'Rather like you, actually, Stevie,' Rice had said when he had given them to her as a thirtieth birthday present, during a dinner at Le Colombier in Chelsea.

All was quiet up at Brown's villa, painted pale grey and set among dark green spears of oleanders. The entire valley had recently been bought, house by house—nine in total—by the Russian president, whom Stevie in her prudence always referred to by the codename 'Brown'.

Brown had left the existing houses as guest cottages and built himself a large villa at the top of the valley, facing out to sea. At the back, facing the road, he had planted an entire grove of two-hundred-year-old olive trees. At the front, reaching down to the bay, he had created an artificial lake studded with massive palms.

It was a villa more suited to the south of France and its popular excesses—not hideous, but too grand, too perfect, an imposition on the landscape rather than an extension of it. The Costa Smeralda had traditionally drawn a different kind of jet set: people who wanted to walk about in bare feet at sunset, to feel close to the wild mountains and winds, close to the sea. The houses were most often shaped organically, rounded and whitewashed and nestled into the massive boulders that inspired their creation. The floors were red brick or terracotta and no one dreamt of air-conditioning. The heavy stone walls and wooden shutters kept out the worst heat of the day, and sheltered the occupants from the violent storms that swept in sporadically.

The gardens were dry and rocky—the odd one with the luxury of a lush lawn—but most making full use of the hardy plants, the natural vegetation that gave the island its distinct perfume. Even now, if on a winter's day somewhere far away Stevie caught a whiff of cistus, or curry bush, or myrtle, she was instantly transported, with goose bumps, to the island. She had been coming almost every summer since she was a year old—thirty years already—and the place was set in her bones.

Six men patrolled the grounds of Brown's Villa Goliath at regular intervals, dressed in green T-shirts with *Giardiniere*—gardener—stencilled across the shoulders. But they carried radios on their belts and Stevie was sure, from the breadth of their shoulders and their fiercely short hair, that they were a lot more than groundsmen.

The land was ringed by a low, dry-stone wall—very much like those of the surrounding villas—but a hedge of oleanders obscured the view and surveillance cameras, planted at twenty-metre intervals, suggested that the owner of the Villa Goliath was more nervous than most.

Brown was at a peace summit in Scandinavia, but he had lent

Krok and his family the villa. From what Rice had told her, Krok did business with Brown on a regular basis—weapons, mercenaries, ammunition, transport logistics—but the loan of Brown's private summer palace equalled a lot of business indeed.

It was quite impossible to get close to the place without compromising oneself and so Stevie had to be content with watching from a distance. There were security men everywhere—Brown's dressed in the green gardeners' T-shirts, Krok's men all in black.

Vaughan Krok wouldn't have been the first of Brown's guests to bring their own security, and no doubt the accommodation of his men had been easy, but there seemed to be a lot of them.

Stevie's mission—could she call it that and not sound ridiculous?—was to find out to what extent the threat to Krok and his family was real and immediate. What were his existing security measures like? Were they good enough? Appropriate? Apparently his wife had her doubts, afraid her husband was using the spectre of violence to keep her imprisoned (her words, according to Rice; not Stevie's). She had yet to meet the woman—that pleasure awaited her tomorrow.

But for now, all was quiet. The occupants of the villa appeared to be resting after their lunch. She hadn't been able to see their faces clearly—they had been mostly obscured by a pergola—but she had spotted what looked like scampi, and a bottle of local *rosato*. It was unlikely they would stir until the cool of dusk. Through the binoculars, she followed the paving stones as they meandered through the lush gardens—hibiscus, palm, oleander—towards the small private beach. Six wooden sun lounges stood in a neat row, all empty; a large sign, VIETATO in poisonous red, warned off the curious.

A small boy in a red and white striped T-shirt was playing with pebbles at the water's edge. He had a dark mop of hair, and looked to be about six years old. It would have to be Emile Krok, only child of Clémence and Vaughan. He seemed a little forlorn—as much as anyone could tell a thing like that through binoculars, from a boat. He was walking slowly up and down the beach, his ankles in the water, now crouching down, probably to examine some treasure.

A shadow flickered on the outer edge of the binocular's circle of vision. Stevie turned to follow it and saw a hulking man dressed all in black, with black army boots and a black cap. He was standing at ease with a sub-machine gun resting casually in his hands. He towered over the child, a dump truck watching a sand crab.

*The bodyguard.*

Stevie saw the man glance at his watch then say something to the boy, who dropped whatever he held in his hand and obediently stepped out of the water. She kept watching until the two mismatched figures disappeared up the garden path.

The wind was picking up. Stevie knelt at the bow of the dinghy and began hauling on the anchor chain, her arms working hard to drag it up from the depths. Then she pull-started the fifteen-horsepower engine, ancient but utterly reliable, and motored slowly in to the tiny stone jetty below her grandmother's house.

**The water in the old** garden hose was still warm from the sun as she hosed off the salt of the day. The stones on the path beneath her feet radiated heat and she felt at peace for the first time in a long while. This business with the Kroks was not going to crack her stillness—she wouldn't let it. It had taken her almost six months to find some inner quiet after all the blood of Russia and she wasn't going to let it go now.

She slipped on an old Pucci kaftan in swirling aquamarines, the cotton worn thin with age, and began climbing the steps to the roof terrace. Behind her, she heard a faint tinkling and Ettore the dachshund appeared, wearing his little red collar.

He visited Stevie every evening at sunset and stayed until his owners across the road, hoarse from calling for him, went back indoors. They had no idea where Ettore went and Stevie never told them. It was their little secret.

'*Buona sera*, Ettore.'

The small dog waved his long tail and looked up at Stevie with bright, intelligent eyes. They headed up to the roof together.

If she stood on her toes, Stevie could just see the roof of the Villa Goliath. Someone had lit lanterns in the garden, and the place was dotted with soft light—not security lighting.

The cameras would have night-vision filters; it was that sort of set-up.

Stevie poured herself two inches of sweet vermouth from an *aperitif* tray she had brought up from the kitchen, added a hunk of ice, a slice of orange peel. The sun was setting over the horizon and the entire bay was bathed in pink and gold. It was impossible to think of evil, only of harmony—and of the lonely tug the perfect sunset seemed to cause in her heart.

*Did all beauty do that?*

From somewhere across the terracotta rooftops, Stevie heard the notes of a flute. Every evening at dusk, the same flute, the same tune. It sounded vaguely Middle Eastern, or perhaps Indian. Stevie did not, unfortunately, have any kind of ear for music and, much as she enjoyed singing, she was often gently—or sometimes not so gently—discouraged from doing so.

She raised her binoculars and scanned the neighbouring houses.

Pino Maranello in the stone bungalow behind—former pro-fessional soccer player, many beautiful daughters, many beautiful wives and girlfriends, unlikely flute player—was sitting on a rattan chair on the lawn, smoking a cigarette and reading the newspaper. He was still terribly handsome and made good use of his looks. Several women in jewel-coloured shift dresses bustled about with plates and napkins under the bamboo pergola, chattering like gay parrots.

Stevie lowered her binoculars. '*Buona sera*,' she called.

Pino looked up from his paper and flashed her a grin. '*Ciao*, Stevie. *La nonna sta bene?*' He always asked after Stevie's grandmother. 'Will we see her this summer? It's been too long.'

'Perhaps this summer. I know she misses Sardinia.'

Pino nodded and raised both palms to the sky. *Of course, everyone misses Sardinia when they are elsewhere.*

Stevie turned her binoculars to the house to her right: the Biedermeiers had obviously just arrived—still pale as butter. They were eating their dinner outside. It was early for dinner, but they were German—from the north—and had perhaps acquired this custom in the long winters. Frau Biedermeier, tall and fair, Herr Biedermeier, round and fair, two good-looking, fair-haired children—not flute players either.

She swung to the left but the music ended there, a last graceful note hanging in the powder-blue air.

*If only all mysteries were as charming.*

Across the road, a woman was calling for Ettore—'*Ma dove sei andato?!*'—the exasperation in her voice growing.

Stevie looked down at her companion. 'Perhaps you had better . . .' And little Ettore was gone.

The sun was sinking steadily into the glassy sea. Stevie's grandmother Didi used to tell her to watch for the green spark—electricity, she called it—that you might see, if conditions were right, if you were very lucky. She remembered sitting beside her father on the sun-warmed wall, just as she was doing now, and the sound of her mother's singing voice rising from the kitchen. Days long-gone, almost as if they never were. Stevie kept her eyes focused on the sliver of planet, pale pink and disappearing fast, until—there! The green flash.

At least some things never changed.

# 5

At the easy hour of eleven o'clock, Stevie stood at the end of the long wooden jetty at Hotel Cala di Volpe. She spotted the launch in the distance: right on time. The sun was already hot, burning through her silk kaftan—this one a wiggling Missoni print in turquoise, pink and yellow; the kind of garment a happy and high-living acquaintance would wear for lunch on a yacht in the Mediterranean. Stevie was, after all, incognito.

She had had a brief moment of doubt on the drive over: was the turban too much? She touched the turquoise headpiece gently, making sure it was as she had arrranged it.

Too late for second thoughts—the launch was pulling up to the jetty.

The *Hercules* was moored off the coast, visible only as a white dot from the jetty. Stevie knew it had been built by an ultra-discreet German firm that had been designing since the warships of World War I. There had been much talk and speculation in mega-yachting circles over the project—know only by its code 999—but the ship-builders and everyone else associated with the project had remained tight-lipped.

Almost no one knew who the owner was, nor how it was possible that project 999 bore such an uncanny resemblance to the latest $100 billion US naval project, codenamed DD(X), a super-fast, compact warship designed for littoral defence, perfect for shallow water and small waterways. It was designed to chase smaller attack vessels and submarines and it was armed with three kinds of torpedoes and missiles.

Stevie had seen pictures of the DD(X), a sleek, pointed ship with a single turret far back on the length of the ship, all hard-angled blades. Even so, she was still not prepared for the sight of the *Hercules*: the giant head of an albatross, six storeys high. The bow was three storeys high and sharp as a needle, drawing back to a towering living space, then cutting away, straight into the sea. The *Hercules* was at once extraordinary, hideous and quite breathtaking; an ultra-modern warship in gleaming white.

It was cold in the port shadow of the beast and Stevie was glad to hop aboard and step back into the sunlight.

'Get those fenders down properly, you morons, before you dent her.' A man's voice, deep and pebbly. Stevie looked up towards the upper deck: the figure of a man, stocky, large arms, silhouetted by the sun.

*Krok.*

Stevie lightly drew breath and assumed her persona. She waved, hand high above her head, gold bangles tinkling, and let out the universal cry of the swanning society swan:

'Yoohoo!'

The man slowly turned his head. 'Clem!' he barked.

**Clémence Krok possessed all the** charm her husband lacked. She was a beauty in her early forties and as polished as diamonds, which she seemed to have a fondness for. Lithe and tanned and perfectly blonde, she wore white linen pants and a turquoise and orange bolero jacket made largely of feathers. As Clémence went to kiss Stevie, palms raised in studied delight, wonderful smile flashing, Stevie decided she was glad she had worn the turban after all.

'Oh, it was at the Serpentine party, Vaughan,' Clémence was saying. 'We promised to meet up if we ever found ourselves in the same patch of sun. And here we are.' She kissed Stevie on both cheeks.

Krok stared at Stevie. 'And here you are.' He wore a salmon-coloured polo shirt, but was not quite tanned enough to pull it off.

Stevie affected airiness, giving a small laugh as she inwardly cursed David Rice.

A crew member appeared, immaculate in white: 'Lunch is served.'

Clémence rose. 'We lunch early, Stevie. My husband likes to get up with the sun, says it keeps him ahead of the competition.' She put her perfectly manicured hand on Krok's arm.

*Did he stiffen?*

Clémence carefully removed her hand and smiled widely. Both Vaughan and his wife wore sunglasses, so it was hard to tell what their souls were up to.

*Were there no other guests on this mega-yacht? Where was Emile, their son?*

Stevie knew better than to ask pointed questions, especially around a man like Krok. She simply slipped her eyes into soft focus and gazed lazily about her, following Krok and Clémence forward.

There seemed to be very few windows, not unusual in a warship, but certainly uncommon in a pleasure craft. Perhaps the *Hercules* used other technology to show guests the view. Stevie noticed a small insignia on one of the small portholes as they passed: bulletproof glass.

'What a wonderfully original design. I've never seen anything quite like it.'

Krok looked back sharply. 'Nothing like it in the whole world. Made by Schorr and Hess. Cost me two hundred and seventy million US.'

Stevie nodded with what she hoped was suitable awe.

'One hundred and eighteen metres long, fourteen guest cabins, forty-six staff.' Krok telegraphed the statistics, his hundred-yard stare scanning the sea. He turned his head and barked into the open doorway, 'Long Island iced tea!' A well-built crew member appeared almost instantly with a long glass on a silver tray.

'Don't you worry about pirates?' Stevie asked in a hushed tone, her eyes suitably wide. Her own experience aboard the *Oriana* was still fresh in her mind, and she also wanted to learn more about this most extraordinary vessel. Krok was only too glad to oblige.

'There's a powerful water cannon on board—can sink a boat at a hundred metres. If they get closer than that—which I doubt—we've got a sonic gun that'd shatter the eardrums of every pirate in an attack vessel.' He fixed Stevie with a rather mad stare. 'And there's a high-speed escape boat. But we won't need that. My crew can defend themselves just fine.' He said this with a smirk and Stevie had no doubt, looking at the massive arms of the tray carrier, that they could do just that, and more.

They sat down in the shade on the foredeck, a huge white expanse of prow stretching before them, tapering to a sharp point.

Wave-piercing technology, thought Stevie. No wonder she goes so fast.

*Could you still refer to a warship named* Hercules *as 'she'?*

Stevie smiled and patted the white leather upholstery. 'Well, it's certainly lovely and roomy.'

Clémence directed the staff with soft clicks of her fingers—
'Champagne over there, prawns here, finger bowls there, there and
there, lemons . . .'

Another very muscular crewman emerged with a huge platter
of oysters and laid them on the table near Stevie. As he turned, Stevie noticed the white leather holster hanging almost invisibly from
the white belt on his shorts. From it emerged the handle of a white
pistol.

*A ceramic gun? Was that possible?*

She smiled a little harder. Clémence sipped a flute of champagne and turned to Stevie. 'We've been in the Med for a month
already. I feel like it's been forever. Does London still exist? How is
the weather?'

'Actually I flew in from Turin. It's been months since I've been
in England.'

*Always keep your lies as close to the truth as possible.*

'So you don't live there. For some reason . . .' Clémence had
not done her homework.

Stevie jumped in. 'Oh, I spend a lot of time there, but I was
visiting friends in Turin. I actually live in Zurich. My grandmother
is there. I find the town a perfect antidote to modern life—with all
the conveniences.'

'We always stay at the Baur au Lac when—'

Krok's mobile phone interrupted, ringing with Wagner's 'Ride
of the Valkyries'.

*How appropriate.*

Clémence stopped mid-sentence.

Krok grunted a few words and hung up, turned his attention
back to the table. 'So, Stevie, you decorative or useful?' he barked
without looking up. He shoved a prawn head into his mouth and
sucked noisily, tossed it onto a pile with all the others.

Stevie dipped her fingertips in the finger bowl. 'Oh, neither, I'm afraid. I get by being in the right place at the right time, I suppose.'

'Married?'

'No. Not married.'

'Ever been?'

'No. Never been.'

'So you're down here in these parts husband hunting.' He plunged a hairy hand into the finger bowl and squeezed the lemon quarter to a messy pulp. 'Rich pickings?'

Stevie blushed despite her cover. She hoped it could be blamed on sunburn.

'Not really my scene,' she laughed, hoping she sounded convincing. 'I'm quite happy to have myself all to myself.'

'That's what they all say. Won't admit to wanting a rich husband, but show them a man with money and their legs go up like the sails on a windmill.'

Stevie took a rather large sip of the (extremely good) champagne and swallowed.

*One must not rise. No. However, one was beginning to find it a struggle to rein in one's tongue.*

'What a wonderful image.' She smiled. 'Aren't you clever, Mr Krok?'

'Oh, call him Vaughan, Stevie, darling. Don't be too intimidated by the ruffian.'

But Stevie could see that Krok was secretly pleased. So she had done well.

She now knew that Krok was a man who liked to goad people for sport, to press until he got a reaction. He was also vulnerable to flattery. This was useful information; Stevie only hoped her self-control would last.

Fortunately Vaughan Krok seemed to have a short attention

span. He stood up before Clémence had even finished eating, shoved his chair back and shouted at one of the crew.

**A clay pigeon pull had** been set up on the aft deck. Krok broke his twelve bore, over and under shotgun and thrust in two cartridges.

'Pull.'

A black disc went flying high across the back of the yacht. Krok pulverised it with a single shot.

'Pull.'

This time low—pulverised.

Krok broke and reloaded, cartridges hopping out like grasshoppers onto the deck. He shot well, ostentatiously, a man obviously used to more powerful weapons.

Clémence moved closer to Stevie, murmured, 'I almost messed that up—the comment about London.'

Stevie turned to her. The other woman's skin, even up close, was unlined perfection. *How was that possible?*

Clémence shook her head and added, 'He can't hear us. He has his earplugs in.'

'Clémence, is this subterfuge really necessary?'

The reply was edged with a sudden ice. 'I can't imagine it's taken you long to get the measure of my husband, Stevie.' The painted mouth was hard now. 'How do you think he would have reacted if I had turned around and said, "Darling, I'd like a second opinion on your threat assessments. I really think you might be overdoing it. How about calling in my ex-lover from London?"'

So Clémence and David Rice had been lovers. That stung a little. Stevie wanted to know more but could hardly ask.

She laid a companionable hand on Clémence's arm. Krok was

the sort of man who noticed everything; that's why men like him survived. 'It just seems like you are running an unnecessary risk,' Stevie said quietly but with a smile. 'The tiniest suspicion, a careful background check, it wouldn't be hard to find out what I do.'

'Perhaps, but look at you. You hardly look like you belong in the risk-analysis business. It's most unlikely that Vaughan will take any interest in you beyond the male perspective—and even so . . .' Clémence lowered her glasses and looked Stevie pointedly up and down. She had startlingly violet eyes, hard as crystal. 'You're not his type.'

No, Stevie thought, that would be unlikely. She wasn't many people's type, as far as she could figure out. Slight to the point of fragility, with the bones of a bird, she had a sharp face—not conventionally pretty, not a beauty. She was blonde, but her hair was cropped into a little bob that left the nape of her neck bare and sat just below her ears.

Clémence pushed her glasses back up to cover her eyes. 'Do you swim?'

Stevie nodded. 'Of course.'

'I rarely do, but feel free . . .' Clémence gestured towards the pool.

Shaded by an overhang, the deep blue tiles transformed the water into a mirror. Reflected in its surface was a centaur, rendered in tiny brown and gold tiles, and rippling gently as the ocean breeze disturbed the skin of the water. It looked to Stevie more like a sacrificial bath than a swimming pool—like one of the dreadful eel pits of Ponza.

Once, when visiting the island, she had gone to explore the Roman remains. The ancient emperors exiled their unfaithful wives to the island; the women in turn amused themselves by ordering pools to be dug into the cliff face and a series of tunnels with water channels that flowed into them. The sluices to these channels could be opened and ravenous eels would swim down into the larger pools. Into these pools the disgraced noble ladies then hurled their slaves. It was an amusement.

Stevie, walking the tunnels and too fascinated for words, had missed her step and fallen into the pool. Never had a bird moved so swiftly as Stevie, leaping out of the eel pond. She had been assured that the eels had long since gone, but how certain could you be of something like that?

Stevie felt suddenly claustrophobic, swaddled by the luxury of the yacht, the empty decks, the periodic explosions of the shotgun.

'Thank you, Clémence, but I prefer the sea.'

Quickly she unwound her turban and slipped off her kaftan. Underneath she wore her favourite navy blue swimsuit—Eres—with its modest boy leg and scooped back. It was elegant enough for the yacht, but you could swim seriously in it if you had to.

Stevie stepped onto the railing, three storeys up, and held the nearest pole with one hand. Then she raised herself onto her toes and fell in a perfect swan dive into the glittering sea below.

For a moment all was silent and cool and still. She opened her eyes. There was nothing but blue—deep blue bleeding into navy, into the black below. No fish, no rock, only the gleaming hull of the behemoth.

The yacht extended a further two storeys below the waterline. And there was some sort of bulge . . .

Stevie would have liked to swim down and find out just what it was, but her lungs were burning and she turned and kicked her way up to the surface.

'Steve!' Krok was leaning over the parapet, his eyes yellow behind his shooting goggles. 'Get up here and have a shot. I have a four-ten here—a real ladies' gun. I bought it for Clem but she won't touch the thing, hates guns.'

Stevie began to protest but there was something about Vaughan Krok that pulverised protest as fast as his shotgun did clays.

Stevie found herself, still in her swimsuit, cropped hair hastily towel-dried, with a loaded shotgun in her hand.

'How much more time have you got, Steve?' Krok's grating voice was close to her ear. 'Do you hear the clock ticking in your sleep? An unmarried woman after twenty-eight has gotta be having a few sleepless nights . . .'

Stevie slowly raised the gun to her shoulder and closed an eye.

'Pull.'

Two clays, one high, one low, zipped across the aft deck. She knew the four-ten had a small shot spread and aimed accordingly. Stevie tracked them with the tip of the barrel—one, two, smashed to smithereens.

She broke the gun and breathed in the smell of gunpowder, now feeling remarkably better. She turned to Krok and found his yellow eyes hard on her.

Stevie realised it might have been more prudent to miss.

**Clémence and Stevie strolled along** the bottom deck to the prow. The ship was almost 400 feet long, so it was a good walk. The wind blew their voices out into the open sea.

'I'm no innocent, Stevie. I knew what I was getting into when I married my husband. He's powerful—I'm attracted to power— and generous with his money; he provides the funds, and I provide the lifestyle.'

She stopped and lit a Vogue Slims menthol cigarette, her feathered jacket ruffling in the ocean breeze. 'Does that shock you?'

Stevie shook her head. 'You wouldn't be the first couple to have bonded over such an arrangement.'

Clémence took a long hard look at Stevie Duveen. 'You're one of the romantics of the world, aren't you? I can see it in your face. You believe in true love—well, perhaps you're still young enough for it . . . just. But I'll tell you this: money can buy happiness, if you know where to shop. Oh, it's not in the clothes and diamonds and cars per se; it's everything. It's all this.' She waved her hand over the Sardinian coastline, glowing pink in the afternoon sun. 'It's never having to fly commercial, it's linen napkins at breakfast, it's never having to wait for a table anywhere, ever; it's feeling totally cocooned in the most marvellous way from the rest of the world. Who wouldn't want that?' Clémence stared out to sea. 'When you marry a man with money—and I mean serious money—there is nothing you can't do.'

Stevie watched a small wooden fishing boat chug past, nets aloft, gulls wheeling in its wake. She turned to Clémence, her voice soft. 'Then why am I here?'

For a long while Clémence said nothing. Then the rumbling of the engines started up and the anchor chain began to disappear noiselessly into the prow. The *Hercules* would be docking at Porto Cervo tonight.

'Vaughan is my third husband, Stevie, and my richest— although I haven't done too badly out of the other two. The reason I have always been so successful is I see my marriages as work, a job, and I take them very seriously. I cater to my husband's every whim. I make him happy. If I didn't, I know there are plenty of other women who would. I obey the golden rule: he who has the gold makes the rules. My husband, Stevie, has the gold.'

Now the *Hercules* was underway; surprisingly quiet, it (she?) seemed to glide across the surface of the deep blue sea.

'I'm still not sure I see the problem, Clémence.'

'He has the gold, and he also has my son.'

'Emile.'

Clémence nodded. 'He's at the villa today with his tutor. My husband is very concerned for his safety—to the point of what I would call paranoia. Emile can't go anywhere without bodyguards, he's not allowed friends, and this spring my husband pulled him out of his school. Said it wasn't secure. Now he's tutored at home. Emile is being crushed. He barely speaks. It's no life for a child.'

Stevie glanced aft; the wake was a wall of white water roaring out behind them. 'Does your husband have reason to fear for your son? Anything specific?'

Clémence shook her head. 'I don't really know. I mean, I ask but he won't tell me. He says it's for my own good. He just talks about dangers, risks, situations . . . Sometimes I think it's his way of controlling me. My husband is, I'm afraid, growing more erratic every day, his moods more unpredictable, more explosive . . . I know he has a lot on his mind—his work is extraordinarily taxing—but I feel like I am going mad.'

She turned back to Stevie and took her sunglasses off to emphasise the point. 'Of course, I can't argue with him—that would go against the golden rule. And in any case, you don't argue with a man like Vaughan. I could handle it for myself, but Emile . . .'

The *Hercules* slowed down as it steamed through the narrow heads of Porto Cervo. It could just fit on the very end berth of the old port. All the others would have been too small. Two grey Zodiacs zoomed out to meet it like gadflys on a pond.

Clémence stared up at the little church perched on the hillside high above the marina, with its curved white walls and softly undulating roof. 'Stevie, I need you to find out if there really is a terrible danger hanging over Emile, or if my husband's delusions are taking over. I'm too afraid to do anything myself—too afraid for me, and too afraid for Emile.'

Stevie felt a wave of compassion for this self-confessed hardened fortune hunter, but the whole thing still puzzled her. 'Clémence, I'm not a private investigator; I'm not a psychiatrist. I don't know what David Rice has told you but I can only offer you a limited amount of help. I could do a basic risk assessment for you and Emile and see how it compares to the situation your husband has painted for you. Beyond that, I'm not sure what I can do.'

Clémence turned to Stevie. Her eyes were blazing—they were not the eyes of a defeated woman.

'There's no one but David I can trust. He told me I could rely on you, that you had principles and courage and knew when to keep your mouth shut.'

Stevie blushed, flattered by David's description, by the fact that he had described her that way. She liked to imagine him thinking of her when she was not there, talking to other people about her. It was a silly vanity she would never have confessed to anyone.

The men in the grey inflatables—the Zodiac cowboys—were guiding the boat in, stern first. One pressed a soft nose against the prow of the yacht, the other on the opposite side of the stern, like supercharged thrusters. Their drivers stood, guiding the outboard motors with one foot on the tiller, the propellers churning the clear water white.

Clémence turned away, her gaze now on the Aga Khan's villa, spreading discreetly between the church and the old port, with its low white walls, green lawns and riotous bougainvillea.

'I've always felt invulnerable and in control,' Emile's mother continued. 'Sure, a lot of the time I pretend to be weak because it pays off when it comes to getting your way with men, but I've always known I wasn't. And then I had Emile.' Clémence glanced quickly behind her. The crew, darting about with ropes, were too far away to overhear their conversation. 'Do you have children, Stevie?'

Stevie shook her head.

Clémence put her sunglasses back on. 'When you have a child, you give a hostage to fortune. There are suddenly so many more ways that fate—or someone—can hurt you. Do you understand now?'

Stevie nodded slowly. She did see the picture, and it was very unlovely.

# 6

It was with no small measure of relief that Stevie, flying along in her ancient emerald green jeep, turned into Via Cappucini. She loved the old car—her grandmother's—the doors on their leather hinges long gone, the canvas rotted away. She felt so glad to be away from the claustrophobic luxury and quiet madness of the Kroks; life at Lu Nibaru was a whole lot simpler.

The house had been built in the early 1960s by her grandparents. A whitewashed beach bungalow cooled by the sea breezes, it was surrounded by friends and family, and a stone's throw from the little beach.

It was a place full of memories for Stevie, full of ghosts—her mother and father had lived great summers here before they had been taken from her. When she was five, they had spent a glorious month by the sea; then that fateful trip to North Africa that had turned Stevie's world upside down . . .

But on an evening like this one, heavy with the smell of the sea-salted bushes, the green foliage popping with oleander pinks and whites and hibiscus reds, the last of the light turning everything an impossible gold, it was almost as if nothing had changed, as if time had not passed and all the shattered pieces were whole again.

Stevie was just finishing a phone call to Josephine Wang, head of the Confidential Investigations department at Hazard, when she turned into the gravel driveway of the house and stopped dead. A white station wagon was parked in the bamboo-roofed carport.

'**I'm so sorry, Mark, I** must have forgotten all about you. I'm sure Didi would have told me . . . she's always so organised. I just can't remember her mentioning . . .' Didi had certainly not mentioned Mark's visit because, had she known, Stevie might have taken some precautions, like booking a cruise in Scandinavia for a week.

She saw little of her very distant cousin who lived in Leeds and had never shown any interest in Lu Nibaru—or Didi, for that matter.

'Mark, there are mosquitoes everywhere! Can't you get in here and do something?' The voice drifted up the tiled stairs to the kitchen.

*Simone.*

'Coming.' Mark disappeared.

Stevie sat down at the table, her head in her hands.

*Disaster.*

Suddenly a smooth furry warmth at her feet—Ettore. Stevie had never been so glad to receive her visitor. 'What am I going to do, Ettore?' She stroked his lovely fur and then felt ashamed. Mark was family, however tenuous the bond, and she should make an effort. That was what Didi would do, she reminded herself.

I'm going to be nice, she told herself. Nice, hospitable Stevie. There's no reason why we shouldn't all share the house. Possibly, I've remembered them all wrong.

Stevie drew in her stomach and raised her chest and breathed deeply, hoping it was all a dream. Good manners start with good posture, she reminded herself, and poured out two inches of good gin. On second thoughts, she poured two more glasses, added ice and lemon, arranged a plate of olives.

Unfortunately, good posture was not enough to get Stevie through the next hour. Simone had allergies, it turned out, to lemon rind, green olives and dogs. She also hated gin. Ettore was sent home early, much to his bewilderment and Stevie's dismay. They headed up to the roof terrace to view the setting sun.

As soon as they reached the terrace, Simone flashed her hand at Stevie—a large square-cut diamond. 'We're getting married. Did Mark tell you?'

'Ah, no . . . um, how lovely. Congratulations.'

Mark, a proud smile on his face, put his arm around his fiancée.

Simone was a Manila girl, every inch of her groomed, plucked, plumped and polished: the most beautiful fingernails, gleaming white teeth and jewels, improbably blonde-streaked hair falling in perfectly straight lines to her chest. She wore towering cork wedges and the latest Gucci minidress—slinky black satin against her dark skin. The overall effect was not unpleasant but oddly artificial, as if perhaps there might be a slot for two double-A batteries somewhere down the back of the hot little dress.

At least they looked happy, thought Stevie.

Simone was staring at Stevie, still in her turban and sitting cross-legged on the stone wall—dark, hungry eyes that missed nothing.

'What kind of pearls are they?' she asked bluntly.

Stevie looked down at her chest. 'I inherited them from my mother when she died—they were her grandmother's. They have great sentimental value.'

Simone was staring at a dark blue enamelled egg the size of

a large raindrop that hung from the lowest strand. A tiny diamond embedded in it drew the light.

'Is that Fabergé?' Simone's voice rose an octave.

Stevie blushed a little. 'It was a gift from a friend, after a Russian adventure.'

*Henning. Dear, handsome, sexy, exciting Henning.*

He had given her the jewel after their first night together—she remembered he had rather quaintly called it a 'love token'—with that wonderful crooked smile of his. They had been bonded by their wild adventures in Russia and beyond, by their strong physical attraction—it had felt like love. But that sort of bond was impossible to sustain. If they had stayed together, their whole story might have been a Great Romance and, to paraphrase Wallis Simpson when she became the Duchess of Windsor, Great Romances are very hard to live out. Stevie was afraid to give her heart to someone as mysterious and magnetic as Henning. Her life was too full of uncertainties without also entertaining emotional turmoil. And so she had allowed them—forced them—to drift apart. She missed his touch now and ran her hand lightly over the pendant at her throat, the memories still vivid.

'I guess it's only small.' Simone tossed her mane disdainfully. 'You know, you can't swim in your pearls.'

Stevie shrugged. 'I never take them off.'

'The salt water will ruin them,' Simone declared.

'I figure, they come from the sea and are probably happy to return to it.' Stevie smiled, seeking to lighten her contradiction.

Simone ignored both the comment and the smile and stared at the antique clasps. 'You should have them valued. They might be worth more than you think.'

Stevie blushed again—this time for a very different reason—and looked away, now following Mark's gaze.

'I came here once as a small boy. I don't remember much. But I do remember everyone whispering about what happened to your parents, and they would always stop when they noticed I was there . . .'

'They always did that to me when my parents divorced,' Simone broke in. She turned to Stevie. 'How much is this place worth? I heard property values are in the tens of millions for land around here.'

Stevie glanced at Mark, looking for help, but saw the hunger in his eyes and understood.

'Didi will never sell Lu Nibaru,' Stevie said, forcing a polite smile, 'so it's quite irrelevant.'

'But seriously, she can't live forever.' Simone turned to her fiancé, accusing. 'You told me she was really old.'

Here Mark at least had the good grace to look a little embarrassed.

*Possibly Simone might lean a little too far over the edge in those cork heels and—*

Stevie stopped her evil thoughts and recalibrated.

'Are you thinking of staying long?' she inquired lightly.

Simone ignored her and slapped at her thigh. 'Oh god, mosquitoes. Can't you spray or something? I'm allergic to mosquito bites.'

'But,' Mark persisted, 'wouldn't Didi be glad of the money? Instead of having it all tied up in this old house? I mean, it's falling apart. It's a bad investment.'

'He's right,' Simone said. 'The tiles are all cracked, the shutters are rotting and the bed sheets are so old they're worn through. And the bathroom smells funny. It's pretty shit for a villa.'

Mark leant in earnestly. 'When she dies, they'll have to sell, Stevie.'

Stevie looked out at the bay, the sea as smooth as silk now. She would have liked to cry. Mark and Simone just wanted money, but with Didi gone, Stevie would be completely alone in the world.

She took a deep, fig- and myrtle-scented breath and saw light at the end of the tunnel. Stevie turned to her tormentors with an innocent smile. 'I agree it is all a bit rundown here, but there are some lovely hotels in the area—very exclusive—that I could recommend . . .'

'Why waste the money when we can stay here for free?' Simone raised her tortured eyebrows. 'I want to do some serious shopping—I'd rather have shoes, even if it means we have to sleep here.' Her nostrils flared ever so slightly in distaste.

It became abundantly clear that, when she had first heard about the house on the Costa Smeralda, Simone had begun to entertain Visions. She was a girl who had come far and planned to go a lot further: from a father who sold air-conditioners in the Philippines, a mother who entertained lavishly and had groomed herself for an existence of fame and fortune. Although there was a comfortably large income, life had never quite lived up to Mrs Carpos' Imeldan ideals. Being the queen of Manila society was one thing, but Europe hovered perpetually, the tantalising mirage . . .

Simone took on her mother's ambitions and injected them with a new vigour. Europe was to be conquered, first with an engagement to Mark Benson of Leeds. As a travel agent to aspiring billionaires, Mark's job was to organise superyachts, private jets, helicopter transfers and Ferraris—all rented, all designed to make the rich look mega-rich. This had given Simone a taste of what was possible—but so far out of reach. Ambition now took the form of a villa in Sardinia, the jet set. Simone was moving up in the world and the view from the heights was dazzling her.

However, the Visions had been disappointed by the

reality—she complained bitterly about the lack of air-conditioning and television and asked where the 'servants' were—and she had moved on to plan B: sell the villa and grab the cash.

Simone had the lightness of touch of a carthorse and the delicacy of a baboon. It was more than Stevie could bear, no matter how many gins she bolstered herself with.

'I'm starving, Mark,' Simone whined. 'There's nothing to eat in the fridge.'

'I've got some lovely *pecorino* cheese,' began Stevie, 'and—'

'For dinner? Cheese?' Simone made a face at her fiancé.

'What about going into Porto Cervo to look at the big boats?' he offered his princess. 'Only you'll have to come with us, Stevie—I don't remember the way.'

*Interaction with the happy couple might be easier with some dilution.*

Stevie smiled broadly. 'Shall we take the jeep?'

**Down at the old port,** the evening *passeggiata* was in full swing. All the yachts were in for the evening, hosed down and polished, lights on, large floral displays on the stern decks. Those aboard sat in full view, mixing cocktails, showing their good fortune, while the strollers ambled from boat to boat, enjoying the show.

Simone's eyes lit up for the first time and she began to toss her hair. (She had insisted on the station wagon; the jeep would ruin her blow-dry.) Stevie, as quiet as it was polite to be, led the way to the old café bar on the corner.

The grizzly-bearded owner called out, '*Buona sera*, Stevie.'

Stevie waved to Franco and headed for her favourite table, under the fig tree. The soft scent of the leaves filled the early evening and she began to feel better. Then Simone opened her mouth. 'Oh god, what is that smell?' Her little nose wrinkled in disgust. Stevie sniffed cautiously but could only detect a botanical scent.

'It's the fig tree,' Stevie said mildly. 'Don't you like it?'

'It's so strong—it reminds me of rotting jungle at home. I can't sit here.'

She stood and moved to a distant table, one more visible to the street parade. Mark and Stevie had no choice but to follow.

Nothing was right, of course: Franco's toasted sandwiches 'tasted funny', the olives were green, there was lemon rind in her water, the mosquitoes were eating her alive and . . . A wasp landed on the bowl of olives and Simone leapt up, shrieking. As she launched into a full denunciation of the insect life of the island, Stevie was almost tempted to take up Clémence's offer to dine on board. Instead, she finished her prosecco and white peach juice, an inspired combination and the perfect dockside *aperitivo*, and suggested a stroll.

At the very end of the wharf sat the *Hercules*.

A small crowd had gathered to gaze at the mega-yacht and opinion among them was divided as to whether it was visionary or utterly hideous. Stevie glanced discreetly about. Security was extremely tight. The underwater lights were all on; designed to deter approaches by divers and submersibles, they turned the water around the boat a translucent green and even the smallest fish were visible. The retractable gangplank was in, and the area of the dock immediately in front of the yacht was roped off and guarded by six impeccably dressed *carabinieri* cradling polished sub-machine guns and relishing the chance to participate in the evening's spectacle. Three black Range Rovers with mirrored windows were parked in readiness should plans include a trip ashore.

Krok's own men were less visible in white pants and shirts

against the gleaming white background, but their brown faces stood out, alert and still. Stevie thought about the white gun. More than anything she had seen or heard aboard the *Hercules*, the white gun disturbed her.

Stevie's afternoon call to Josie Wang at Hazard had caused a stir—as much as it was possible to stir an indomitable woman like Ms Wang.

'Are you sure the gun was ceramic?' Josie's voice was sharp. 'Officially ceramic pistols don't exist; they're impossible.'

Stevie described the gun and holster she had seen.

There was a silence on the end of the line, then, 'Stevie, what were you doing anywhere near a man like that?'

'It's just a lunch or two with the wife, nothing more. But the gun intrigued me. I've never seen anything like it.'

More silence.

'Josie, David asked me to do this. You know he wouldn't have if it was a dangerous job.'

Josie's silence grew deafeningly unimpressed. She believed Stevie was half in love with David Rice, a fact Stevie denied vehemently, the man being almost old enough to be her father, and her protector in more ways than one. But Josie had her theories and could rarely be swayed. She remained completely convinced of her ability—which was admittedly quite extraordinary—to recall every quirk and behavioural trait and weakness of the names in her massive files. While her energies were most often directed towards the collection of criminal, warlord or terrorist specimens, her friends and co-workers also found themselves neatly labelled and placed in her 'greenhouse of human nature', as she called it, subject to her dissections.

Stevie imagined Josie consulting her mental file for Stevie Margaret Duveen, noting the extreme stubbornness, weighing up the options with a specimen such as she.

Josie gave a pained sigh. 'There are rumours of the existence of a small automatic pistol made entirely of ceramic material. The bullets are also ceramic and the magazine is loaded into the handle. The spring driving the bolt/slide mechanism is supposedly made of plastic.'

'I know they've had some success with plastic guns. Wasn't there a furore over—'

'That was the Glock 17.' Josie clicked her tongue impatiently. 'Component parts made of plastic, including the grip and the trigger guard, but still at around eighty per cent metal if you're going by weight—more than enough to set off a magnetometer. No, Stevie, this is something completely different—if indeed it is what you think. These guns would be completely invisible to a metal detector.'

Josie continued, warming to her subject. 'The problem with glass guns has always been that the pressure in the chamber is so strong it causes them to explode when fired, to literally blow up in your face. Apparently this has been resolved by igniting the propellant in two stages, which keeps the chamber pressure low. The bullet operates almost like a cannonball with a charge of powder behind it.

'According to the rumours, it has been developed in a secret CIA lab, but all queries have elicited a 'no comment' from the Agency. If the crew aboard the *Hercules* are carrying ceramic automatics, it means your man either has weapons labs that are on a par—if not more sophisticated—than the CIA's, or he has some pretty extraordinary connections.' Josie let the pause hang a moment too long then said, 'Do I need to repeat myself, Stevie?'

'I know, Josie. I won't do anything reckless. I am staying firmly on the reservation this time. I don't think I could go through another adventure like . . .'

'You don't have the strength, Stevie.' Josie's voice was stern. 'You were lucky to make it out of the Swiss Alps alive, and you know as well as I do that your Russian friends could still be looking for you. We're counting on their short attention spans—not a very sure gamble.'

Stevie felt a chill of fear touch the back of her neck.

*That's all over. It's time to forget.*

'Ahoy there!' Stevie looked up and saw Clémence on one of the upper decks of the *Hercules*, waving a thin arm now covered in silver bangles. 'Stevie, darling! Come up for a cocktail.'

'Who's that?' Simone hissed, her hand on Stevie's arm.

Stevie called back, 'We were just on our way home.' She took an ignoble pleasure in denying Simone the satisfaction. Call it payback for hoping Didi would die. 'Some other time, though, I'll accept with pleasure,' she added.

Stevie felt Simone's nails dig in.

'Are you sure you can't stay for dinner, darling?' Clémence replied. 'Plenty of room for all of you aboard.'

As the nails dug harder, Stevie wondered if Simone's desire would leave scars. She shook her head. 'Thank you, though, and please thank your husband for today.'

Clémence gave another regal wave and disappeared.

Simone's disappointment manifested itself first in manic questioning: *who why what where when . . . how much?* She scurried along, her claw still on Stevie's arm. When Stevie claimed to have forgotten the woman's name, or her husband's, or anything else about the boat or the owners—'so absent-minded, it's awful'—the mania gave way to a petulant silence. Stevie wasn't at all unhappy about the silence.

**Back at the house, Stevie** prepared a simple risotto with saffron; the night was so still they could have their dinner on the roof. She had begun to feel a little sorry for Simone, stewing in her thwarted desires, and decided to put a bottle of champagne on ice. That was sure to cheer her up, and by tomorrow, the girl might have mellowed.

By now, they had missed the flute player and night had fallen. Steve lit candles on the roof and their reflections danced on the worn white walls.

'I almost forgot,' Stevie said as they sat down at the rickety wooden table, the risotto steaming in the middle, 'I have a surprise. Wait here.' She flew downstairs and grabbed the bottle, three flutes, and emerged triumphant back on the roof.

'*Voilà!*'

Simone looked up from her plate. Her mouth flattened sourly, her eyebrows arched in disdain. 'Is that the surprise?'

Without a word, Stevie set the bottle on the table. She peeled back the foil, twisted the wire helmet open, softly popped the cork into her hand and poured three full glasses. She handed one to Simone and one to Mark; she took the third glass in her left hand, the champagne bottle in her right, then turned and walked away.

The garden was dark and trilling with cicadas. Stevie headed for the fig trees by the back wall. There, she topped up her glass, tied the bottom of her kaftan into a knot above her knees, and climbed up into the oldest of the trees. The scent of the fig leaves was strong around her and Stevie knew she would be safe.

While at first she had tried to consider the possibility that she might even be glad of the company of Simone and Mark . . .

'. . . I now find myself considering the possibility that I might push Simone off the roof.' This idea pleased her and she said it aloud, liking the sound of the words in the night air.

'It would of course look like an accident,' she continued. 'Heels too high, masonry too old, a little too much to drink . . .' She sipped her champagne and plucked a fig from the tree. They were tiny and green and wonderfully sweet.

'I may have to stay up here tonight,' she said to the tree. 'I'm not sure I could face Simone or my dear cousin without resorting to physical violence.' She sighed deeply.

'All I can say is, Oh dear.'

A chuckle came out of the darkness and Stevie almost fell out of her tree in fright.

'Your grandmother Didi could be very fierce when crossed. I fear for your cousins.'

Stevie sat as still as a fig.

'Are they really that bad?' asked the voice in the night.

Stevie debated whether to acknowledge the voice.

'Is that why you are hiding up a tree,' it asked, 'in the dark, plotting murder?'

With as much dignity as she could muster in the situation, Stevie answered, 'I'm having a glass of champagne, in private. It was the only safe place.'

'Oh dear.' Another chuckle.

Stevie peered into the blackness but could see no one. There was no moon and the starlight was blocked by the fig leaves. The voice seemed to be coming from the roof of the garage next door— but that was impossible. The roof, Stevie knew from daylight, was made of thin slats of bamboo. They couldn't bear the weight of a man, and it was a man's voice speaking.

'You may mock,' she added, her indignance growing, 'but you haven't met Simone.'

'What's so terrible about her?'

Stevie took a steadying breath. 'The girl lacks any trace of elegance—of manner, of mind, of character. And she's praying Didi dies soon so her husband-to-be, my cousin, will come into some money.'

'Ah.'

'Exactly.' Stevie took a sip of champagne. 'The trouble is, they're staying put. I don't know how to get rid of them, short of something desperately messy.'

From the house, the noise of a woman swearing.

There was a pause in the conversation as the man stopped to listen. Then came the low remark, 'Yes, I think I see . . . Perhaps you could concentrate on the things that you find charming, on the things this woman can't ruin for you. She is a speck of dust in the blissful whole. Now, you can choose to focus on the speck, or you can see it for what it really is, insignificant in the universal scheme.'

Stevie raised her glass. She was feeling a little tipsy, but it could have just been the odd situation up the tree. 'In principle, I would agree. If Simone were a work assignment, it would be nothing—I've handled worse, believe me. But in my heart all I want to do is slap her.'

This time, a belly laugh from the darkness.

'She's on your turf . . . Have you suggested a charming little *pensione* up the hill?'

'Of course!' Stevie replied. 'And I know Issa would make room for them at the Pietra Niedda, no matter how full he was, if I begged him to. But she wants to save the money for shoes.'

That maddening laugh again.

'I can see you're finding this hilarious—whoever you are.' Stevie was beginning to feel quite cross. 'Perhaps *you* should take them in.'

'It does all seem funny—you should see it that way too. If you can see this woman's antics as amusing rather than infuriating, the whole thing will become playful. You won't even have to make an effort.'

There was more swearing, then the sound of a door slamming. Hopefully it was the bedroom door, thought Stevie, and she could return to the house in safety.

The voice in the darkness was right. It was the only way to deal with Simone. She would begin tomorrow. 'Would you care for a glass of champagne?' she asked tentatively, but the night made no reply.

# 7

Stevie awoke early the next morning, absolutely famished, having only managed three figs and the greater part of a bottle of champagne for dinner. She slipped on her swimming costume and padded in bare feet down the stone path to the little beach below. The bay was washed in a soft pink light that turned the coarse sand gold and the water a silvery mauve. No one was about: the Biedermeier doors were still closed, the Liptons next door were quiet, and the two Olivetti houses—built by the famous Italian industralist brothers in the 1960s—were dark.

The first Olivetti house now belonged to a British fashion designer and his wife; the second remained empty. Years ago, one of the Olivettis had been kidnapped and held for months in a cave not that far away. When he had finally been returned, the coast had lost its magic for his family and they sold their pair of small, curved, stone and glass houses.

Stevie slid into the water and swam briskly out to the farthest buoy. She clung to the rubber ring on the top and looked back up the valley. The shutters were open at the Villa Goliath and there were *giardinieri* in green moving on the terrace. Stevie remembered that Clémence had said her husband liked to rise early.

A man in his line of work would certainly attract enemies—most likely rivals, and unsavoury ones at that—but it took a lot of energy and risk to go after a man as well-protected and connected as Krok. It didn't make much sense. Surely he had confidence in his own systems, his own security? Was Clémence right about the paranoia? Or was Krok deliberately keeping his wife imprisoned in fear?

Stevie shivered. The water felt cold now that she was no longer moving. It didn't seem to her that Clémence had any intention of crossing her husband, nor of fleeing. Clémence had mentioned Emile and her concern for him. Perhaps they had clashed over the boy and Krok was punishing her? It was an unpleasant thought for such a beautiful morning.

Stevie dived underwater, then struck out for the shore.

She couldn't risk breakfast at home so she threw on her old denim shorts, a worn shirt that had belonged to her father, a pair of white plimsols, pearls, Rolex and Ray-Bans, and set off for Bar Spinnaker, which was frequented mainly by locals and the yachties off the sailing boats in the marina. There you could buy newspapers in six languages at the tiny newsagent next door and the coffee was good. In the evening, a little restaurant opened in the courtyard and they served salt-crusted fish and squid-ink pasta. Stevie wanted a word with Sauro, the owner of Spinnaker and a tremendous source of local gossip, but it was still reasonably quiet and he didn't seem to be about.

Stevie stood at the bar and ordered a black coffee and chose a *cornetto*, still piping hot from the café's oven and filled with apricot jam, then went and sat at one of the small marble-topped tables. The papers brought news of an earthquake in China, people killed because local developers had skimped on the proper foundations, not believing that the laws of nature applied to their buildings—or possibly not caring.

The colour supplement blew open at the social pages—a

party given in Venice two weeks ago at the Palazzo Guggenheim. There was a photo of Clémence looking rather serpentine in silver lamé, Krok close beside her scowling, stocky and pink.

A convoy of black Range Rovers with mirror-tinted windows roared past at high speed.

*Krok's men.*

The numberplates were even personalised: STORM.

Stevie frowned behind her dark glasses. Vaughan Krok was a man who ought to know better. The most effective way to avoid unwanted attention was to preserve as much privacy and anonymity as possible. This meant simple things such as unlisted phone numbers and addresses, avoiding flashy watches, jewellery, clothing and luggage; it meant getting rid of personalised numberplates and very noticeable vehicles. It also meant entertaining more modestly and staying out of the social pages.

While Krok was certainly not the flashiest billionaire Stevie had come across—not by a long shot—he seemed to take a certain pleasure in doing things very much his own way and this attracted notice. *Hercules* was the talk of the boating world; Clémence's jewels inspired equivalent chat among a certain set of women. There were the STORM cars tearing about, the parties, the highly visible security detail in their set-designed uniforms . . . such ostentation was not the mark of a man who was afraid.

'*Hai visto?*' Sauro flicked his chin at the passing motorcade and pulled out a chair at Stevie's table. He was a good-looking man, tall, with a mop of dark hair and kind brown eyes. 'Every morning is the same.'

He kissed Stevie fondly on both cheeks, pinched one of them. 'You look a bit thin.'

'I missed dinner last night.'

Sauro spread his hands wide. 'You should come up here. My

sisters are visiting from Bologna and the food is especially good this summer. They are making their own ravioli, all the pasta . . .'

The barman brought Sauro a *caffè corretto*—espresso with a shot of grappa.

'Is your *nonna* here? It's been so long since I saw her.'

Stevie shook her head.

'Did you see what is happening in Liscia? That Russian—'

'Sauro, don't say his name.' Stevie lowered her voice to a whisper. 'I know who you mean. Let's call him Brown.'

Sauro laughed and ruffled her hair. 'Ah, *bellina*.'

'Trust me, Sauro, you never know who is listening.'

Something in Stevie's eyes must have convinced him she was serious, for he continued, 'So, this Brown . . .' He downed his espresso in a single gulp. 'He has bought all the houses in the valley, one after the other. Has he come to you yet?'

Stevie shook her head again. 'I don't think Lu Nibaru is what Brown's after. How did he convince these people to sell? Some of them have been here since the beginning. Like Bettina—she wouldn't have sold just for the money.'

Sauro made a pistol with his thumb and forefinger and pressed it hard to Stevie's temple. For a split second, Stevie's nerves registered metal—her heart leapt in fright, the memory of another gun at her head, a snowy night in the Alps . . . She shook herself.

*Fool.*

'Really, Sauro?'

He only shrugged. 'You never know who is listening, *carina*.'

He gave her a wink and ruffled her hair again. Sauro always made her feel like she was seven or ten, a kid sister. Stevie didn't mind. It had been forever since she had felt like that.

Sauro got up and went inside the café, leaving Stevie to sit and watch Issa Farmishan wheeling a cartload of milk from the supermarket to his little three-wheeled truck. He ran the *pensione* on the point next door to Brown's compound. The Pietra Niedda was a lovely soft pink house with a series of little bungalows dotted about under pergolas of bougainvillea. Issa had come to the Costa Smeralda decades before. His hotel was one of the first to have been built and many guests stayed there while they finished building their own villas. Having had the pick of locations in the bay, he had chosen well. Several times people had tried to persuade him to sell his promontory but, even though Issa was not a rich man, the Pietra Niedda was his heart and home and he wouldn't think of selling.

After what Sauro had told her, Stevie was relieved to see him on what seemed to be an emergency milk run.

He caught sight of Stevie and waved. '*Ciao*, Stevie,' he called. 'We had another blackout—the fridge went out and all the milk is off!' He grinned. 'My guests want their breakfast.' Stevie couldn't remember ever seeing Issa without a smile.

His little son Farouk waved at her from the van and Stevie walked over to him.

'Farouk!' She opened her mouth wide in mock surprise. 'You're so big now—how old are you?'

'Six and three quarters exactly.' The tiny boy was proud as punch at having earned himself such high numbers. He was a beautiful little thing with a basin cut of dark hair and huge, limpid eyes.

'I go to school,' he said, beaming.

'Only very grown-up boys go to school. Your papa must be very proud of you.'

Issa shut the van doors and climbed into the driver's seat. 'He is my sunshine, Stevie.' He reached over and put his arm around the little man's shoulders, grinning from ear to ear. 'When are you going to have one?'

Stevie shrugged, a little embarrassed.

Issa grinned. 'Things take their own time. *Insha'Allah*, when it is right, you will be blessed.' He gave a honk of his horn and roared off; Farouk stuck his little hand out the window and waved enthusiastically at Stevie until they were out of sight.

Stevie had just wandered back to her car when her tiny phone rang. It was Rice, calling from London. Stevie sat in her jeep and took the call.

'You had lunch with Clémence?'

*I'm very well, thank you, David, and how are you?*

'Aboard the *Hercules*. It's the most unusual yacht I've ever seen. It's—'

'I've seen the photos, Stevie,' he broke in. 'What did you find out?'

His voice was taut and strained. Stevie exhaled silently. Rice was in a mood.

'Clémence thinks her husband is paranoid and growing more so every day. She says he tells her their family is in great danger but won't specify what kind. His men are everywhere and neither she nor Emile, their son, can move without close personal protection.'

'So, you think Clémence is right?'

'I'm not sure yet. Krok is a vain man but not the type that needs extremely visible security to feel important. And he is a man who would conceivably have many powerful enemies—especially if he is that close to Brown . . .'

'Stevie, I wish you'd quit using your ridiculous codenames.'

Stevie decided to ignore him. His shortness was beginning to irritate her. She was doing him a favour, after all.

'. . . which would justify the security,' she continued. 'But he doesn't behave like a man who is truly afraid.'

Stevie told Rice what she had observed of Krok's outfit so far.

'Does he suspect Clémence will leave him, then,' Rice asked, 'or have an affair?'

'Certainly I don't think she has given him any reason to; she seems totally dedicated to making him happy for the long term—or at least that was her plan until he started acting wild.'

There was a long silence on the phone. Stevie wondered if Rice was jealous of Krok.

*Serves him right.*

'Josie was supposed to get me the full report on the Kroks,' Stevie added. 'But I don't think she approves of my mission.'

'I don't give a damn who approves of what. It's an order and she'll do it. You'll have the report by this afternoon.'

Rice was not a man to throw his weight about like this. He had the utmost respect for the members of his team. Stevie's irritation faded and was replaced by concern.

'David, are you alright?'

There was a silence, then, 'I'll be in touch.' And the line went dead.

Stevie put her phone down on the seat next to her. She felt empty. Rice sounded terrible, his voice as thin as tissue paper, and she was worried. He was strong and fit, but he was no longer young. Things were obviously not getting better.

She picked up her tiny phone—the smaller the better because she hated the things—and scrolled through her numbers.

*Henning.*

This was the second time in two days she had thought of him. She missed him. Missed his romantic view of life; missed his way of knowing exactly what she was thinking, all the time; missed the strength of his arms when he held her, the crush of his lips on hers. Actually, if she were honest, she thought about him most days, if only briefly. Had she done the right thing in pushing him away? Had the risk to her heart really been that high?

She shook herself. Henning was a tall, dashing man who disappeared at a moment's notice, who left too many things unsaid, who reeked of mystery and Turkish tobacco; Stevie would not have been surprised if there were women in the background, and her heart couldn't take that uncertainty—she needed to feel safe. They would be friends, and it would end there. Just friends.

So there was no reason why she shouldn't call . . .

'Stevie.' The pleasure in his voice warmed her after her chilly call with Rice.

'Where are you, Henning? It sounds like a Turkish bazaar.' Tinny, Middle Eastern music was blaring in the background.

'I'm in Persepolis—some Persian poetry books, aeons old, have come to light. Fascinating stuff. Did you know that the paisley pattern was originally Persian? And that the motif is actually a flame—or some argue, a cypress—the symbol of life and eternity, the essence of Zoroastrianism? They call it *buteh*. It was used as a decorative motif in the Sassanid dynasty.'

'That is interesting.' Stevie smiled into the phone. 'I'll never look at paisley the same way again.'

'Precisely. I've picked up some incredible examples of the stuff—Samarkand is wonderful for that sort of thing.' There was the briefest of pauses. 'I'll give you some if you like—very useful for pyjamas and robes and whatnot . . .'

'How lovely.' Stevie suppressed a giggle, rather fancying the idea of paisley pyjamas. 'I couldn't be further from Persepolis.' Here she felt a pang of disappointment. 'I'm on the Costa Smeralda.'

'Need rescuing, do you?' She could tell from his voice that he was smiling.

'Not at all—why do you say that? I'm on holiday, my grand-mother's place.'

Henning laughed. 'It sounds charming, I wish I wasn't so far away, but . . . I've just remembered—my mother's in Porto Cervo. How perfect.' The sound of a rooster crowing in great alarm in the background. 'I'd better go, darling; I think Alidod might need a hand with the shopping. I'll arrange for her to have tea with you tomorrow.'

'Oh no, Henning. Really. I'm sure your mother's lovely but I—'

Henning laughed. 'She's not what you're thinking, or I wouldn't send you. I'll be in touch tomorrow.'

Stevie groaned inwardly. That was the last time she would give in to impulses to call Henning.

She turned her mind to work. Perhaps solving this little puzzle for David would help him, take some of the pressure off, even if it was only a tiny bit. To that end, she needed to do more scouting, get a feel for the dynamic between Krok and his wife; Rice had promised that Krok's full dossier would be in her hands by the afternoon, so that left the reading for later.

Stevie rang Clémence's phone. It was answered by her husband.

# 8

The Villa Giardiniera was a long, low pebble-stone house built on a headland jutting into the sea. It was set into a hillside garden covered with the greenest, most perfect lawn imaginable, the grass growing over the top of the back half of the house, and over the courtyard that linked the back to the front. From here, you looked south to Cala di Volpe, or north towards Porto Cervo, the void creating a window right through the headland.

The house belonged to a Milanese industrialist called Dado Falcone, according to Clémence, a sometime business associate of Krok's who manufactured guidance systems for missiles. When Stevie arrived with Clémence and Krok by Riva, the lunch party was already in full swing.

A small grey man in a beige suit and large black glasses was dancing slowly with a Nordic goddess well over six feet tall, luminous in an emerald silk dress and high gold wedges. Nestled in her most wonderful bosom was the largest emerald Stevie had ever seen, all set about with diamonds, and so heavy it pulled the already-revealing cleavage of the dress down to new glories.

As he shuffled to the music, the grey man stared straight ahead in rapture, his eyes perfectly level with the jewel.

Three young girls in white crocheted bikinis and white

high-heeled espadrilles stood smoking, huge sunglasses hiding their faces, printed silk scarves tied around their hair.

When a white-jacketed waiter offered champagne, neither Clémence nor Stevie refused.

A lithe blonde in a red lycra jumpsuit, a thin white belt circling the waist, sashayed past giggling to another blonde in a white sundress. 'Don't you love Italian men?' she whispered in accented English.

'That's Princess Loli Hanau-Schaumberg and her sister, Princess Ludi-Brigitte von Anhalt. Vaughan's mad about them.' Clémence's eyes narrowed dangerously. 'Fortunately they barely speak a word of English between them.'

'But I just heard her—' began Stevie.

'Well, not a lot of English, anyway,' Clémence replied quickly. She reached for another glass of champagne. 'I suppose the whole Euro-royal thing might be interesting for a moment,' she continued, 'but I've told Vaughan I'll never give him a divorce. And really, their titles mean little these days and most are as poor as church mice—relatively speaking.' She gave the pair one last, appraising look. 'They are young, though—mid-twenties. That's an asset. Most of the time.' She turned back to Stevie. 'Then again, experience has its own allure . . .'

Clémence could definitely hold her own, thought Stevie. Certainly she would not go quietly if Krok ever tried to end their marriage. Did this constitute a motive for keeping her under lock and key? Stevie did not know much about these matters but she imagined that a transgressing wife would be more useful to a man contemplating a separation than a devoted one . . .

Clémence shimmered in a silk coral dress with tulip sleeves, and gold sandals. Diamond bracelets rippled on her wrists whenever she moved her fine brown hands, and her ears sparkled with large pink diamonds. Stevie caught the other guests glancing her way, dazzled by the jewels. Clémence Krok's reputation preceded both her and her husband, and there would be no doubt anywhere in the room that the giant rocks were real.

Clémence and Stevie wandered over to the windows where Krok was standing. Dado Falcone was moving towards them, wearing a pale apricot linen suit and a light blue shirt, a combination that suited him and his party to perfection. He kissed Clémence's hand then stood back to admire her.

'*Stupenda—una favola*, a fairytale.'

Clémence, her laugh and her bracelets tinkling, took Vaughan's big, freckled forearm.

'How much did this place set you back, Dado?' Krok barked by way of a greeting.

Falcone smiled broadly. 'It was built by my father, it passed to me. What is money when sentiment . . .?' He raised his hands.

'Only people who haven't made their own money talk like that.' Krok's eyes were watery and pink. 'I'm self-made, and I'll tell you something—*money* . . .' he pointed a large freckled sausage finger at Dado's chest, '*is back*.'

Clémence whispered to Stevie, 'Please, darling, a large vodka. I daren't leave Vaughan when he's like this.'

Stevie nipped to the bar trolley in the corner and poured four fingers of neat vodka into a crystal tumbler.

Clémence handed it to her husband, who took it automatically and drank it in one gulp.

'Are you looking to purchase a villa, Vaughan?' Dado's manners were flawless.

'Thinkin' about it.' The vodka had mollified Krok somewhat. He lit a cigarillo with a battered Zippo lighter. 'But there's only one piece of land I want on this whole goddamn island.'

'The Villa Goliath?'

'The Russki can keep that. I want the land next door.'

Stevie's ears pricked up. She did not like the idea of Krok buying into the neighbourhood any more than she had rejoiced at the arrival of Brown and his menacing black helicopters. Moreover, she feared she knew exactly what piece of land Krok was talking about: the Pietra Niedda. Well, Issa would never sell.

'The villa there is rubbish,' Krok continued, 'but the land—it's a whole promontory. A man could build a castle there.'

Stevie glanced around. The crewman who had arrived with them in the Riva stood a little behind Vaughan and Clémence. His immaculate white uniform, white beret and mirrored sunglasses set him apart from the guests and the staff. He stood as still as an icicle, surveying with invisible eyes.

Stevie, wanting to create space for a private chat with Clémence, stepped out onto the lawn where several people in various shades of gelato-coloured clothes were lounging on cane lawn chairs.

An older man in a perfectly crisp marigold-yellow shirt was telling a story to a small group of people, gesticulating with a free hand. 'But I tell you, they weren't always professional. That's why so many got killed. You remember Dorigatti?'

'The tyre king?' asked a man in sugar-paper blue trousers.

'Him. He had a villa down at Romazzino, by the water. There was a beautiful daughter, about thirty, spoilt—you know the type— I think her name was Valentina or Valeria, something like that.'

'Valeria Dorigatti,' confirmed a woman in orange and red palazzo pyjamas. 'I remember her.'

'Anyway, every summer she brought a different boyfriend to stay,' continued the marigold man. 'Dorigatti didn't like it, but he usually tolerated it because he loved Valeria with the distraction of a father. This particular summer, though, she had taken up with a much older man, very much interested in her money—a gigolo. He was distinguished-looking, well-dressed . . . but aren't they all?' Here the marigold man chuckled and took a sip of his drink.

'It was at the height of the kidnappings,' he continued. 'Some men broke into the villa at Romazzino and kidnapped the gigolo, thinking it was Dorigatti. When the kidnappers called, Dorigatti himself got on the phone and offered them money to keep him.'

The group laughed, feeling safe enough; those things didn't happen very often on the Costa Smeralda—not anymore.

Stevie could see Clémence and Krok inside. He was still talking to Dado, standing very close, his fish eyes darting about. Clémence had installed herself on a pop-art pink sofa with an elegant lady of sixty, swathed in shades of caramel and cream. Krok's security man—one of his white knights, as he called them—stood directly behind her, closer than was prudent or necessary for personal protection, close enough to hear what the two women were saying.

Maybe Clémence was right in her suspicions that her husband was up to something. Either that or he was curious about what Clémence and her companion might be talking about.

'Stevie, come and join us,' Clémence called, and Stevie felt the mirrored eyes of Krok's man swivel towards her.

'This is Elisabetta Falcone,' she said when Stevie approached.

'Signora Falcone.' Stevie took the older woman's hand.

'Lisa, please.'

'Your guests were telling the most extraordinary stories about kidnappings out there,' Stevie said, trying to begin a conversation that might turn to useful gossip. 'The man in the beautiful yellow shirt seems to know a lot about it.'

'Dario? He was head prosecutor for organised crime in Torino before he retired—early. It is not a job that is good for the health.'

'Some people are still afraid of the *banditi*, aren't they?' asked Stevie casually, taking a sip of her champagne.

'Usually it is people who have something to be afraid about. Their conscience tells them so. But these days I suspect it is not so much the *banditi* that are at work . . .'

When Lisa didn't finish the sentence, Stevie added, 'Although it must be a temptation—the jewels, the yachts, the incredible cars that sit like gold nuggets in the scrub. I might be tempted to pocket one if I were a desperate sheep farmer.'

Lisa raised her palms. 'People these days want to show too much.'

Stevie noted that Elisabetta Falcone wore only small golden rings in her ears, and a wedding ring of thick gold; her watch was a plastic Swatch but her clothes were silk and cashmere, her suede loafers quietly expensive.

'I agree,' replied Stevie. 'Living discreetly is really the best defence against—'

Clémence interrupted, obviously growing annoyed with the direction of the conversation. 'Oh, yes, yes, but what fun is that?' She pointed at the white knight behind her. 'The best defence is a large man with a gun.'

Stevie wasn't sure if Clémence meant what she was saying or if it was being said for the benefit of her husband, who had now moved within earshot.

'You wouldn't understand that, Stevie.' Clémence levelled disdainful violet eyes at Stevie, clearly wanting to put her back in her place. 'You know nothing about the real possibilities of massive wealth.'

'Probably not, Clémence,' Stevie replied mildly. 'I only know that some people live in prisons of their own making—they make money their motto and then it holds them captive in return.' She smiled. 'I try to use the little money I have to be free.'

Sensing a dangerous topic, Lisa deftly turned the conversation onto another tack.

Stevie heard Krok's voice grow loud: '. . . and I tell you what, they're operationally perfect and totally risk-free. Officially, nobody controls them, and they don't work for any government—so there is no recourse. They can disappear as quickly as they appear, and the most beautiful thing is, they are totally, utterly deniable. It's an amazing investment opportunity.'

Stevie froze as Dado began to protest, but in a much softer voice.

Stevie smiled as Lisa said something about the new restaurant in the port, and nodded at Clémence's reply, but her ears remained tuned in to Krok and Dado. Her mind was reeling. She hoped the white knight didn't suspect eavesdropping; she giggled and took a canapé just in case.

What were the two men talking about? Krok's mercenaries? Perhaps. But he had mentioned that no one controlled them, that they were deniable . . . She wondered if that was a good description of Krok's soldiers of fortune. And why would Dado be interested?

Beside her, Clémence lifted her chin and allowed her cheeks to be kissed by a handsome man in red trousers.

'Piero, darling.'

'Come and sit on the grass, Clémence. Martina and I have brought friends from Milano. I want you to meet them.' Clémence stood and followed Piero onto the lawn. Krok and Dado moved over to the bar, out of earshot now, and Stevie excused herself.

She walked across the lawn and sat on the grassy roof above the courtyard. She could see Clémence at the centre of a gay little group down below. She seemed to be telling a story and the others were laughing. Stevie tried to reconcile this Clémence with the troubled woman who had appealed to her for help.

Was Clémence really such a good actress that she could totally mask her terrors under this laquered façade? If so, she was one of the best Stevie had ever seen. Or was she perhaps a woman who, bored, sought extra attention by manufacturing dangers and fears and then begging for help? Stevie had seen a few of those in her line of work too.

Vaughan Krok's head appeared below. He scoped the garden then saw Clémence and went still, fixed in her direction like a sniper. Stevie felt glad she was nowhere near the man.

**Lunch had been laid out** on a magnificent narrow table under the bamboo pergola, with small cane chairs for fifty. Stevie found herself seated between Piero, the man in the red trousers, and a young man with tawny lion's hair and wide turquoise eyes. Both stood politely as she arrived at the table and Piero pulled out a chair.

Clémence was on Piero's other side. Dado, the host, had placed Krok at the far end of the table, but Krok ignored the place card and sat down opposite his wife, scraping back his chair and leaning forward on his elbow, talking over Princess Loli, addressing Dado. Stevie noticed his eyes darting between Clémence, Piero and the man in the marigold shirt, also sitting beside his wife.

The first course was a beef carpaccio done Harry's Bar style— cut slightly thicker than usual and dressed with a mustard sauce. Piero was talking to Clémence—Stevie could hear her tinkling laugh—while the man on her right was talking to Lisa Falcone, so she had ample time to scope the guests.

The women at the table were amazing, like beautiful birds of paradise in their coloured silks and jewels. They weren't all young, but they all shimmered with animation and style. There were a few young men like Piero and the tawny man next to her, but most of the men were older, all glossy with grooming and money.

Krok stood out as a hard man among them—muscular, his hair cropped, dressed like an off-duty soldier—but he was not, Stevie noted, the only man at the table with frightening eyes. Stevie could suddenly smell the danger—even under all the polish. These were Krok's friends, she realised, not Clémence's. Her roving eyes stopped on a man seated at the far end of the table, broad nose and shoulders, dark hair slicked back, tortoiseshell sunglasses: Socrates Skorpios. He felt her gaze and turned, nodded once in acknowledgement: he had recognised her too. Stevie found her eyes locked on his, unable to look away. Fortunately, the man to her right turned and introduced himself with a smile. 'Mi chiamo Osip.'

'Like the poet?' Stevie held out her small hand.

The man nodded. 'My father is a lover of the arts.'

'Is he here today?' Stevie wondered whether handsome men with clear eyes turned into the spoilt, ruthless men she saw around her—was it simply a matter of time and cruel intentions?

Osip shook his head. 'Lisa is an old friend of my mother's. She rang and asked me at the last minute—one of the other guests had fly out to America and the numbers were off. This is not my usual . . .' He seemed unsure how to finish the sentence.

'So you're here as eye candy?'

'Possibly you could put it that way.' Osip smiled. 'I haven't heard that phrase before. I suppose men can be *bonbons* too.' His accent was French, not Italian, and his voice was ever so vaguely familiar, but Stevie couldn't place it . . .

'Are you a friend of Lisa's?' he asked.

Stevie shook her head. 'I came with the Kroks—I'm a friend of Clémence's.'

'I don't know them personally.'

'Tell me, what do you think of them? I mean, as an outsider, watching the two of them, what are your impressions?' Stevie wasn't quite sure what impulse had led her to ask Osip this, but she had a feeling his reply would be perceptive.

Osip fixed his gaze on Krok first. 'His reputation precedes him, of course, but even if I had no idea of the man and his friends, I should still say he was a violent man—erratic and angry. See how he sits on the edge of his chair, and his fingertips are white on his fork? Look at how aggressively he cuts his food. He is not a man at ease. And yet he is protected by his bodyguard. He has demons, possibly, or a guilty conscience; they might be one and the same.'

Osip turned his eyes to Clémence, who was fluttering her feathers and chatting animatedly to both Piero and the man in the marigold shirt.

'Clémence Krok is more difficult, I think. Is she the trophy wife who lives to please Krok and wear diamonds, to chit-chat amusingly and be envied by the women? Or is there something much tougher under that face, a steel plate, perhaps . . .'

'Might it not be possible that she's both?'

Osip smiled at Stevie, his eyes an electric blue in his tanned face. 'Indeed it might, but usually it shows more—the steel, I mean. She seems to bend like a willow in the winds of the men around her.'

Stevie watched Clémence a moment—now laughing gaily with her male neighbours—and thought that Osip was right.

Vaughan Krok was watching too.

He was shredding a bread roll with his stubby fingers, rolling pellets on the linen tablecloth. Suddenly he shoved back his chair and stood, knocking over Princess Loli's large glass of chilled rosé.

Krok's eyes were bloodshot. 'We're leaving.'

Clémence looked up, her eyes wide. 'Darling, so soon? Why don't we finish lunch? I'm sure you and Dado—'

'Now.'

'Oh, Vaughan. Why don't I join you in an hour? It won't—'

Two powerful palms covered in freckles clamped down on the table, making the silverware jump. 'Clem!' he roared. The bull's head lowered a moment, then came Krok's voice, gravelly and dangerous: 'I own you.'

Quickly, Clémence stood, nodded to Lisa with a brilliant, unfocused smile, then followed her husband, the white knight falling in behind her, her napkin still clutched in her hand.

As soon as they were out of sight, conversation at the table naturally turned to the just-departed couple.

'Well Susanna told me he killed his first wife—and I wouldn't be surprised if it were true.'

'He's like Bluebeard the pirate!'

'No, no, *no*, darling, you got that all wrong. It was her—*she* killed her first husband, and her second died in mysterious circumstances. Apparently she drives all men wild with jealousy . . .'

'Of course she stays for the money. That's why they married.'

'He certainly owns her in that sense, but where is her dignity? I'm not sure I could stay with a man who treated me like that for any amount of money.'

'But did you get a good look at her jewellery? I'd love diamonds like hers. And he's probably not even home half the time. Just the odd holiday. Not such a bad price to pay.'

'He's mixed up in all sorts of things that are hidden behind his mercenaries.'

'It's a dirty business regardless, I know . . .'

'But he takes it to another level.'

'You shouldn't cross him—important people are in his debt.'

'I'm not impressed. The man's a pirate.'

The scene with the Kroks, far from dampening the spirit of

the party, seemed to electrify it. Soon after the *babas au rhum* were served, the women were dancing, along with some of the more colourful men; others sat in knots smoking their various tobaccos, drinking espresso and small glasses of *fil 'e ferru*, the local grappa, named after barbed wire for both historical reasons (the mountain peasants used to hide it down wells, attached to a length of wire) as well as for the quality of its mouth feel. Stevie stayed seated, watching the scene unfold before her.

Osip, still next to her, looked away from the dancers and turned to Stevie. 'Do you think they are as happy as they look?' he asked lightly.

Stevie considered a moment, head to one side. 'Yes,' she said slowly, 'I think they might be. Not all of them, not all the time, but I think they are happy.'

'Is it the money, do you think?'

'No. The money helps them to be free and have more fun, but I think they seem to have a capacity for joy. That is the key to happiness.'

'To find pleasure in the small things, the everyday things,' Osip echoed.

Stevie smiled and nodded. 'I've seen people with enough money who fixate on getting more—of everything: diamonds, cars, handbags, clothes, houses . . . They can't consume fast enough. And they always seem to be the unhappiest people—the men can't relax and they grow fat; the women get these horrible pinched mouths. They become mean. They can no longer take pleasure in a perfect dawn, or a warm bed, or raindrops on the window pane.'

Osip grinned. 'You are quite the poet yourself.'

Stevie shook her head. 'My soul is terribly unromantic. In my business—' She stopped abruptly. She had almost forgotten herself.

'I plan parties,' she explained with a smile, 'and in my business, I see too much of people behaving badly.'

Osip looked at her curiously. 'You remind me of someone.' His eyes bored into hers and she felt her colour rise.

*Damn the curse of blushing!*

'The cousins,' he said simply. 'You're the girl with the cousins.'

Stevie was thunderstruck. *How did he know about Simone and Mark?*

'The fig tree,' Osip went on, smiling. 'The champagne bottle. I knew the voice was familiar.'

Stevie blushed even deeper. All she could manage in response was a carefully controlled, 'Oh.'

Osip laughed and looked away, sparing her more discomfort. 'Have you managed to get rid of them yet?'

Stevie shook her head. 'Alas, no. I fear it will be impossible.'

'Everything in life is possible,' he replied, 'that is the beauty of it. Why don't you come over tomorrow afternoon? We're neighbours after all. You can meet my sisters—although I think perhaps you know them already?'

'Nicolette, Marie-Thérèse and Severine,' Stevie replied, putting the pieces together. 'We used to play on the beach as little girls. You're the *Barone's* son.'

'Adopted son, but in all other ways, yes. We are a very close family. Come over. It will be a reprieve from your cousins at least.'

'Thank you,' Stevie said, 'I might do that.'

Osip excused himself, saying he had a windsurfing appointment with a friend in Baia Sardinia. He kissed Stevie on both cheeks and left the party.

Stevie stood and walked about. She didn't feel like dancing; she wanted to learn more about Krok and his world. Three men in pale linen trousers and light summer jackets were seated at the far end of the pergola. They were deep in discussion, their eyes hidden by sunglasses, although the sun had far passed its brightest point and the light under the bougainvillea was dim. One of them was Dado Falcone, the other was Skorpios.

Stevie's instincts told her these were the men whose conversation would be most useful, but she could hardly just sidle up, yawn, and lie down under their lounge chair, no matter how innocent she looked.

Then she had a thought.

Many of the houses on the Costa Smeralda, having been built by the same handful of architects, had similar features. One of them, as was the case at Lu Nibaru, was sunken bathrooms with low windows opening up at terrace-floor level. Many a conversation had been accidentally overheard because of this unlikely design. It was possible that the Falcones' villa might have such a bathroom. There was a window not too far from one of the men's feet.

Stevie slipped into the house and followed the cool terracotta steps down. The bathroom was on her left and she opened the door with great caution. Sure enough, through the window high above the toilet, she could see a tan loafer, a silk sock in pale pink. She twisted the handle on the window to open it, silent as a humming-bird, then lowered the cistern lid and sat.

Anyone peeking in would be embarrassed to find a young lady engaged in private business.

Fortunately for Stevie, the men spoke Italian, rather than a regional dialect that she would have found impossible to understand.

Dado dropped a lit match and she smelt cigar smoke. 'When times are economically uncertain, it's unwise to offend one of your best customers. The man may be a vulgarian, but he buys more of my systems than Germany or France. It is the relationship, not the man, that I nurture.'

'But, Dado, you have no idea where he on-sells your systems to, nor to whom. He's a mercenary, not a registered arms trader. I can only imagine he sells to places where others won't.' Stevie craned her neck to get a better view. Dado's confederate was a man with thick white hair—a shock of snow above his tanned face. 'I've heard he runs barges off the coast of West Africa—floating gun supermarkets for anyone who wants them. Think about the customers: from Sierra Leone, Nigeria, the Congo. The picture is not a pretty one.'

'Someone will always sell to a pariah,' a third man's voice broke in. Although Stevie couldn't see his face from where she was sitting, she recognised Skorpios' Greek-accented Italian.

'You Swiss,' he chuckled. 'You'll worry yourself white, Aldo. Business is business and money makes the rules. As I have more money than both of you put together, I say Krok is sound. Our syndicate finds him useful and until he is not useful, he stays.'

The man with the white hair—Aldo the Swiss—began to protest. 'He is not a man we can control. This new venture smacks of madness. I don't—'

'We don't need to control him,' Skorpios said. 'We only need to profit from his activities. If anything goes wrong, we deny all association.' He shrugged his giant shoulders. 'Of course, let me remind you this is not our first time, friends; we are hardly a gathering of virgins on their wedding night.'

There was a pause, then Dado spoke. 'But I do agree with Aldo that the man seems to be growing less predictable. That destabilises the relationship.'

'Does he still buy from you?' Skorpios asked. 'Does he still find customers when no one on the open market seems to be buying? Does he allow you to keep your hands perfectly clean?'

Dado nodded.

The Greek turned to Aldo. 'And does he still run his money through your banks?'

Aldo raised both hands in a gesture of resignation.

'Does he still make me a fortune?' Here Skorpios laughed.

The three men stopped talking as a waiter brought a fresh round of espressos and a plate of colourful marzipan fruit.

Stevie recognised Skorpios' hand—the signet ring—take a plump sugared peach.

'Besides,' he went on, 'the man has the best connections this side of the Pillars of Hercules. Totally clean, totally professional—even we don't know who he is. If we did . . . well, Krok might be less useful. But I've seen what his men can do and it is . . . impressive.'

'His connections are extraordinary.' Dado neatly tapped the ash from his cigar into a silver pocket-ashtray.

'He is linked to every villainous head of state and warlord on the planet.' Aldo shook his head. 'Gentlemen, profit is one thing and I don't deny I have a love of money, but what about conscience? Things are going too far. This is completely unethical and immoral. Our profits so far have been excellent. Let's close this door before Krok blows the building down with us in it.'

Skorpios laughed again. 'What an imagination you have, Aldo. I didn't think the Swiss had it in them.' Then he leant forward, his deep voice almost a whisper. 'You can never have enough money, Aldo. Money is power. Conscience is an unnecessary mental obstacle to greatness; it troubles mere mortals. Morality, ethics, laws—what are these to people who can make their own? These things do not touch men like us.'

Stevie, sitting as still as a stone in the bathroom, remembered their conversation in the jet above the Rub' al Khali desert.

Aldo set his espresso cup down, his hand trembling slightly. 'I'm afraid I cannot include myself in your select group, Socrates.

Your greed will be your undoing. As a Greek, you should well understand the concept of hubris.'

This time there was no chuckle from the Greek, merely a dangerous silence that none of the men seemed inclined to break.

Aldo rose. 'There are other banks, other bankers, willing to lend a hand. My withdrawal will not affect the syndicate. I am content with my profit share so far and require no more. Please do not contact me ever again. You can rely on my absolute discretion. I know my life depends on it and the years I have left are of great value to me.' He gave a little bow and walked away.

Stevie, shivering in the cool dark of the bathroom, didn't dare breathe. She had definitely overheard too much. If she got up and flushed, the men would become aware of someone nearby. She would have to stay put until they moved.

But the two men seemed to have little intention of going anywhere.

Skorpios lit his own cigar—a fat, stinking affair—with a delicate gold lighter that looked like a toy in his large palm.

Dado was the first to speak. 'Aldo has a wife, grandchildren. I think we can trust him.'

Skorpios simply lifted his great bullfrog throat and laughed.

# 9

When Stevie awoke, the sunlight filtering through the cracks in the dark wooden shutters was already hot. Her mind was still spinning a little from her experience at the Villa Giardiniera and she needed coffee desperately. She could hear Simone in the bathroom blow-drying her hair. Possibly now was a good time to get the kitchen to herself . . .

The shutters in the little kitchen were still closed. Stevie flung them open to the hot pink and orange bougainvillea that grew over the kitchen window, so ancient and so large that it threatened, every year, to come crashing down. She spooned coffee into the metal coffee pot then lit the gas, singeing her finger with the match.

She could think only of Skorpios and the conversation she had overheard from the bathroom. She felt shaken—but did it really have anything to do with her assignment for Clémence? She had managed to establish that others too—even his associates—thought Krok volatile and unpredictable and dangerous. He seemed to have some new venture or deal afoot that all but the Swiss banker wanted in on.

Clémence hadn't returned her call and Stevie hoped she was—

But before she could finish the thought, Simone entered the

kitchen, already in full make-up and high heels. Stevie looked up brightly, hiding her dismay.

'Good morning, Simone. Did you sleep well?'

Simone scratched a carefully waxed brown arm. 'That room you've got us in, it's full of bugs. I can't sleep—I'm exhausted. And I've got this huge bite on my arm this morning. It's disgusting.'

'Oh dear.'

The coffee pot boiled over impatiently as Stevie found two old blue cups. She held the pot aloft. 'I've just made coffee. Will you have some?'

Simone wrinkled her nose, shook her head and opened the fridge. 'Does nobody in this country eat, like, pancakes for breakfast? We tried to get brunch yesterday and it was impossible. I thought Italy was supposed to have this amazing food, but you can't even get poached eggs for breakfast.'

Stevie made a sympathetic face. 'I don't think Italians are big breakfast people. They generally just do coffee, maybe a biscuit or a pastry. Eggs aren't breakfast food here.'

Simone stared at Stevie as though she had just explained that earthworms were considered a most sophisticated *aperitivo* in Sardinia.

A manicured hand extracted the milk carton from the fridge. 'And that's the other thing—the use-by date on the milk here is so close. It's practically off.' Simone's large diamond gleamed in the sunlight. 'Actually, I will have coffee.'

As Stevie filled Simone's cup, she wondered at her house guest's lack of grace. Simone had had every material advantage: two loving parents, a university education, every luxury she could think of, and yet she had managed to slide through life without picking up any manners.

Stevie stood on one leg, resting the other on her knee, and

cocked her head in thought. Perhaps it was because Simone came from a slave culture, having grown up with housemaids and drivers and porters that her parents never taught her to respect; perhaps it was this attitude that Simone was unfortunately exporting from her home town into the wider world.

'What are you and Mark doing today?' asked Stevie, praying they were planning an excursion of some hours' duration.

Simone began fanning herself exaggeratedly with her hands. 'Bloody Mark, he's a lazy shit.' She plopped heavily onto the kitchen stool. 'It's too hot here, I can't move, let alone leave the house. I can't believe you don't have—'

'Perhaps you should try the hammock. It's quite cooling.' And with that Stevie refilled her own coffee cup and fled to the roof terrace, where she could contemplate the bay in peace.

The sounds of gay laughter drifted over from the *Barone's*. On the roof terrace, three young women in brightly coloured bikinis were sunning themselves on raffia mats: Nicolette, Marie-Thérèse, and Severine—straight out of a Slim Aarons photograph. Stevie admired the fact that the crasser aspects of modernity had not touched the French women next door. They lived suspended in a universe of elegance and beauty and utter self-containment.

A yelp of pain, followed by several curses, disturbed her thoughts. It had come from the terrace below. Stevie peeked over. Simone was headed for the hammock and, waddling on her heels to keep her freshly painted toenails out of the dirt, she had stepped on a thorn.

Stevie watched her reverse her backside awkwardly up to the hammock then raise one leg unsteadily into the cloth sling. She lay back gingerly and lifted her other foot carefully off the ground . . . Suddenly, balance lost, the hammock twisted violently, trapping Simone. She now lay upside down like a candy in a wrapper, with only her painted feet sticking out. Her cries, muffled by the thick cloth, were barely audible, and struggle was pointless.

Stevie took a small sip of her coffee and allowed herself a moment of silent delight, then she crept her wicked way back to the kitchen.

A message from Henning was waiting on her phone: tea at eleven at the the Yacht Club Costa Smeralda. Stevie's reluctance to meet Henning's mother had faded somewhat in light of her pressing need leave the house and its guests.

What should she wear? she wondered. Nothing too outrageous; Henning's mother was quite possibly old and frail. She decided on a raw silk shift dress the colour of raspberry sorbet and some flat snakeskin sandals.

At the appointed time, she pulled up outside the yacht club, a sleek affair in granite, all sharp, clean lines, limestone floors and large canvas umbrellas. The yacht club had been founded in 1967 by His Highness the Aga Khan and sailing was taken very seriously here; the Rolex Cup, the Swan Cup, the Loro Piana Superyacht Regatta and many other prestigious international yacht races were held there every year.

Stevie, feeling unaccountably nervous about meeting Henning's mother, made her way slowly to the terrace.

A waiter appeared.

'*Buon giorno,*' Stevie greeted him. 'I'm meeting . . .' Henning had forgotten to mention his mother's name. She cast about wildly.

'Henning's mother, darling.' A tall, slender woman stood and waved from a corner table. 'I'm over here.'

It was hard to get an impression of Henning's mother as she was mostly covered by a giant yellow sunhat of supreme elegance.

'Stevie.' She held out both hands and smiled.

Up close, Stevie noticed the razor-sharp profile, the high

swelling of the cheekbones, the fine, painted mouth. Henning's mother was a Beauty in the true, old-fashioned sense of the word.

'I'm sorry.' She returned the smile. 'Henning quite forgot to mention—'

'My name is Iris,' said Henning's mother. 'But call me I. Everyone does.'

'Does that ever get confusing?' asked Stevie as they sat.

'Only for people who don't know their own mind.' Iris smiled again. 'Will you have a drink?'

By now, Stevie felt sufficiently awed by this woman to long for something stronger than tea. But she could hardly—

'*Due* gin and tonics *por favor, garçon*, and *charges-les*,' Iris called out to the hovering waiter.

Stevie wondered for a moment if Iris had Henning's uncanny ability to guess her thoughts, and sincerely hoped not.

'So, Henning is in Atlantis or Constantinople or Alexandria or somewhere else impossible—as usual—and I suppose he must have thought I was the next best thing to his company. Poor Stevie. I'll bet you didn't feel like having tea with an old lady when you got up this morning.'

*Oh dear.*

'I absolutely did, I.'

'Well, I'll try to be interesting.' Iris grinned under her sunhat.

Stevie stared at the bracelet circling Iris' left wrist. It was made of gleaming jet and studded not with jewels, but with seashells of all sizes and shapes. The effect was wild—half gladiator, half Neptune's nymph.

'It's a pretty thing, isn't it?' Iris glanced at her arm. 'I had it made especially. Jewels can sometimes feel ordinary, don't you think? And when you're by the sea, it feels quite appropriate to wear shells.'

'It's beautiful,' Stevie agreed. 'I've never seen anything quite like it.'

'Of course, it has a *pourquoi*.' She slipped off the bracelet to reveal a tattoo of a Japanese dragon in fiery red, yellow and blue, circling her wrist where the bracelet had been. 'Sometimes I like to show him, sometimes I like to keep him under wraps.' She smiled at Stevie, looking at her closely.

Their drinks arrived and Iris raised her glass. 'I am happy you came for tea, Stevie. Henning talks about you, you know. I wanted to meet the girl who takes up so much of his attention.'

Stevie felt Iris' gaze hot on her and couldn't help blushing. 'We went through quite an adventure together. I think it brings you closer.'

'But not close enough, it seems.' Iris' eyes were still on her.

Stevie took a very large sip of her gin and tonic, then another. 'I adore Henning. He is a remarkable man.'

Iris said nothing.

'I'm sorry if that sounded trite, I. To be honest,' Stevie continued, 'I'm still quite confused about what happened. We get on desperately well, and yet . . .' She trailed off, then tried again. 'I feel so close to him, and yet I also feel I know nothing about him. It makes me nervous.'

Possibly the gin was making her say more than she should, and yet Stevie felt comfortable with Iris and she hadn't talked to anyone about Henning. It was almost a relief.

'Even I don't always understand Henning, and he's my son.' Iris laughed. 'Henning is my youngest. His two older brothers run the shipping company we inherited from Timo, their father, and they're rather good at it—serious boys, dedicated to the family business. Henning is different.' Iris took a small sip of her drink. 'He's always marched to his own beat, that boy. Of course, he has the money to do anything he wants in the world, but he loves his musty old books and manuscripts with a passion. Every now and then, we dust him off, pop him in a smart suit and send him round to talk to our clients. He's a wonderful figurehead for the family and the most charming of my boys. He smooths feathers and launches ships and generally spreads the family presence around the globe.'

'Sounds like a good job . . . I had no idea.'

'He didn't tell you anything?' Iris was surprised.

Stevie shook her head. 'I didn't even know he had brothers, or that his father died . . . ' Stevie's voice trailed off as she thought of her own parents. She turned back to the conversation. 'There was one thing he would never tell me about: the tattoo he has of the owl.' Stevie saw it in her mind's eye, the bird on his finely muscled forearm.

Iris smiled. 'Yes. He has what you might call a real fellow-feeling with the creatures. He says they symbolise the ability to see things that are hidden. They represent freedom, insight and swiftness, but also stealth, secrets and deception. They say owls see without seeing, and can hear what is unspoken.'

Stevie smiled. 'That sounds exactly like Henning.'

'So maybe you know him better than you think.' Iris placed her glass on the table and sat back. 'Is it a matter of courage?'

Stevie frowned. She didn't like to think she lacked courage.

'And I mean on both sides, Stevie. My son isn't always as forthcoming with his feelings as his mother. It's because I am part American and part Iranian. You can only imagine the internal conflict, darling.' She laughed and, raising a hand to the waiter, ordered two more drinks.

'*Garçon, deux* more, *por favor.*'

Iris slid the magnificent bracelet back on, hiding the dragon. 'I think you should both just relax and not worry, if I can be nosy and offer advice. Just let things be. Emotions can't always wear name tags and live in neat boxes, and if it's meant to be, well, let it be. Take a chance!' She paused and glanced out to sea. 'You only ever regret the things you don't do—take it from an old lady.'

A stocky man in a white linen shirt and large tortoiseshell sunglasses appeared with a retinue of four in tow. With a start, Stevie realised it was Skorpios. He waved a large hand at Iris and approached. He kissed the lady's hand, holding it like a silk glove in his heavy paw.

'*La bella Iris*,' he said in his Greek accent. Iris did not let her hand linger too long in his. She turned to introduce Stevie.

Stevie, now wondering how and why Henning's mother knew Skorpios, quickly extended her hand and said, 'We know each other.'

Skorpios smiled, eyes searching Stevie from behind the toffee-coloured lenses. He was possibly as surprised as she was to find Stevie popping up wherever he went.

'We lived an adventure together,' explained Stevie to Iris, not wanting her to imagine unimaginable things.

'Oh?' Iris' tone was surprised, cautious.

Skorpios smiled charmingly. 'She saved La Dracoulis—my glorious Angelina—from Somali pirates.'

'Good heavens,' said Iris mildly, her eyes on Stevie again. ' Did you want to join us, Socrates?' Iris made a languid gesture that conveyed that the request, however sincere, had no real energy behind it.

'Thank you, but perhaps we would disturb.'

'Well, another time, then,' said Iris, neatly shutting the door on the prospect.

When the man had been seated at his table, Iris adjusted the brim of her hat to shadow her face. 'The trouble with having been married so many times, Stevie, is that one picks up all sorts of friends that are very difficult to lose. Once you know someone, it is very hard to unknow them. Believe me, I've tried, and it's always the ones you most wish to lose that are the stickiest. In the end, I decided it was easier to submit to their acquaintance—and to wear a large hat.'

'So, Skorpios was a friend of your husband?'

'First husband, Henning's father, many years ago. The dear man died in a plane crash and no one has ever lived up to him since, not really.' The waiter arrived with fresh drinks and a bowl of olives, and whisked the empty glasses off the table.

Iris continued once he was out of earshot. 'Skorpios is in shipping, so was Timo. They knew each other, although Timo never particularly trusted Skorpios. He told me Skorpios used to run fleets of rust buckets that were overdue for the wrecker's yard, all nicely painted and reregistered, but he lost ships, and many crew went down with them. Timo thought his carelessness with human lives was gross.' She gave Stevie an appraising look. 'I have to say I was surprised that you knew him.'

'And not entirely approving?' Stevie smiled. 'In my line of work, I too meet a good many people I wouldn't wish to know privately. It's a hazard but, unlike you, I'm more easily forgotten.' She twisted her glass on the table, wondering how much she should be saying to Iris. 'Skorpios was at a lunch party I was at yesterday,' she added. 'It's funny—we seem to be on the same orbit.'

Iris gave her a long look. 'You don't want to be on the same orbit as that man. He attracts misfortune, Stevie, dear. I can look after myself; I am powerful in my own way. I've had sixty—well, fifty-five perhaps—years of dealing with men like him. But Henning has implied that you are a magnet for trouble, and Skorpios's world is not one you want to be drawn into.'

———

**On leaving the yacht club,** Stevie decided to walk through the marina and clear her thoughts. The intrigue of Iris—their conversation about Henning—and the chance meeting with Skorpios, mixed with the two gin and tonics, whirled about in her head.

There was a lot of activity on the dock—the first of the yacht races would start in a week and most of the boats had been brought over and the crews flown out, and everyone was getting ready for the Sardinia season. The Ferragamo brothers were there, Prince Frederik of Denmark, Ernesto Bertarelli . . .

It was past noon and most of the boats that were planning to go out that day had left so the Zodiac cowboys had little to do but refill their fuel tanks and buzz about catching the breeze. Stevie spotted Domenico, one of the most experienced cowboys, by a Wally chase boat painted a sleek dolphin grey.

'*Salve.*' Domenico smiled up at Stevie, his teeth gleaming in his tanned face. Stevie had never seen anyone more tanned. 'Did you want a lift across to the *porto vecchio?*'

Stevie shook her head. 'I was having a drink at the yacht club.'

Domenico raised his eyebrows. The yacht club was not one of Stevie's usual haunts.

'Not a boyfriend, Domenico,' Stevie laughed; the whole of Italy seemed to put love first. 'An older woman—a most remarkable woman, actually.'

'If a woman has substance, years will only improve her,' he responded. 'It's the empty vessels that crack with age.'

Stevie grinned. Italians had some rather marvellous philosophical pronouncements when it came to the opposite sex.

'*Senti*, Domenico, what's the word on the *Hercules?*' Stevie could see the huge ship still in port. 'What are people saying?'

Domenico raised his palms. '*È un mostro.* We've never seen anything like it. There's even a *sommergibile*, a submarine, underneath.

Pilù found out when he went to connect the power lines from the dock.'

Domenico had worked the port for over twenty years and had seen pretty much everything. The Zodiac cowboys were important to the superyacht owners because it was they who decided which berth went to which yacht. Many had been slipped generous tips to ensure that a particular yacht would take prime position on the dock, thereby cementing the aura of power and influence that the boat owner was keen to project and protect.

He frowned. '*Ma c'è qualcosa che non va* . . .' He made a sign to ward off the devil with his forefinger and pinky.

'The crew?'

Domenico shrugged. 'They are very arrogant in their little white hats. They won't let anyone near the boat except when we're guiding her into the berth—as if we haven't dealt with thousands of mega-yachts! Their security *è al massimo*, more even than Khashoggi or the Sultan of Brunei.'

'Does the owner have a reason to be afraid, Domenico?'

Domenico stared at Stevie with his dark eyes for a long moment. 'Why do you ask me this?'

Stevie could see she had offended him. '*Ti chiedo scusa*, Domenico, I didn't mean anything by it. I just know that you and your boys are always the first to hear the rumours—you're the most important people in the port, after all.' She smiled.

He returned the smile, all forgiven. 'I haven't heard anything, *non un fischio*. But then, his troubles probably have followed him from home. These days, the problems are less and less local. These bigshots with their mega-boats, all trying to outdo each other, they are importing their own crime wave. It has nothing to do with the *banditi* of the *massiccio*.'

As Stevie walked back to her jeep she thought about what

Domenico had said. Perhaps it was true—these men with their fast new billions from the oil fields of Russia or the conflicts of Africa or the contracts of the Middle East flew down in their private jets, trailing enemies behind them like a wake. These high-value targets (HVTs) would be less well protected on holiday, no matter how tight the security, and their guard would lower as they relaxed.

It was hard to believe anything bad could happen in a place like this. But every glittering scene has shadows and on the Costa Smeralda they were long ones, stretching back to the 1960s, when the slice of coast had first been established as a playground for the jet set.

The jet set was a much smaller, more exclusive group then: jet travel was new, and few people flew or took overseas summer holidays, and even fewer owned yachts. The jet set life was the preserve of a small number of glamorous people, often titled, or from big industrial families like the Guinnesses or the Olivettis, who all knew each other and met up in airport lounges and alpine villages or on wonderful beaches, instantly turning the place into a riotous cocktail party. Jetting about the world meant luxury, power and a permanent tan. There was no mass tourism, only stylish gangs in search of *divertissement*, who flitted from villa to cabana to yacht to chalet. It was rich and it was private. It was not a rapper throwing cases of Cristal off the jetty while plastic women lap-danced in bikinis for attention.

Sardinia had been a desperately poor island, with the local population retreating up into the mountains to farm their sheep and goats, leaving the valueless land—too salty to grow crops, too vulnerable to centuries of pirate attacks—to the women. So it had been the women who had done well when the Aga Khan and his partners had come in and bought a large swathe of land on the north-east coast of the island. The *bijou* people had come to relax in the land of the granite people, and the contrast as the two rubbed together was the cause of so much trouble to come.

There had been banditry from the beginning. The inland roads were not safe. Stevie's grandmother liked to tell the story of the time she and Camillo were driving inland and saw some peasants by the side of the road, sawing down a huge tree by hand. They thought nothing of it until they heard the next day that a bus full of tourists had been stopped at a roadblock made by a felled tree and robbed of all their valuables.

Kidnappings had been rife, with victims being snatched and held in caves in the mountains, completely protected by the steep granite and thorny scrub, and the wall of silence that the local people built around themselves. There was no hope of finding the victims; the only choice for the family was negotiation.

But those times had passed. Things had calmed down—or had they?

Stevie's phone rang just as she was starting her jeep. It was Clémence and her voice was quiet and as brittle as tin.

'Stevie, I need to talk to you privately, without the guards. It's very important. How can we meet?'

Stevie's mind raced, picturing the Villa Goliath, its myriad cameras and ever-present soldiers. Then she had an idea. 'Go down to the beach in front of the villa at three,' she instructed. 'Swim out to the buoy directly in front. It's a big orange ball not far from the end of the stone jetty. I'll meet you there. It should be safe enough.'

'But, Stevie, I never swim. What will Vaughan think?'

'If he asks, just complain that you've put on a few pounds and feel fat, and that you've heard swimming is the new boxercise. I doubt he'll question it.'

Stevie stopped off at Spinnaker for a *panino* and a glass of fresh orange juice. Sauro was reading the paper in the corner and Stevie sat down with him.

'Tell me, Sauro, the man you see drive by in the convoy every morning, the one staying at Brown's villa . . .'

'Who?'

'Brown.' Stevie made a face, willing Sauro to remember.

He smiled. 'Ah, *si*, Brown . . .'

'Do you think this man is afraid of the local *banditi*?'

Sauro shrugged. 'Everyone with a lot of money is at least a little nervous. The security has improved things a lot but still, this is Sardegna, and its heart is still as wild as it ever was.' He stared at Stevie a moment. 'But if this man is friends with Brown, and has so many guns . . .'

'What?'

'*Lupo non mangia lupo.*'

*A wolf doesn't eat a wolf.*

'Unless the wolf has a personal grudge against the other wolf,' Stevie suggested wryly.

'*Carina*, why are you so interested in wolves? You should be full of sunshine and flowers and my sisters' cooking.'

Stevie smiled. 'Well, I'm here, aren't I?'

**At ten to three, Stevie** put on her swimsuit and a black bathing cap. The cap would make her less recognisable and lend credibility to her cover persona if spotted: a rather precious *signorina* out swimming laps. She swam breaststroke (less splashing) to the buoy opposite the Villa Goliath and reached up, clinging to the blue ring on top. She was careful to keep the buoy between herself and the beach; it was big enough to hide her completely.

After a few minutes she saw Clémence walk down the beach and enter the water slowly, her hands fanning out with reluctance. She too wore a bathing cap, but it was white and emblazoned with the Chanel Cs, and matched her white swimsuit. She looked very glamorous and Stevie hoped she would make it as far as the buoy; aboard the *Hercules*, Clémence had mentioned how rarely she swam. An emergency water rescue would hardly be a stealth move for either of them.

Once in, Stevie realised Clémence was actually an excellent swimmer: neat, swift overarm strokes, her shoulders parallel to the water. She reached the buoy quickly, not even a little out of breath.

'I thought you hardly ever swam.' Stevie spoke in a low voice that wouldn't carry.

'Just because I don't doesn't mean I can't,' Clémence whispered back. 'I swam the English Channel with my sister when we were sixteen. Vaughan doesn't know, of course. He's not a strong swimmer. It would only create problems.'

Stevie looked back. Two bodyguards in white berets stood at ease on the sand. They looked hot and bored. 'What's happened?'

Clémence looked at Stevie for a moment, her face quite naked with her hair under the tight cap. She seemed a little older, a little more tired than usual, despite the perfect red lips. Stevie had seen the look before.

'It's Emile,' she said softly.

'What's happened?'

'Nothing yet, but this morning after breakfast Vaughan received a phone call on the house land line. Someone threatened Emile. They said he would be kidnapped.'

Clémence's eyes filled with tears and Stevie's heart went out to the woman.

'What exactly did they say?' she asked firmly but gently.

Clémence shook her head. 'Vaughan wouldn't tell me—he said I didn't need to know. Only that it was an anonymous call and that the man—I assume it was a man—had threatened to kidnap Emile.'

Stevie thought for a moment. 'Did the caller ask for anything? Make any terms?'

Clémence shook her head and looked away, fighting tears. 'I don't think so. It was a short conversation—my husband took the call on the balcony.'

The indigo sea felt like it was cooling around them and Stevie began to shiver. 'Why would someone warn you that they intended to kidnap your son? It doesn't make sense unless they set terms. Why let you know? Why not just go ahead and do it?'

They bobbed in silence for a minute, both grasping the orange buoy.

'I'm afraid, Stevie,' Clémence said finally. 'I'm afraid of my husband's enemies, I'm afraid of his friends, I'm afraid of my husband, and I'm desperately afraid for Emile.'

'What does your husband think you should do?'

'Well, I suggested the police, even though I knew he would laugh in my face. And he did. But I told him we had to do something. He suggested a cruise. He thinks the *Hercules* is impregnable and we will be safe there. Perhaps he's right . . . It's a warship after all.' She glanced quickly over her shoulder at the guards on the beach. They were growing restless, beginning to pace.

'We leave tomorrow for Corsica. I want you to come too, Stevie.' Before Stevie could object, she hurried on, 'You can't refuse me this. David promised me you would help and I need you with me. I can't think or see straight. I need you to be my eyes and ears and make sense of all this. Anyway, I've already told Vaughan. A few of the others are joining us—you'll fit in perfectly.'

One of the bodyguards was becoming curious. Stevie saw him pull out a pair of binoculars. She let go of the buoy.

'Be at the *porto vecchio* by nine tomorrow,' Clémence hissed as Stevie took a breath and dived under.

She swam as far and as fast as she could underwater, away from Clémence and the buoy and the dark shadows lurking under the surface, then rose nonchalantly for air and resumed her gentle breaststroke.

**As she made her way** up the path, the black stones burning under her bare feet, Stevie caught Simone's voice drifting down from the roof. Her heart sank a little further. Mark was with her, and a plump woman in a pastel pink suit and sunglasses. She was Italian, struggling with the English terms, but Stevie understood right away: 'The value . . . it is high, very high. Here is expensive, *molto* expensive area . . .' The newest intruder was an estate agent. Rage boiled in Stevie. Simone and Mark were getting a valuation of Didi's house. It was all Stevie could do to stop herself from running up to the roof and pushing all three off it.

Then she remembered Osip. She was not usually one for accepting invitations but Stevie felt she could not face Simone and Mark; she wanted to be cocooned in the *Barone*'s world, even if it was just for an afternoon. She snuck into her bedroom and threw on a white cotton tunic dress she had once bought in Bali. She glanced in the mirror. The swimming cap had flattened her hair so she grabbed the Hermès scarf David had sent and tied it, turban-style, backwards. Then she lined her eyes with kohl and slipped back out through the garden, up the fig tree and over the stone wall, into the grounds of the *Barone*'s villa.

From somewhere beyond the olive grove, voices drifted about, chattering in Italian, French, Spanish. The air was warm off the granite, and fragrant with cistus and curry bush and wild fig. A bougainvillea had exploded in hot pink and orange on one white-washed wall of the house. Stevie felt a little shy, but the thought of Mark and Simone drove her forward where she may have otherwise hesitated and turned back.

She saw Osip first, more handsome than before, in white trousers and a linen shirt in faded blue, the first three buttons undone. He was mixing Bellinis, smiling and shaking his head as one of his sisters teased him about his mane of hair, wild from the salt and sun. The little group were gathered around the granite swimming pool, talking and laughing, some lounging on straw mattresses, others sitting in old cane chairs looking out towards the sea. Stevie took a deep, steadying breath and stepped out onto the terrace.

Osip looked up and beamed, then walked over and kissed her on both cheeks. 'Have you met my parents?'

A handsome older man with silver hair and a perfect tan rose from his cane chair to kiss Stevie. 'You were very young, but I recognise you.' His wife had the same silvery hair and tan, and she wore amber jewellery and a pale purple kaftan. As she kissed Stevie she said, 'Your mother and I were great friends, you know.' She stepped back. 'You have her eyes.'

Stevie smiled. 'It's been a long time . . .' she said softly.

'But we have never forgotten her, or Lockie.' The baroness squeezed her hand. 'They were a handsome couple—*les plus beaux du quartier*.' She turned as three girls approached. 'My daughters are around your age. Perhaps you remember them? Severine, Marie-Thérèse and little Nicolette.'

'We used to play together on the beach when we were tiny,' said Marie-Thérèse as Severine handed Stevie a Bellini.

'Do you remember Palmiero?' her sister chimed in. 'The little boy who used to show off so much on the windsurfer?'

Stevie nodded. He had been a god to the little girls too young to lift a sail yet.

'That's him over there.' Marie-Thérèse pointed to a tall man with shoulder-length dark hair and a beautiful smile. 'I think I may have to flirt shamelessly with him tonight.' She laughed and looked over at Palmiero again. 'I think I might have loved him since the windsurfer. His parents moved to South America after that. He only came back last year.' Palmiero glanced over at Marie-Thérèse and smiled. She blushed and looked away, then turned to Stevie. 'Do you think it's possible to love someone and not realise it for so many years?'

Stevie thought it over a moment and decided that definitely it was. She said so.

'Then maybe tonight I will be brave enough to tell him,' said Marie-Thérèse, lifting her eyebrows in merriment.

Stevie smiled and felt as if she had come home.

As the daylight turned from soft gold to pink, Stevie reluctantly withdrew herself from an animated discussion on the best way to make osso bucco and made her way towards the back courtyard. She was due to phone Hazard and needed a moment of privacy. The roof was probably her best bet. Her feet dragged up the stairs—she didn't want to talk to Rice, not with the way he was right now. She didn't want to come away from their phone call feeling deflated and cold, not now, not the night before she was leaving for some pleasure cruise of the Mediterranean on a ship full of villains. Still, work was work. She took her second deep and steadying breath of the afternoon and dialled.

Rice's direct line was answered by Josie: 'Rice's line. He isn't taking calls right now.'

Stevie was relieved. 'It's Stevie. How are you, Josie?' There was silence on the line. Josie hated small talk. 'I'm supposed to report in on the Kroks,' Stevie went on, speaking as quietly as possible, and ducking down out of sight behind a low wall. 'I never got the dossier Rice was supposed to send, so this is all just my observations.'

'Okay, shoot,' replied Josie.

Stevie filled her in on the situation at the Villa Goliath, and aboard the *Hercules*. 'And Clémence Krok want me to go on a cruise with them, leaving tomorrow morning.'

Josie's response was swift. 'That sounds like a very foolish idea, Stevie. The man is the head of the world's largest private army; he is surrounded by bodyguards armed with ceramic guns; he is unstable, irritable, violent, unpredictable and deadly. What part of that doesn't put you off?' she asked drily.

'The thing is, Josie, Krok is up to something. He's running some syndicate with Dado Falcone and Socrates Skorpios.'

'A weapons manufacturer, and a billionaire shipping tycoon of *very* dubious reputation—of course they are up to something. Men like that are always "up to something". But what does it have to do with you? It is all the more reason to stay away.'

'Josie, I can't stay away. I'm doing a job for Rice. He asked me to do this as a favour.'

'I don't think he fully knew what he was getting you into, Stevie. I don't think he would have asked you if he had. I'm going to tell him as soon as he comes out of the crisis room—which probably won't be for days,' she sighed exasperatedly.

Stevie's heart thudded. 'Is it still terrible?' she asked quickly. 'Is David alright?'

'David looks terrible,' said Josie, pulling no punches. 'I wouldn't be surprised if he has a heart attack. The pirates are driving him to his death.'

Stevie swallowed the huge lump in her throat. 'Don't tell him anything, Josie,' she whispered. 'Please. He doesn't need any more worries on his plate. I will quickly and quietly finish the job. It's the least I can do to help him.'

'It sounds like you've seen enough. Pack it in.'

'The threats to Emile Krok are becoming more specific. There's something not right going on. I can't get a good picture of who might be threatenening the child if I don't have some sense of what Krok is up to. In a way, the cruise is the perfect opportunity to watch and learn.'

'You make it sound like a sewing circle,' Josie replied acidly, but Stevie could hear the concern in her voice as she said, 'Don't do anything stupid, Stevie. David's not worth it.'

'He is to me, Josie,' Stevie said softly, and ended the call.

It was then that she heard the first notes. The pink light was fading to pale blue as Stevie peeped over the low wall that hid her from view. Osip was sitting cross-legged on a reed mat and playing a flute. Stevie sat still and listened, enchanted by the music, as the sun sank slowly into the sea.

The last note of the flute died with the sun and Osip wrapped his flute in a cloth and stood. '*Ciao*,' he said; he must have caught sight of the top of her head, Steve realised.

'I'm sorry if I disturbed you, Osip,' she said quietly, straightening up from behind the wall. 'I came away to make a phone call. You know, I hear that melody every evening and I've always wondered who was playing.'

Osip smiled. 'I could sense someone listening.' It was almost dark now and the scent of sandalwood rose from the terrace below; a light breeze came up off the water and danced around their faces. Osip's eyes turned an impossible blue as he stared at her.

'Do you play for any special reason?' asked Stevie, looking for something to say to break the rather intense spell of the moment.

'None,' he replied, gesturing with his free hand. 'I play because it is charming to me, and because I know the music drifts around to the other houses in the bay. I know people wonder who is playing the strange melodies, but I think they like the mystery.'

'It is a charming mystery,' Stevie agreed. 'I won't tell anyone.'

'It's okay.' Osip grinned. 'I see it as my contribution to the universe—that one tiny moment of beauty.' He took her hand. 'Do you find that silly?'

Stevie shook her head. 'No. Not at all, actually. It makes perfect and wonderful sense. I think everyone should do that. Only I'm not sure what I could add . . .'

'This is where I should say something like, "Your beauty is enough", right?'

Stevie laughed. 'No! Definitely not.'

'I'm not good at seductions like that. I should be: I'm French. But the art seems to have eluded me. Perhaps something hidden deep in my background . . .'

'I'm sure you do just fine, Osip.' Stevie raised an eyebrow and gently removed her hand from his.

'The moment of beauty can be as simple as giving an unexpected compliment, or putting a flower by the bed, or cooking something for a friend. The important thing is that you are giving back to the universe—creating something—as well as taking from it. There is a balance to strike.'

Stevie thought of her afternoon on the yacht, the party at Dado Falcone's house, Simone. Everyone wanted something, everything. 'Maybe you are right,' she said slowly. 'Maybe it is that simple: the intention to give back is enough, however small. I think a lot of people only think about what they can take from the world and other people. Giving is seen as weak or as somehow harmful to their own interests.' She wondered if she was like that, taking too much, giving too little. Perhaps this favour for Rice was a way of giving. She would like to see it as that, to see it as something that would give him strength in some way, fix things. She wanted to think about David, but right now Osip was gesturing down the stairs where dinner awaited.

The glitter of the sunlight had been replaced with candles now, set the length of a long wooden table on the terrace, and dotted around the pool. The terracotta tiles were warm under Stevie's bare feet as she found a chair and sat—prudently, she thought—a little way away from Osip. An enormous fish cooked in a heavy salt crust was served, with salad and grilled vegetables from the garden, and a local rosé. For dessert there was ice-cream made of white rice and covered with a mysteriously delicious reduction of grape must called *saba*. As the plates were cleared, three musicians appeared and the dancing began.

Stevie sat on a cane chair and watched the dancers, sipping on a small glass of pungent *mirto*, the local myrtle berry liqueur that was a dark shade of purple.

Osip came and sat beside her on the still-warm stones. 'Are you worrying about your cousins?' he asked.

Stevie's mind had been on David, but she nodded. She was worried about them too. 'They had a real estate agent over this afternoon.'

'But the house is not theirs to sell?'

Stevie shook her head emphatically. *No.*

'Then, really, there is no problem.'

Stevie looked at him in surprise. 'But they want my grandmother to die so they can sell the house.'

'Wishing won't make it so—isn't that the saying?' Osip replied. 'They seem terribly unhappy, your cousins, because they are constantly looking to the future and fantasising and saying "when we have this much, we will be happy"—but of course they won't. Because the worm is within.'

'So I should do nothing?'

'I think you should let them torment themselves with visions of what could be, and ignore them. They will depart soon, and go back to their covetous little nest, and leave you and your grandmother in peace.'

'It's that simple, is it?' Stevie asked sarcastically, but then she realised Osip was right. The worst Mark and Simone could do was to annoy her and offend her sense of what was right. And even that was only if she let them. She would take back that power and let them go.

'It's that simple.' Stevie smiled at her new friend and touched her glass gently to his. 'To learning to let go.'

# 10

As the guests came aboard the *Hercules*, the staff served warm lemon-butter croissants. A crowd had gathered behind the security cordons on the dock, eager to catch a glimpse of who was boarding, and to see the monstrous albatross of a boat under steam. Stevie had arrived early to avoid the circus and slipped aboard unnoticed. She had resisted the temptation to wear white—not wanting to be mistaken for one of the crew—and had instead chosen a silk dress printed with toucans and tigers on a background of emerald green. Sometimes standing out was even better camouflage than blending in. Stevie had long ago learnt that invisibility was becoming exactly what people expected to see.

Vaughan Krok was nowhere to be seen but the boat swarmed with his men in their white berets with their white ceramic guns. They glanced at Stevie but made no attempt to address her or check her identity. She assumed they had been shown photos of the invited guests and knew exactly who was expected aboard.

Stevie left her sandals in the raffia basket by the gangplank and went looking for Clémence.

She found her by the shaded centaur pool, long brown legs stretched out on a chaise longue, her face mostly hidden under a large red sunhat. She was reading a yachting magazine.

Stevie wandered over but Clémence did not notice her approach. 'Have you heard anything more?' she asked the reading figure. Clémence looked up and Stevie jumped in fright.

Mrs Krok's face had changed. Overnight, it appeared to have sharpened; it was the same, yet somehow strangely altered. Perhaps it was the mouth . . .

The corners of it now twisted up in a strange smile. 'What are you and my sister plotting, I wonder? Something's up, only she won't tell me what. I suddenly have a feeling it has something to do with you.'

As Stevie returned the gaze, she felt as if she were staring into a reptilian kaleidoscope, irises of fragmented colours, without any warmth in them at all. It took all her self-possession to flop down casually on the chaise next to the predator, put her feet up and wave a small hand in the air.

'Your sister was going to get me an appointment with one of her masseurs. Apparently the man works miracles with circulation and especially *cellulite*.' She hissed the dirty word under her breath. 'It takes months to get an appointment.'

Clémence's sister fixed her with her strange stare. 'Really?' The word was laced with boredom and contempt. Another of her sister's spoilt, vacuous friends, she was obviously thinking.

*Mission accomplished.*

Stevie lay back, closed her eyes and nodded. 'It's the scourge of the twenty-first century.'

There was a faint jangling sound, followed by a whiff of gardenias as Clémence sat down on the third chaise. 'Hello, Stevie. I see you've met Marlena. Is she playing nice?'

'Charming, charming,' muttered Stevie.

'We were born identical, Stevie,' continued Clémence, 'only life has shaped us differently. Now, I think, you could tell us apart.'

Stevie opened her eyes and studied the two sisters. Seen together, they were remarkable. Two jaguars swathed in designer silks. Only there was a slight difference between them: Marlena's eyes were narrower, her cheekbones more prominent; she was Clémence with a harder edge, and a slightly more muscular build.

'Clémence is younger by almost a minute. It shows, don't you think? The younger twin is always a little frailer, a little weaker—and of course her eyes are an uninterrupted blue . . .'

'They're violet,' snapped Clémence.

The twins broke off their bickering to watch a small commotion on the dock. Two women in their early thirties had roared up in a silver convertible Porsche Boxster—one blonde, one dark, both in the enormous oval sunglasses so popular that summer. They parked across two spaces then got out. Both wore platform stiletto heels and babydoll dresses, one blue, one yellow, and carried enormous designer handbags. Their jewellery flashed in the morning light like sun on the sea.

They looked vaguely familiar . . .

Suddenly Stevie remembered where she had seen the girls before: Tara and Tatiana—Stevie couldn't remember which was which—had been hanging off the arms of Alexander Yudorov, oligarch and husband, at his chalet in the Swiss Alps.

Clémence had lowered her sunglasses 'Do you know those girls?'

'Vaguely . . . Tara and Tatiana, St Moritz last winter, the polo on ice.'

Clémence slipped her glasses back over her eyes. 'I saw them in Cannes, at the festival, attached to the enormous son of a Hollywood studio head. He was so big the director's chairs couldn't be trusted to support him and the organisers had a special one secretly reinforced, just for him.'

'Goodness.' Stevie's mind boggled at the thought.

Clémence was still watching them. 'Their husband hunt was obviously unsuccessful and they've moved hunting grounds for the summer.'

'Clémence, dear,' said Marlena, 'don't you think it's a little *de trop*, all this coming from you? These girls are just following in your footsteps.' Marlena was losing interest in the sideshow on the dock. 'I only hope they don't plan to wear those shoes aboard a yacht. The owner will crucify them for ruining the deck.'

Clémence reapplied her lipstick, then poured herself a Pimms from a jug on the table before answering. 'Those girls will never get the husband they think they deserve. They've got it all wrong. They think if they act like princesses, their prince will come. Let me tell you, that is not the way of the smart fortune huntress. These two, they go after the good-looking, flashy men. They're often the ones looking for a rich wife!'

Marlena cackled with delight. 'Our parents made that mistake. Both thought the other had money—what a disappointment. Clémence is absolutely right.'

'The really successful fortune huntress will do anything to please the object of her attentions.' Clémence grew energised as she spoke. 'She cooks, she flatters, she's always happy and fun. Those girls pout and complain and demand. Why wouldn't the men just take the eighteen-year-old from Brazil with the incredible arse who only wants to have a good time and land a few trinkets?' Clémence shook her head in dismay. 'Big mistake.'

Marlena nodded in amused agreement. 'Even real princesses don't behave like that—look at Loli and Ludi-Brigitte. They're tremendous fun, even if they are a bit dim. That's why the airline hostesses have more success marrying big money than the *nouveau riches*. Watch Clémence—she is a master.'

Her sister took the comment as a compliment and warmed to her theme.

'One of the most important things is to know when to mind, and when not to. If I minded every phone call from his ex-wives, every mention of his other children, every Christmas spent with the ghosts of his past at his disapproving mother's house, well . . .' Clémence lowered her glass. 'Well I wouldn't be in this position. No,' she continued, 'I'm afraid the only person who will marry either of those two girls is someone looking to please their father, or someone who doesn't know better and mistakes their petulance for class.'

'Well now—' Marlena smiled wickedly and raised her glass '—they'll deserve each other, then, won't they?'

The engines of the massive ship started and she began to shift slowly out of her berth. Two Zodiac cowboys nosed the port bow, outboard motors churning, keeping the *Hercules* from colliding with her neighbour. The behemoth turned in a tight circle and was soon steaming out to sea, leaving the old port to shrink in the distance.

**It wasn't until the guests** were getting ready for pre-lunch drinks that Stevie got Clémence alone.

'Is Emile on board?'

Clémence nodded. 'Of course. He's in his playroom with the tutor and the bodyguard. They're watching *The Little Mermaid*.'

The irony was unmissable—the little boy with the world at his fingertips, exploring the wonders of the sea via a cartoon on television while floating above the real thing.

'There was another call last night.' Clémence kept her voice low. 'I was asleep. I think it was around eleven thirty. This time the caller said nothing—but it was him.'

'Does anyone know, apart from your husband?'

Clémence shook her head. 'Probably Vaughan's head of security—Megrahi. You haven't met him yet, have you?'

Stevie shook her head. She would remember a name like that.

'He's doggedly loyal, a Libyan, missing a thumb.' Clémence glanced quickly over her shoulder. 'Gives me shivers.'

'Clémence, did you invite the guests or were they your husband's idea?'

It seemed strange to Stevie that a man as security-aware as Vaughan Krok would have invited guests aboard if he suspected kidnappers were prowling. Surely every extra friend and crew member was an added security risk? They would all have to be carefully vetted.

'It was my idea. Vaughan decided that from now on, we would only be safe aboard the *Hercules*. I'm not sure I could handle weeks at sea alone with him and his moods. I insisted we bring friends to . . . dilute.' After a pause, she added, 'I even invited the princesses, to keep him happy.'

'And does Marlena know about the threats?'

Clémence paused before answering. 'I met my husband through my sister. They used to work together, once upon a time.' She stopped again. 'I prefer not to discuss him with her at all. I love her deeply but I'm not always sure I can trust her—if you can understand that.' Clémence noticed the interest in Stevie's eyes and clammed up. 'If you want to know about Marlena, you'll have to ask her yourself.'

Their bond was strong, thought Stevie, despite the things that Clémence had said about her sister. They were twins, after all. She would do well to remember that.

Lunch was served as they steamed towards La Maddalena. Stevie marvelled at how perfectly contained the superyachts were from their surroundings. They were floating on a swelling sea, shimmering with summer sunlight, and yet they would have been just as untouched by the environment if they had stayed indoors on land. Perhaps that was the attraction . . .

Stevie preferred to feel the elements on her skin and to know where she stood on the planet.

Lunch revealed the other guests invited along for the cruise. Seated around the table were Vaughan Krok, Clémence and little Emile (who was allowed above deck for lunch), Marlena, Dado and Elisabetta Falcone, the princesses Loli and Ludi-Brigitte in matching jumpsuits, and a young man named Stéphane from Liechtenstein with incredibly soft hands.

Stevie had Stéphane on her right, but there were two chairs empty, one immediately on her left. Suddenly a large figure dressed in a lemon-yellow cardigan appeared in the doorway.

'Apologies to all—my tardiness is unforgivable, but Indian politicians will keep you on the phone for an eternity.'

Skorpios.

He bowed to the assembled guests, then to Stevie alone, before sitting down, a smile on his bullfrog face. 'Angelina sends her apologies,' he announced to the table. 'She is in her cabin with a migraine.'

Stevie smiled, noticing that Marlena's eyes had seemed to blaze at the mention of Angelina . . . or was it just Skorpios's presence that had produced that reaction? Stevie hoped Angelina would remember her promise to say nothing about Stevie's work, to keep her secret safe. She turned back to Stéphane, who was recounting a cycling holiday in Austria. Her mind teemed with Iris' warnings; Skorpios seemed to be everywhere.

She had dealt with many powerful and even dangerous men,

but even so, something about Skorpios made her hesitate. She would have to tread very carefully. He was no fool.

So Stevie said very little and left her ears wide open. However, it wasn't long before Skorpios turned his toffee-coloured lenses on her: 'You perch on your chair like a songbird that has lost its song. Have you?'

'Lost my song?' Stevie replied lightly. 'I'm reluctant to shatter your image of me as a songbird, charming as it is, but I'm a terrible singer.'

'Terrible, eh, Miss Duveen?' He laughed.

Stevie nodded and picked at her roll, studying his face from under lowered lids. Skorpios was not a handsome man—he was not tall enough, was too broad in the chest and arms—but Stevie could feel his magnetism. His eyes were dark and heavily lidded behind the glasses, giving him an air of sensuality and perpetual sleepiness. His mouth was wide and generous, and his nose stood like a monument in the centre of his face, proud and strong.

Beside him, the men at the table could have been made of tissue paper. Stevie wondered how close Iris had been to Skorpios . . .

Stevie felt a gaze on her and turned; Marlena was watching with her harlequin eyes. It was not a friendly gaze and Stevie hoped she hadn't made an enemy of Clémence's twin.

'Socrates is a man of excess in everything, Stevie,' she drawled in her curious accent, her voice now laced with bitterness. 'Except the truth.'

Skorpios glared back at her, his sudden silence resting heavily between them. Stevie wondered what their relationship was. Had they once been lovers, perhaps? There seemed to be thunderclouds thickening with every word spoken. *Was Marlena jealous?*

To lighten the mood, Stevie raised a pointed eyebrow and said, 'I've always been rather frugal in my appetites.'

'What a pity.' Skorpios leant imperceptibly closer. 'Because I think you have a fire inside of you.'

Stevie froze; she felt like a fly caught in the tacky strands of the spider's web. She had to play this one very carefully. She had her cover—as well as her dignity—to think of.

She waved a world-weary hand. 'Is all this really necessary? I mean—' and she flashed her tormentor a smile '—I'm charmed and all, but it's only lunchtime. Such advances are a little . . . heavy for the daylight, don't you think?'

Skorpios smiled. 'Forgive me, Mademoiselle. It is a habit. Every woman is a potential mistress to me, and that is how I approach her.'

'And Angelina?' Stevie asked quickly.

Skorpios smiled but said nothing.

'I just hope you don't make her unhappy,' she added, softening her tone.

A platter of lobsters arrived and the conversation broke up, drifted towards their route through the Mediterranean, gossip from Paris and London and New York, scandals and deaths and third marriages.

Skorpios was not so easily distracted however. He stared at Stevie for a long moment before he spoke. 'In a woman, unhappiness can be sexy.'

Stevie started. 'What an amazing thing to say. I can't imagine you really believe that, Mr Skorpios.'

'Why not?'

'Well, for one thing,' she replied quietly, 'it's cruel.'

A waiter, passing with a bottle of wine, stopped to freshen Stevie's glass. Skorpios took the bottle from him and filled Stevie's glass himself. 'A woman chooses to be happy or unhappy. It is not men who make her so. Women who think that ascribe too much influence to us.'

'And men who take that point of view, in my experience, are often the worst misogynists. Why do you think that is?' Stevie put down her fork. 'Maybe it gives them an excuse to behave badly.'

Skorpios stared at her, then smiled slowly. 'I think I was right about your passionate nature.'

Stevie flushed and took a sip of her white wine. She had revealed too much. It had been a mistake. Now Skorpios would take an interest in her. The thought made her very uncomfortable.

Fortunately, at that moment Vaughan Krok stood and announced that he had two planes circling O'Hare airport in Chicago and they were running low on fuel. He grabbed his drink and left the table. Emile jumped up and started after his father. Without a backward glance, Krok called out, '*Sit.*'

Emile dropped quickly back into his chair, crushed.

Marlena rose a moment later and disappeared through the same doorway.

Stevie turned to Stéphane. 'What on earth does he mean?'

'Vaughan is addicted to Flight Simulator—the computer game. He never lets business or pleasure interrupt his obsession.' Stéphane took a sip of his wine and dabbed his lip with a napkin. 'I don't understand it myself. The man has several airfields and private planes—why not just fly for real?'

Halfway through lunch, Clémence's phone rang. She glanced at the screen and went pale, stood and took the call by the railing. Even from a distance Stevie could sense the tension in the slim shoulders. Stevie stood and went to her. She turned, her face a ghastly white, her red lipstick jumping out like a gash of fear.

'The threats?' Stevie whispered.

Clémence nodded. 'They called my phone this time—it was a man. He just asked me if I loved my little boy and said that if I did I had better be very careful.' Her manicured hands were trembling.

Stevie glanced quickly at the table. No one was paying them any attention. Then Marlena reappeared at the door. Her eyes focused on Stevie and her sister, but Stevie couldn't worry about her now.

'Can you tell me anything about his voice?' she asked gently.

'There was nothing really unusual—a man's voice.' Clémence was struggling for control. 'He spoke quite slowly and very softly—not much more than a whisper. Maybe he had a little bit of an accent, but it was very hard to tell.'

'And he made no demands?'

Clémence shook her head again. 'I'm so frightened.'

Stevie paused and collected her thoughts. 'I think that seems to be the whole point. But why go to all the trouble? What would someone gain by frightening you and your husband? It's malicious, certainly, but it also seems a little senseless.'

'I don't want Emile—anyone—to know.' Clémence glanced back at the table.

Stevie smiled gaily. 'Of course not.' Then louder, so the table could hear, 'Oh, she'll get over it, Clémence. She just has very bad taste in men. Always has.' A thought struck her. 'Quick. Give me the phone—I'll talk to her. You go back to your guests.'

Stevie looked up the call register to find the number of the last call received and was surprised to find it wasn't a private number but a local one, an Italian mobile. That was strange. She selected the number and called it. The caller would almost certainly have turned the phone off or changed the SIM card, she reminded herself, but it was worth a try . . .

Stevie froze as from the hatch, came the opening bars of Wagner's 'Ride of the Valkyries'. Abruptly it was cut off.

*Krok's phone.*

Stevie felt the icy claw of fear on her neck.

*Impossible.*

Stevie sat back down at the table, pocketing the phone, just as Krok appeared in the doorway.

Under the table, Stevie opened her own phone and copied the number from Clémence's call register to Josie Wang at Hazard HQ with a text message that read:

*Can you trace location? VVVIP Stevie.*

She smiled brightly, took a large sip of wine and helped herself to a scampi, her insides burning with anticipation.

It had to be a coincidence. Krok's phone virtually never stopped ringing.

Josie would type the number into her StarSat programme; that would run a GPS trace, based on repeater triangulation. It should give the location with a pretty high degree of accuracy.

Josie seemed to be taking an awfully long time with the trace. Finally the reply came:

*Latitude 41°12'55.548"N–Longitude 9°24'36.792"E.*

Stevie memorised the coordinates and looked out to sea. They were just passing the port on the island of Maddalena, with its Romanesque villas in yellows and pinks and oranges, its rows of neat palm trees and block stone seafront.

To the far right was the American naval base, home of the warships and submarines that prowled the Mediterranean, relics of the Cold War.

Stevie couldn't wait for the lunch to be over. She felt Marlena's eyes on her every moment; Clémence was having a low, agonised conversation with her husband, who was intent on demolishing the pile of scampi on his plate, carcasses piling up in front of him, like some demented Roman emperor. His expression gave nothing away.

The other guests chatted on, oblivious—but then, they were probably used to the strange dynamic of Mr and Mrs Krok's relationship. Several had, after all, all been present at the lunch party when Krok had exploded at his wife . . .

Then finally, mercifully, it was over and most of the guests retired to their cabins for a siesta. Stevie yawned and got up, thanking Clémence for lunch. She made her way sleepily into the saloon and paused by one of the charts pinned to the wall. It showed most of the Mediterranean Sea.

The saloon was dark and deserted, the teal blue carpet muffling all sound. Stevie peered casually at the chart.

Latitude 41°12'55.548"N–Longitude 9°24'36.792"E.

Stevie traced the coordinates lightly with a finger and came to a stop on the small circle that marked the port of Maddalena.

It was close enough. They had been sailing past the port at the time of the call. Surely it would be too much of a coincidence that the person behind the threatening phone calls should be on the island itself . . . No. The much more logical conclusion—and the more frightening one—was that the caller was aboard the *Hercules*.

Stevie spun around: someone was watching her, she could feel it. But there was no one there, no sound, not even the hum of the engines. The yacht was too well insulated for that.

Feeling desperately uneasy, Stevie made her way back to her cabin along the deserted hallway.

Examining charts was an innocent thing to do when out sailing, wasn't it? And yet it was not really something likely to interest a party girl. It could look suspicious to the wrong eyes. Well, there was nothing she could do about it now. She would have to be more careful from now on.

She saw a flicker of movement to her left and stopped. A pair of large brown eyes peered out from behind an ornamental table. It was Emile.

*Had it been Emile watching her in the saloon?*

Stevie stopped and crouched down. 'Hi,' she said softly. Emile darted back under the table. 'What are you doing?' she asked.

There was no answer. Then she heard a muffled crash from behind the door to the stateroom. Krok's voice shouting, furious, came to her through the heavy maple doors. Clémence's reply was barely audible. Emile didn't need to hear the words to know that his parents were fighting. His large, dark eyes told the story. She held out her hand to the frightened boy. He stared at it for a moment then crawled out and took it. Stevie stood and led him slowly away from the door.

# 11

The island of Cavallo sat like a flat French rock as far into Italian territory as it dared go, surrounded by treacherous reefs and hidden rocks. The waters were practically unnavigable without detailed charts, good local knowledge and calm seas. Even then, the island could really only be safely approached by tender.

The entire island was private property. There was no public port or jetty, in fact, no public access at all. Even mooring close by was forbidden. This suited the über-VIPs who frequented the island, among them British royals, famous actors and Vittorio Emanuele di Savoia, the exiled pretender to the throne of Italy; Cavallo was as close to his home country as he could get without actually setting foot on Italian soil.

Stevie was surprised when the *Hercules* steamed straight for the island and anchored not far off. The captain must know the waters well, she thought; he'd done this before.

Stevie went out on the aft deck and looked about. The crew were pulling out diving gear and stacking it neatly on one of the retractable platforms.

Marlena was stalking about in a cheetah-print swimsuit, examining the masks and giving orders to the crew. She looked up and saw Stevie.

'You'll dive, won't you, Stevie.' It was an order rather than a question but Stevie was more than happy to get into the water. Plus, she was dying to get a better look at the underside of *Hercules*—perhaps even catch sight of the submarine Domenico had mentioned.

Stéphane and the princess sisters were also coming on the dive. The girls wore matching yellow wetsuits. Stevie struggled into a small steamer—she knew that the water would be cold after a few minutes, despite the heat of the sun above the surface.

Marlena swung her tank onto her back with no effort. She wore only fins, no wetsuit, and a diving knife strapped to her calf. Stevie noticed she was still wearing her red lipstick. Clémence's sister pointed at one of the smaller tanks. 'The crew filled that one for you, Stevie. You don't look like you use much air.'

Stevie did as she was told. She had done over a thousand dives and several underwater-rescue training courses, but she thought it best not to let any of that show. She pretended to struggle a little with the buoyancy control device, deliberately stumbled.

Mask on, vest inflated, she was ready to leap in. The sea was calm and clear—it ought to be a pleasant dive. One of the crew gave a quick briefing: some underwater currents to watch out for—nothing too strong; good visibility all round.

Something made Stevie turn and glance back up to the deck of the monstrous yacht. A squat, dark-haired man in whites was standing at the railing, staring down at her. One of the crew? she wondered. She gave him a light-hearted wave; after a beat he lifted a hand in reply. Stevie saw it was missing a thumb. Her heart suddenly felt heavier than her weight belt. Had it been Megrahi, Krok's head of security, watching her in the saloon?

She shook the thought from her mind, now more glad than ever to be escaping the ship for the underwater world where she would feel safe, at home, and at peace.

She made a thumbs-down sign to the other divers and slowly sank below the surface chop. Immediately, the sound of the bubbles and her hollow breathing soothed her. Diving was like meditation. She drifted slowly towards the bottom, fifteen metres down, then looked up towards the shimmering surface. The others were descending slowly, feet first. Only Marlena swam downwards with purpose, the muscles on her lean legs standing out in the blue light.

The hull of the *Hercules* was clearly visible now, a great white mass shaped like a V. Stevie could see the bulge towards the stern and the faint outline of a portal of some kind. The submarine.

She saw the white hull of a launch hit the water on the other side of the ship. The propellers started—loud and high-pitched underwater—and after a moment it took off in the direction of Cavallo.

Stevie waited for the other divers then set off; one of the crew members was leading the dive. The sea floor was mainly massive granite boulders piled in stunning formations. Sea urchins clustered in the crevasses and large silvery fish swam about, matching the silvery rocks. It wasn't a colourful dive, no corals or tropical fish, but there was a beauty in the aridity of the sandy floor, the massive boulders and the endless blue.

The water was clear but dark, almost dense, and the forms in the distance quickly melted into shadows. Stevie swam to one side of the group, hanging back enough to feel that she was alone; only Marlena swam behind her, slightly above. She had an underwater camera, Stevie noticed, and was peering carefully into every crevasse, hunting for something to photograph.

The little group swam deeper, down to a cave fringed with small anemones. Inside, the light was dim and the cave was filled with the black spines of sea urchins. A trapdoor of blue light beckoned at the bottom: an opening.

Marlena swam past Stevie and into the cave. She disappeared for a moment into the blackness, then Stevie caught sight of her fins slipping through the far opening. The others decided not to follow.

Stevie hesitated, but the lure of the quiet, dark cave, with the glint of blue at the end, beckoned and she swam in.

The cave was deeper than it had seemed. Stevie realised she had descended five metres; the water was colder and she had to take care not to catch the top of her tank on any rocky outcrops. She reached the opening and looked through it: a vista of the big blue, endless ocean, the colours of a sky at dusk—that little perfect moment just after the sun has set, but before the curtain of the night has fallen.

Stevie hung there for a moment, perfectly still, soaking in the charm of it, the wild, empty beauty. She suddenly felt dizzy and giggled, now slightly breathless. She held the rocky opening firmly and breathed long and deep.

A headache began to creep towards her temples, hints of nausea.

She glanced at her dive computer. She was deep and would have to ascend soon if she didn't want to risk decompression sickness, but she still had time and air. Her head swam, her vision blurred a little. Now a feeling of fear began to seep into her guts, like a trickle of water into a mask.

*Something's wrong.*

She held up a hand to her face, trying to focus her eyes. The beds of her fingernails were dark, dark brown. For a moment, her mind swam with confusion, then her heart began to pound.

*Contaminated air.*

One of the symptoms of carbon monoxide poisoning at depth was cherry-red nailbeds. Underwater, of course, red looked brown. She had to surface quickly, before she became more disorientated or lost consciousness altogether. With a massive effort, Stevie pushed herself through the small opening and out into the big blue. She looked about but none of the other divers were in sight.

Stevie began to swim upwards, putting all the strength she had left into kicking towards the surface. She glanced at her depth gauge to see how much further she had to go. To her horror, Stevie saw the numbers were ascending: she was moving in the wrong direction; she was swimming deeper.

Panic threatened; she was afraid to breathe too deeply, but it was unavoidable.

*Watch your bubbles, Stevie.*

Her dive instructor's voice came back to her from a wreck dive they had done one dark night.

*Watch your bubbles.*

Stevie stopped swimming and breathed out. Her bubbles streamed out sideways and she realised she was lying horizontal in the water. She straightened up until her bubbles flew up overhead, then slowly began to fin in their direction, eyes on the bubbles, thinking of nothing but the bubbles, fighting the urge to vomit, to sleep.

Suddenly it became too much. Stevie was gasping for breath, even though her regulator was in her mouth. She knew she was going up too fast, that she risked the bends, but she had no choice. She mustn't pass out, but every cell in her brain wanted to succumb to the blackness.

Stevie took a breath of the poisoned air. She was about ten metres from the surface now; she could see the hull of the boat, the black fins of the other divers floating on the surface. But no one was looking down.

She released her regulator, put her finger in her mouth and bit as hard as she could.

The pain focused her mind for just long enough. Her buoyancy vest fully inflated, she began to swim like the devil for the surface, letting a small stream of bubbles escape from her lungs as she ascended, as she had been trained to do.

She felt that her lungs would burst. She mustn't breathe in— the air in her lungs would expand as she ascended; she would make it.

The surface shimmered like a silver net, just too far away. Her vision was growing dark, as a if a storm cloud had covered the sun.

Suddenly her head broke the surface and she bobbed up with the power of the air in her vest. Stevie just managed to turn over onto her back before she lost consciousness.

**When Stevie finally came to,** she was in her cabin, breathing pure oxygen through a mask. The ship's doctor was with her. The doctor, a neat man with blond hair clipped short and the physique of a battlefield soldier, put a large hand on her shoulder and told her not to stand.

'You had carbon monoxide poisoning. The only treatment is rest and fresh air. I've supplemented your air with oxygen.'

Stevie nodded her thanks behind her mask.

There was a knock at the door and a steward entered carrying an enormous fruit platter. 'Mrs Krok thought you might need some refreshment.'

The elaborate pineapple centrepiece swam in and out of focus.

'Thank you,' Stevie mumbled from behind the perspex.

'Doctor . . .' She turned her head. 'What happened?'

'It's quite a common diving accident: the tanks are filled downwind of a generator exhaust or some other source of carbon monoxide. The contaminated air is compressed and then breathed at depth, concentrating the poisonous gas. You were very lucky to make it to the surface. Your poisoning was already quite severe by the time we got to you.'

Stevie coughed. Her lungs hurt and her throat felt raw. 'So it was an accident?'

The doctor stared at her, his eyes a strange shade of swamp green. 'It was an accident,' he repeated quietly.

She wished she had said nothing.

'An unfortunate instance of carelessness on the part of the diving staff,' he continued. 'They are to be given a refresher course on the correct procedures for filling tanks this evening, and all the remaining tanks are to be checked. Mr Krok is particularly concerned that this incident not be repeated.'

'Of course.' Stevie smiled wanly. 'How kind.'

'Lie down for another hour then see how you feel. Ring if you need anything, or if you feel worse.'

He turned to go, then stopped. 'Oh and, Miss Duveen, Mr Krok is also most anxious that word of this unfortunate accident does not spread. You'll be right as rain—no need to make a big fuss is there, hey?' He glared down with his jungle eyes. 'Be a good girl and you might even make dinner.'

The door closed behind him and Stevie was alone. Her mind was whirling, somersaulting, clearing for patches, then fogging up again. Gradually the dive pieced itself back together—she remembered everything up until the cave, swimming in. After that . . .

Her finger was throbbing and she saw deep bite marks, a little blood. Someone had painted them in iodine. Were they hers? She measured her teeth against the bite: a perfect match.

*How mysterious.*

More mysterious than unexplained bite marks, however, was the contaminated air. It was something that could and did happen, especially when filling tanks in small, enclosed spaces, such as on a ship. But Stevie couldn't help wondering . . . She recalled Megrahi's stare as she floated in the sea, ready to go down. Had it really been an accident?

What a simple way to get rid of a nosy guest—an unfortunate diving accident, the body never found, deepest regrets. Stevie knew she could easily have ended up lost to the big blue.

But surely she was imagining things. Why would Megrahi want to kill her? She was nothing to him. Unless it was on Krok's orders . . .

Krok was a man who killed for nothing, a voice reminded her, and her nosiness might be enough. Had she really rung Krok when she had dialled the number of the anonymous caller? She couldn't be sure, but given the location Josie had confirmed it was hard to deny the strong possibility. And someone had noticed her interest in the nautical charts . . .

Once suspicions were aroused, how simple to find out that Stevie worked for a risk assessment agency. This meant nothing in itself, but it could be enough to tip the balance against Clémence's new little friend.

A diving accident was a wonderfully deniable way to dispose of an irritation.

There was a knock at the door and Clémence came in. She was wearing a red wig.

'Oh, darling Stevie. How simply awful. Are you alright? I hate diving—it's just so dangerous. I don't know why people insist on going under like that. It's just as wet up top, and a lot safer. Are you feeling any better?'

Stevie nodded. The oxygen was helping and she was feeling much clearer and stronger.

'Will you join us for cocktails? It's almost six. I hate to think of you down here all alone and everyone's so worried. We could prop you up on pillows in the corner and you can hold court. In any case, we're having guests. We just had a radio message from the *Petrina*. Essam Al-Nassar wants to pop by for a drink. You must meet him. Extraordinary eyelashes.'

Clémence was looking paler than usual, drawn despite her lively chatter. Perhaps it was the effect of the red hair . . .

'How is Emile?' Stevie croaked.

Clémence stared up at the tiny porthole. 'In the playroom watching *Pirates of the Caribbean*.'

'Don't you think he'd like to join us on deck?' Stevie asked slowly. 'Your husband has enough guards for a whole classroom of children. Does Mr Al-Nassar have any children? Perhaps one might come and play?'

Clémence looked at Stevie as though she were a little mad.

'It might do Emile good,' Stevie continued, thinking of the dark eyes, blank with worry, the pale face. 'He seems to be with adults most of the time. We can't be much fun for him.'

'Vaughan doesn't like other people's children.' Clémence sighed and got up, shimmering in a teal blue sheath dress, a blue chiffon scarf looped casually around her throat. 'Sometimes I'm not even sure he likes his own.'

**Everyone was indeed concerned for** Stevie. She was propped up on large velvet cushions, like a small string of pearls in a display case. She accepted a glass of Krug from Clémence, for reinforcements— oligarchs and arms dealers always drank Krug, Stevie noted—and found herself perfectly positioned to watch the arrival of the guests. She had heard a lot about Essam El-Nassar, notorious Saudi arms dealer, and she was keen to see the man in person.

The *Petrina* was visible on the horizon, a floating palace. Soon three launches came zooming into view and docked nose to tail on the sheltered side of *Hercules*. Music could be heard, the quick, plaintive tones of the Middle East, and then a group of musicians appeared on the deck—maybe ten or twelve—all swathed in red and gold chiffon. Still playing their instruments, they formed a corridor of sorts. Down this phalanx danced a dark-haired medusa dressed all in gold, undulating her wondrous belly, an enormous sapphire lodged in her navel. She wore tiny cymbals on her fingers and the toes of her hennaed feet were adorned with golden rings. Then she tossed her head back and began to sing, her beautiful voice warm in the soft night air.

Two more dancers followed, tossing rose petals behind them as they swayed and swirled, perfuming the air with each spin, sandalwood and rosewater. Then Essam Al-Nassar and his wife Lamia appeared.

He was a small man, rotund, dressed in a dark suit, his feet neatly shod in patent leather. He looked more like a prosperous shopkeeper than the King of All He Surveyed, but there was no doubting the charm and energy that radiated from every pampered pore.

His wife Lamia was almost his physical opposite: a tall, buxom blonde with enormous hair and cool, blue, almond-shaped eyes. Her magnificent décolletage cradled a massive diamond, emerald and ruby necklace; she wore earrings to match, and a diamond wedding ring that covered the entire lower half of her ring finger.

She had been born Laura Donata in Milan and had met Al-Nassar at only seventeen. Like his first wife Petrina, she changed her name and became a Muslim when she married Al-Nassar.

Stevie was transfixed; despite the über-wealth she quite often found herself surrounded by, Lamia took things to the next level: there was not even a nod to modesty of any kind. More was definitely more.

The couple headed for Clémence, and Al-Nassar took his hostess' hand in both of his. 'I beg your forgiveness for this intrusion and hope you will accept a small token of my appreciation for your hospitality.' He handed Clémence a long, slim box. She opened it and held up a massive ruby necklace.

Clémence smiled graciously and kissed Lamia on both cheeks. 'Quite unnecessary, I assure you,' she murmured, and swept her guests towards the most comfortable divan.

Stevie overheard Al-Nassar's silken, rosewater voice continue the serenade of apology.

'Our musicians and servants are here to allay any distress the intrusion of our party might have caused you, dear Clémence. You must sit by me and enjoy this magnificent Mediterranean evening.'

Al-Nassar had, of course, brought his own security men, who melted into the shadows. Stevie wondered if there was a vessel anywhere as well protected as *Hercules* at that moment.

Krok was standing by Clémence, deep in conversation with a tall, impeccably dressed young man who seemed to be Al-Nassar's right hand this evening. Clémence's husband appeared quite relaxed for a change, even smiled at his companion. The two men were soon joined by Skorpios, dressed in a crisp white shirt and a double-breasted navy blazer; he and Al-Nassar's man looked to be old friends.

Stevie's unease returned. She wanted very much to hear their conversation. The smiles had gone and the men were obviously talking business. Al-Nassar sat discreetly to one side, within earshot, Stevie had no doubt, yet for all intents and purposes merely engaged in exchanging social niceties. Stevie was fascinated by the magnetic little man's cunning, and the obvious adoration he engendered in those around him. Stevie caught Clémence's eye, and she waved Stevie over. Angelina appeared beside their hostess, a vision in forest-green silk and a feathered headdress.

'Darling, can you walk?' called Clémence.

Stevie stood and swayed a little. One of the *Hercules* crew immediately appeared at her side and took her arm. Stevie actually felt fine, if a little weak, but she realised she could learn a lot from Clémence's strategy, and decided it could be to her advantage at this point to appear more fragile than she really was. She kissed Angelina hello, willing the diva to remember her promise.

Clémence turned to Angelina, 'You two know each other?'

'Oh yes,' replied the diva. 'Stevie was the most wonderful travelling companion when I went on that dreadful cruise. She kept me sane.' Angelina's face betrayed nothing, not even the tiniest flicker, and Stevie knew her secret was safe.

Essam Al-Nassar really did have the most extraordinary eyelashes she had ever seen. And very polished manners. Stevie sat back in her chair, as wan and pale as a Regency heroine, and smiled at the room in general.

'We almost lost poor little Stevie this afternoon—it was terrifying.' Clémence made her sound like a small dog, or a pair of precious sunglasses.

'I'm fine.' Stevie placed a hand on her chest, her cherry-red nail beds and bright red lips giving her a slightly vampiric quality and heightening her frailty.

'Yes, too terrible,' Clémence continued. 'One minute she was happily jumping into the water with all the others to go diving, the next she was bobbing around unconscious.'

Lamia covered her voluptuous mouth with a jewelled hand. 'How dreadful. I could never go under the water. The fish frighten me.'

'My wife has ichthyophobia, you see,' Al-Nassar chimed in. 'The unfortunate condition confines her to swimming pools.'

'Oh, much safer,' murmured Clémence, and she hastily summoned the chief steward and instructed him to ensure no fish was served at dinner. She glanced nervously up at her husband, but he appeared to be taking no notice of her.

With eyes half closed and ears pricked, Stevie strained to hear what Skorpios was saying to Krok and Al-Nassar's man.

'The cargo of helicopters that disappeared off Puntaland last week has been, shall we say, "found", stingers and all.'

Krok took a swipe at his whisky. 'Somalia. The place is filthy with pirates.' He glared at Skorpios a moment, then turned back to the other man. 'The *Morning Star* of Panama—one ship among over twenty hijacked in the last three months.'

'She is now the *Crescent Voyager*, registered in Istanbul. As for the crew—a few Filipino and North African galley slaves—they'll be released eventually, I'm sure.' Skorpios smiled without warmth.

'Cargo's more valuable than crew,' barked Krok impatiently. 'The men who want it will pay anything—because they can. They've offered three hundred million US, but I'm thinking we might do better.' Krok smiled. 'I hear your friends are thinking of starting a civil war. Those helicopters would be very useful.'

Skorpios glanced at Al-Nassar's man and took in his expression. 'Don't become too greedy, Vaughan,' he said slowly. 'It never ends well: gout, syphilis, financial ruin. I should know—I lost an empire, only to have to build another. One is more cautious the second fortune around.'

'You are, of course, insured in case this cargo goes "missing" once more?' Al-Nassar's man spoke for the first time. 'Our contacts expect one hundred per cent reliability and punctuality. There are no second chances in these matters.'

It was Krok who answered: 'Heavily insured.'

An arms deal, thought Stevie; they're negotiating to sell a shipment of stingers.

Stinger missiles were the weapon of choice for shooting down low-flying aircraft and helicopters, popular with both regular and irregular fighters. They were lightweight and portable, weighing only about ten kilos, and were able to be used by a single operator. The missile used an infra-red seeker to lock on to the heat in an engine's exhaust, and could hit nearly anything flying up to three and a half thousand metres, with a range of about eight kilometres. In other words, if you could see the plane, the stinger could bring it down. And the missiles were extremely accurate.

Lamia's accented English overlapped the voices of the men, much to Stevie's dismay. 'This one is my wedding ring, so naturally it is more special to me.' Mrs Al-Nassar was waving her hand about like a branch in the breeze, showing to good effect the precious rocks that perched thereon. 'It is forty carats.'

'It certainly has presence,' Stevie remarked, her eyes quite blinded by the glittering egg that covered the lower half of Lamia's ring finger.

'It is not the size that matters, darling.' Lamia took in Stevie's lack of adornment—four simple strands of pearls around her neck—with an air of slight puzzlement. 'Naturally it is the sentiment that counts.'

Stevie nodded her assent. 'As you can see, I am not the sentimental type. Perhaps my pearls . . . They were my great grandmother's.'

'The Fabergé egg?' Essam Al-Nassar had noticed. Stevie blushed but Lamia saved the day.

'I believe in inherited jewellery,' she interjected. 'It has a certain patina of sentiment that I find irresistible.'

Stevie suspected there was little in the way of jewellery that Lamia could resist. Well, at least the woman had passion, and she smiled warmly and often at her husband. There seemed to be real affection there.

Stevie leant her head back, suddenly feeling tired from the day, the champagne, the anxiety, the poisoned air . . . She caught Krok's words again—he appeared to be in the middle of a sales pitch.

'I have contacts right through Africa and Southeast Asia, but what I really want, and where the big money is now, is the Middle East. But I need the connections. I need someone who can put deals and people together. That's what EN does best. He's been doing it since before the Americans in Iran—the arms for hostages deal— and now he can do it for us.' He stared hard at Al-Nassar's man. 'We can get our hands on anything you want: missiles, helicopters, guns, ammunition, guidance systems, submarines, even chemical and nuclear weapons. We have a, er, particularly creative way of getting hold of specialty cargo. Nothing is impossible, nothing is traceable back to us, and we pay a very generous commission on all deals brokered at no risk to EN. Just connections, connecting.'

The sound of a motor launch distracted the men. A boat had pulled up alongside carrying some more guests from the *Petrina*. The musicians darted towards the ladder and formed a new cor-ridor, swaying and playing.

The first person aboard was a dour little woman in a dour little brown woollen dress, the front of which was buckling under the weight of pearl brooches and necklaces; she was followed by a brown little man who could only have been her husband.

The next couple made Stevie catch her breath—the beauti-ful Iris, resplendent in polka-dotted chiffon and moonstones, and behind her a tall man in his late thirties, blue linen trousers, dark-haired and craggy-faced.

*Henning!*

Stevie's heart did an involuntary somersault of pleasure that was quickly replaced by confusion and suspicion.

*What are Henning and his mother doing on the Petrina? Why are they here?*

Skorpios swooped on Iris; Stevie noticed Henning, too, needed no introduction. Why was she surprised? How much did she really know about the man? And, as she had discovered in Moscow, he seemed to specialise in unlikely friends . . .

Neither Iris nor Henning looked in her direction, although Stevie knew Henning had seen her. She had felt his blue eyes hot on the side of her face. Likewise, she gave the couple no more than a cursory look of mild and shallow curiosity.

Something was up.

Skorpios brought the couple over to Stevie. 'You know Iris, I believe.' Stevie and Iris shook hands. 'And this is her son, Henning.' Henning took Stevie's hand and smiled right into her eyes.

'Charmed,' he said softly in his deep voice.

Stevie realised with a jolt just how much she had missed him—his touch was electric on her hand—but she merely smiled politely then turned away towards Clémence, an inane query about dinner already forming on her lips.

Clémence, on the other hand, was showing some interest in the new arrival, and was casting admiring looks at his strong, lean figure, his fine suntanned hands.

'I'll seat this one next to you at dinner,' she whispered to Stevie with a slight raise of the perfect eyebrows, then glanced nervously towards her husband. She did this often, Stevie had noticed—her eyes flicking up to his face with the small, rapid movements of a gazelle. Krok was paying her no heed and she seemed relieved.

Stevie's gaze shifted to the mousy woman who had arrived

with Henning. Who was she? Her thinning grey hair was caught up in a tight bun and she wore large glasses with clear plastic frames; a matching chain assured that the glasses would stay on her person if they did slide off her nose. She kept pushing them up with a thin little finger—a nervous tic, perhaps, thought Stevie.

The woman wore sensible beige shoes with white rubber soles that were completely at odds with the encrustations of pearls that hung on her front: at least eight strands of large white pearls, several pearl brooches pinned in no particular pattern, and a pearl tiara fixed firmly to the front of the head. The effect was not unlike a display of antique jewellery at a flea market, laid out with pins on a rough dark cloth, though Stevie could tell that the pearls and their settings were magnificent.

Her husband wore a tweed jacket, similar glasses and shoes, and had obviously fought a losing battle to control the wiry tufts of grey hair that insisted on sprouting almost at random on his balding scalp. He was otherwise undecorated, except for a gold wedding ring and the most enormous gold tie pin, crowned with a diamond that, in another setting, would have had to be fake.

They were sitting together, each with a glass of Pimms, saying nothing.

The little knot of plotters had broken up with the arrival of the new guests and Stevie decided to indulge her curiosity. She stood, somewhat unsteadily, and made for the odd couple.

'Good evening, I'm Stevie Duveen.'

The couple stood and replied as one, 'Good evening, I'm sure.'

The woman spoke first. 'I'm Primula White. This is my husband, Professor Peter White.'

'It's a pleasure to meet you both.' Stevie smiled. 'Do the musicians travel everywhere with you? It's rather a lovely idea, don't you think?'

'Oh no, not always,' Primula White replied. 'They play on social occasions mainly. They wouldn't follow Mr Al-Nassar to a business meeting, for example.'

Professor White broke in, 'Although there was that one time in Smyrna . . . There was a Greek merchant—or was he a Cypriot? I can never quite get my facts straight in the heat.'

'He was a Greek trader, Professor, and the circumstances required a musical accompaniment.' Primula White's voice was sharp and precise, cutting through the fog of her husband's reminiscences.

Stevie's mind boggled trying to imagine the kinds of business deals with Greek traders that might require musical accompaniments. Instead, she said, 'It sounds like you are regular guests of Mr Al-Nassar. How fortunate for you.'

'We are indeed very fortunate, Miss Duveen, to be the recipients of such generosity. However, perhaps you labour under a misapprehension. I am engaged as a governess to Mr Al-Nassar's youngest son, Ali. Most kindly, the Professor is welcome to join us whenever he is free to.'

'Whenever I am free to, yes.'

'It must be a charmed life, full of adventure,' remarked Stevie. This explained a lot, but still not the pearls and the tie pin.

'Miss Prim watches over us all. It's really very reassuring.'

Stevie didn't need to turn her head to know exactly who was standing next to her. Miss Prim, as he called her, was actually blushing.

'Do you need much watching over?' Stevie mustered up the courage to turn and look smack bang into Henning's eyes.

His expression was serious, but the left corner of his mouth danced in the way she knew so well. 'Anything can happen at sea— and frequently does, wouldn't you say, Professor?'

'Oh, er, yes, frequently does. Indeed.' He was blushing too.

Henning had certainly made quite an impression with the bookish couple. But then again, that was what he did best.

'Poor Miss Prim had her arm twisted to join us this evening,' Henning continued. 'EN insisted that she put all her jewels on and be ready at seven.'

'I told Mr Al-Nassar I didn't have any jewellery—only the ear-rings my mother left me, and they are back in England, in the bank, for safekeeping.'

'So Essam festooned poor Miss Prim with something from his own stash—or, rather, Lamia's.'

'It really was very kind of him to lend me such beautiful pearls.'

'Even the Professor didn't escape.' Henning gestured towards the tie pin. Peter White shuffled his feet, embarrassed.

'Come on,' said Henning. 'Let me refresh your drinks.'

'Oh, Mr Henning, really, I should start to feel quite tipsy and—'

'Dear Miss Prim, your reputation is under the protection of your husband and several hundred bodyguards. It is unassailable.'

Henning refilled the glasses, adding a little extra gin to the Pimms for good measure then poured himself a whisky and soda. The couple tottered back to their chairs and Henning cornered Stevie.

'Is it responsible to spike the governess' drink?' she asked, feigning horror.

'She's a lovely woman really, but she needs to relax. She's held together so tightly I worry she'll pop something one day.'

Stevie pictured Miss Prim's bun exploding like a champagne cork and giggled. 'By the way,' she said, 'what on earth are you doing here?'

'Didn't you call?'

'No. Well, yes, but days ago. And you were on the other side of the world.'

'Actually, Persepolis is closer than people think.'

'Not the point, Henning.'

Henning looked at her long and hard. His laughing blue eyes grew serious, his voice quiet. 'Clémence told me about your dive. After today's misadventure, are you really telling me you don't need rescuing?'

Stevie took a large sip of her champagne and looked away. 'I'm perfectly alright, thank you. And you couldn't have known that was going to happen,' she added, 'so that can't be why you're here.' She realised she felt faint and looked surreptitiously around for a chair, hoping Henning wouldn't notice.

He pushed a cane armchair over but remained standing. 'Don't forget I'm on your side,' he said gently.

Stevie sat but said nothing. She didn't quite know where to begin. Drawing Henning back into her world was not something she had thought she would do. Still, she needed friends, needed someone to talk to, especially as Rice was impossible these days. After some time, she spoke, her voice almost a whisper.

'I'm just an observer.'

Henning leant against the railing and looked at her. 'Observing what, exactly? The Kroks? Their friends' amorous intrigues?'

'Pretty close.'

Henning looked sceptical. 'It's a new line of work for you.'

'It's a favour for someone—not strictly, strictly business.'

Henning's face hardened. 'Rice.' He turned away to face the lights flickering on the mysterious island of Cavallo. His voice drifted back to Stevie. 'He has no right.'

'I'm here as Clémence's guest—she knows everything. It's safe.'

'Really?' Henning turned, his eyes going to Stevie's red nails. 'He has no right,' he repeated, taking a deep sip of his whisky.

'I could have said no,' Stevie said sharply. She had a strong will and mind of her own and Henning had best not forget it.

'Rice knows only too well the influence he has over you. He pretends not to, of course—much easier on the conscience . . .' He placed his glass on the handrail and looked at her. 'But he can make you do anything.'

Stevie suppressed a thunderball of anger rising in her throat. It would not do to show her fury, draw attention, lose control. Not now.

'I remember another friend who once asked me to do him a favour.' Her voice was icy. 'To help a friend.'

'And I should never have asked.' Henning's expression was grave. 'I'll never forgive myself for putting you in so much danger.'

'Well . . .' She softened a little. 'We would never have had that mad adventure together. I don't regret saying yes.' She added, even more softly, 'To any of it.'

They were quite alone. Stevie suddenly longed to kiss him again. The other guests were mingling around Al-Nassar; it was unlikely anyone would notice. Henning's low voice brought her out of her reverie.

'Vaughan Krok is a devil. You shouldn't be anywhere near this man.'

Stevie raised an eyebrow. 'I suspect he's not the only one on board tonight that matches that description.'

Henning broke off to draw a fresh cigarette from a crumpled soft pack. He was about to offer Stevie one, then stopped. 'Sorry. Probably not the best thing for you right now, considering.'

Stevie smiled as he put the packet away. 'Probably not.'

'It's not a coincidence I'm here, Stevie.'

She waited for him to continue, and when he didn't she suggested, 'Your mother?'

'Partly. She heard you were cruising aboard the *Hercules* and wondered if it was such a good idea.' Henning did not meet her eyes.

'And she called you back from Persepolis.'

'My mother is not a hysterical woman, Stevie. Quite the opposite. I have seen her demonstrate the most extraordinary sangfroid when bear-like men have quailed. When she tells me something is not quite so, I listen.'

'Your mother is fabulous.' Stevie glanced rather enviously over at Iris, as tall as a milky reed in a cream silk blouse and pencil skirt. She was laughing lightly at something Vaughan Krok was saying to her pearly chest (he stood almost a head shorter than Iris), the dark waves of her bobbed hair dancing in the evening breeze. Her red lips were perfect and there was not a note of falseness in any of her gestures.

'I think she rather enjoyed you too, little Stevie. Certainly enough to take your welfare to heart.'

Stevie said nothing for a while. The notes of Al-Nassar's court minstrels danced about on deck. Finally, 'Well, now that you are here, Henning, you may as well make yourself useful and—'

But Stevie's plotting was interrupted by the sound of a motor launch. It seemed to be going quite fast for such a dangerous approach, and in the dark. Krok's crew moved like ghosts to the edge of the boat, hands on holsters, staring into the darkness. Stevie saw Marlena move swiftly to Megrahi's side and say something in his ear before moving away towards the stern. A navy blue Wally chase boat pulled up alongside and a dark figure in a dinner jacket jumped onto the stern platform without waiting for the speedboat to dock. The boat took off again into the night, as quickly as it had appeared.

The new arrival was a young man with dark curls and black eyes. He made his way towards the party with confidence bordering on arrogance, completely sure of himself, of his power. In that, he reminded Stevie of someone . . . Ignoring all the other guests, he made straight for Marlena, like a bull in the ring. She watched him approach, then let the man take her into his arms and kiss her. There was a murmur in the crowd, before people turned back to their conversations. Many eyes, however, remained subtly turned the couple's way. It was hard not to be curious, thought Stevie. She caught sight of Skorpios, standing with Krok, and immediately saw the similarity. Henning said quietly, 'Aristotle Skorpios, son of Socrates.'

'Lover of Marlena, so it seems,' added Stevie.

'It's a new affair, but Aristo is apparently very taken with her. Possibly all the more so because his father can't stand it.'

A loud clanging interrupted their conversation a second time. Krok was ringing an old-fashioned ship's bell with great vigour. The chief steward stepped forward. 'Dinner is served.'

A more wicked collection of people would have been hard to find around the dinner tables of the Mediterranean that evening, and the atmosphere was electric. Like the moments before a bushfire crests the nearest hill, everything carried on as usual, but every gesture crackled with sparks and life and menace. It was getting harder and harder to breathe.

Krok was drinking straight whisky with his dinner, growing dangerously drunk, his small red-rimmed eyes glittering with malice as he glanced around the table, looking for a victim. Clémence, at the opposite end, eyed him nervously, hands fidgeting with her hairpiece. Marlena sat next to Aristo, who smouldered like a hot coal. He darted glances at his father, thunderbolts, while Marlena herself appeared utterly unfazed and as cool as marble.

Stevie was rather fascinated by the magnetism of the couple. Then she sensed eyes on her and turned: Iris was watching her from across the table. She felt uncomfortable, but smiled, hoping it didn't show. She also hoped Iris wouldn't make some comment about her and Henning—he was just to Stevie's right and dangerously within hearing. When Skorpios—seated on Stevie's left—excused himself to take a phone call, Iris inclined her head a little and said softly, 'Apparently Skorpios threatened to dispose of Marlena, unless Aristo did so himself.' She took a small sip of her champagne. 'But Aristo won't do that. He's madly in love with her.'

'Do you think Skorpios would really hurt Marlena?' Stevie asked in a low voice.

'It's a credible threat,' replied Iris, raising an eyebrow. 'It was never going to make for harmonious relations between father and son.'

When Skorpios returned he ignored his son and lavished attention on Angelina, who had surfaced resplendent with fury from her chrysalis. She had caught her lover trying to lure Princess Loli into an empty stateroom that afternoon and the injury had still not been redressed. Fortunately they spoke in French, not Greek—a language that Angelina said made her feel passionless. Stevie could hear Skorpios's chocolate tones saying, 'Angelina, I am an animal. Only you can tame me. What is a flirtation compared to what we have together? A pebble before Vesuvius. *Rien!*'

Angelina flicked her head imperiously but Stevie knew her well enough to see she had been conquered. She rose from the table—ostensibly to powder her nose.

Skorpios turned his attention to Stevie. He must have known she had been listening.

'Men and women can only ever be making love, or making war. There is nothing in between.'

'That's a rather exhausting idea.'

'It is the truth. Beautiful women cannot bear moderation; they must have an inexhaustible excess of everything.' He drank his whisky. 'And Angelina is very beautiful. She has a very passionate soul. She has already forgiven me. *Tout passe.*'

'Perhaps,' replied Stevie softly, 'but it leaves scars on the heart. How much can one organ bear?'

Skorpios leant back and pulled out a cigar, eyes still on Stevie. 'You have been wounded and now you are afraid to love.' He lit the cigar and puffed with satisfaction. 'Only because you have not met the right lover,' he continued. 'The right man will make you forget everything, all the past, all the tears. And what is pain for? It tells us we are truly alive. How can we be truly happy if we have never truly suffered?'

Stevie glanced over at Henning—she couldn't help herself. Was he listening? She hoped not. She turned back to Skorpios. 'Have you ever truly suffered—I mean, for love?' Stevie doubted it. The man was a tiger.

He looked at her for a long moment. 'I am a great romantic.' He smiled. 'You pine for Iris' son.' He had noticed the glance. 'He's not for you. He has looks and charm, but he will break your heart. He will not make a good husband. I think—' he gave her a trader's appraising look '—that you can do better. You are elegant and frail. Many men like that—the delicate quality. I myself have had occasion to fall for its charms. You could go far.'

Stevie swallowed the first two replies that came to mind and settled for a milder, 'I'm happy where I am, Mr Skorpios, and I don't pine for anyone.' But the man with the toffee-lenses had guessed too much already.

'Everyone pines for someone. The heart abhors a vacuum.'

'I thought it was power . . .'

'Love is power, is it not? Make someone love you and you have power over them.'

Stevie struggled to keep her voice even. 'That's rather a horrible way to look at it.'

'Miss Duveen, you live in a fairytale. Can you really believe the things you are telling me? Is this a faux naivety for my benefit, or have you really not seen enough of life to know?' His eyes narrowed. 'I could teach you many things.'

Skorpios poured Stevie a fresh glass of champagne, his fingers unexpectedly gentle around the crystal stem, the golden scorpion gleaming on his signet ring.

'I prefer my women experienced,' he continued, 'with that faint tinge of scandal about them. Women like that understand men like me.'

'Women like Angelina?' Stevie stared right at the dark lenses, hoping she had found his eyes. 'Why do you torture her? You seem to do it on purpose. Why not let her go if you don't love her. Leave her to the man who does.'

'Zorfanelli?' Skorpios laughed. 'He is nothing.'

'And what are you, that you are so proud of yourself? Are you any better than these other men?' Stevie couldn't stop the words coming out of her mouth.

Skorpios' face darkened and she braced herself for a tempest. 'Yes, I'm a disgrace. I'm a murderer. I'm a thief . . . But I am also a billionaire, and powerful. I will never give up Angelina, and I will use whatever means necessary to keep her. Everything else can go to hell.'

Suddenly it was as if the air had been sucked out of the space around them. Stevie was afraid to move. Had she made a terrible enemy?

*I'm a murderer.*

Angelina's lacquered nails landed lightly on Skorpios' shoulder, breaking the spell. Stevie looked away in relief and caught Marlena staring at her. She gave the woman a small smile that Marlena did not return.

Aristo was smoking a cigarette and as he turned, the profile of his proud nose and heavy brows stark against his white shirt, Stevie was struck by the resemblance to his father. There was no doubt that Aristo had a charisma all his own, quite aside from the draw of his father's money. Although few would call him handsome, he was strong and graceful and proud—if a little arrogant. She could see what attracted Marlena to him, even though he was twenty years younger, only just out of his teens.

Skorpios was also now watching Aristo, and Stevie felt his silent regard flow like poison. Angelina noticed it too.

'Is it because you want her too?' she asked him, her eyes glittering dangerously.

Skorpios dismissed her provocation with a wave of his hand. 'Women like Marlena are a necessary education.'

'You are jealous of Aristo, of your own son. I would have thought he would make you proud by taking a lover like Marlena.'

'She is a whore.'

Angelina laughed. 'Because she won't sleep with you?' The diva leant across the table seductively, her pale skin reflecting the candlelight, the dancing shadows accentuating every curve. The woman was a phenomenon. 'Aristo, tell your father he must marry me.'

'Angelina, I can't do that.' Skorpios' voice was sharp. 'This is a user pays arrangement.'

The diva jerked back as if she had been slapped. She stared at her lover with her huge eyes. 'Skorpios . . .' Her incredible voice trembled. 'You are a monster.'

Slowly she stood, as if unable to trust her legs to hold her, and left the table.

Stevie struggled between the impulse to go after her, and her desire not to get involved in the love affairs of others. She realised she felt very tired. For now, she would wait.

Stevie looked to one side and saw Skorpios, a man who refused to stay with one woman; at the other end of the spectrum was Krok, a man who refused to let one go. Did these two men represent the choices in love? Did love exist in a straight line, with two opposite points—Krok and Skorpios—between which some accommodation had to be found?

The thought depressed her and she turned her gaze up to the few stars that were visible beyond the lights; darkness forever. The suggestion of eternity comforted her, she didn't know why. Actually, she did know why—it was that the very word 'eternity' was filled with the breath of freedom. It was the opposite of being trapped, confined, locked up, owned and beholden. It was a state of complete and perfect liberty.

Would she one day meet a person who made her want to change that—take the gloss off her utter independence? Unlikely. She hoped any man she fell in love with wouldn't demand that of her . . . or was surrender a pre-condition to true love?

Did people simply attract what they themselves put out to the universe, like to like? Clémence had learnt how to trap a man and keep him—now she was kept in a vice of iron; Angelina thrived on the drama of passion and she had met a man who would keep her swinging from ecstasy to despair. Stevie couldn't live like either of them. And then there was Henning: what might he demand of her if she let him get too close? The thought frightened her. A winter love affair was one thing; one that stretched to two—even three—seasons, quite another. Stevie did not feel ready for what that might lead to.

Henning caught her gaze and smiled; he was dangerously charming, Stevie thought, and too real to sustain her fantasy of him. Best exit. If she let him have her heart, she would be at his mercy. She would end up like Angelina.

———

**The diva was weeping hysterically** in her cabin.

'Angelina . . .' Stevie stood by the door for a moment, waiting for the sobs to lessen. When finally she raised her head from the pillow, the woman's face was swollen and contorted with pain.

'Angelina, why do you stay with him?'

Angelina gulped. 'Will you pour me a drink, Stevie, darling?'

Stevie handed her an inch of vodka from the room's bar.

The diva swallowed it and it seemed to calm her. She shook her head. 'When slur follows slur, and insults pile upon insults, the love that is left makes no sense, but it is also indestructible.' She turned to look at Stevie. 'It is a madness of sorts, and nobody chooses to be mad.'

Her false eyelashes had come unglued and fallen in front of her eyes like drunken spiders—she did indeed look a little demented. Stevie reached into Angelina's purse, pulled out her compact and held the mirror up to her.

'Tell me, Angelina,' she said softly. 'Is any man—any love—worth this?'

Angelina took the mirror, stared at her deformed face, and began weeping afresh. Stevie closed the cabin door quietly and left her to her tears.

She was halfway up the stairs when she heard voices in the main saloon. 'Damn that bitch, I could—' The end of the sentence was swallowed by a burst of collective laughter from the deck. Stevie recognised the voice of Skorpios. Then another voice spoke—Dado Falcone?

'You tried, but you did not succeed.'

'Who says I won't try again?'

'It's an unnecessary risk. You don't—'

Their conversation was interrupted by a woman's scream, high, loud and as clear as crystal.

*Angelina!*

When Stevie reached the cabin door, she found the diva attempting to commit suicide with a letter opener. Fortunately, the letter opener was not as sharp as it looked and, as anyone who has tried knows, it is actually quite difficult to stab oneself with enough conviction to cause a serious injury. Angelina had managed a small—though no doubt painful—flesh wound that would not do any lasting damage. She refused to let Stevie touch her.

When Skorpios and Falcone appeared in the cabin door a moment later, they were treated to a dramatic tableau: the diva was sitting on the edge of her bed; her black dress had slipped off the shoulder exposing her milky left breast. Her head was thrown back, exposing her long and famous throat, and a trickle of bright blood crept towards her cleavage. In her fist she clutched the letter opener like Cleopatra's asp. She gave a small moan.

Skorpios bellowed, 'Leave us,' and ran to his lover.

Stevie was only too glad to close the cabin door on the scene.

She smiled politely at Falcone as he stepped back to let her pass in the narrow passageway, wondering if she was the irritant the two men had been talking about. Was there murderous intent disguised as chivalry and *bon ton* in the man behind her? Her shoulder blades burnt in anticipation of the sharp sting of a knife.

None came and Stevie felt both relieved and a little foolish as the hubbub of the after-dinner conversation came through the open door. The guests had left the table and were mingling on the deck.

Henning was whispering to Princess Loli, making her laugh, her eyes bright; Iris was deep in conversation with Lamia. Stevie saw Clémence glide over to where her husband stood talking to Al-Nassar and his right hand and watched as she tried to join the conversation—but Krok just turned his shoulder and blocked her, pushing her away with the back of his arm. He didn't even pause his words.

Clémence looked momentarily lost and Stevie slipped over to her side, taking her elbow.

'Darling,' Stevie said gaily, 'I haven't seen you all evening! Come and sit by me.' She led Mrs Krok to some empty chairs a little to the side of the party. As they passed, Stéphane, the aristocrat from Liechtenstein, handed them two glasses of champagne with a little bow, his eyes fixed on Clémence.

'He seems very interested in you,' Stevie remarked, glancing at the dark-haired European.

'He's interested in my money—in Vaughan's money I should say.' She drank from her glass. 'I'm not being cynical, Stevie. It's hard for Stéphane. Behind his world-weary gestures and disdainful laugh is the insecurity of an aristocrat without a country, clinging to a meaningless title that gets him invited to the right parties. Trouble is, Stéph's tastes are very expensive—sports cars, travel, gambling, fine art, the life of le jet-set. He needs a fortune to finance his aspirations.'

Clémence looked around. 'I'm the richest woman here, apart from Lamia. And even Stéphane is not that stupid. Why not? I'm still attractive—if Vaughan and I divorced I would be entitled to a huge chunk of his wealth.' She finished her champagne in one long swallow. Her voice was low and hoarse when she spoke again. 'Sometimes it's as if he can't stand me, can't stand the sight of me.'

'Would you ever leave him, Clémence? Surely his fortune isn't worth your health—not to mention Emile's life. And as you said, it's not as if you would be left with nothing.'

'My dear Stevie, you don't understand, do you? A divorce would be far too expensive—even for my husband—and too dangerous. I know too much about Vaughan, his business . . . You don't get to be as powerful as he is without doing some very bad things. After sleeping with Vaughan for nine years, I'd have to be pretty stupid not to know at least one secret that could destroy him. He will never let me go.' Clémence glanced down at her nails, her rich perfume hanging about her like a protective cloud.

'He will never let me go,' she repeated, 'and if I tried to leave . . . he would kill me. I'd be found on the floor of one of my bedrooms in a pool of my own vomit—a drug overdose, a tragic suicide. I've heard him talk to people about my barbiturate addiction.'

Stevie stared at her. She didn't seem to be—

'No, Stevie, I don't have an addiction. That's the point. He is laying out the groundwork for my murder like a game of solitaire, card by card. And he knows I see it. It's one of his more delightful forms of bullying—to remind me of how lightly I tread on this earth, to remind me that I breathe because he allows me to.'

Stevie shivered and stared down at the oil-black sea where the lights of the *Hercules* were dancing to the tune of Al-Nassar's musicians. The ship was full of bullies and thieves and Stevie could feel the desperation—Clémence, Angelina, Stéphane, how many others?— creep along her spine.

A steward appeared with a tray of cognac and announced to the party: 'The games in the saloon are about to begin.'

# 12

Stevie did not like games. Nor was she very good at them. Even ones that people might have supposed she would be quite suited to were somehow beyond her. Generally she was able to avoid them, though children's birthday parties could be problematic, and English country house parties were perilous. In that situation, a well-timed urge to take the dogs for a long walk usually did the trick.

However, shipboard with a sociopathic weapons dealer and mercenary definitely classified as a situation where games would be difficult to avoid. Stevie gathered her skirts and wondered whether she could convincingly fake a faint, considering her condition . . .

The guests were assembled in the saloon and the round central table had been transformed for the games with a green baize top. Piles of striped chips and stacks of playing cards were collected to one side, under the protection of the chief steward-cum-croupier. Chairs had been set out around the perimeter of the room and a large screen in the corner hinted ominously at the possibility of electronic games—something equally dread-inspiring to Stevie.

She crouched quietly on a banquette, taking care to sandwich herself between two deflectors: Henning (tall and broad) and

Clémence (attention-swervingly glamorous). She concentrated on making herself invisible—a rare talent she had that most of the time worked very nicely.

Once all the guests were seated, Krok appeared, cigar in one hand, the other hanging heavily in his jacket pocket. Stevie noticed the outline of a snub-nosed revolver straining at the white linen of the pocket.

'Games. Mark of a man—how he plays a game.' His voice was loud and hoarse from the whisky, the smoke and the goblins within—a bark. 'Can't trust a man who doesn't play games.' He turned his boiled eyes to his wife and Stevie felt the skin on Clémence's arm, resting lightly against her own, chill a few degrees. 'Or a woman for that matter.'

He stared around the room, his eyes aggressive, as if daring someone to give him an excuse to explode. Then he suddenly smiled and gave another bark. 'Russian roulette?'

He removed his hand from his pocket and drew with it a small white gun, like those carried by his crew. He raised it and fired at the crystal chandelier hanging from the ceiling. The sound was furiously loud, even in the carpeted and cushioned room. Someone let out a squeal, quickly stifled.

A single crystal drop fell from the chandelier into Clémence's balloon glass of cognac. A smoking hole was left, round and perfect, in the panelled timber ceiling above her head. The glass in Clémence's hands began to shake. Stevie saw Marlena reach over and take it out of her sister's hands, place it on the side table. The twins exchanged a glance that, to Stevie, was unreadable.

Stéphane leant towards Clémence. 'Are you alright?' he whispered.

Clémence forced a tight little laugh, 'Of course. It's just the gun . . . I hate guns—hate the noise, the smell, can't bear to touch

them.' She reached for her glass and took a sip. 'No doubt why
Vaughan insists on firing them for party tricks,' she added, and
smiled at the room in general.

Krok was laughing now. 'It's much more fun with other
people's lives,' he said. 'Trust me.' Then, his eyes on Stéphane and
Clémence, he added, 'Don't look so shocked. My wife will tell you
I'm only joking.' He smiled like a crocodile. 'What shall we play
first? I have every game you can think of and lots you can't. Battle-
ships, *quinze*, poker, *boules*, backgammon, *pai gow*, roulette, craps,
Monopoly, World Domination . . .' His eyes were ablaze with genuine enthusiasm. This mad love of games was a trait that might
have humanised someone else, could maybe have made them more
endearing. It only made Krok creepier.

Stevie was not the only person who felt this, it seemed. In the
saloon full of people, not a peep could be heard. Men leant back and
lit cigarettes, women sipped daintily at their drinks and smiled in
their jewels, but no one said a word. Not even Stéphane, depend-
able lubricator of every social situation.

Krok's talent for cruelty now displayed itself, his antennae
obviously subtle and sensitive despite the boorish impression he
had crafted. He homed in on Stevie.

'You. Pick a game.'

Stevie felt the familiar flush of terror—hot then cold all over.
She straightened up, breathed, and raised her chin. Bullies were
more dangerous if you cowered.

She only remembered the rules to two games: Charades and
Snap. She glanced over at Skorpios' huge brown paw resting on the
table nearby, the heavy signet ring, and she recoiled. 'Charades,' she
said in a clear voice, her skin prickling with self-consciousness as
the room turned its face to her. 'Let's play Charades.'

The silence deepened. Stevie continued to hold her chin high, backing her suggestion with a confidence she did not feel in the slightest.

Krok stared at her. Finally, just as her neck was about to crick painfully in its unnaturally assertive position, he smiled and barked: 'You heard the bird. Charades.'

The game was to be played in two teams, with each person choosing the title of a movie, a book, a song or a play, writing it on a slip of paper and popping it into a silver bowl on the table. The titles on the slips of paper were kept secret from those in the other team. It took a while to form the teams. It seemed people could not decide whether it was better to be on Krok's team, or playing against him; the matter was finally decided by the steward.

At one point, Stevie did wonder whether there wasn't something to Krok's theory—that you could tell a man by the way he played a game. She was on the opposing team to Krok, with Angelina, Stéphane, Dado, Princess Loli, Lamia, Professor White, Aristo and Clémence. Megrahi and the right hand were nowhere to be seen.

Angelina, her dark hair tumbling over her shoulders, her wound bandaged, chose Ophelia—which technically was a personage and not a play or a movie or a book, but it suited her idea of herself: tragic, gorgeous love suicide. Stevie wondered for a moment how she would pull off such an unlikely casting . . . However, Angelina was not La Dracoulis for nothing. With a gesture, the swelling Greek womanhood disappeared and in its place appeared the lovesick girl. Without moving from her spot by the grand piano, she conveyed Ophelia's madness, her fragility, her devastated heart, her wretched death by drowning.

The other team was busy guessing, spirits and voices buoyed by the cognac and the miracle of talent before them. Then a voice louder than all the others called out: 'My wife.'

Patchy laughter.

Krok continued, 'Ask her where she got that scar on her wrist.'
He barked out his laugh. This time only Marlena joined in, although
she seemed to be laughing for a different reason, her gaze on Krok
and not her sister. Several pairs of eyes drifted to Clémence's wrists.
Stevie's followed; Krok's wife did indeed have a vertical scar on her
left wrist . . .

Had Clémence been lying to her?

Clémence must have seen Stevie's hesitation. Her own face
was brittle and pale, and showed nothing. 'A bicycle accident, Stevie,' she said stiffly. 'When I was a child.'

Marlena lit a cigarillo and threw back her head, exposing her
pale, slender neck—so vulnerable to slitting or strangling, thought
Stevie. She caught a whiff of Marlena's perfume, violets and something . . . Unusual and slightly bitter, it suited her. Marlena blew
a perfect smoke ring and watched it ascend. 'O for Ophelia,' she
announced lazily, drawing Krok's attention away from his wife. 'Am
I right?' She knew she was, Stevie thought; Marlena was a master of
charades.

The sound of outboard motors interrupted the game. Krok
lifted his bull head from the bowl of his glass and almost smiled.
He got up and left the saloon without a word. A few of the guests
followed, including Stevie.

Out on deck, the noise was louder—it sounded like several
dinghies close by . . . Krok stood, ham hands resting heavily on the
rail, gazing out to the black sea. There were no lights visible, no
boats. Nothing.

Al-Nassar said something over his shoulder and his right
hand appeared. The man stepped up to the rail, closer to Krok. The
sound of engines was growing louder—deafening almost—but still
there was nothing to see. More guests had gathered on deck by now,
drawn by the vibration of the motors.

A shout from the darkness, sudden synchronised silence, a feather-bump on the hull of the *Hercules*.

Krok held a hand aloft—then dropped it like a flag. A flood-light exploded the sea, the deck, and the glittering guests with light. Below them in the water bobbed a monster the likes of which Stevie had never seen before: a single Zodiac inflatable, about twelve metres long, painted white-pointer grey, and powered by eight three-hundred-horsepower Evinrude engines. It had been custom-fitted with massive fuel tanks and was designed to have a low profile in the water. Stevie understood straight away what it was: a high-speed, uncatchable smugglers' craft.

'It's light, it's fast, it's unsinkable. We've had similar inflatables running across the English Channel three times a week—just a blur on the coastguard radar. Not one caught yet.' Krok spoke directly to Al-Nassar. 'The beauty is you can beach these, run them right up. Takes the hassle out of offloading your cargo. And they'll catch anything they chase.' Krok's eyes glinted in the reflected light. 'I call them "Medusas".'

'How much?' It was the first time Al-Nassar had spoken outside the cocktail-social context.

Krok hooded his eyes, looked a little bored, contemptuous about talking money. 'In US dollars, about seven hundred thousand. How many does your client want?' He grinned wolfishly. 'We might even do a little discount for orders over a certain number.'

The right hand said something to his boss in a low voice; Al-Nassar replied in the same hushed tone. It was the right hand who spoke. 'Impressive, Mr Krok, indeed. And yet we have not seen them in action. What can they do? We feel our clients would need to be . . . convinced before they would confide their operations to vessels such as these. Fibreglass craft have done just as well so far.'

Krok snorted. 'Fibreglass is too visible, too vulnerable. Fine for the Caribbean rum runners, but this is a step into another league.' He puffed on his cigar. 'I will blow their towel-head minds with this.' The right hand visibly stiffened, then relaxed at a soft gesture from one of Al-Nassar's perfect little hands.

'Prove it,' the arms dealer said softly.

Krok stared at him, each assessing the other's intent. The right hand's phone rang, breaking the deadlock.

He answered in abrupt Arabic. As he listened, his eyes grew dark with displeasure. He said a few harsh words that Stevie could not understand, then relayed something to his boss in softer tones.

Al-Nassar pursed his lips and gave a wave of his hand. 'Dump them,' he said in English.

Krok turned to the guests still marvelling at the monster below. 'The show's over, folks, as they say. Champagne and dessert in the saloon.' Krok's guests took the hint and began drifting back into the saloon. Only Stevie remained, hidden in the shadows.

'The ship that is transporting the SAMs for our African client has been spotted,' Stevie heard Al-Nassar explain quietly. 'The Corsican coastguard is following it.'

'Someone must have tipped them off . . .' The right hand's voice was bitter. Al-Nassar made a tiny movement with his hand and his man stepped back.

'Our client will be very . . . disappointed, I am afraid.'

'You have a transportation issue. I am in the transportation business.' Krok narrowed his eyes. 'Do you want me to fix this problem?'

'In exchange for a direct line to him, I presume.'

'Of course. An introduction and a recommendation he source through STORM exclusively.'

Al-Nassar nodded minutely. 'It is done.'

Krok smiled, called out for Marlena. She appeared at Krok's side almost immediately and he spoke to her in a low voice, his words inaudible to Stevie. Then he addressed the right hand. 'Tell Muammar to check his Christmas stocking tomorrow evening.' He smirked, triumphant.

Stevie, invisible to all, watched from the shadows as Marlena stripped off her cashmere shawl and, in her tight black jeans and shimmering midnight-blue blouse, leapt down into the boat. The driver—a figure in black—stepped aside deferentially. She tied an Hermès scarf tightly around her head and fired up the engines as if she had done this before. Many times.

Moorings were cast off and the engines roared into life, deafening the spectators. The Zodiac peeled off at high speed, a wall of wake leaping up behind, then racing towards the *Hercules* and coming to crash like surf against the hull. Then Marlena and the monster were gone.

'Someone must have tipped them off,' the right hand said again, out of earshot of Al-Nassar, his laser gaze directed at Krok. Krok merely laughed in his face, threw the cigar stub overboard and went back inside.


**That night Stevie slept fitfully,** her slumber filled with vivid dreams that made her cry out in terror. When she woke around three, the moon was shining in her porthole and her face was wet with tears. There were demons at work inside her that she had never faced, never managed to quell, and when she was tired or tense or otherwise vulnerable they came to her: the memories of her parents, of their murder, of all the blood she had seen in Russia, of the heartaches, people lost, loves lost . . . When the pink of dawn came it was a relief and Stevie swung her legs over the edge of the bed. She took a cool shower, clearing her head of the night's turmoil. The sea outside was as still and perfect as a lake, mirroring the pale pinky-blue of the sky. Remembering Marlena's departure the night before, Stevie decided to take a jet ski out to see what she could find. She doubted there would be anything to see, but she needed action to drive the shadows of the night from her mind, and it was as good a plan as she could think of that morning.

All the jet skis aboard were gold. The man needed to be seen—she hadn't realised that about Krok initially: he was vain as all hell. She took off fast and roared out onto the sea, heedless of the rocks which were clearly visible under the glassy surface; the jet ski's draft was too shallow to be bothered by them. She let herself enjoy the speed and the warm air and the feeling that she was leaving everything behind, perhaps forever.

Out of the corner of her eye, she saw another craft. Following her? She turned up the throttle; Krok's jet skis were fast. So was the one racing behind her. A prickle of fear—the memory of the near-fatal dive was fresh.

She could outrun it, she thought, if she had to. But where to run to? Was the *Hercules* safe for her?

Far out to sea, a dim blur grew into a boat. Stevie headed for it. Perhaps safety lay that way. As she drew nearer, she could see it was a white luxury motor cruiser, almost indistinguishable from so many other day boats in the Med. But it appeared to be drifting. There was no anchor chain—it was too deep anyway—and the engines were switched off. Stevie forgot the jet ski behind her and headed straight for the cruiser. Perhaps those aboard were in trouble.

Circling the boat, she could see no sign of life. She drove up to the stern and cut the engine, drifting in. She called out but there was no reply. There was no ladder either, and the platform was up, making it difficult to board. She pushed her way along to the starboard side, now hidden from the direction she had come, fastened the jet ski, stood up on the seat and grabbed the lowest rail. She could just reach. She swung her tiny frame up and clambered successfully—if rather gracelessly—aboard. She could hear no movement, see no sign of people on board. Curious. Her skin prickled again. Something was wrong . . .

The sound of another jet ski pulled her thoughts away from the mysterious ship. Her pursuer was approaching, heading straight for the boat. Her moored jet ski would be plainly visible to anyone circling the boat. Stevie crouched down out of sight and grasped the diving knife she wore strapped to her calf. She hoped it would not come to that. Her training was all very well, but she had yet to stab anyone for real. Although, she reminded herself, she had come very close that night in the Swiss sanatorium . . .

The sound of the engine was upon her. Steve peeped from a hole in the rail. The jet ski in pursuit was purple—not one of Krok's. Who then?

There was a soft bump against the hull, the cutting of the engine. The top of a man's head and one shoulder appeared over the rail. Stevie's heart jumped. She would recognise that shoulder anywhere.

'What are you doing here?' She leapt over to Henning.

Henning vaulted the rail in one quick move and grinned at her. 'I knew what you would do—I had a hunch you'd head out to try and discover where Marlena went in that beast of a boat last night. Turns out I was right. I had planned to do the same thing myself. Too curious to stay away . . .'

'I'm glad you're here I suppose.' Stevie bent to sheath her knife. 'Although you gave me a scare. I thought someone was chasing me.'

'Well,' Henning winked, 'someone is. But you know that already.' He smiled again, eyes hard on her.

Steve grew warm. She was unprepared for such a sally. Her knife was of no use in this situation. She looked into Henning's ice blue eyes, gaze glancing down and off the two smooth brown shoulders, the finely muscled arms, the tattoo of an owl in full flight on his inside forearm. She swallowed hard: it wasn't even seven am and she wanted him. There was no hiding from that. She wanted him with every cell in her body, here on this abandoned yacht, this ghost ship, with all its dangers and its menace.

She moved imperceptibly closer to him and suddenly Henning's arms were around her, holding her so tight it was hard to breathe.

His breath was warm in her hair as he whispered, 'My god, how I've missed you, little bird.'

For a second, Stevie wanted to sink for eternity into this moment, to be held by Henning forever, the world be damned. Then she shook herself. Focus, Stevie. Open that door again and you may never be able to shut it. Not a second time. There is too much behind it. Things had almost got out of hand after Russia but she had managed to slam the hatch shut after a torrid few days—run away might be a better way to describe it. She could still remember him calling after her in the *bahnhof* as she bolted for the train, love in his voice, amusement: 'Run, Stevie. But I will catch you. It is only a matter of time, my darling.'

She had not seen him in the months before Sardinia. The fact that he had not insisted, that after a few phone calls that Stevie had not answered he had stopped calling, had made it easier to get him out of her head. But seeing him again like this brought all her feelings flooding back. She was capable of anything out on this slate-smooth sea. It was a most extraordinarily dangerous position to be in and Henning must absolutely not guess any of it. If he did, he might try to persuade her to change her mind, to come back, and she might find herself unable to refuse.

She cleared her throat. 'Where is everyone?' Her voice was husky. She coughed. Everything now depended on breaking this mad and unwelcome spell. Fortunately she was wearing her sunglasses; she hoped it would be enough to stifle Henning's rather uncanny ability to read her mind. She turned away and headed for the gangway. Whatever dangers lay below were less, at that moment, than the ones that lay within.

Henning put a hand on her arm. 'Wait.' He slipped past her, torso just brushing her shoulders. 'I'll go first.' He crept nimbly down the stairs, moving surprisingly quickly, Stevie thought. But then, there was just so much about him that she still didn't know.

On the table in the cabin below were the remnants of someone's dinner—two people; flat bread, some soft cheese, tabouleh.

'It seems they left in a great hurry.' Stevie sniffed an empty glass. 'Arak,' she said. 'So they were Middle Eastern, maybe North African, at a guess.'

'A good one.' Henning nodded to the Mars Légères cigarette packet lying empty beside the ashtray. 'I know they smoke those in Tunisia.' He headed below to check the cabins but reappeared quickly. 'Not a soul. But I did find piles of clothes lying about— men's clothes.'

Henning fired up a computer sitting in the corner. 'Everything seems to have been wiped,' he said finally.

Henning and Stevie split up and combed the ship for clues, meeting up in the hold a few minutes later. It was empty save for a few old towels and some rope that had been recently cut. Stevie held up a small piece of straw. 'Packing straw?'

Henning examined it. 'Unlikely to have been for animals' use. Where did everyone go?'

Stevie sniffed the air. There was a faint smell of violets . . . She struggled to place it, then it came to her in a flash. 'Marlena's scent.

She was wearing it last night. She came here in that boat—she and Krok are mixed up in whatever this is.'

As they made for the ladder Stevie asked, 'Henning, did you notice there is no name on this ship, nor registration markings?'

'I didn't find any registration papers either.' He shook his head. 'It's odd because she's in perfect condition, and I'd say worth around five hundred thousand euros. You don't just abandon a ship like this.'

'She's a ghost ship.'

There was something floating in the sea to port. Stevie grabbed a pair of binoculars hanging from a hook and went to the porthole. 'What is that?'

She squinted in the direction of an indistinct shape on the horizon. It was a small, punctured inflatable, barely afloat. Stevie lowered her binoculars. 'I'd lay money on it being the tender. There's lettering on the sides but I can't read it.'

Henning took the binoculars. '*Bel Amica*. Must be the name of this ship.'

Stevie looked at him with some amazement. 'You have extraordinary eyesight.'

Henning grinned at her. 'I see everything. Don't forget that.'

'I won't,' said Stevie, rather alarmed. They were silent for a minute. Stevie's mind ticked. 'What was Marlena doing here last night, and what was Krok plotting?' she asked.

Henning suddenly stooped and reached for a crumpled piece of paper, half torn and jammed behind some wires. As he smoothed it out his face froze.

'What is it?' asked Stevie nervously.

He handed her the paper. It was an end user certificate, issued by South Yemen, for twelve surface-to-air missiles. 'EN's stingers,' she murmured, then looked up. 'South Yemen no longer exists.'

Henning frowned. 'I know.'

'So where do you think she really took them?' The stingers had gone with Marlena; it had to be. Henning led the way back to the main cabin. There was a pile of maps under some magazines on a side table. He found one of the Mediterranean and traced his finger north from the island of Sardinia.

'This is roughly where we are—and with a boat like that, calculating a fuel storage capacity of around fifteen thousand litres, she has a lot of options. But . . .' He ran his finger lightly south. 'I'm guessing she was headed for Africa—most likely Tunisia.' He pointed to a peninsula that jutted out into the Med. 'Either somewhere on the Cap Bon peninsula, or further west, the Ichkeul National Park. Those would be the best places to land cargo like this, and she could make that distance quite easily.'

'Tunisia,' mused Stevie, leaning over his shoulder. 'Who would want SAMs in Tunisia?' She searched her mental database for rebel groups interested in shooting down helicopters or civilian aircraft— the most popular use for the covetable portable missiles. Henning turned to her, their faces suddenly very close in the cabin. 'It's not Tunisia,' he whispered, his eyes on Stevie's. 'The weapons are bound for Libya. EN's man is ex-Libyan secret service. I recognised his face. He was involved in a boating "accident" off Cavallo last year; two men died and his face was in the papers. It makes perfect sense.'

'Didn't the UN lift the arms embargo in 2003?'

Henning nodded. 'Yes. But there are any number of people and groups in Libya that they could be going to, and government forces could still be high on the list.'

'So who would be chasing the shipment? The CIA?'

'Likely. Or anyone working with them. I don't think there would be many friendly governments who would want rogue SAMs floating about.'

Stevie thought for a moment. 'And the tip-off to the French coastguard came from Krok. Of course. He saw it as a chance to prove Al-Nassar and his client couldn't do business without him.'

'I think you might be right.' Henning nodded. 'The man loves to play games . . .'

Stevie squinted at the horizon. 'It won't be long until the coastguard picks up the ship, not if they were alerted to its possible contents. We should get out of here.'

'Yes, sticky questions and all that.' Henning looked at her for a moment, then said, 'Although you could stay—get taken back by them for questioning . . . it would get you off Krok's yacht.'

'I'm needed there,' she said almost inaudibly.

'By whom?' There was a note of bitterness in Henning's reply. He leant in, a hand on Stevie's tiny shoulder. The pressure was strangely comforting. 'I'm sorry.' He shook his head. 'I'm worried about you on that boat. Come and stay with us on the *Petrina*. EN would be only too delighted to have you. You're not safe where you are.'

Stevie shook her head. 'I'm fine, Henning. Anyway, we dock in Bonifacio this evening. I think I can look after myself for a few hours.'

Henning kept his hand on her shoulder. 'A minute is all it takes.' Then he lifted it off. Without the pressure, Stevie almost felt like she could float away.

'You have a hole in your shirt,' he remarked. Stevie looked down. She must have torn it climbing onto the ship. 'I could mend it for you,' Henning offered.

'You sew?' she asked sceptically.

'I learnt in the army.'

'When were you in the army? Which army?'

Henning grinned.

'And,' Stevie continued indignantly, 'you never told me you had brothers!'

Henning's grin grew wider.

'Why do you have so many secrets?' Stevie insisted. Before she could resist, Henning had pulled her close and was kissing her, his lips salty from the sea spray. Stevie returned the kiss with a fervour that surprised her, her arms holding his strong shoulders close, her insides tumbling with nerves and desire.

When she broke away, Henning made no move to stop her but merely said, 'You know everything about me that matters—mostly, how I feel about you.' His fingers touched the tear in Stevie's shirt. After a moment, he said, 'If you were mine, I would take better care of you. Excellent care, in fact.'

Stevie's head was spinning, her cheeks burning as she leapt aboard her jet ski and powered off.

**By the time Stevie got** back to her cabin and changed into white shorts, a pale pink silk shirt and some very dark glasses, it was breakfast time for the guests aboard the *Hercules*. Clémence picked at a croissant; with her wig off—her hair back to blonde—and her sunglasses hiding her eyes (and most of her face actually, noted Stevie, they were so huge), she looked almost normal. Angelina never rose before noon so Stevie did not expect to see her at the table. Marlena was also missing. Having seen what she had that morning, Stevie was not surprised.

Krok was in a good mood this morning, laughing with Skorpios, waving his cigar about as expansively as a wound-up warlord can. No wonder, thought Stevie. He had made a good deal last night, if his trial was successful: the monster inflatables would be sought after by gun and drug runners the world over.

The morning papers were spread over the table. Stevie glanced distractedly at *Il Corriere* as she poured herself a cup of coffee and pulled the knob off the top of a perfect little brioche—still warm— and popped it in her mouth. There was news of a Saudi tanker, the *Andromeda*, that had been seized by Somali pirates six weeks earlier. The Saudi owners had taken a pragmatic view and finally negotiated a ransom payment. A small plane dropped fifteen million dollars in cash onto the deck of the tanker, using a parachute. Apparently the pirates had a machine that mechanically counted the money and that could also detect fake bank notes. Stevie wondered at the level of organisation and professionalism of the pirates, and remembered David Rice's misgivings.

Then her eyes hit another headline and she stopped mid-chew: SWISS BANKER ASSASSINATED. She forced herself to swallow, knowing immediately who the victim was. These sorts of things didn't happen to ordinary Swiss bankers.

Aldo Meienfeldt had been found bleeding by the side of the pool at his Sardinian villa, his body riddled with bullet holes. The *carabinieri* suspected a semi-automatic weapon due to the mess and number of bullets, but were at a loss to find a motive. His neighbour, Graziella Burano, described him as '*un uomo preciso, discreto e pulito*'—a clean, discreet and precise man—and could not think why anyone would want to kill him. She blamed the Russians.

The chief of the *carabinieri* was a little more poetic in his assessment of Aldo, but had come to pretty much the same conclusion: 'These stupendously wealthy men with their maleficious connections come south for the sun and trail evil in their wake. These are not crimes of the Costa, but crimes of the cities and gangsters of Europe.' He was more correct than he knew, thought Stevie. She risked a sly glance at Krok. What did Richard III say in Shakespeare's play? *Why, I can smile and murder while I smile.* There was no doubt in her mind who had been responsible for Aldo's killing, that it had been done messily and publicly as a message to the others; and Aldo's killer clearly felt no remorse, no compulsion to at least pretend to be distressed by the gruesome death of his partner. She would make sure to stay in the sunlight and surrounded by guests until they reached dry land.

As the *Hercules* weighed anchor, the guests began to drift from the breakfast table towards the sun lounges. They were headed for Corsica that morning, only a short distance away. Stevie wandered about, trying to look aimless. In the saloon, she found Emile sitting on a sofa. He was reading a comic book about the Phantom. She went and sat down next to the small boy, who looked up at her in surprise.

'Hi,' she said, smiling at him. 'Is the Phantom your favourite superhero?'

'He's not really a superhero,' Emile said quietly after a moment.

'Let's see.' Stevie leant in and they began to look at the drawings together, the boy explaining the story so far. Out of the corner of her eye, Stevie saw a pile of charts sitting on a table by the computers. Curiosity began to burn like fire somewhere between her eyes: she needed to see those charts. She got up and on cat-like feet made her way towards the pile. Her skin tingled with nerves—it would be so easy to get caught, and yet . . . She glanced at the top chart.

To her surprise it mapped the waters of the Bab-el-Mandeb, off the coast of Somalia—nowhere near the Mediterranean waters they were currently in. *What did they need it for?* The water and parts of the coastline were marked with red dots—there would have been about twenty marks. Stevie glanced quickly over her shoulder. Emile was watching her. She looked back at the charts. Underneath were others, this time for the Bight of Benin, off Nigeria, the same dots . . . and suddenly she knew exactly what those red marks meant. She darted back to Emile and smiled, putting a finger to her lips. 'I'm like the Phantom, you see? You must pretend you never saw me, okay?' The little boy nodded, eyes even wider now. Stevie kissed the top of his head and slipped off to find somewhere she would not be overlooked.

From the depths of a sun lounge, by the rooftop spa, Stevie sent a text message to Rice, cc-ing Josie, just to be sure: *Aboard Hercules. Found charts of Somali/ Nigerian coastline with markers all over. Pretty sure they correspond to pirate attacks in the area. Why Krok? Is he involved? S*

Then she carefully deleted her sent message and lay back, her Panama hat shading her face.

# 13

The evening light was soft on the great limestone cliffs of Bonifacio. The Old Town appeared, innumerable stone buildings with minuscule windows clinging like barnacles to the edges of the precipices overlooking the open sea. The bottom of the cliffs had been eaten away by the booming waves of the winter storms and the houses now appeared to hang precariously over the water below, as if they might lose their grip at any minute and tumble into the sea.

As the *Hercules* steamed past, Stevie looked up. The cliffs would have been close to seventy metres tall and the effect was vertiginous, even from below. She wondered what it would be like to live in one of the old stone dwellings, to sleep jutting over the jaws of the sea. Some had been there since the ninth century.

The wind had picked up in the afternoon and, as they approached the port, several small sailing boats headed for the shelter of the bay. The town itself had been founded in AD 828 as a defence against the pirates that had terrorised the coast even then. A great rusted ring was still set into the rocks at the mouth of the port where once a chain was strung to keep out the marauders. Later, in the seventeenth century, the pirates that operated in the Mediterranean were known as the Corsairs, and although some were European, most were from the coast of North Africa: what is now Tunisia, Algiers and Morocco—the Barbary Coast. They plundered other ships and also coastal towns, regularly capturing entire populations of men, women and children and taking them back to the slave markets on the Barbary Coast. Often the slaves were condemned to the misery of rowing the pirate galleys, the wind being unreliable in the Mediterranean; the women were often sold into the harems of the rulers of the Barbary Coast. Ransoms were demanded of the families back home, and eventually the problem was so bad that families of some of the captives from England petitioned the House of Commons for help.

Bonifacio was only a short boat ride from Sardinia but it felt a world away. Stevie had never been able to step ashore without feeling the sense of something sinister settle over her. The port town had been the biggest staging point and recruitment centre for the French Foreign Legion and perhaps something of that pervaded the walls as well. Although Stevie had to be grateful to the Legionnaires, since they had been the ones who had found her in the jeep when she was a girl . . .

They docked in the port and arrangements were made to go ashore for dinner. Stevie was glad they would be getting off the boat; it was starting to feel very claustrophobic. As the sun began to sink in the sky, the guests of the *Hercules* set out to make the lung-busting climb up to the *haute ville*. The road was wildly steep and paved in cobbles. All the women were sensibly shod in flat shoes—most of them had been to Bonifacio before. Only Angelina had begun the climb in heels, though she soon discarded them by the side of the road, saying she felt like Sophia Loren walking barefoot on the cobblestones. By now, the wind had picked up and a veritable gale was blowing out to sea. The narrow stone streets acted as wind tunnels: sheltered from the wind one moment, you would turn a corner only to be almost knocked off your feet by a gust of cold sea wind.

Their destination was a dark *cave*, or cellar, in the Old Town, and the party was glad to duck in through the low wooden door and out of the buffeting wind. Stevie blinked and looked about: the medieval stone walls were limestone like the cliffs, the ceiling low and crisscrossed with dark beams. The only light came from candles and oil lamps set about the cellar and along the length of a large wooden table that occupied the centre of the room. Fishing nets and old cudgels hung on the walls, but not for effect—these were obviously relics with a family history of toil on the sea, and pirate attacks. At one end of the room was a great open fire where the chef—a huge man in a charcoal-stained T-shirt—roasted and mixed and stoked the flames like some Dantean devil. The rustic room flickered and danced with shadows, the flames picking out, here and there, a dash of emerald or a blaze of diamond, the rich shine of silk as the incongruously elegant guests sat around the table.

A huge bouillabaisse had been ordered and now arrived in a steaming cauldron in the middle of the table. Bowlfuls of mussels and octopus tentacles and fish were ladled out; bread was toasted on the open fire and rubbed with garlic. Stevie tasted the scalding soup—magnificent. Bouillabaisse was done differently in every seaside town; in Corsica it was called *aziminu*, and it was delicious.

'So where will we cruise to next, Clémence?' Ludi-Brigitte asked. Dressed in yellow silk Capri pants, she was struggling with a mussel; she burst out laughing as it flew from her fork and landed in her sister's bowl with a clang.

'I don't know,' mused their hostess. 'I'm getting rather bored of quaint little sea ports. I fancy some action . . .'

'Vaughan has organised a shooting competition,' said Loli, dipping her bread in the soup, 'with a big prize.'

'What a good idea, darling,' Stevie heard Clémence say. She supposed Clémence was rather good at feigning enthusiasm where her husband was concerned.

Krok grunted and drank the rest of his soup straight from the bowl. 'Winner gets the new Riva,' he said between gulps. Stevie thought that was a competition she might quite like to win . . .

'What about Venice, darling, the Biennale?'

'Oh yes,' chorused the princesses. 'Divine idea.'

'Lord Sacheverel is having a party—his *palazzo* has some wonderfully creepy frescoes.' Stéphane was warming to the idea of Venice.

Angelina, dressed in her customary black, announced that Sacheverel had asked her to sing. 'I might even do it . . . La Serenissima is so inspirational.'

'The perfect excuse, then—not that we need one,' said Stéphane. 'I'll phone Sacheverel.' He turned to the young man at the end of the table, wreathed in cigarette smoke and his own thoughts. 'Aristo, will Marlena come?'

'I don't want you there with that woman,' broke in Aristo's father, laying his hand heavily on the table and making Angelina's glass jump.

His son's eyes glittered dangerously in the dim light of the cellar. After a moment he asked, 'What is it about her that you object to so much, Papu?'

'I know her,' Skorpios sneered. 'I know her past, her secrets, her sins—I don't want her anywhere near you.'

'Because you, of course, are blameless,' shot back his son, voice full of bitter sarcasm.

'She has you by your anatomy, dear Aristo. It is nothing that a good fuck won't cure.'

Stevie almost expected the boy to launch himself at his father from across the table, but Aristo did not move. When he spoke, his voice was quiet, but there was no mistaking the fury behind it. 'You should watch what you say, Papu. Marlena might become my wife one day. And you can hardly expect me to listen to advice from you, of all people. I despise you.'

'At least I am sensible enough not to marry my whores.'

There was a cry like that of a wounded animal. Angelina stood, sending her chair crashing to the ground. 'Socrates!' she screamed, then ran out of words. She turned and dashed for the door, flinging it open and launching herself into the night.

'Angelina,' roared Skorpios, shooting daggers at his son as he leapt to his feet to go after her.

Krok was laughing. 'She's as mad as Clem. Better go and stop her from throwing herself off the cliff.'

Skorpios ignored him, but he stopped at the door and turned back to his son. 'You're a fool, Aristo,' he growled. 'I would disinherit you, but you are my only son. If you don't get rid of Marlena, I will.' And then he too vanished into the night.

The room went suddenly very quiet; only Krok was still laughing. Stevie watched him as he leant back and lit a cigar with obvious satisfaction. The man derived a great deal of pleasure, she noticed, from other people's discomfort—a great deal.

The conversation had only just resumed when the heavy wooden door opened once more and, like a highwayman from times of old, a figure was silhouetted against the night—a slender, billowing silhouette that swore in French and whose hips swayed when she walked.

*Speak of the devil.*

'Bonsoir,' cried Marlena. 'Bonsoir, tout le monde.' She circled the table, stopping only to kiss her sister. 'Did I miss anything?' As she looked around the room, the rubies in her ears caught the candlelight and glowed like blood. She went and sat down by her young lover, draping an arm, like a snake, casually over his shoulder.

The conversation exploded as everyone rushed to fill her in on the drama. Marlena smiled her curious smile but remained unmoved by the passion that she had incited, by Angelina's distress. The local firewater was served in tiny glasses, the stone bottle left on the table. The party grew louder and merrier, but Skorpios and Angelina did not return. Stéphane suggested a walk on the clifftops by moonlight to feel the pirate ghosts come alive; a walk was deemed a good idea and the party set off.

As they left the restaurant, they passed an entrance to one of the narrow tunnels that ran from the base of the cliff and wound its way along the face and up to the top. 'We'll be out of the wind in here,' Stéphane declared in his role as entertainment director. He did, after all, have to earn his keep.

'Legend has it that Louis of Aragon's troops built these secret tunnels in one night and so attacked the city unawares and took it. Probably, though, it was the monks who built them over the years to bring up water and supplies on windy days.'

The tunnels were dark and none of them had thought to bring a torch. The limestone of the walls had been worn smooth after years of footsteps, and out to sea a great yellow moon hung low over the rippling silver water. Stevie tried to imagine being on pirate watch, seeing the black outline of masts and sails on the horizon, heading for the port—the fear, the panic, the mad scramble to ready the defences. And it seemed the pirates were still at it.

As she turned to follow Stéphane in front of her, she felt a hand grab her by the upper arm and pull her back. For a moment, Stevie's rather alcohol-addled mind imagined it was the hand of a skeleton and she jumped. Instead it was Clémence who hissed in her ear, 'Wait for me when we exit. I need to talk to you.'

They came out at the very top of the precipice. Stevie stepped to one side and bent over her foot, as if dislodging a pebble from her shoe. The party passed her by; Clémence stepped next to her in the shadows.

'I'm frightened,' she whispered without preamble. 'He's gone too far this time.'

'What is it?' Stevie's mind teemed with possibilities.

'Vaughan's having me admitted to a clinic when we get back.' Stevie could hear the rising panic in her whisper. 'A psychiatric hospital in Austria. If I go in, I know I will never come out again.'

'So,' Stevie said cautiously, 'refuse to go.'

'I can't.' Clémence fumbled for a cigarette in her little Fendi baguette. 'He says if I don't agree, he will start proceedings to have Emile taken away from his unfit mother. He can do that—he can do anything he wants. And then he will find a way to admit me against my will. Who knows what they will do to me in there?' She turned hunted eyes on Stevie. 'I'm trapped.'

As Clémence's story sank in, Stevie was slowly gripped by the horror of it. Clémence's child was being used as a weapon against her and she was powerless to protect herself or her son. Stevie now fully understood what she had meant that day when her hostess had first explained her situation.

'Can't you run?' Stevie asked, knowing already what the answer would be.

Clémence didn't even bother to reply. They both knew that Krok would find her anywhere, no matter how far she ran. Stevie did not know what to say.

They were interrupted by Krok's bellow. 'Clem, you mad broad, where are you? I don't trust her around these cliffs.' Clémence pressed her lips hard together and stared at Stevie a moment before turning and tripping up the cobbles. 'Here, darling.'

Stevie wondered that she did not choke on the endearment. It was, she supposed, a better plan to remain seemingly acquiescent and happy for the time being. It might put Krok off his guard . . .

The man was never off his guard, Stevie reminded herself. He probably slept with one eye open.

She could not face the group just yet. She needed a moment to let Clémence's predicament settle in her mind. The wind was fierce up on the high cliffs, almost enough to lift you off your feet. Stevie went to stand at a low wall, jutting out over the sea far below. She needed the wind to blow through her, to scour her clean of the evil that surrounded her, that was dragging her soul under. She stretched her arms out behind her and breathed in the salt air. She found she could lean slightly forward, so strong were the gusts, and the wind would hold her. She cleared her mind of all but the feel of the wind and the sound of the waves, and closed her eyes. It was almost like flying; the possibility of beauty returned slowly to the world.

In her trance, it seemed the wind reached out the softest hand to the small of her back and puffed. Stevie's eyes flew open as she felt her balance go. Her centre of gravity was already too far forward, her arms began windmilling and her head arched back in a desperate attempt to reverse her momentum. The sea was chopped silver below—too far down for her to hope to survive a fall that no one would see.

For the longest second of her life she teetered on the edge of the Corsican cliff, suddenly feeling that she very much wanted to live. Then she fell.

It was not the graceful dive into nothingness that she had imagined in her terror; she hit rock and gravel almost straight away, and a sharp steel bar dug painfully into her thigh, but she had stopped falling. Stevie lay as still as she ever had. Not since that awful day in the back of her parents' jeep had she felt like her entire life hung on not making the slightest movement, not making the slightest sound. She was too afraid to turn her head and see what had caught her, lest the movement disturb some fragile equilibrium and send her tumbling to finish the rest of her death fall.

She closed her eyes and began to mentally feel every inch of her body beginning with her toes. This calmed her and when she finally mustered the courage to open her eyes, she realised what had happened. Unseen below her had been the remnants of an old balcony that had succumbed to gravity and fallen into the sea. Its remains had stopped Stevie's fall but only just. She lay on the tiniest shelf, held in place by a steel construction bar, rusted over and deadly sharp. Had she fallen differently, she might have been impaled on it.

She reached gingerly forward to touch her hands to the cliff wall. It felt solid enough. A bracket of concrete . . . she opened her eyes. The bright moon showed her the top of the cliff—was there something fluttering up there? No, a trick of the light . . .

She inched closer to the wall and took a hand-hold, then another. She did not turn around or look down. She began to climb the cliff like a spider, slowly, inch by inch. Her foot slipped on some loose limestone shale and her heart leapt into her mouth, almost chocking her with fear. The adrenaline was everything. She clung with her nails, feeling them tear, but not the pain of it, not caring for anything but the top of the cliff, and life.

Finally she reached her upper hand as far as she could and grasped the clean hard edge of the wall. She hauled herself up and over, and lay, panting and shaking, against it.

She was not sure how long she lay there but when she did finally rise to her feet, she was exhausted. The adrenaline had worn off and she could hardly walk down the steep cobbled streets towards the port. A dark suspicion had begun to creep across her mind: was it really the wind that had pushed her, or had some-one been standing behind her? It was hard to be sure. The push, if human, had been so gentle. And the shape she had seen at the top of the cliff when she was lying on the ledge—had she imagined that? Someone had tried to kill her on the dive; it was possible that they had tried again tonight. Stevie trembled, this time from fear.

Stevie was not a naturally brave person but she did try, when circumstances presented themselves, to do what was right. Some-times this resulted in brave acts, but for Stevie, bravery was only ever something that she recognised, in retrospect, as an act of neces-sity rather than choice. Right now, she did not feel at all brave. She wanted to go home to her flat in Zurich and run in the woods and swim in the ice-cold lake and drink *apfelmust* on her balcony in the evening, surrounded by the scent of apple trees.

The *Hercules* appeared below in the port, lights ablaze as always, the gangplank still extended and a man standing guard. Ste-vie stopped. Could she, should she, get back on board? The killer had to be someone on the ship. The risk was not worth contemplat-ing. Suddenly she heard her name being called: a search party had obviously been sent out to find her. It would be a good chance to disappear, she thought, and ducked behind the wall of the old fort.

*Let them look forever.*


**It was Henning who found** her, asleep near the church, curled up like an alley cat. He insisted it had been purely by chance: 'A party of us came ashore at Bonifacio, and my mother and I were the only two energetic enough to make the climb to the Old Town. Mother has a thing for churches, so we stopped. It was actually she who found you. I believe her exact words were, "Henning, darling, have you lost something?" I was a little confused, but Mother can be enigmatic at times, then she said, "I've found something that I think belongs to you.'"

Stevie blushed fiercely and rather angrily—much to Henning's obvious amusement. She did not belong to anybody. But the irritation faded quickly in the light of the gratitude she felt for having been discovered by friends.

'I must have passed out,' she mumbled. 'I was quite exhausted.'

'Yes.' Henning stared hard at her, concern in his eyes. 'I don't wonder. When I saw your hands . . . I knew you mustn't return to that ship. I called Clémence and told her I'd found you asleep on the bench of the scenic lookout and that your hangover was so bad you refused to walk. I told her I would take care of you. She is having your things packed and sent over to the *Petrina*.'

'They're all off to Venice for the Biennale,' Stevie croaked, her throat still bone dry from shock.

'Yes, they mentioned that. I think a few of our lot are lobbying for Venice too; they're a bit sick of the ship. They plan to check into the Danieli and drink hot chocolate for breakfast and buy crystal chandeliers for their chalets.'

They were sitting at the prow of a tender to the *Petrina*, looking back towards the massive cliffs, monstrous jaws now, receding behind them.

'I'm not sure I'll be in a hurry to visit Bonifacio again.' Stevie smiled, but the terror had not quite left her eyes.

Henning rested a tanned hand on her knee. He understood. He always did. 'So, will you finish your holiday in Sardinia?' He hesitated, then added, 'You're very welcome to come with me to Athens, you know.'

Stevie shot him a look. 'I was almost arrested the last time I was in Athens. I'm not in a hurry to go back there either.'

'What on earth for?'

Stevie shook her head. 'You don't want to know.'

Henning grinned. 'It sounds like the world is getting too small for you, Stevie Duveen, little as you are—all these places where you seem to be persona non grata.' He said these words softly, lightly, taking out the sting. 'Where to next for you, then?'

Her telephone beeped; there was a message from David Rice. *Headed Venice. Your mission terminated as of now. Get ashore where you can. See you in London. D.*

Stevie stared out at the horizon, eyes searching eternity for a different answer to the one she already knew she would give. She turned back to Henning, her short blonde hair ruffling in the wind like feathers. 'Why, Venice, of course.'

# 14

The late summer storms hung in the sky like a hem of black lace, shedding water over a city already sinking. The lagoon had turned pewter in the half-light, and the *vaporetti*, their lights glowing in the gloom, bucked the wind as they ferried back and forth. Stevie leant into the red leather seat of her water taxi and looked out at La Serenissima through the downpour. The raindrops dragged down the earthy colours of the *palazzi*, the Moorish window frames, the hidden gardens, heavy as chain mail, into the canals. In this weather, the floating city seemed sad, awash, doomed.

Stevie's phone beeped. A message from Rice: *Caffè Florian at 1800*. She tossed the phone back into her bag. David had been rather cross when he had heard she was in Venice, but she had explained that she was now aboard the *Petrina* and could not get ashore until Venice. It was, she suggested, a happy coincidence that he too would be in Venice and they ought to meet. He had been suspicious, but reluctantly agreed. A message had arrived not long after their discussion, this time from Josie. Stevie and Rice would be attending the party at Lord Sacheverel's *palazzo*—a *ballo mascherato*. 'Bring mask' had been the instruction from her colleague in London. It seemed like a very long time since Stevie had seen David, and his reassuring figure was just the thing she needed to dispel the last of

Aldo Meienfeldt. 3) Krok was somehow involved in the plague of pirate attacks off Somalia and Cape Horn, possibly Nigeria—a well-connected accomplice handled the ransoms, name as yet unknown. 4) He also sold 'invisible' speedboats for smuggling contraband and, the thought occurred to Stevie, possibly for use in future pirate attacks. 5) Krok was arrogant, vain, unpredictable, ruthless and cruel—a very dangerous combination. Altogether, Stevie reflected, it was a very unlovely picture; the man was practically a psychopath.

All this information, Rice could decide what to do with. She was done.

By the time she left the restaurant, the rain had begun to pour down again and the *calle* was dark. With every footfall, Venice seemed to sink deeper into the sea. Stevie found a little shop among a maze of smooth stone alleys, boarded windows; the smell of rotting canal water was strong here. She went in and looked at the masks. At first tempted by the rhinestone, ribbon and pearl extravaganza in the window, in the end she chose the most understated mask she could find: a black and white Pierrette.

**A little before six, Stevie** caught a water taxi to the Florian. As it docked, she thanked the captain and leapt nimbly onto the shore. The silk Missoni kaftan rippled and danced like mercury in the wind, and she wore large amber bangles on her wrists and flat leather sandals; only the uninitiated ever wore heels in Venice. The cobblestones would break your ankle if the shifting jetties didn't first. Wellington boots might have been more appropriate, she thought, as thunder rumbled across the sky then cracked into a jagged shaft of lightning. The strange light of storm weather had turned the lagoon an opaque shade of jade green and fingers of red now shot out from an invisible setting sun. It was weather fit for the end of the world.

She hurried into the covered *arcata* as the heavens opened and sluiced the city with more water. The marble floor, worn by so many millions of feet, was slippery with rain. Stevie dodged a conga line of tourists, snaking past in identical cheap plastic raincoats with pointed hoods. *Tout comme les préservatifs.* The phrase came to her in French, and she smiled. She brushed her hair back off her forehead and hoped her eyeliner had not run. She wanted David to see an elegant woman before him, rather than a drowned rat.

He was waiting for her in a dim corner of the bar. Stevie felt a flush of pleasure as she closed the door behind her and moved towards his table. David stood and kissed her on both cheeks, handsome as ever, and smelling rather intoxicatingly of sandalwood shaving soap. 'How are you, Stevie?' he asked with genuine affection, his voice low and gravelly. Stevie would have liked to hug him but knew he would consider it unseemly. She sat opposite, drawing back her shoulders and lifting her chin ever so slightly. All presence began with good posture—her grandmother was very strict about posture—and Stevie tried hard to keep it in mind.

'What will you have, Stevie?'

'A Negroni,' she answered, gesturing to his half-empty glass.

'*Due Negroni, per favore,*' Rice said to the hovering waiter. Despite speaking Italian with a very English accent, no one would have dared to treat Rice as a tourist. His every movement exuded suppressed power, and total control. The man was a lion.

'I have quite a bit to tell you,' Stevie said as the drinks arrived.

'I rather assumed you would, Stevie.'

Stevie took a sip of her drink: gin, Martini Rosso and Campari. It was strong and she was glad of it. 'Clémence Krok's husband is a madman,' she began. It was the only way she could describe

Krok. 'He has a dictator's sense of destiny, cunning and craving for power, coupled with the tyrant's classic paranoia and ruthlessness. He has an added penchant for cruelty and games that tends to spice things up a bit.'

Rice sat back. 'Ah,' he said quietly.

'Yes, Clémence is not crazy. Although her husband is out to make people think she is. He plans to have her committed to some Austrian clinic, and she is terrified that she will never come out.'

Rice said nothing, his lined face set in stone now and all traces of warmth gone. The grey light outside was fading; the waiter brought a candle. The soft, dancing light only exaggerated the shadows under David's eyes, the hollows in his cheeks. He had aged; his face above the crisp white of his shirt looked tired.

'David,' Stevie started, extending her left hand towards his. He didn't seem to hear her and her hand, losing confidence, stopped short of completing the journey. He woke abruptly from his reverie and glanced down; Stevie had gone for the single glove in the end. After all, it was a masked ball.

'What happened to you on that ship?' he said, his voice almost a whisper. He was looking at a large scratch on her wrist that even the glove could not hide. Stevie stared at him: didn't he know? She had told him about the diving incident—though not yet, she realised, about the cliff fall. Still, that was not, she sensed, what he meant. She filled him in—rather hurriedly—on everything she had discovered about her host; David listened in silence. 'And the glove?' he asked finally, as if everything Stevie had told him meant nothing. 'You have too much style to wear that for no reason,' he added.

'Someone tried to kill me in Bonifacio,' Stevie said quietly. 'Someone tried to push me off the cliffs. I'm pretty sure of it.' She watched his face. 'The glove is to hide my rather mangled nails.' She described what had happened, eating three olives, one after the other, as she did. To her surprise and horror, she saw his eyes moisten with tears. Instantly she forgot her own fears and feelings—something had to be horribly wrong if David was tearing up. Then the liquid shine disappeared and the steel returned to Rice's gaze.

'This time it was my fault and that is unforgivable. I knew Krok was dangerous but I never thought he would go after you.' He glanced up at her. 'How did he know?'

'Know what?'

'That you were not what you seemed to be—just a friend of his wife.'

Stevie had wondered about this. She had decided that it was unlikely that Krok had found out her secret. It wasn't his style to say nothing, and Clémence would have warned her if he had. Possibly his paranoia had driven him to unfocused suspicions about her, but there really was no satisfactory answer to this. If he had thought that she was an enemy or someone dangerous to him, he would have killed her, certainly. But he would not have failed, and certainly not twice. A bullet to the head while she was sleeping was all it would have taken. Burn the pillow and sink the body. Easy. No, the attempts on her life had been too subtle for a man like Vaughan Krok.

'There was no one else on board who would care what I do—or am . . .' She took another sip of her drink. 'His security men would hardly have acted without explicit orders. And he doesn't look like he would make a mistake, let alone two. Something doesn't feel right. Or so it seems to me, anyway.' Stevie turned her glass in her hands. 'So, what's tonight about?'

Rice gave her a long, searching look then drained his glass. 'Lord Sacheverel is having a party at his *palazzo* for some Biennale bigwigs from the States. I believe Angelina Dracoulis will perform.'

'Ah, La Dracoulis. She's rather magnificent. Have you ever seen her?'

When David ignored the question, Stevie, suspicious now, asked, 'So, who is this Lord Sacheverel? A friend?' She raised a careful eyebrow.

David glared at a point somewhere over Stevie's shoulder and clenched his jaw. 'Sacheverel was an admiral in the Royal Navy, a man of not insignificant independent means, Maltese mother, superior to the point of arrogance and with a serious sadistic streak. He lives in London, with offices in an old submarine moored on the Thames. He has connections to all sorts of unsavoury people, mainly organised crime syndicates. MI5 tell me he was behind the syndicate that left all those illegal cockle pickers to drown on the sand bar in Cornwall.'

'So,' Stevie said cautiously, 'if he's such a vile man, why are we going to his party?' Rice was silent. 'I deserve to know, David, don't you think?'

Rice ordered two more drinks and waited until they arrived before he replied. 'I'm not expecting any trouble, Stevie, or I'd never have agreed to take you with me.' When Stevie didn't comment, Rice went on. 'Sacheverel has been trying to buy Hazard for some time now. I have refused repeatedly, despite the financial and logistical pressure we are under from the pirate attacks on our ships. I have no intention of selling up, and if I did, it would certainly not be to a man like Sacheverel.'

When Rice did not continue, Stevie asked, 'But why does he want Hazard so badly? Surely he can buy his own protection?'

'He can't buy our good reputation. Everyone trusts the Hazard name. He needs that trust.'

Stevie sensed she was not seeing the whole picture and, when Rice seemed reluctant to say any more, she prodded him again. 'So, what happened to change things?'

'The other day, a man came to see me—ex-SAS, until very

recently he worked for STORM. He told me his name was Jim Clarke and that he wanted a job, a new job for him and his men. I turned him down straight away, saying I didn't like Krok's outfit and couldn't take on anyone who had served under him. Then Clarke told me a story.

'Apparently his men were out in Somalia. As you can imagine, it's pretty hairy work—in some parts of the country they have a standing order to kill any Caucasian on sight. Clarke and his men wanted a pay rise; they felt Krok wasn't paying them enough for the amount of time they had to spend in that mess of a country. Krok waited and stalled, then four of the men fell ill with malaria. Krok refused them access to medication until they agreed to relinquish their demands for more money. The men caved, but two of them died anyway.'

David took a long sip of his drink. 'Clarke is out to get even, as well as find a new post. He gave me Sacheverel as a gesture of good-will.' He looked at Stevie. 'It makes perfect sense now—why our ships seemed to be suffering so heavily in the attacks. Sacheverel—and STORM—were targeting them. It was his way of forcing me to sell my company.'

'He turned the pirates on you?' Stevie shook her head. 'How is that possible? Why would they obey him anyway?'

'Krok and his mercenaries have been training the pirates, arming them, and using them to make deniable and untraceable assaults on all the shipping transiting the area. The sums exchanging hands are phenomenal—and that's just Somalia. Apparently STORM are branching out to the Gulf of Guinea, off Nigeria—another piracy and kidnap hotspot. They sell arms to the pirates, and take the lion's share of the ransoms and the bunkered oil.'

Stevie remembered the oil wells in the Niger Delta, shut down because of local militants. She had some sympathy with the militants, whose land and livelihood had been completely destroyed by the drilling, but it was also one of the most dangerous areas in the world. The theft of oil—bunkering—was worth billions.

'They have recently muscled in on the drug trade. There's a triangular cocaine-smuggling route, from the Canary Islands to Cabo Verde and Madeira. The STORM-trained pirates have been attacking the drug ships and seizing cargo, killing all on board. These attacks obviously go unreported, but it's a nice little sideline for both the syndicate and Sacheverel.'

'Hence the Medusa speedboats,' observed Stevie. 'They could catch any vessel the drug runners might be using.'

Rice nodded. 'It's a massive business. As far as I understand it, Sacheverel's the man handling the ransom payments for the Somali pirates in London. All the ships—not just ours. Sacheverel and Krok—there may be others—are hijacking the vessels, onselling the cargo and holding the crew for ransom. They then repaint the vessels and reregister them under a new flag of convenience; these can then be on-sold to buyers who are willing not to look too closely. Others become ghost ships, floating in international waters, untouchable by law, ferrying all sorts of illicit cargo—arms, drugs, people—around the world to points where it can be offloaded by smaller speedboats and smuggled ashore.'

'But where does Hazard fit into this?' asked Stevie. 'Why does Sacheverel want us?'

'Acquiring Hazard was just part of a plan for expansion.'

Stevie waited for him to go on, but he didn't. 'This is great!' she exclaimed. It would fix Rice's problem with the pirates, and Clémence's problem with her husband. Stevie, in her enthusiasm, chanced a hand on David's arm. 'With Jim Clarke's evidence, surely we can get them both!' She sat back and waited, but Rice's face did not give her the reaction she was hoping for.

'Get them,' he repeated softly, almost to himself. He started on the second drink then pushed it away, losing his thirst. 'We are not in the business of "getting" people, Stevie. We are not the police; we are not intelligence. We protect people, we do not go after them—that's where all trouble begins, and you know that better than anyone on my staff.'

The point stung but it was fair. Stevie had been reckless before and she had sworn to her boss that she would not be so again, on pain of losing her place at Hazard. She took a breath and tried again, slowly, calmly. 'I understand. But we have a real chance of stopping a whole swathe of these pirate attacks.' There was a long silence from the other side of the table—too long. Stevie's ears were filled with the sounds of pigeons and Polish drifting in from the crowds outside.

'And . . .' Her argument died on her lips. Rice was right. She knew that, but still she persisted. 'Surely, when one can see the full picture—David, can't we do something, or at least tell someone who can?'

Rice shook his grizzled head wearily. 'We could tell people, but we no longer have the witness. Jim Clarke is dead.' Rice ejected the last word from his mouth like an olive pit. 'A fatal car accident while on leave in Paris.'

Stevie waited for a few respectful moments, struggling with her frustration and rising anger, then said, 'David, the monsoon season ends soon in Somalia. There'll be a new rash of pirate attacks.'

Something in Rice's eyes flickered. Suddenly Stevie knew—she felt, she guessed—David was saying all this to stop her getting involved: he had a plan, it just didn't include her. That stung even more. She made a strategic decision not to pursue it, to let David think the matter was resolved in her mind. He would be less guarded that way.

'Well,' she said archly, 'sounds like this party could be fun.'

**They arrived together by water** taxi, Stevie's arm linked through David's. She looked up as they swooshed through the canal. There was a figure at the lighted window of the *piano nobile*, the silhouette of an elegant man, smoking a cigarette and looking down onto the water traffic below. Above his head, Stevie could see the exposed beams of the ceiling, the sparsely furnished room, so elegant. In another universe, on a night like this in Venice, she and David might have been lovers. She let the word linger in her mind a moment, soften and melt. Glancing up at David's face, she clearly saw that no such thoughts were on the warrior's mind: his expression was all steely resolve. He released his arm from hers and placed his mask— a black velvet band—over his eyes. Stevie did the same, but added a smile for effect. It was, after all, a party.

The vast wooden double doors of the water entrance were wide open, two footmen in velvet knickerbockers and white powdered wigs grabbed the painter and held the taxi fast while Stevie and Rice alighted. A wild wind blew in unpredictable gusts, pressing the silk tight to Stevie's lithe frame. She closed her eyes for a moment and felt the damp air on her face, breathed it in; for an instant she was far away from all this, deep inside her head. Then she opened her eyes and looked up at the *palazzo*. It was painted oxblood red with pale grey Moorish detailing around the windows and balconies; a lush garden bordered by huge oleanders and a high, spiked wrought-iron fence spilt out onto the canal on the left; to the right, another canal disappeared from view.

The taxi pulled away from the mooring and a beautiful old Riva, this one with turquoise leather upholstery, took its place. A masked figure in a dinner jacket was seated in the back. Something about him was familiar, but the mask covered all except the mouth, a purplish plaster cast with a cartoonishly large nose—a Renaissance villain. David followed her gaze, stared at the figure, then turned back.

'Shall we?' he suggested, and they went inside. Climbing the vast marble staircase that hugged the left wall, they saw that all four walls were covered in the most extraordinary frescoes. On the one closest to them, a wonderfully voluptuous woman was being carried over a river by a centaur. It was enough to stop Stevie in her tracks. The figures of the woman and mythical beast were dark, obscured by the dim light and four hundred years of candle smoke, much of the walls pitted with damp and water damage, peeling, but this only made the figures seem more alive. Stevie turned to the wall ahead: here the centaur was trying to rape the woman, but a large arrow was sticking out of his chest, blood pouring from the wound. The right-hand wall showed the same woman, horror on her face as she stared at a smoking pool of blood on the floor of her bedroom. Deianeira, thought Stevie, at the moment in which she realised that the blood of Nessus the centaur was poison. When her husband Heracles had shot him for trying to rape his wife, Nessus, with his dying breath, maliciously told Deianeira that his blood would make Heracles true to her forever. When Deianeira feared Heracles was straying, she daubed his shirt in the centaur's blood. Too late she realised the terrible trick. Stevie turned, and there on the wall behind her was Heracles, three metres tall, burning to death. A chandelier covered in dripping candles was the only lighting in the space, and its unsteady flame made the tortured figure dance.

David and Stevie entered the reception rooms on the *piano nobile* in time to see the masked guests moving to one end of the room. Double doors gave onto a stone balcony that overhung the canal. It was lit with hundreds of candles, and on the balcony stood the glorious figure of La Dracoulis. She wore black, a white gardenia in her hair, held there by the famous tortoiseshell comb, and her eyes were cast down.

The music from the orchestra stopped; Angelina seemed to

be moving into herself, retreating from the party, gathering herself in readiness to sing. Stevie and Rice joined the guests at the windows and waited for the diva to begin. Stevie, from force of habit more than anything, scanned the crowd. She spotted Clémence and Stéphane, behind elaborate sequinned creations; Krok was nowhere to be seen. Then her eyes bounced off a familiar cut of shoulder, an old dinner jacket in midnight blue with the smallest moth hole, a familiar silk shirt the colour of milk . . . her heart gave a tiny leap. *Henning.* It gave another leap as she took in the willowy blonde on his arm. Even with a mask, Stevie could tell the woman was beautiful. She carried herself that way, and her shoulders were perfect. Stevie was surprised to find that a tiny flame of jealousy had ignited inside her and was threatening to blaze. She glanced quickly away and up at David. His eyes, too, were searching the room, but they did not seem interested in willowy blondes.

Rice's gaze came to rest on a man who stood right at the front, to the side, in a velvet dinner jacket, his thick white hair standing out against his dark skin, and combed back on either side of a distinctive widow's peak. He had, thought Stevie, the face of a hawk: sharp curved nose, thin lips, eyes hidden behind a red satin band—a predator. He wore his trousers an inch too short, showing his red socks and a pair of velvet slippers embroidered with a skull and crossbones. It could only be Sacheverel. The man certainly had a sense of theatre, Stevie deduced, and went to a deal of trouble to produce the right effect; he was a man who had the money and leisure to do it properly.

La Dracoulis breathed and raised her eyes; the crowd immediately fell silent. And she began to sing, low notes hovering in the warm air like an uncertain hummingbird, before gathering strength and conviction and soaring to celestial heights. Stevie felt the hairs on her arms raise as Angelina sang of Euridice and the price of love, here in this pirate's lair on the canal. Stevie noticed the man in the purple mask again, close to the front; she saw the signet ring with the golden scorpion and realised why she knew him: Skorpios. Of course. Half-hidden behind another mask, all white, was Dado Falcone.

A tray of drinks passed by, held high by another powdered footman. Rice took a glass of champagne for Stevie but refused anything for himself. Then, without warning, Henning was upon them. He smiled at Stevie and kissed her cheeks before she could say anything, then he turned and shook Rice's hand. Neither man hid his suspicion of the other. Stevie was introduced to the blonde—Anastasia—and was glad her mask hid her eyes. A smile was easier to fake than a gaze.

'What are you doing here, Henning?' Stevie asked lightly. 'I thought you were going to Athens.'

Henning gestured towards the crowd and Stevie caught sight of Iris' unmistakable silhouette. 'My mother can be quite persuasive, as you know.'

Stevie did not reply.

Sacheverel was heading towards them and Henning, sensing he was not wanted, elegantly removed himself and his Anastasia. Stevie made a concerted effort not to turn and look after the sinuous blonde.

'Rice,' announced Sacheverel.

David nodded but the two men, Stevie noticed, did not shake hands. They were the same height and had a similar build, although Sacheverel had grown a small prosperous paunch that David had not. Rice did not introduce Stevie.

'Drink?' Sacheverel gestured towards a passing waiter carrying a tray of flutes.

'Thanks,' David replied curtly, 'I'll wait until I can get a whisky.'

Sacheverel nodded to the waiter who went off in search of a bottle.

'So, what was so important you had to see me, Sacheverel?'

'You know exactly what or you would not have come all the way down here.'

Both men spoke cautiously, verbally circling each other, wary as cobras. Stevie noticed Sacheverel wore a large signet ring with a red city seal, unusual in a man of his class. Rice glared. Stevie wondered that the other man did not quail in the face of it. But Sacheverel was no shrinking violet, she remembered; he had served as an admiral in the navy. He met Rice's stare head on.

'You may have the time and inclination for games, Sacheverel. I do not.'

Sacheverel gave a small smile. He was superior and he knew it: wealthy, titled, magnificently powerful, and in possession of a full head of hair. The man was untouchable. 'Sell me Hazard, Rice, if you know what's good for you.'

'What for?' The voice was cold, toneless.

Sacheverel took a sip of his champagne. 'I plan to expand into maritime protection—think of the possibilities.'

'For what?'

'Do I need to spell it out?' His voice, thought Stevie, was odd.

'We servicemen are dense.'

Sacheverel sighed wearily, as if the weight of dealing with such small things weighed on his shoulders every day. A man put-upon. Stevie realised what it was—the man's voice was faintly sibilant, with the hint of a snake's hiss. It was most unusual. 'The pirates are frightening everyone. Given Hazard's reputation, well, why would anyone go anywhere else?' He took a tidy sip of his champagne and continued, 'It's no concern of yours what happens once the company is mine . . . is it?'

Rice kept his voice even. 'Some of us still believe in right and wrong, in duty, in honour.' He laid particular emphasis on the last word. 'I know what you are planning to do, Sacheverel. Jim Clarke came to see me before his . . . accident.'

Sacheverel hesitated, then said smoothly, 'Jim Clarke, of course. A tragic collision in the tunnel. One can't really trust a man who has survived cerebral malaria . . .'

Rice said nothing and Stevie was proud of him; she knew he was the greater man, but she also knew he had the greater heart and sometimes that was a weakness.

Sacheverel, after a long pause, was forced to go on. 'If you won't sell, then join us. Many vessels carry, shall we say, "friends" as part of the crew; sometimes even the captains are in on it. They give our men details of cargo and coordinates in exchange for a slice of the pie. Lately, however, the insurance companies have been getting het up. Ever since Lloyds declared the Gulf and the Malacca Straits "war zones" for insurance purposes—we're rather proud of our role in that actually—the companies are now insisting their more heavily insured vessels take an escort. You know, ex-marines, that sort of thing—much like, in fact, the service your outfit provides. With you as a partner, we could make sure the insurance companies hired Hazard men to guard the ship. Your men would, naturally, be lightly aggressed—for authenticity—but nothing that could not easily be compensated for with cash.' He took another sip of his champagne and went on, 'Your men are "taken" by our pirates, and exchanged for ransom paid by the ship owners—or rather, their insurance companies—which we would naturally share with you. You would get, say, twenty per cent of the profits from the ship and cargo itself, and—' his eyes narrowed '—total deniability. We take all the risk and provide all the hardware. It's a win-win situation for everyone.'

Stevie stood as still as ice. So that was what David had found out: Sacheverel wanted to use Hazard as a Trojan horse for his pirates. No wonder he was angry.

'Except the ship owners and insurance companies,' she heard him reply, 'and the sailors injured, killed or held captive for months.'

Sacheverel waved a hand in the air, as if to music. He did not give a damn. A silence that was thick enough to repel all sounds of merriment from the party around them.

'I despise your offer, Sacheverel.' Rice's voice was frigid, venomous, quiet. 'I despise you for making it. What kind of man are you—if we can call you a man at all?' The colour was rising to Rice's neck.

'Don't be a fool,' Sacheverel spat, his upper lip curling. 'The only man who can prove anything is dead. Your outfit is being run into the ground. You have no choice.'

'I know what Clarke told me and I will find other ways to prove it, mark my words. I will take you down.'

Sacheverel laughed mirthlessly. 'There's no need to get all heated, Rice. It's just a mad adventure. Think of us as a band of thieves . . . If you want no part in it, so be it. It is, frankly, your loss.' He took a glass of whisky from a passing waiter.

'It might have started as an adventure for you, Sacheverel, but you have crossed over to the dark side. And you actually seem to be enjoying it,' Rice added.

Sacheverel smiled again and handed David the whisky. 'The dark side . . . you sound like the Spanish Inquisition. Drink up and enjoy yourself. It's a party. Oh, and Rice? May the best man win.' And Sacheverel turned on the heel of his velvet slippers and walked away.

Stevie could sense Rice's fury bubbling beneath the cool exterior of the dinner jacket.

'Got to get back to London,' he murmured to himself.

'Perhaps you should stay and have a drink, David,' she said mildly, suddenly concerned that her boss's rage would boil over. She put a hand lightly on his arm and felt the muscles as tense as iron. Rice stared down at her, but Stevie could tell he was not really looking at her. Then he raised the glass and downed it in one gulp.

# 15

It was the moment that Stevie would replay over and over in the terrible days that followed. After Rice's collapse, an ambulance boat had been called. Stevie had leapt upon the prone figure of her hero and checked for vitals. He had stopped breathing, the pulse was so faint. Without a second's hesitation, she tilted his great head back, pinched his nose shut and began artificial respiration. She could smell the whisky still. Was it poisoned? The thought crossed her mind as she lowered her mouth to cover his; what if it got her too? But she didn't care. She had to save this man. Nothing mattered except the rhythm of her breathing and the inflation of his chest.

She stopped her breathing a moment to check again for a pulse. Nothing. The adrenaline in her blood was cold; she felt no fear, no shock, saw none of the people standing in a ring around her. She knew what she had to do. She began CPR, her arms pumping his chest with all her strength, almost superhuman now, not caring if she fractured a rib, just willing that damn heart to start beating again.

Henning bolted towards them, tearing off his mask, the paramedics close behind. He had to physically pull Stevie off Rice's body. Tears were pouring down her face as the paramedics leant over her boss.

They tore open David's shirt and charged the defibrillator. Someone—Henning?—put a shawl around Stevie's shoulders, but she shook it off. They held a glass of brandy and sugar to Stevie's lips. The heat of the drink woke her from her trance. Rice had been loaded onto a stretcher and was being carried down the vast marble staircase by the paramedics.

'*Salvatelo!*' she cried, when she was finally able to speak. '*Dovete salvarlo!*' Her whole body was trembling wildly after her efforts, the adrenaline pumping with nowhere to go. She got to her feet and tore down the stairs after him, her world resting on the shoulders of the men in the ambulance uniforms. Arms held her back as he was loaded onto an ambulance boat. The doors closed in the rain and Rice was ferried away; in her agony, Stevie read the name of the boat: *Charon*.

**And now David lay dying** in a hospital in Zurich. His heart had been successfully restarted by the Venetian medics and his condition had been stabilised. But the doctors had warned Stevie that the danger was far from over. Her boss was dying and needed very specific equipment that they did not have. Perhaps Rome . . .

Perhaps not, Stevie had decided. Henning had taken the matter in hand and called Rega, the Swiss medivac service. Stevie was a member, and they had sent a small plane the same day and flown him to the special hospital by the lake where David could receive the care he needed. Stevie spent hours by his bedside, holding his hand. He remained in a medically induced coma to protect his brain from further danger. The doctors gravely explained that there was no way of knowing yet if the brain or other organs had been permanently damaged. Only once he awoke—if he awoke—could anything be determined for certain.

No one could tell any more than that it had been a massive heart attack. Stevie was sure there had been foul play and insisted as much to the doctors. They had told her there was no way to tell what had caused the attack, but Stevie remained convinced that someone had poisoned her boss. The doctors tried to persuade her to go for long walks by the lake, to get out, to go home, to sleep; Henning seemed to float in and out, talking to the doctors in his precise German, bringing her food she barely touched. For two days Stevie did not leave David's bedside, her mind churning.

On the morning of the third day, Henning appeared in the room and put a gentle hand on Stevie's shoulder. 'I've called your grandmother. She's coming to see you.'

Stevie looked at him through a blanket of sorrow. 'I know how he did it—Sacheverel.'

Henning's expression of concern infuriated her. 'I'm not crazy, Henning. I'm angry and sorry and desperately worried. Don't look at me as if I'm mad.'

'I'm sorry, little bird. I'm feeling much the same at the moment.'

She relented and gave him a tiny flicker of a smile that vanished like a wax match in the rain.

'It was Sacheverel.' Stevie's eyes glazed over as she watched the scene replay in her mind. 'He offered us champagne but David said he would wait for a whisky. Sacheverel put his heinous offer to David, then he took a glass of whisky from a waiter.' Stevie's eyes were focused on the heart monitor, but her mind was back in Venice. 'David was so angry. We were both distracted. That's when Sacheverel poisoned the whisky.' Stevie looked up at Henning. 'I remember he was wearing this massive ring on his pinkie. I thought it was a European affectation, but now I know what it was: a poison ring.'

'You mean like the ancient Romans?'

'Exactly. My grandmother has one in the display cabinet at

her house. My grandfather bought it in Egypt in the 1920s. The stone flips up to reveal a hidden cavity. The Romans used to fill it with poison powder which they could then discreetly empty into an enemy's glass.'

'Do you really think so? That's a very underhanded—'

'That's Sacheverel,' Stevie snapped. 'Who do you think we are dealing with here? A knight of the round table with definite notions of what is honourable and what is not?! The man thinks he is above us all, a law unto himself.'

Henning was quiet.

'And the worst part is—' Stevie's voice broke '—I told David to drink it. He was so angry, I thought it might help. He downed it in one go, and I told him to do it.'

Henning said nothing for a long time.

'It's going to rain this afternoon,' he said, looking out at the black clouds gathering at the far end of the lake. A summer thunderstorm.

Stevie turned to him, exasperated. 'Did you hear anything I just said?'

Henning turned to her. 'Yes, of course I did. But Rice's poisoning is not your fault, Stevie, and you should be smart enough to see that. Your emotions are clouding your judgement.'

'I'm not emotional,' Stevie said coldly, furious. 'Why don't you leave me alone, Henning? I can take care of this myself. Thank you for your help but this is my concern now. I can't think of you both. I don't have the energy.'

'Is that what you really want?' Henning asked mildly.

'Yes. Just leave. Go away. Stay away. Please.'

Henning turned away from the window. He stopped to rest a light hand on the back of Stevie's bowed neck then headed for the door.

Stevie heard him greet someone in the doorway as he passed through it.

Stevie turned to see her grandmother. She wore her olive corduroys and a blue blouse, and came smelling of earth and apples. She hugged her granddaughter tight, saying nothing. Then Didi moved to the bed and took David's hand.

'You poor man,' she said softly. 'You poor, poor man.'

Stevie was so grateful to Didi that she felt tears well up in her eyes. That was exactly the sentiment she had been looking for beneath her anger and her guilt. Didi had found it and shown her the way.

**Stevie and her grandmother walked** around the lake, the late summer air warm and heavy with the promise of a mountain storm. People cycled by the lake, sailed, rowed, some swam. The white and yellow striped awnings were up on the windows of the Baur au Lac, and window sills everywhere were bursting with red geraniums. Stevie told Didi everything that had happened, including her role in David Rice's poisoning.

'Stevie, that's not your fault, and just as I have told David a million times that your parents' death was not his fault, he won't forgive himself for giving them the wrong advice. But—' she stopped and put her arm around her granddaughter '—he is still alive, and where there is life, there is hope.' Her face darkened. 'What I am more concerned about,' she continued quietly, 'is what you told me about the diving accident, and the incident on the cliff top. I know you are not accident-prone. And you know it too.'

Stevie nodded. She had recounted both incidents, explaining them both away as accidents, but her grandmother was too sharp for that. She had worked in naval intelligence in the UK during the war and she didn't believe in coincidences.

'Do you think it was this Krok?' the woman asked.

Stevie shook her head. 'It makes some sense, but the accidents weren't his style. He had so many other chances to get rid of me . . .'

'Maybe a lackey acting on his orders?'

'Again, I just don't think I'd be walking here with you if Krok wanted me dead.'

The clouds had covered the sun and a gust of warm wind skimmed the lake, wrinkling the pewter-grey surface, stirring up a few early autumn leaves that had fallen to the ground. They passed the *schwimmbad*, renovated that winter. The swimmers and sunbathers were packing up their towels, pulling on shorts and summer dresses, glancing at the dark clouds. Time to get going.

As they passed the newsstand at the entrance, a headline caught Stevie's eye and she stopped. 'Didi, one moment.' She ducked under the awning and bought a copy of the newspaper. There was a small headline on the bottom of the front page: ARMS DEALER HOIST WITH HIS OWN PETARD. She had a strange feeling, her instinct telling her who it was even before she read the article.

Vaughan Krok had apparently been on board the *Hercules* and enjoying a clay-pigeon shooting contest. A small bore cartridge had been slipped in instead of the twelve bore, so the gun had not fired. Krok had inserted another cartridge, fired, and the gun had exploded in his face. Many hunters had died exactly the same way. Krok had survived the accident, rather miraculously, and been flown to a clinic in London. The article did not know whether Krok would recover but he was alive at time of press.

Stevie looked up at her grandmother. 'Another accident.' She shook her head. 'I don't believe the guests on the *Hercules* could be so clumsy. Perhaps the ship is cursed.' She folded the paper. 'I imagine Clémence will welcome the temporary respite from her husband.'

They dined on vegetable soup, bread and cheese under Didi's grapevine in the garden. The first drops of warm rain hit as they were finishing and they hurriedly cleared the table and went inside.

As the rain poured down the window panes and the forest grew black around them, Didi lit the lamp and cut two slices of *Apfelkuchen*. 'Are you sure you want to go home tonight?' she asked Stevie. 'You can sleep in the attic room. Peter would love to have you, I'm sure.' Peter was Didi's cat—well, the cat that Stevie had rescued one day in Zurich, hairless and hungry, and brought to live with her grandmother. His fur had grown back but he had never left. Life was comfortable and good with Didi and he had grown to love her, and she him.

At the mention of his name, Peter leapt heavily into Stevie's lap. He had put on a considerable amount of weight since his rescue. Steve fondled his ears and accepted a glass of plum schnapps. 'I'll be fine, Didi. I'm only down the road. It'll be nice to sleep in my own bed again after everything.'

She only hoped her sleep would be undisturbed. Stevie still suffered from nightmares about her parents' murder—they recurred as some kind of psycho-physical response to stress or extreme fatigue.

In the end, though, when she tumbled into the soft white featherbed in her little flat, her sleep was deep and dreamless, lulled perhaps by the sweet smell of the fresh forest that came through the open window.

At dawn, she rose and put on her tracksuit. The air was still cool from the evening's rain but the sun was up and shining at a low angle through the trees. She set off on her *vitaparcours*—exercise course—through the woods. It felt good to run in the cool crisp air, under the dark green light. She needed to clear her head and release the tension she had been carrying since Venice, and before. She ran along the narrow track, crossed a tiny footbridge and swung on the parallel bars, feeling her core taut and strong, the muscles in her arms working hard. Her body took over from her mind, and she let it happen.

When she got back to the flat, she had a shower and ate a bowl of muesli. She would head off to see David as soon as the hour was decent.

At the hospital, there was no change in David's condition and the relief Stevie had found in the evening spent with her grandmother evaporated as she entered and saw her boss still attached to all the tubes. What would she do if he didn't make it? It was not a possibility her heart could entertain and yet her mind knew she had to. Along with Didi, David was her rock in a drifting world. What was this world she was in, this violent orbit that threatened to take those around her? David had warned her it was not a white world when she had asked to join Hazard. She had taken that risk on for herself but she hadn't thought about how she would feel when those close to her were threatened. She wasn't sure she would handle it well.

Stevie stepped out onto the balcony, hoping the fresh air would restore her. There seemed no point to anything, no point to all the work she did when she could not even protect the people closest to her. A gloom filled her and she felt heavy; her neck ached and her head throbbed. Was this the end of the road? She could give it up, do something else, something very different. She had no idea what . . . perhaps gardens. Yes, something to do with gardens, where there were no people, only plants and quiet. She would hide there from the world. Enough was enough.

Her tiny phone rang, making her start. She didn't recognise the number . . .

'Stevie? It's Issa Farmishan, from Liscia.' Stevie was startled. The hotel owner from Sardinia had never called her before.

'*Buon giorno*, Issa.' She tried to force some cheer into her voice but failed.

'Stevie, I'm sorry to call you like this, but Sauro suggested it. You must help us. I don't know what to do.'

Stevie recognised too well the tone of despair in the voice. She felt a chill come over her and prayed she was wrong.

'What is it, Issa?' she asked.

'Farouk,' he said, his voice breaking as he spoke his son's name. 'They've taken Farouk.'

**At certain times in life** there is no choice; sometimes there is only one possible course of action and everything else recedes. This was such a time. For Stevie, all thoughts of gloom and depression were swept away, horror flared then was replaced by a determination. By the afternoon, she had organised for Josie to come out and sit with Rice, grill the doctors, and take care of anything that needed attention; she was on a plane to Olbia.

Farouk was six years old and she couldn't get his face out of her mind—the limpid brown eyes, the happy smile, his father's pride. A rage was boiling inside her. She was so angry—angry that there were people who did this, people who took children, who had no sense of morality or empathy or of law; people who thought they were above and beyond that, people who could come crashing into a stranger's life and destroy it. What right did they have? By what right did they do this?

Stevie was angry that people could take the lives of others for their own gratification and greed, angry that there were men and women who thought that the laws of humanity and the cosmos did not apply to them and that everyone was either an asset to be squeezed, or a liability to be crushed. They killed as an afterthought. These people who fostered pressure systems of destruction all over the world and were rarely brought to justice. She clenched the armrest and politely refused a glass of Orangina and a salami *panino* from the siren of a stewardess, all tanned limbs, shapely curves and large brown eyes.

Twenty-four hours after Farouk went missing, Issa received a telephone call—an Italian voice, local dialect—telling him they were holding his son. The kidnappers made no specific demand at the time but told him they would call back with a ransom amount and instructions. Issa tried to warn the voice that he was not a rich man; the call was terminated. All Issa could do now was wait for the next phone call. The poor father told Stevie this as she emerged from the terminal at Olbia airport. The heat and oleander-scented air felt poisonous to her that afternoon; the crowds of holidaymakers had thinned and it was mostly sailors bearing large canvas bags, arriving for the regattas of September. Issa's face was pale and drawn, at odds with all the tanned and relaxed faces drinking *caffè* and *spremuta*, a glass of prosecco, while they waited for the next flight from Milan or Rome.

'Issa, tell me everything, from the beginning,' she whispered as they walked quickly and purposefully out of the terminal and headed to his white truck.

'He was playing in the garden, down by the water. I never

worry because he is already such a good swimmer—it was the first thought that crossed my mind when he didn't come back. I was out till darkness searching the coast, the water, in my boat.'

Stevie felt a shudder of horror at what Issa must have been feeling in those awful uncertain hours.

'And then they called.' He started his truck and pulled out. They sped past the low granite hills and dry grasslands dotted with sheep and olive trees. The sun was glowing red, low on the horizon, turning the odd small cloud purple with its dying rays. The roads were quiet.

Good, thought Stevie. It would be easier to spot a tail that way. So far, they appeared to be unaccompanied.

Issa continued his story: 'The next day, they called again. This time it was a woman, also local, I think. She said she knew I had been offered fifteen million euros for my land and that I should accept at once, hand the money over, and then my boy would be returned.' Issa's face had taken on an unearthly glow in the sunset; he kept his eyes on the road. 'That's how it works here. The rumours move so quickly they are better than any newspaper—people hear things . . . I thought the days of the *banditi* were over, but I guess not. I only wonder why they went for me and not one of the rich people with holiday villas and Ferraris.' He shook his head in weary sorrow.

'I tried to contact the man who had made me the offer,' Issa continued, 'to accept—but the number he had given me went to voicemail. I left so many messages, but no one has called back.' He turned a panicked face to Stevie. 'That's when I called you. I didn't know what else to do. Sauro told me you do this sort of thing in your work. Please. Please help me.'

Stevie's eyes filled with tears and she blinked them away, her gaze on the horizon. She had to appear totally strong for Issa. It would give him strength in turn. 'Of course I will help,' she said softly. 'My work is usually on the other end of things. I organise protection to stop this sort of thing from happening. But I do know the process and there are people I can call who will help us.' She paused before asking, 'Did they tell you not to go to the police?' asked Stevie.

Issa shook his head and Stevie frowned. That was odd; perhaps the kidnappers were amateurs, nervous themselves, and they had forgotten to add the standard warning. Amateurs worried Stevie: they were more inclined to go off half-cocked, to get scared and panic; the victim was more likely to get hurt—or worse. This thought she kept to herself.

'The *carabinieri* came to find me though,' Issa said. 'They already knew Farouk was missing. I don't know how—the rumour mill again . . . I just shook my head—I didn't want to talk to them. I thought it might be dangerous for Farouk if anyone found out.'

Stevie thought a moment. 'I might just go and pay a visit to the *carabinieri*.' When Issa looked alarmed, she explained, 'It's important in a situation like this to try to get the best possible picture of what has happened—any information at all is helpful. Even if we just discover how the *carabinieri* found out. Someone might have seen something. The more we know about who has taken Farouk, the stronger our position when we negotiate his release: we will know better how to handle the kidnappers, how far to push them, what buttons to press and so on.' Then she asked, 'Have you got a photo of Farouk?'

Issa reached into his pocket and pulled out a picture of the boy, grinning, a bottom tooth missing.

Stevie put it carefully in her bag and laid a hand lightly on Issa's arm. 'You can drop me on the other side of Porto Cervo,' she said. 'It will be okay,' she added with a confidence she did not feel.

He stopped the car at a bus stop hidden from the road by a massive pink oleander bush, and Stevie jumped out.

She ducked into one of the covered passageways that led down to the piazza, turned abruptly at the bottom and went straight into the nearest shop. It was a luxury boutique that sold furs. Stevie pretended to browse among the massive pelts, keeping one eye out for anyone coming down the same passageway. She was clear.

A tightly wound saleslady with a bleached beehive that channelled Ivana Trump was keeping a suspicious eye on Stevie. She now approached, proffering a hideous purple fur that fell to the floor. Stevie smiled icily and allowed the woman to place it over her shoulders; the air-conditioning was freezing but Stevie still wondered whether anyone actually bought the creations, let alone in the peak of summer. Her question was answered by the door opening to admit a large man in a lime green suit and Panama hat, and two pneumatic-breasted women in little more than Swarovski crystals. The saleslady immediately switched her attention to the trio, accurately sensing better opportunities for commission; Stevie silently exited.

She mingled with the crowds on the piazza, then made her way down towards the wooden bridge and across to the old port. The *carabinieri* station was just up the hill. Stevie smiled at the young officer on duty and explained that she needed to see the chief immediately. This was not, apparently, possible. Stevie smiled and repeated her request, adding that she was a concerned family friend who might be able to help with an investigation dear to the chief. She added another, hopefully winning, smile and tilted her head to one side to show she was harmless. The young officer caved and led the way down the hall. The *carabinieri* always looked so immaculate, she marvelled, in their navy trousers with red stripe and navy jackets with silver buttons. The officer knocked on a door; a voice shouted, '*Entra.*' The officer smiled at Stevie again and showed her in, closing the door behind her.

The chief was a handsome man with black hair combed off his forehead. He smiled and spread his hands. 'Excuse me, Signora, for not standing, but . . .'

Stevie realised why: the chief was in his underwear, boxer shorts and a singlet. His jacket and trousers were hanging neatly behind his chair so that they would not crease. The generally unflappable Stevie was, for the briefest of moments, discombobulated. She recovered quickly and smiled, extending her hand. 'I quite understand,' she said. 'The heat . . . I'm Stevie Duveen.'

'How can I help you, Signora Duveen?' He gestured to a chair in front of his desk. '*Caffè?*' Stevie nodded.

'It is a delicate matter,' she began, sitting on the edge of the chair, staying close to the chief. She found persuasion was more effective with physical proximity, for all sorts of reasons. 'A young boy, a family friend, has gone missing. His name is Farouk Farmishan. You know this already, I believe.'

The chief looked at her hard for a moment, assessing how much to tell this stranger. He took in the slight frame, the long neck decorated with pearls, the blonde hair, the large green eyes lined in imploring black, and relaxed. 'We are aware of the situation.' He nodded. 'We contacted his father but he was not . . .' the chief spread manicured fingers, 'willing to cooperate. We cannot do much in such an eventuality.'

'Perhaps he is afraid,' Stevie suggested gently. 'And,' she added, looking the chief in the eye, 'the sight of the *carabinieri* can also be very . . . intimidating for some people.'

The chief visibly swelled with self-importance. He leant in. 'Perhaps you are right, Signora. Perhaps I did not take this possibility into account. One tends to forget . . .'

Stevie smiled. 'Quite,' she replied.

There was a knock on the door and the young officer appeared with a tray and two cups of espresso and some sugar. He put the tray down on the desk and left. The chief stirred three sugars into his coffee; Stevie accepted hers plain.

'Do you have some information you wish to share?' he said, after taking a sip of his coffee.

Stevie sighed. 'I was rather hoping you might be able to help me. I want the boy's father to cooperate with the authorities. I believe you and your men are the best chance we have.' The chief was nodding in agreement. Stevie continued, 'But his father is afraid. He asks me how the *carabinieri* can know things so quickly; he is worried about informants. He doesn't have quite the same faith in your force as I do, I'm afraid.' Stevie smiled again and was pleased to see the chief do the same. She leant in a little. 'If I could only tell him how you found out about his son—and any other details you can share that might reassure him—I might have some success.'

The chief thought it over and made up his mind. 'It was a guest of a neighbour of his, actually, who rang the station.'

'He reported the disappearance?'

'Not quite. He called because he was afraid for the safety of his own son. He said the boy next door had been kidnapped but he was certain it was a case of mistaken identity.'

The blood rushed to Stevie's face and she hoped the chief had not noticed. 'Really?' she whispered, widening her eyes. 'Does his son look like Farouk?'

The chief swivelled in his chair and reached for a slim file. He opened it and handed Stevie a photograph. She knew, even before she saw the young face, that it was a picture of Emile Krok.

Clémence's son did indeed look a lot like Farouk—she wondered that she had never noticed the similarity before—only Emile wasn't smiling in the picture. 'How remarkable,' she said vaguely and handed the photo back. 'Do *you* believe it was a case of mistaken identity?' she asked, treading as lightly as she could.

The chief downed his coffee and nodded, lighting a cigarette. 'This is the line we are following at present. It makes more sense. The neighbour, Vaughan Krok, is a very wealthy man, a holiday-maker, a man who would attract the notice of others. Issa Farmishan is a local, a man of little interest to anyone around here. And, as you noted, the boys look very similar. It would be an easy mistake to make.'

Stevie's mind raced. Was the chief right? Had Farouk been taken by mistake? It was possible . . . Stevie accepted a cigarette, giving herself a moment longer to think.

Maybe Vaughan had been right about the threat to his son. Maybe he had known things that he had not shared with his wife. And there had been the strange phone calls on board the Hercules . . .

Stevie exhaled slowly and turned to the chief. 'An easy mistake, as you say,' she said as mildly as she could. 'But then why did the kidnappers ring Issa Farmishan and not Vaughan Krok?'

The chief stared at her suspiciously and took a deep drag of his cigarette. 'The ways of the criminal, like the snake, are often circuitous, Signora,' he said, speaking as a man who has had long experience in the ways of the underworld.

Stevie nodded thoughtfully.

'After all,' added the chief, 'as Mr Krok pointed out, Farouk's father doesn't have fifteen million euros . . .'

The sum hung in the air and it was the last piece of evidence Stevie needed. She thanked the chief quietly and accepted his card. 'Call me anytime, Signora. We are here to serve. This is my mobile number—day or night.' She thanked him again and let herself out.

There was no doubt in her mind who was behind the kidnapping and why. She was burning with fury. It all made twisted yet perfect sense: Issa had almost no money of his own, but fifteen million euros was the sum that Krok had offered him for his land on the promontory. Kidnap the boy, force Issa to sell his land to him, then get the money back in ransom; use the ruse of kidnap threats to Emile to throw any potential investigations off the scent. Just like with Clémence and the suicide threats, he had been laying the groundwork. The threats to Krok's son had the added benefit of terrifying Clémence. It was the sort of cruel, devious plan that Krok would find pleasure in. He didn't even have to worry that anyone would put the pieces together, as Stevie had done. The man was untouchable—there was no proof. What could a man like Issa do against the power of Vaughan Krok? Issa would have to give up his land to the monster. That was the price that evil would extract from Issa, and Issa was prepared to pay.

But then the accident had intervened. Krok was possibly unconscious; he might even die. What would happen to Farouk then? What were the orders? Were there any contingency plans? So many things could go wrong. Stevie needed to make sure that Farouk came back safely, at any price. Justice they could seek later. The boy was all that mattered to her, and all that mattered to Issa: his whole world was in hostile hands.

# 16

As Stevie's taxi pulled in to the drive of Lu Nibaru, it almost ran into Mark and Simone's white station wagon reversing out. Stevie had completely forgotten about her cousin.

Mark rolled down the window. 'We can't stay, Stevie. Sorry. There's been a kidnapping right near here—Simone is terrified for her life and, frankly, I agree with her! We're going home.'

Stevie raised a hand in farewell, her mind far away, 'God-speed,' she managed to say, and waved without smiling as the car took off up the dirt driveway.

Despite having repossessed her solitude, Stevie hardly slept that night. Her mind churned and when the sun began to show itself, she got out of bed, glad that the night had ended and that there would be time now for action. She took a pot of black coffee to the roof and, wrapped in an old blanket against the cool morning air, sat on the low stone wall and watched the sea turn from pink to mauve to blue. The beauty of this arid coastline was stunning, but she wondered at how much pain and evil was hiding in its cracks today—like scorpions, she thought. Her tossing in the night had given rise to the beginnings of a plan, or at least a first step. She had not told Issa of her suspicion about who was behind the kidnapping; she was afraid he might do something rash and make the situation worse, if that was possible.

Issa said he had tried to contact the potential buyer for his property many times—the source of the ransom he would pay for Farouk—but he could not reach Krok. Stevie knew this was because Krok was in hospital in London and out of action. However, Clémence was the next best thing, and she could reach her. Stevie took out her phone and called.

Clémence answered after two rings. 'Stevie!' She sounded surprised.

'I just wanted to see how you were doing, Clémence, all that horrible business about Vaughan's accident.' Stevie wanted Clémence off her guard.

'Oh, you're too sweet. I've been with him 24/7 until now. They say he will make a good recovery.' Stevie could tell by Clémence's bright, brassy tone that someone was probably listening.

'Are you back on the *Costa*? I heard a rumour . . .'

'I am, Stevie, but not at the big villa. I rented a place in Piccolo Pevero. Marlena's with me but Emile is in London with the nannies. You should visit us sometime . . .'

When Stevie rang off, she wondered if Clémence knew what her husband had done, if she cared. It was all drama when it was her son, but would she feel the same if someone else's boy was in danger? She would soon find out.

Clémence's villa in Piccolo Pevero was a much more modest affair than the Villa Goliath. Stevie fired up the old jeep and, dressed in a loose yellow linen sundress and flat sandals, Rolex watch and Ray-Bans, knife strapped to her upper thigh, set out to do battle.

An armed major-domo let her into the house and motioned

towards the patio. There a woman in a purple and green bikini and matching turban was reading a newspaper; an identical woman in a red voile kaftan sat bare-headed in gold sunglasses looking out to sea. Marlena and Clémence, only Stevie had to move closer to see which was which. She had been hoping to find Clémence alone. Both sisters turned towards her as she approached. Marlena put down the *Wall Street Journal* and looked up.

'Still trying to figure out which one of us is the evil twin, Stevie?' Her smile was like glass. 'Is it Marlena, the smuggler, the pirate runner, the drinker? Who loves a fight and won't back down?' She turned to glance at her sister. 'Or is it dear, sweet Clémence with her doe eyes and her painted talons, clutching at anything with money until she tears its very hide away?' She laughed as her sister got up and walked inside.

'We both knew we were destined for better things than the basement flat on the Avenue Foch,' Marlena went on. 'Our mother always told us so. We just went about it in different ways. Who is to say which is the most noble—' she flashed another of her brittle smiles '—or the least ignoble?' Her smile vanished. 'Are you judging us, Stevie?' she taunted.

Stevie shook her head. 'No, I'm not. Not on your past. What is that to me? I didn't live it with you. Decisions were made based on the circumstances you found yourselves in.' Stevie took off her aviators and folded them carefully away into their old leather case. She looked up at Marlena with her emerald eyes. 'But I will judge you on the choice you are about to make—with your sister.'

Marlena's eyes narrowed. 'Let me tell you something. We grew up in the worst flat in the best district in Paris. We were friends with everyone who had money, but we had none of our own.' She leant forward and took a cigarette from an onyx case. She smoked menthols. 'Our mother was determined to change that. She was a seamstress at a great couture house.' Marlena lit her cigarette and slowly exhaled. She was obviously playing for time to figure out what Stevie was up to; Stevie did not interrupt her, curious to see what this dangerous woman would say. 'Our father was Polish and a bad gambler. He rarely won, and if he did, he would buy things like lobster and champagne, but we never had more than one pair of shoes. Our mother would bring back scraps of material from her work—silks and fur and sequins—and she would sew them onto our plain cotton dresses. We used to call them "pieces from heaven". But then we grew up and the scraps were no longer enough. Clémence married her first husband at nineteen because he offered to buy her a bicycle.'

Marlena turned her feline head and gave Stevie a burning stare; Stevie returned it, betraying nothing, saying nothing. Often silence would make a person say more than they intended.

Just then, Clémence came clacking out with a jug of sangria, her gold bangles jangling. She smiled at everyone and no one and sat down on the Versace sun lounge.

'Marlena, don't be a bitch.'

Marlena looked away and said, her tone bored, 'What do you want, Stevie?'

'The boy,' she said simply.

'What are you talking about?' Clémence stopped mid-pour.

Stevie turned her eyes on Emile's mother. 'Farouk Farmishan,' she said, ice in her voice. 'Your husband had him snatched so he could get his hands on his father's land. I want him back.'

'I don't know what you are talking about.' Clémence's mouth was an O of surprise. 'Krok hates children.'

'Krok is indisposed at the moment.' Marlena's lip curled in a tiny smile of cruel amusement. Stevie did not know if it was for Krok or Farouk or her sister—or all three.

'He had a terrible accident,' Clémence added, in the tone of dazed astonishment usually used by Southern belles. 'Awful guns. I won't touch them myself.'

'That's why I am here,' countered Stevie flatly. She turned the force of her gaze onto Clémence. 'Where is the boy?'

'I don't know,' Clémence insisted, her eyes large with an expression of amazement that did not quite convince Stevie.

Marlena smiled. 'Go home, Stevie,' she said. 'My sister has had enough to deal with without your accusations.' She reached out and took Clémence's hand in hers; their nails, Stevie noticed, were painted matching iridescent green.

Stevie waved away the proffered glass of sangria. She could not help but notice it was the colour of blood. 'It is nothing to you,' she spoke directly to Clémence, 'and everything to the boy and his father. You, as a mother, know that only too well. Call your husband or his henchmen or whoever you have to and find out. Either you rise to the challenge of acting like a human being—with all its implications—or you do not. There are no grey areas.' She said this softly, murderously, her eyes still on the woman in front of her.

Clémence looked away; Marlena's smile did not give Stevie much confidence. 'Why would we help you, Stevie?' Marlena said. 'Even if we could? These people mean nothing to us.'

Clémence put a placating hand on Stevie's arm. 'Vaughan is mad with anger. He is totally irrational right now, desperate to find out who tried to kill him.'

'It wasn't an accident?' Stevie said.

'Of course not,' broke in Marlena. 'He has so many enemies. He is too dangerous even to talk to over the phone right now. I'm afraid we can't help you.'

'We have too much to lose,' added Clémence, a note of pleading in her voice.

Stevie got up slowly. 'You have already lost.'

'What do you mean?' Clémence reached for Stevie's arm again but Stevie stepped away.

'You have lost your human credentials.' Stevie said, then she made a decision. She looked down at Clémence. 'I am not leaving. I will sit in your house until either of you change your mind, or I can get Krok on the phone myself.'

Marlena shrugged. 'Suit yourself.'

**Stevie chose a white-painted cane** chair under a shady canopy of bougainvillea. The scene should have been marvellous—a pool nestling among natural granite boulders, the heady scent of thyme and cistus, the trill of the cicadas. But she could think only of Farouk. A small green scorpion appeared from a crack in the rocks. She moved her foot carefully away. *To think of all these scorpions in the sun . . .* She looked back at Marlena and Clémence, tanning themselves. *Evil likes to enjoy itself too.*

She didn't know what she would do next, but she wasn't leaving. The twins were her only lead to Farouk right now. To distract herself from her pounding rage at their indifference, she picked up a book of Slim Aaron's photographs sitting on top of a pile on the coffee table. The photographer was a well-known documenter of *la dolce vita* and the international jet set. His gorgeous photographs captured the great and the good and the fabulous at play in their hideaways all over the world. Interestingly, he had begun as a war photographer. One day the death and tension became too much for him and he decided to walk on the sunny side of the street, as he put it, for the rest of his life.

Stevie flipped through the photos, trying to think of something that would help Farouk. She saw pink swimming pools on the Mexican coast, tree houses in Brazil, ranches in Arizona, chalets in France and Switzerland, yachts on the Mediterranean, a safari in South Africa . . . She was about to flip the page when something gave her pause. She looked more closely at the photograph. A group of four—two couples by the looks of it—stood in the foreground of a luxurious camp, dressed in tailored khakis.

The woman on the right caught Stevie's eye: she was tall and lean, her hair swept into a long, high ponytail, a pair of large gold sunglasses pushed back on her forehead. Her nails, rather incongruously given the background, were painted aquamarine. The face—Stevie could have no doubt—belonged to Clémence. Her boot was resting on the head of a huge wildebeest, and she cradled a shotgun in both hands. No one else in the picture was holding a gun and there could be no doubt that Clémence had shot the beast herself, in a former life, with a former husband. Clémence Krok, the photograph told Stevie, was not afraid of guns at all. From the look of it, she was very much at ease with them. As Josie always said, even criminals stick to what they know. And Stevie suddenly knew who had tried to kill Vaughan Krok.

She carefully set down the book, page open, and called to Marlena as she passed, on her way into the house. Marlena stopped and glared at her, but her curiosity was aroused by Stevie's small, beckoning hand. She came.

'I have a proposition for you, Marlena.'

Marlena smirked in contempt. As if Stevie had anything she wanted, it seemed to imply.

'I know it was Clémence who tried to kill Krok.'

'What?' A short, sharp retort, like a revolver shot.

'You didn't know?' Stevie studied Marlena's face, but it betrayed nothing. It was possible she didn't know.

'She could never do that, not in a million years would she have the strength to do that.'

'I think you underestimate your twin, Marlena.' Stevie pointed to the open page.

Marlena's eyes followed and she froze. Then, recovering quickly, she snapped, 'Stupid girl. Her vanity was always her weakness.' Her eyes flashed. 'It doesn't prove a thing.'

'Maybe not to a court, or to you . . . but it will be enough to convince her crazy husband that she did it, and who knows what he will do to her?'

Marlena blanched visibly. Stevie had struck home. She felt a pang of regret at having to use blackmail in such an insidious way, but greater things than scruples were at stake. She swallowed to keep her voice cold and calm. 'So I propose a trade: your sister's life for Farouk.'

Marlena said nothing for a time, her eyes on the reclining form of her twin by the pool. Clémence, oblivious, waved at them, her bangles tinkling. Marlena looked back at Stevie and said, in a voice Stevie had never heard her use before, 'I don't know where the boy is, I swear.'

Stevie nodded. 'But you can find out. And you will. And we will get him back safely.' She took out her phone and photographed the picture of Clémence, then she looked at her watch. It was almost midday. 'You have until seven this evening. Otherwise this photo goes to Krok with a suitably provocative message.' Stevie stopped and stared Marlena full in the face. 'And you know there's no point running. You know better than I do that he can find you anywhere and he will never stop looking. Your only hope is to help me. My company will get a copy of this message, and instructions to send it on if anything happens to me. Bear that in mind also. And now I think I will leave you to make your inquiries. Time is short.' She nodded to Marlena. 'I will be back at seven.'

**Stevie passed the day in** restless activity. She swam out to the buoy in front of her grandmother's house, she did her calisthenics on the roof, activating her muscles, stretching out the knots that had accumulated with tension and hours spent on hospital furniture. She left a message for Josie, asking after David's condition. Everything else would have to remain unsaid; she did not want to risk worrying David, if he did come to.

She did take the precaution of emailing herself the photo and a brief description of the situation, with the subject heading: *In Case of Missing*. If she did disappear, Josie would check her emails and find it. Not that it would do much good at that point, she thought. The power of the photo was in the deterrence.

Perched on a granite boulder at the edge of the crystal sea, soaking up the last of the warm afternoon rays, Stevie asked herself the question she had been dodging since her encounter with the twins: was she prepared to go through with her threat to expose Clémence to her psychotic husband? She could only hope it didn't come to that. She knew she had to believe she would in order to have any power over Marlena; the woman's instincts were finely tuned to any sort of weakness and she could not afford to show any doubt or Farouk would remain missing, if not worse. The twins had made a choice when they got involved with Vaughan Krok, and they had made another choice when they refused to help Stevie; these choices had consequences.

Back in the small kitchen, Stevie made herself a simple dinner of prosciutto, bread and cheese, some olives. She would need the strength. Then she dressed carefully: she had to be ready for anything. She put on her blue swimsuit, then a pair of loose black silk pants, a navy blue cotton safari jacket. She filled the pockets with sugar lumps, a powerful torch and her phone. She could not know what the night held, but it would certainly be best to attract as little attention in the night shadows as possible, no matter what. She strapped her knife to her calf and set out to find the twins.

Stevie parked the jeep a short distance away from their villa, facing downhill. The engine was noisy and she wanted to surprise them in case they had had any clever ideas about calling Krok's men themselves.

All was quiet at the villa; the lights were on around the pool. Stevie climbed over the granite boulders that surrounded the pool and looked in. It seemed that Marlena—it would have to be Marlena—had given the security men and staff the night off. The sisters sat side by side on a cane lounge, deep in conversation. They were holding hands. All looked as it should. Stevie crept through the boulders like a ninja then appeared suddenly by the pool's edge. The sisters started.

'Good evening,' said Stevie, walking towards them, exuding a sangfroid she did not feel.

They looked up at her. Marlena, for the first time since Stevie had met her, looked vulnerable, even frightened. There had been a change.

Stevie stood in front of them. 'Where is the boy?'

'They're holding him on Cavallo,' Marlena replied softly, her usual sneer gone. 'In the boatshed of the yacht club.'

Stevie needed to keep the advantage. To do that she had to take complete control, and she made a split-second decision.

'Where does Krok keep those Medusas?'

---

**Down at the marina, it** was quieter than usual. The yachties were mid-regatta and having an early night; the parties had not yet begun. The season was over and many of the big yachts had moved on, most towards the Caribbean, where the season was just beginning. The *cantiere* was deserted, the boats in dry dock under tarpaulins. Marlena led the way. The twins had changed out of their customary resort wear. Clémence wore dark, slim-fitting jeans and a midnight-blue windbreaker, Marlena a black neoprene wetsuit and holster. The butt of a silver gun showed. Of course she would be armed, thought Stevie—however she had no choice but to trust Marlena.

They reached a shed by the water with a great steel door and several new locks. Marlena produced a set of keys and began to unlock them one by one. The heavy door finally creaked open. Stevie shone the flashlight: eight Zodiacs were stacked in twos. A ninth sat in the middle of the room on a trailer. 'This is the one you saw.' Marlena pointed at it. 'I refilled the fuel tanks when I got back. It should be all ready to go.'

'What are they all doing here?' asked Stevie, looking around the dark shed.

'Ready to fill orders, but everything is on hold at the moment. Only Krok can give the nod and he's got other priorities right now. Megrahi will probably take care of them in the next day or so.'

Stevie gave a little shudder as she remembered the man with the missing thumb. Krok and Marlena were not, she reminded herself, the only dangers that lay in wait. 'Out of interest,' Stevie ventured, 'where did you go that night?'

Marlena gave her a long look. Finally she sighed. 'I don't suppose it matters now.' She started lifting off the tarpaulin. 'Tunisia. We had a load of MANPADS. They fit nicely in the lockers of the boat and they're very popular in Africa and the Middle East.'

Stevie drew a sharp breath. She and Henning had been right,

that day on the ghost ship. MANPADS: shoulder-launched surface-to-air missiles. They were usually guided and a favourite weapon to use against aircraft and helicopters. They were loved by terrorist groups and rebel groups alike for their portability and affordability, and for their ease of use. They would be a pirate's delight.

Stevie looked at the Zodiac. 'I'm surprised you would use a boat like this to send a few MANPADS to Africa . . .' Some older missiles could be bought for a couple of hundred dollars. It seemed like a waste of resources.

'It was a demonstration of what these boats can do.' Marlena's eyes narrowed defensively. 'And the MANPADS were Starstreaks. They go for a quarter of a million dollars or more, and they're very hard to get. Controls are tight.'

Stevie froze. Starstreaks were beam-guided missiles that homed in on the target along a laser beam—called beam riding. They were particularly frightening because they were pretty much immune to most missile countermeasures. They could wreak untold havoc in the wrong hands. She shook herself. There would be time to think about that later. The matter at hand was Farouk.

She helped Marlena and Clémence push the trailer out to the water's edge and launch the boat. They jumped in. Marlena stood at the wheel and started up a single engine. They puttered discreetly past the dark boats, the rounded church lit beautifully from below, the lighted windows of the Luci di la Muntagna hotel.

Once out of the heads, Marlena set the compass for Cavallo. 'You'd better buckle in if you want to stay on board.'

Clémence and Stevie buckled into the special bucket seats loaded with massive springs for suspension; Marlena wedged herself between the wheel and her twin. The eight three-hundred-horsepower engines roared to life.

The sound was extraordinary. The Zodiac picked up speed,

nose climbing vertically at first under the weight and churn of the engines before planing and gathering even more speed. The wind rush was incredible. The closest thing Stevie had come to this was skydiving. Only here they bounced and flew as the fibreglass hull hit wavelets, and everything was pitch black.

*Here's hoping Marlena's good at the wheel.*

Fortunately, Marlena drove the beast with great skill. As they approached their destination, she slowed. Stevie remembered the dangerous shoals—were they mad to attempt this at night? But there was no other way. She was about to speak up when Marlena, without looking down at Stevie, said, 'Relax. I know these waters like the back of my hand.' And she steered the craft expertly towards the small lights of the island before cutting the motors.

They unbuckled their belts. Stevie's hair was standing on end and her cheeks felt whipped, eyes watering. The momentum carried them in a way, then the wind, which by good fortune was blowing behind them. When they were close enough to make out the outline of the empty houses in the starlight, Marlena motioned to Stevie to drop the sea anchor. They could not put a real one down for risk that it would get caught in the rocks below and delay their escape. A rocky outcrop and the inky darkness made sure the dinghy was invisible to anyone on the shore. Marlena pointed a painted fingernail at the dark shape of a shed at the other end of the jetty. A crack of light suddenly appeared then disappeared again. Someone had just gone in, or out. They needed to get closer, find a way to look inside.

Was Farouk in there? How many others were there? How were they armed? The rescue party had the element of surprise and a very good getaway vehicle in its favour, but that was about it.

Stevie whispered, 'I need to get a look inside the shed. I'm going to swim in.' She stripped off her outer layers and rubbed a little engine black on her face to stop it gleaming like a moon. Before she slid overboard, she reminded the sisters that Josie and others had the photograph and the message, and should anything happen to her . . .

'Just go,' hissed Marlena. Stevie slid soundlessly into the inky black sea and began swimming.

She swam right up under the jetty until she was directly under the boathouse and stayed there a moment, treading water. Looking up, she could see slivers of light between the planks. The radio was on, playing Italian pop music. She could hear no other voices. A shiver of cold and fear ran through her. What was she doing? It was madness to attempt this. She wanted out. She was frightened. Then she thought of Farouk, and Issa, and of how far they had come already. There was no choice but to go ahead.

She crept silently out of the water and onto the rocks. The boatshed was built against a sea wall made of granite boulders and Stevie was small enough to fit between the boulders and the wall of the shed. There was no window, but a point of light led her to a hole where a knot of wood had fallen out. She put her eye to the hole.

Curled up on a blanket in the corner, like a lost puppy, was Farouk Farmishan. He was shackled to the wall by one ankle. The bile of rage rose in Stevie's throat when she saw the chain, saw the little ankle rubbed raw by the steel clamp. A man sat in the other corner; Stevie could only see his legs from her spyhole. He was sitting by the radio smoking, reading a newspaper. There did not appear to be anyone else in the shed. And after all, what could a six-year-old boy do to escape? Stevie's mind raced, searching for a plan. Should she go back and get Marlena? Marlena had a gun, and they would be two against one.

Stevie moved away from the peephole and was making her way back down to the water when her foot dislodged a small rock. It bounced on a rock below and fell into the sea. She heard the floor creak. The man inside was getting up. She froze. Had he heard? Surely the radio was too loud. The door to the boatshed opened, light spilling out. The man stepped towards the edge of the jetty and looked out to sea. There was something familiar about the body language and Stevie realised the man was getting ready to take a pee off the edge of the jetty. It was now or never.

She clambered up like lightning and unsheathed her knife. She heard the clink of a belt buckle, a zip. She crept closer. The man's focus would be on the task at hand; this was her chance. She spotted a boat hook lying on the jetty and resheathed her knife. Distance was best. She lined up behind the figure, who grunted in relief and let loose a stream into the sea. With all the might of her small but muscular arms, Stevie swung the boathook like a bat and caught the man on the temple. Without a word or a noise he toppled forward into the sea. A face appeared beside the body: Marlena.

'Turn him over,' whispered Stevie. 'He'll drown.'

'Who cares?' Marlena whispered back, but she did as Stevie asked. She began tying the unconscious man's hands high on the legs of a sea ladder.

Stevie crept into the shed and knelt by the door. 'Farouk,' she called gently. 'Farouk, little sunshine.' It was Issa's pet name.

The boy looked up and for a moment didn't recognise Stevie. Then a light dawned in his eyes, but no smile.

'Your papa sent me to find you,' she said, creeping closer, not wanting to frighten him into shouting or crying. 'Do you remember me? Stevie?'

He nodded once.

Stevie looked around and found the key to the shackles on the desk. She freed Farouk and picked him up in her arms. He felt as light as a feather. 'Are you ready to come with me, Farouk? We will have to swim.'

He nodded again.

Stevie and Farouk climbed carefully, quietly, down to the water's edge.

Marlena swam over to them. She pointed at the unconscious guard. 'He won't drown, but he's not going anywhere.'

Stevie put Farouk on her back. 'Now hang on, Farouk, don't let go.'

She began to swim with her precious cargo, Marlena following behind. The water was cold and dark but there were no shouts or noise and soon the Zodiac came into view. Clémence hauled Farouk aboard, dripping wet, and wrapped him tightly in a towel. Stevie climbed in and found the sugar lumps. She put one in Farouk's mouth and the rest in his hand. 'Eat these one by one.' They would help stave off shock. Stevie ran to pull up the sea anchor.

Suddenly the guard tied to the sea ladder woke up and began to shout.

'Damn you and your bleeding heart, Duveen,' Marlena swore, and gunned the engines. 'You should have left him to drown.' More shouts followed as men came running with torches. The powerful beams swept the sea in arcs, searching for the source of the monstrous noise, but the Zodiac was just out of their orbit.

'Buckle up and get ready,' Marlena snarled over the noise of the engines. Stevie took Farouk on her lap and buckled them both into the seat. A speedboat had already been launched in pursuit. Marlena held the wheel with her knee and pulled out her gun. She turned, took careful aim, and fired. There was a scream in the dark, followed by a volley of return gunfire.

Stevie leant over Farouk, shielding him. 'For god's sake, Marlena, just get us out of here.'

Marlena slammed the accelerator with her palm and the boat flew forward. A silver cigarette boat was now in pursuit, and bullets were firing into the dark. Marlena couldn't resist the provocation and slowed to fire another round. She let out a cry as a bullet from the return volley tore into her flesh. Clémence screamed and Stevie shouted, 'Where are you hit?'

'My arm—flesh wound. Bastards!' she swore.

'You can't drive like that. Swap seats—you hold Farouk,' Stevie ordered, pushing Marlena down into her own seat and jumping behind the wheel. 'Put pressure on it,' she called over the engines.

'I know, damn you. It's not the first time I've bloody been shot,' Marlena shouted back, her face pale with pain. Clémence leant over and began winding a scarf tightly around her twin's arm, Marlena telling her to pull tighter, not to be a milksop, goddamnit. Stevie took the wheel and they shot out into the darkness, with Marlena shouting directions, guiding Stevie away from the shoals. Stevie tried not to think about the cigarette boat in pursuit; she knew a boat like that could probably match the speed of the crazy Zodiac. She concentrated fiercely on the dark water as Marlena shouted and swore, the blood now soaking through Clémence's scarf, running down her arm and pooling on the floor.

There was a burst of automatic weapon fire and Stevie crouched lower over the wheel, hearing a crack as one of the bullets slammed into the fibreglass. She could not risk being strafed with bullets, not with little Farouk on board, not with so little protection.

*How would they get away? Could she run them onto the rocks?*

She doubted it. Then she remembered a story David had told her of the old days in Hong Kong, the people-smuggling Triads and their snake boats. She had been fascinated by a tactic used by the Son of Sabre chase boats that pursued them. It had worked then, in similar circumstances; fingers crossed it would work again. She certainly had the advantage of surprise . . .

The pursuers were almost alongside now, burning their

engines at seventy knots. The metallic paint of the cigarette boat was glinting silver in the starlight. A rigid hull and structure would be even better for the plan, thought Stevie. She took a slow breath and centred her courage, then she slammed the accelerator to full and sped past the pursuers.

'Hang on!' she screamed at Marlena and Clémence, then, flying at around eighty knots, a few boat-lengths ahead of the cigarette, she spun the wheel and turned the Zodiac a full ninety degrees. The engines screamed and Stevie felt herself lurch violently sideways, almost winded by the seatbelt.

The speed and power of the Zodiac sent up a monstrous wall of wake behind them, right across the path of the hunters. In the dark, at that speed, the pursuers had no chance of seeing it coming.

The cigarette boat hit the water wall with a smash that sounded like a car wreck, then veered wildly off course and into the rocks. The vessel splintered. Stevie spun the Zodiac back on course, engines roaring in protest. She did not slow down to see what had happened, but when she did risk a glance back, there were no longer any lights, nor the sound of engines behind them.

**Stevie, heart hammering, made two** calls as they pulled in to the little stone jetty at the end of her beach. The second was to the chief of the *carabinieri* on his mobile. There had been, Stevie reported, a shoot-out on Cavallo, a little boy spotted, men with flamethrowers . . . (It was best to over-dramatise, she thought, to make sure the armed response would create a sufficient stir.) Maybe even a bomb, she added. If things went according to plan, the *carabinieri* would call the gendarmes in Corsica and both would descend like

Thor's hammer on the little island and take everyone holding arms into custody; this would give credence to the rumour she intended to start that it was the *carabinieri* who had rescued the boy. If Krok's men did decide to hunt for Farouk anyway, the delay would give Stevie and Issa a good headstart.

The first phone call had been to Issa. It was not safe to take Farouk home, and Issa was not safe there either. The little party retreated to Didi's house. It was hidden from the road and near the butt of a dead end. They would be safe from surprise. Issa was waiting for them by the front door and, weeping, he took his son into his arms. Apart from his chafed ankle, and the fear he had suffered, Farouk was unharmed. Unsurprisingly, he sat on his father's knee and did not say a word. Issa, on the other hand, could not stop thanking them, tears periodically welling up in his eyes, his arms almost crushing his little boy with love.

Stevie took Marlena into her bathroom and unwound the scarf from the forearm. Blood pulsed from the wound, but the bullet had missed the bone. It had grazed the arm lengthways rather than piercing it. 'You were lucky,' said Stevie.

'You were luckier,' shot back Marlena. 'You didn't get hit.'

Stevie found an old bottle of hydrogen peroxide and poured it on the wound. Stitches were no good for bullet wounds—they simply increased the risk of infection being sealed inside. They had to heal from the inside out. She put a soft cotton pad on the graze and bound it tightly with a bandage. Marlena's eyes never left Stevie; Stevie ignored her and got on with her work. She fashioned a rough sling and tied it around Marlena's slender neck.

'How are you going to explain—?'

'My injury? Oyster shells.' She glared at Stevie with her hard eyes. 'I stumbled on the rocks and tore my arm on oyster shells.' She said it so certainly that Stevie almost felt like a fool for not believing her. She realised she did not have to look after Marlena; Marlena could look after herself quite well enough. Stevie's usual role was protector. With Marlena, she did not know who she was . . .

'That was a nice trick with the wake wall, Stevie. I might have to try that one myself sometime.'

'Against whom?' muttered Stevie, still struggling with tying the sling.

Marlena laughed. 'Whatever happened to that Henning fellow? He seemed rather keen on you.'

Stevie stared at her a moment. Finally she said, 'I sent him away.'

'And now you wish you hadn't.'

Stevie shook her head. 'It was the right thing to do.'

'Bullshit.' Marlena laughed. 'Don't worry, he'll be back.'

Stevie shook her head again. 'No, he won't.' She went to re-tie the sling, trying to perfect the angle of the arm across the chest.

Marlena stood up. 'For god's sake, Stevie, stop fussing. Let's get a drink.'

They went into the kitchen, where Stevie found a bottle of grappa and poured everyone a medicinal drink. 'How does that rumour mill of yours work, Issa?' she asked. 'If I want to start a rumour . . .'

He looked up at her, uncertain where she was going with her question.

'You tell one of Sauro's sisters, Ornella at the fruit and vegetable stand, and the old *nonna* in the *pasticceria* . . . By noon the whole island will know.'

'We start this one tomorrow: the *carabinieri* launched a daring joint raid with the French police and rescued Farouk. Everyone is surprised because they are not known for their—alacrity? But nevertheless, it was a job well done.'

Issa nodded; he understood.

'You know you can't go home, Issa,' Stevie said, looking straight at him. 'They might come for you there. You will have to hide somewhere with Farouk until it is safe.'

Issa nodded. 'I understand.' He thought for a moment. 'But if Krok is everything you say he is, he will know where I would hide. He will find us.' Issa's hands were trembling.

Stevie knew he was right but said nothing. They had bought some time; sometimes that was everything. Whether Krok decided to come after Issa out of spite was an unknown. It might depend, Stevie thought, on how many distractions Krok had . . . All she could do now was deal with the matter at hand.

'Marlena, we have to get them off the island. I'll need the Zodiac. We need to get to the mainland.'

'Not a chance.'

'Right now, Krok has no idea what has happened; when he investigates, he will hear that the *carabinieri* were behind the raid. No one on the island saw the boat or our faces. Things will be worse for everyone if Issa and Farouk don't get away tonight. It's just a few more hours.'

Marlena said nothing, conceding the point. The father and son were evidence. The further away from her they were, the better. She nodded.

'Call me when you're done with it. I'll meet you at the port.'

'We'll need warm clothes, food, drink and lots of petrol,' continued Stevie. 'I can do food, but the petrol might be a problem.'

Issa woke from his trance. 'I can do that,' he said. 'I have tanks of it in the hotel stores. The generators run on petrol. Alberto will bring it.'

'Alberto?'

'I would trust him with my life.'

Stevie said, 'Well, that is exactly what you will be doing.'

Issa made the call. Stevie changed into warm, dry clothes, a waxed jacket in olive green, jeans. She ferreted around in an old cupboard and found some old corduroy trousers that had once belonged to her for Farouk, and an old ski parka. For Issa, she found a slightly torn windbreaker and a woollen vest. 'The wind will make it cold out there.'

Stevie hunted out the old sea charts from her grandfather's study. Her plan was to head for Genoa under the cover of night. It was a huge port, busy with ships and ferries and crafts of all sorts. Their arrival would go unnoticed. From there, she would arrange for Leone to meet her. He could drive from Turin to Genoa in less than two hours; she would ask him to take Issa and Farouk to his home in the countryside until she could think of a better plan. They would be safe there.

'Marlena, did you know Krok had taken the boy?' Stevie asked suddenly.

Marlena stared at her for a beat then shook her head. 'If you don't look, you don't find.' Then her expression changed and she added, 'No, I didn't know until you asked about him and I made my inquiries.'

Stevie turned to Clémence, her eyes holding the same question.

Clémence looked away, her eyes filled with tears. She did not shake her head.

Stevie took one of Marlena's cigarettes, lit it and inhaled deeply, willing serenity.

'He'll find you eventually,' Marlena said. 'You won't be safe. None of us will be.'

Stevie looked at her, not wanting the boy to hear this. But, thankfully, he had fallen asleep in his father's arms. 'I know that,' she replied. 'But this will do for now.'

'And then what?'

'And then we will think of something.'

Marlena leant back and lit a menthol, an incongruous figure, more snake-like than ever in her wetsuit. 'Krok must go,' she said, exhaling a stream of smoke towards the ceiling. 'It's the only way we will be safe.'

Stevie looked at her. She was right of course, but what was she suggesting? An assassination?

She read Stevie's thoughts. 'Oh no. We won't get near him again. Clémence was in the prime spot and even she failed.' Here she looked at her sister, who glanced guiltily at the beautiful, sleeping Farouk from time to time.

Clémence looked up at Stevie. 'I will do *anything*,' she said, 'anything at all to take him down. He turned me into a monster like him—and I didn't even realise it.'

'We won't get near him.' Marlena ignored her sister. 'But I know people who can.'

'What sort of people?'

'Let's just say, they've been after me for years but they've never been able to get me for anything.'

'The police?'

Marlena smiled, her diffidence returning. 'The police . . . I suppose you could call them that. They are a joint taskforce dedicated to eliminating international criminals—arms dealers, drug dealers, people smugglers, terrorists, and those who supply them.'

'Pirates?' suggested Stevie.

Marlena laughed. 'And pirates. They once offered me immunity if I told them everything I knew about Krok. He's at the very top of their list but they can never get him.' She tapped the fine tip of ash that was growing at the end of her cigarette. 'Or me. But I think we might just be able to get them to do our dirty work for us.'

'Do you know enough for them to take the bait?' asked Stevie cautiously.

It was Clémence who replied. 'Between the two of us, we know everything there is to know about that man.'

Stevie downed her grappa and made a face. She could never get used to the local firewater, but it certainly warmed the cockles. 'So,' she said, 'how do we whistle up this taskforce?'

Marlena leant in. 'It's not safe to use phones or any other electronic communication devices. Krok has extraordinarily advanced eavesdropping technology pointed their way, with programmes designed to pick up on key words, phrases, names and so on. But I have other ways of contacting the man we need. He is in Baku. You'll need to go there.'

'Azerbaijan?' Stevie raised an eyebrow. 'And you?'

*Was she walking into a trap?*

'I'll meet you there. We'll draw less attention that way, and it appears I'm not wanted on your little boat trip so . . .'

Stevie finished the rest of her grappa. 'Baku it is, then.'

**The night was calm and** clear as the three fugitives set off. Stevie kept her eyes on the soft glow of the compass and prayed for safe passage; Issa stared into the blackness, his arms cradling the sleeping Farouk. With the Costa Smeralda behind them, the sea was quiet save for a few enormous car ferries lit up like skyscrapers, and the odd yacht or the occasional fisherman laying nets. Dawn rose as the northern tip of Corsica vanished behind them. The sea was silver and pink and there was not a ripple. The Mediterranean felt like a pond. Out to starboard there was a movement in the sea, rising humps of water . . .

'Dolphins,' shouted Stevie, grinning, and the boy awoke. 'Look, Farouk, dolphins.' A pod of around thirty were undulating their way west, tails sending up silver spray. They had the sea to themselves, as they had once at the dawn of time. It was a glorious sight and Farouk was smiling. That too was good. Stevie felt sure the dolphins were a good omen.

The mainland of Italy appeared as a grey haze in front of them; it was not so much distance as the heat and pollution that caused the venerable old land to smudge on the horizon. With Issa's help, they unbolted six of the engines as Genoa came into sight. The engines sank to the sea floor and, without them, the beast became a normal, if somewhat bigger and slightly misshapen, inflatable dinghy. The engines were easily replaced. Marlena would have to take care of that when she got the boat back. But with Krok out of action, she doubted engine repairs would raise any red flags. That was the genius of these crafts, she thought as a *carabinieri* launch passed by without giving them so much as a second glance; they operated completely under the radar. That reminded her . . .

Stevie took out her phone and dialled the underpanted captain of the *carabinieri*. Stevie wanted to congratulate the captain on a job well done—his men had excelled themselves and brought great honour to the force. The whole of the Costa was grateful. Stevie would not let him ask a single question, her praise rolling over him. The missing boy had been found by his men and everyone was grateful. The boy was being sent to Corsica by ferry that evening to stay with an aunt.

The chief managed to hide his confusion quite well, thought Stevie as she rang off. Hopefully he would go on to the next step and publicly take credit for Farouk's rescue in the newspapers.

She then made a second call, this time to Switzerland.

'Stevie!' Josie snapped when she heard her colleague's voice on the phone. 'I've been trying to call you. Where the devil have you been?'

'Is David alright?' Terror tightened at Stevie's throat.

'Out of the coma—the doctors are very surprised. He's very weak but he can talk.'

'Oh, thank god,' she cried.

'Some paralysis in the left leg,' continued Josie, 'but so far, so good.'

'That is the second piece of good news today.' Stevie smiled.

'Where are you?' Josie's voice was sharp, but Stevie carefully ended the call without another word.

# 17

Having safely settled Farouk and Issa with Leone, Stevie caught a flight to London. Once in the city, she checked in at her favourite hotel by the park, The Gore, where she briefly debated calling Henning to apologise for being so abrupt in Zurich. He had been wonderful with David . . . and yet her message would still be the same, wouldn't it? Leave me alone.

She ordered a vodka and tonic from room service and kicked off her sandals. When the drink arrived, she took a large sip and decided that she should definitely leave things as they were.

The next morning, she went back to Heathrow and bought a ticket to Azerbaijan. London to Baku was a direct route for British Airways, thanks to all the oil rig workers and oil men who came and went every week. This also meant that, apart from a gingery grandmother with a gold tooth who came from Aberdeen, Stevie was the only woman on the flight. The other passengers were, to a man, tattooed, with large forearms, battered clothes and faces.

She remembered the last time she had flown this route—from Baku to London—with a planeload of exhausted workers flying home for leave. When the inflight service began, the passengers had asked for Venezuelans or Bloody Marys. It was quarter past eight in the morning. Stevie had turned to the man beside her, a small, top-heavy oil man with stick legs that made him look like a ventriloquist's dummy. He was so tired that he fell asleep between drinks, always managing to wake when the stewardess passed to offer refreshments. During a bout of wakefulness, he had explained that a Venezuelan was named after a Venezuelan oil worker he had met on a previous trip home. This fellow had ordered a whisky and soda while waiting at the bar in the airport. It cost five US dollars and he only had a ten-dollar note. So he just drank two. Hence, two whisky and sodas were known as a Venezuelan.

No one on today's flight was drinking except Stevie and the grandmother from Aberdeen. The oil rigs had a strict 'dry' policy, so the drinking only happened on the flight home. For nostalgia's sake, Stevie ordered a Venezuelan; the grandmother ordered a beer and raised her glass to Stevie in the aisle. Stevie raised one of hers in return and smiled, then she sat back and opened her peanuts. The in-flight entertainment began with the news. When oil prices came on the news, you could literally feel every ear in the plane prick up. It was followed by a showing of *Garfield*, an unusual choice for such a raw-looking bunch, although she did remember they had shown *Harry Potter* on the last flight, so perhaps it was some kind of airline policy to show children's movies on this route. Perhaps anything with Steven Seagal might have roused unpredictable energies. Stevie reclined her seat, put on an eye mask and settled in to get some sleep.

The man behind her snorted loudly, startling her awake. Just as she was making herself comfortable again, the man behind snorted again. After a few more sharp, gurgling intakes of breath, Stevie grabbed her napkin and turned to offer it to the snorter, muttering, 'For goodness' sake!' A forearm the size of a Christmas ham was sitting on the armrest behind her. It was colourfully decorated with daggers and skulls and a fanged octopus with mammoth tentacles.

On second thoughts, the snorting really wasn't so bad. Stevie started on the second whisky and soda and settled in to watch the antics of an overfed tabby cat.

One chicken Kiev and half a chocolate mousse later, they were flying over Georgia. Stevie craned her neck for a view of the gorgeous Caucasus Mountains, nature spinning glory despite man's violent assaults on man in the valleys and troughs. The sun was setting fast, lighting the peaks a red gold. They were wild and deserted mountains, not a village to be seen. They would be over Azerbaijan shortly.

**It was dark by the** time they started the descent. The city of Baku was spread below in uneven patches of light; the half-finished moon hung low and orange, and the Caspian was so still it reflected the moon like a spotlight. Poisonous-looking clouds the colour of lint hung in dense, eerie clumps. The reflected moon was bright enough to see the oil tankers lined up in rows on the silver lake, waiting to take their fill. She felt a shiver of excitement: this part of the world held so much fascination for her because of her grandmother's time in Persia, and her mother's—and who could not be transfixed by a place where Zoroastrians and caviar and the currents of history collided? The Great Game had been played out here, and in so many ways it was still being played . . .

Marlena and a hard blond man were at the airport to meet her. Marlena did not introduce the man, who had muscles like brick and a stare as hard, and Stevie did not ask. He was obviously the man they had come to see. Their driver—could his name really be Jumanji?—sped like a demon along the highway towards the city. Through the tinted windows of the black four-wheel drive, Stevie saw a huge oil derrick—known as a 'nodding donkey'—made out of neon lights advertising one of the plethora of petrol stations on the road. It felt a bit like Las Vegas—or at least, the way Vegas must have felt when it was just a desert outpost servicing GIs.

'Nice flight?' Marlena asked, finding the question amusing.

'Fine, thank you,' Stevie replied, suddenly feeling quite worn out. 'Where are we going?'

'I thought dinner in a caravanserai . . . Do you want to go to your hotel first?'

Stevie was longing for a shower and said so. They were driving through the old part of town, surrounded by intricate Moorish-style buildings; they passed a giant 'boom' mansion, now the headquarters of the Azeri national oil company. By the early twentieth century, half of the world's oil production was supplied from Baku, and like bees to the sticky black honey-pot came the Rothschilds, the Nobel brothers, Persians, Russians, Jews, Armenians . . . They built great 'oil boom' mansions in the city, glorious stone structures with styles ranging from imitation-Versailles to Gothic gargoyles. Many were monogrammed with the initials of the oil barons who built them.

They drove through an industrial wasteland called 'Black City' and the driver pointed out the Nobel brothers' house. The once-grand mansion was now a ruin; the park around it was completely overgrown and roamed by wild dogs. A rusting slide and a dilapidated merry-go-round squatted in the front garden, looking sad and sinister as only once-jolly places can. Finally, the Maiden Tower rose ahead of them, and they pulled into a small square in front of a building made of blocks of creamy, honey-coloured stone. The hotel. 'We'll wait in the bar,' said Marlena. 'Don't be long.'

———

**The water was steaming hot** and plentiful. No trouble in Baku, where fire burnt just beneath the earth. Stevie felt the scalding shower cascade over her shoulders, releasing the knots. She turned the taps to icy cold, suppressing a squeal as her skin tingled in protest, then jumped out and towelled herself vigorously dry. The hotel had thoughtfully provided a thick-toothed wooden comb. Stevie picked it up and read the inscription: *Greetings from Siberia*. Wondering if it was convict labour or Siberian birch—or both—that the comb was advertising, she smoothed her mop of hair and applied her Louis Widmer moisturiser; there was no need to eschew the beauty essentials just because the situation was tense. Indeed, Napoleon, on the morning before Waterloo, said to his manservant: 'Dress me slowly for I am in a hurry.' Not that she liked to think of what happened to Napoleon at Waterloo . . .

Stevie glanced at the bed, with its deep red terry-cloth spread with gold border, its black leather pillows, and hoped that sleep would be possible in a bed like that. Someone had left the television on and, in the far corner of the room, Peter Andre was singing. When she looked back, the programme had changed: a man appeared to be strapping explosives to the belly of a female suicide bomber. Stevie hoped it was not an omen. She lined her eyes in black and strapped her knife to her calf. Then she pulled on a pair of dark grey jeans, black leather ankle boots with deceptively good grip and a flat heel, a T-shirt covered in indigo sequins and her navy safari jacket. Finally, she wrapped a pale grey scarf in raw silk loosely around her neck. She was ready.

**Marlena's caravanserai was in the** old town. Originally built as a rest house for travellers taking the Silk Road, the camel stables in the ancient stone courtyard had been converted to private dining nooks, decorated with carpets and flags—Nigerian, Venezuelan and Georgian—and having the great advantage that you could not be overheard. A gnarled fig tree grew at the centre of the courtyard, probably since the beginning of the world. It was bedecked with oil lanterns. Azeri musicians played in one of the alcoves and the scene was charming. The restaurant was, however, deserted. Marlena ordered caviar to start, shashlik to follow, and several bottles of wine.

Marlena's companion was a little more talkative within the privacy of the stone walls. His name, he claimed, was John. It may well have been. He was an American, probably. He ate with his hands, suggesting that he had spent time with the Bedouin. He also spoke Azeri, but not to the waiter, to whom he spoke Russian. Speaking Azeri would draw attention to himself here.

Stevie looked at Marlena. Was this man the key to the problem? Where did they go to from here?

Marlena's expression betrayed nothing. She took a sip from one of the goblets that served as wine glasses, then smiled slyly and reached for her onyx cigarette case. 'I'm getting married.'

Stevie started. Her first reaction—which she was fortunately able to quash in time—was to ask, 'To whom?' Instead, 'That's wonderful,' Stevie managed cautiously. Who knew what Marlena would say or do next?

The bride-to-be lit a cigarette and exhaled into the night. 'Aristo asked me in Monaco and I couldn't think of a reason to say no. So I said yes.'

Stevie hid a smile. She knew enough about Marlena to know that Marlena did not do anything she did not want to do and that she therefore very much wanted to marry her young lover. Marlena suddenly seemed more human and Stevie warmed to her just a little.

'Skorpios will be furious when he finds out, of course, as only Greeks can be,' she added. 'He will talk of revenge and murder and blood and the family honour. But I can survive anything, even his assassins.'

At the word 'assassins', John noticeably pricked up his ears. When Marlena did not elaborate, nor qualify the comment, he said quietly, 'We're pretty keen to get to him too . . .'

Marlena sucked her teeth and tapped her cigarette. 'Now, now, don't you get greedy, Johnny. We're only offering you one treat this evening.'

'Johnny' fell silent. Stevie marvelled at how Marlena handled their menacing and obtuse dinner companion.

'It's a wedding present,' she said to John with a smile, 'although this one is from the bride. I can give you Krok.' She picked up a steel shashlik kebab sword and turned it over in her manicured fingers.

'We would need to know exactly what you have to offer,' he countered, playing it cool. 'We might not be interested.'

'You've been after me for years, John. Don't start playing hard to get now.'

'We need to know what you can bring to the table,' he repeated.

Marlena's eyes glinted and she spread her hands on the table-cloth. 'Well,' she drawled, 'you know the headlines: arms to all countries under embargo, and several groups on your terrorist list; false certificates of end user, hardware to drug runners and smug-glers . . . but all this is peanuts.' Her eyes narrowed. 'What I tell you needs to put Vaughan Krok away forever.'

John matched her stare. 'We can guarantee that,' he said with quiet certainty. 'What have you got?'

'The pirates.' Marlena's long slender fingers reached for her cigarette case. She removed a cigarette and put it to her lips. She took her time lighting it, drawing the string of tension between the three of them tight. 'The pirate gangs operating off the coast of Somalia and Nigeria are involved with Krok. He trains the pirates, arms them, gives them intel. Then he takes the pirated vessels and their cargo, repaints the vessels and sells them under new flags of convenience; the crew is ransomed, the pirates are paid. Some ships simply disappear off the shipping register and become ghost ships, sailing the international waters, providing a safe haven for smugglers and pirates and anyone who wants to stay in the shadows.

'Of course you know all that—or suspect it. Well I can prove it.' She took a long drag on her cigarette. 'Krok and his partners have set up what is basically a stock exchange meets syndicate that funds these pirate attacks off the coast. It's run out of Haradheere, the pirate's lair. Our pirates have been making tens of millions of dollars from ransom payments and the rest. I mean, it's the corridor from Asia to Europe. They're very well positioned. It would be naive not to take advantage of the geophysical resources.'

'We've got an international naval force—' began John, only to be cut off by Marlena.

'Which have only driven the pirates further offshore. This is such a big business that our stock exchange now has investors from the Somali diaspora abroad, as well as everywhere else.' She shot a glance at Stevie. 'Including London. We have some very good clients there. Krok set up the exchange to manage the investments.'

'How many syndicates are there?' asked Stevie, furiously absorbing all the information. Rice would be very interested, if he made it back to work. Stevie pushed her doubts to the back of her mind.

'We started with fifteen four months ago. We now have seventy-two. Only ten have actually been operating at sea. Think of the potential—and not just in Somalia. Nigeria, Southeast Asia, even off the coast of South America. Why not?'

'It's organised crime.'

'Darling, it's a community service. The shares are open to everyone, and anyone can help out—either out at sea or on land, providing materials, money, weapons . . . Haradheere used to be a complete hole, and now those little dusty roads are jammed with shiny new four-wheel drives and men in diamond earrings. I went to a marvellous pirate wedding the last time I was there . . .'

John's voice could have been computer-generated for all the interest and expression in it as he added his bit: 'The Western-backed government of President Sheikh Sharif Ahmed is tied up battling hard-line Islamist rebels.'

Marlena broke in, 'He basically controls a few streets of the capital, not much else. The administration has no influence in Haradheere—piracy pays for almost everything there: public infra-structure like hospitals and schools. The locals depend on piracy and the district gets a percentage of the ransom from ships that have been released.'

'It's smart,' said Stevie. 'If the locals depend on you, they will protect you. How much would an average person make?'

Marlena turned to Stevie. 'I met one lady, a rather wonderful twenty-two-year-old divorcee called Sahra. There she was, lining up to get her share of the ransom from a captured tuna fishing boat. She told me she had contributed a rocket-propelled grenade for the operation, part of her ex-husband's alimony, and that she had made seventy-five thousand dollars in a month.'

Stevie raised her eyebrows. This for a population that existed on two dollars a day. No small temptation.

John turned to Marlena. 'But it's Somalia,' he drawled. 'It's a Spanish fishing vessel, Russian timber carriers . . .'

'Chemical tankers, oil tankers, LPG carriers, nuclear waste, weapons—do I need to spell it out? While piracy was in the hands of Somalis, it was going to be disruptive, painful financially and hard on the unlucky sailors. But Krok is an ambitious man; he has plans.'

John's voice sharpened. 'What kind of plans?'

Marlena smiled. 'Aside from controlling the pirate stock exchange, Vaughan Krok now has his own instructors on the ground, training the better pirates in maritime assaults—and they have, naturally, no end of hardware. The best. In fact, Krok is using the pirate attacks to test weapons and hardware—new GPS, ceramic guns, RPGs, you name it. All things are better tested under pressure. You get a more accurate measure of their strengths and weaknesses. His clients enjoy watching videos of their weapons in action.' She sat back and smiled again. 'It's a great marketing tool.'

Stevie remembered the *Oriana*, the professionalism of the assault, the sophisticated weapons, Skorpios' cool under attack . . .

Marlena stubbed out her cigarette and lit another one; Stevie suddenly understood the other woman was nervous, although she wouldn't show it. Marlena knew that the things she was about to say—the things she had already said—had earned her a death sentence if Krok ever found out. She had crossed the Rubicon. She continued: 'Krok is also heavily invested in shipping insurance. Combined with the ransom payments, the on-selling of the ships themselves and the goods they carry, plus the jump in demand for his weapons, he is doing rather well out of his pirates.'

John stared at her, his hard mind computing and calculating. 'What do they do with the money?'

'They used to use the *hawala* system—before the payments simply got too big.'

Stevie raised her eyebrows. Now that was clever. The *hawala* system was an informal Islamic set-up that had been around since before the eighth century. *Hawala* operated outside the international banking system: if a customer in one country wished to transfer money to another, he went to a broker with details of the person to whom the money was to be sent. This broker contacted another *hawala* broker in the destination country with the amount. The destination broker made the payment to the recipient and the account would be settled later. Although a simple, trust-based system, it was massive, to the tune of two hundred billion dollars a year. *Hawala* brokers didn't ask questions, nor did they keep a detailed paper trail of individual transactions. Ideal if the people involved wished to remain anonymous . . .

Marlena stopped to take a sip of wine. 'The payments eventually got too big and the operation had to evolve. Pretty soon, Lord Sacheverel got involved and used his connections in the City of London to organise transfers of cash from one bank account to another, then another. It was a perfect marriage.' She smiled. 'No one wants to touch a man with a title in England. He is above reproach.'

John nodded once then stared at Marlena. 'What about you? What's your role in all this?'

'Surely you don't think I'm going to give anything away to incriminate myself further.'

'It doesn't matter. We're not that interested in your operations. We want Krok—and maybe this Sacheverel fellow. Your part in it all just helps complete the puzzle for us.'

Marlena sighed, glanced at the moon for a second as if collecting her thoughts, then explained, 'Basically, you could call me the Pirate Queen—only I don't mess with tankers and container ships and all that heavy industry. No, my operation is high-end, clean, and very organised. I pirate luxury yachts to order. You have no idea how long the waiting lists are on some of these massive recreational vessels—especially now that all those Russian billionaires have come into the game. And men like that, well, they're not prepared to wait. And so they come to me. They tell me what they want and I go shopping . . .'

'But surely,' Stevie interjected, 'these yachts are recognisable. Surely Interpol or someone has a watch list out. It can't be that easy to resell them.'

Marlena shot her a contemptuous look. 'I never embark on an operation without having a buyer lined up who is fully aware of exactly what he is purchasing. He gets a small discount on the *cantiere* price, he also knocks eight years off his waiting time. I doubt you could tell many of these gin palaces apart—once we've changed the interiors, given them a few different finishes, repainted and reregistered, they're like new.' She smiled again. 'It is a very profitable business.'

'What about the passengers and crew?' Stevie asked.

'Well, we try never to kill anyone or hurt them too badly. It attracts unwanted attention. We are not that clumsy. But if the crew insist on fighting, we will kill them.' She said it simply, coldly. Stevie had no doubt she meant it. 'The Russians and the Korean crews are the worst for that. Luckily most crews are Brits and Filipinos; we usually just set them adrift in a lifeboat or maroon them on a desert island. It's all very buccaneerish.' She raised an eyebrow and Stevie marvelled at the cool of the woman. She had no trouble picturing her at the head of a band of professional pirates, raiding these floating money boxes in the Mediterranean and the Caribbean. It would be too easy, she thought, for a woman like Marlena. The luxury behemoths would be sitting ducks.

'Krok gets a piece of the action, of course. And in exchange, I get access to the best men and the best firepower.'

John opened his mouth to speak but Marlena cut him off again. It was almost as if she feared she would lose the words if she did not get them out of her head and onto the table.

'Krok's latest thing is surface-to-air missiles.' Stevie sensed John stiffen. 'He has Chechen clients, South American clients, now his focus is on Middle Eastern clients. Somalia is a good way of getting their attention.'

John nodded. 'We can get him on that. Since 2004, a mandatory twenty-five-year sentence is given to anyone who conspires to sell surface-to-air missiles. Even if none of it occurs on US soil. If you're saying what I think you're saying, there will also be conspiracy charges: conspiracy to kill officers and employees of the United States, conspiracy to supply materials to terrorists, conspiracy to supply and use anti-aircraft missiles. We can probably get him on money laundering too. Enough to keep him locked up forever.'

'That's how you got Monzer al-Kassar,' Stevie said quietly. Kassar had been one of the world's most prolific arms dealers and it had seemed he could not be caught. Agents had set up a sting operation, and used the same charges to convict him.

'Like with Monzer, we have years of traced calls, paperwork, everything, but so far we've never managed to get anyone to roll on Krok.' He looked at Marlena. 'What changed your mind?'

'Never *you* mind,' Marlena smiled. 'What matters is that I have.' She glanced at Stevie, her face unreadable in the shadows cast by the ancient fig.

There was a pause as a waiter brought more wine, then John said, 'The fewer people who know the details the better.' He looked pointedly at Stevie.

'She's the reason I'm talking to you,' Marlena snapped, 'so spit.'

'I have two agents in mind. Both very experienced field agents. They'll pose as urgent buyers for—'

'It'll never work.' Marlena sighed impatiently. 'Krok always says that whenever there's any urgency to do something, that always means a trap.' It would take your agents months, if not years, to earn his trust, and I'm not sure even then that they would have the skill. The man is a shark. He can smell the smallest drop of blood in the sea. The last man who tried to betray him was fed to a white pointer.' She drained her glass, lifting her chin and exposing her throat. Her eyes glinted in the lamplight as she put the glass back down on the table. 'The only person who can do this is me. I am already close to him. I'll wear your wire. We'll discuss the SAM shipments, his clients, anything else that is pressing that day—just like any other day.'

Stevie was silent. She preferred the idea of John's agents, but she also knew Marlena was right.

'What if he finds the wire?' she said.

'He won't find it because he won't search me. Why would he? We've worked together for fifteen years. He's never had cause to doubt my loyalty. He has never searched me, and he has never hidden anything from me. He knows I am a creature like him.'

'You were,' Stevie said quietly.

Marlena looked straight at John with her strange eyes. 'This is my show.'

**The breakfast room was on** the top floor of the hotel and opened out onto a terrace. The Caspian glittered just over a tree-lined boulevard and gulls were wheeling over the foreshore. In the half-mist of early morning, tankers moved slowly and powerfully, like elephants at the waterhole; beyond them, hovering over the shining sea, Stevie could see the skeletal platforms of the oil rigs. The room was empty, save for a sad-looking waiter in a polyester burgundy cut-away who hovered around the Bunsen burner, waiting for the stale coffee to warm up. At the sight of the mini breakfast buffet Stevie's spirits rose. Not for long. Although several food types were represented at the buffet, there was very little actual food: the cheese plate consisted of four paper-thin slices of cheddar, three tiny slices of salami made up the meat plate. There were some cucumber slices—maybe six—and a small cup of milk sitting mysteriously apart from the rest of the food.

Stevie took two slices of cucumber and a piece of salami. The waiter, after some persuasion, found a slice of black bread and the palest egg Stevie had ever seen. She was wondering if it was perhaps a seagull egg, when in strode Marlena, in her tight suede jeans and lilac cashmere wrap, smelling of violets and taking the waiter's breath clean away.

She sat at Stevie's table and lit one of her cigarettes. 'Interesting man, our John,' she said, with a strong note of sarcasm in her voice.

'Are they all like that?' Stevie meant, were all the people on the other side of the law chasing Marlena that colourless? It seemed, somehow, an ill-matched game.

Marlena laughed. 'John is particularly stiff. There are others . . .' She drifted off with a glint in her eye that made Stevie pity the men and women who had been assigned to pin this poisonous butterfly to a board.

'Gobustan,' she announced, getting to her feet impatiently. 'There are things we must discuss and we can do it there in safety.'

They roared out in Marlena's Toyota four-wheel drive, heading out towards the oil fields of Mordor. Stevie noticed the car had red diplomatic plates and wondered how Marlena had managed to swing that. She stared out of the window towards the far shore of the Caspian, to Turkmenistan, invisible today. After a time, she asked, 'What is John doing in Baku?'

Marlena glanced at her with a small smile. 'Think of the neighbours,' she replied.

Azerbaijan's neighbours were a feisty lot, thought Stevie: Georgia, Armenia and, of course . . . 'Iran,' Stevie said softly. Marlena did not reply, but Stevie knew she was right: Iran, Islamic Republic and eternal thorn in the side of the Americans. It seemed like the currents of history had crisscrossed the region forever, and they continued to do so. If the famous theory of the geographical pivot of the world had not completely lost currency, and if a navel were to be assigned, a point of stillness around which the energies of the world turned, then that centre of energy had to be Baku, the capital of Azerbaijan, on the shore of the Caspian Sea.

They passed a wild Soviet mural in the confident block colours of propaganda: Atlases in overalls cleaning sturgeon for caviar, building oil rigs, marching under red flags; huge hands cupping oil, firemen, cosmonauts and factory workers—the glories of the Soviet Union now slowly being eaten by concrete cancer. A rusted tank sat in a brown field, next to a beach, complete with rusting lifeguard towers and a mural of people at play. Just off the beach, the oil rigs rose from the sea, a rusted carrier lay dying by the rocks. History, thought Stevie, had not been kind to the Azeris. She supposed it was the curse of natural resources, so well documented.

Massacred by the Turks in World War I, Azeris were then invaded by the Soviets under Lenin. Then came Stalin's mad liquidation of Azeri 'elites', killing an estimated hundred and twenty thousand people out of a population of three million; home videos had Hitler taking a big bite of his Caspian-shaped birthday cake and swallowing Baku. He had set his sights firmly on the Baku oilfields during the war but got bogged down in Stalingrad on the way. Continuing the cake motif, de Gaulle stopped off there on his way to discuss the anticipated slicing up of post-war Europe with

Stalin. The USSR collapsed in 1991 and the Soviets pulled out, leaving carcasses of junk metal and a beach full of the most poisonous snakes in the world, let loose by departing scientists from the nearby poisons laboratory. She remembered that only too well, and shuddered. She would never forget when she herself had been poisoned in St Moritz the previous winter; the feeling of the dark cloud of her poisoned blood closing in on her, lulling her to death, almost succeeding. But for Henning . . .

She missed the man. There was a dull ache in her heart and she realised that it was as simple as that. She missed him and wanted to be with him. What were complications and indecisions in the face of massacre and war, of life and the universe? They were restrictions she had placed on her own heart and her own love that were not real and could vanish at the wave of her hand. The only chains that could bind her were those of her own creation; she was free.

At their last meeting, she had told Henning to leave her alone, to go away. It was too late. This was not a film. Sometimes you could miss chances in life and they didn't come around again.

Suddenly she felt cold despite the desert sun and she turned her gaze to the metal jackets of the oil rigs in the distance. She had messed it all up, realised too late that she loved him. She loved him. With these words, her heart began to ache. Stevie swallowed the lump in her throat and blinked back a tear. These thoughts must be quashed until she was completely alone. She wound down the window and let the air blow through her.

Lakes of warm crude spread along the shores of the Caspian, giving off that distinctive sulfuric smell. In the dustbowl ahead of them were hundreds upon hundreds of old oil derricks, for the most part still, a petrified forest of rusted steel. Marlena swung the jeep down a dirt road that led through the oil field. 'It's not strictly on the way,' she said, 'but I can never come to Baku without visiting Mordor.'

The place could not, thought Stevie, have been special to any-one but Marlena. It was ruined, derelict, with crumbling concrete bunkers and broken boulders. But, as they drove on, Stevie noticed that the black pools of oil reflected the sky like perfect mirrors, and that they were now driving through a field of blue sky and high cloud. It was surreal.

'A bit like being in heaven?' Marlena laughed. 'This is the clos-est I'll ever get.' She stopped the jeep and they jumped out. There was not a soul in sight. Marlena leant over a pool and dipped her finger into the oil. 'It's warm,' she said, 'like the blood of the earth.' She licked her finger. 'Taste it.'

Stevie put her finger in the pool—it was indeed runny and warm—but chose to wipe it on her handkerchief instead.

Marlena grinned at her. 'That's the taste of money.'

Back on the road, they passed several police cars and road-blocks but were waved through every time. 'It's the diplomatic plates,' said Marlena, waving at the last officer. 'Otherwise we'd be ripe for a shakedown every two hundred metres.'

The road ran alongside a huge pipeline running to Tbilisi in Georgia, then Ceyhan, in Turkey; telegraph poles led in long lines to nowhere. A truck piled to bursting with watermelons swerved past them, then another carrying fat-tailed sheep destined, no doubt, for the shish kebab. By the side of the road, a man was roasting a whole bull, skin and all, with a blowtorch. The land was flat and dry and the horizon disappeared into a shimmering silver haze.

Soon they pulled onto another dirt road and drove until they arrived at a dusty grey field dotted with mud craters. It was as deso-late as the moon. 'Gobustan,' announced Marlena, and hopped out.

They could have been the first—or last—two people on earth.

Craters of dried grey mud protruded from the earth. Inside, molten mud bubbled under the methane gas jets. 'Put your hand in,' Marlena said.

Stevie looked at her. Was she mad?

'Go on.'

Stevie moved closer to the crater—she could feel no heat, there was no smell. Carefully she leant forward, one eye still on Marlena, watching for sudden movement, and dipped a finger in. The mud was cold. Stevie dipped her whole hand in. The mud felt glorious—cool and smooth. It made her want to leap in naked in the moonlight. Stevie laughed as a bubble of mud popped and splattered her face.

'It's wonderful for the skin,' said Marlena, dipping both her arms in up to the elbow. She sat back on her haunches, arms drying in front of her, like some glamorous cave woman. Abruptly her smile vanished. 'Stevie, we are doing something very dangerous with Krok. There is no going back from here. John has already set things in motion.'

Although she already knew this, Stevie shuddered. Suddenly things were no longer funny.

'Krok is holding a party for his friends and associates. You can imagine what that means. This is our chance. Clémence is organising it and you're invited.' Marlena pulled out her cigarette case with her muddy fingers—now dry and grey like bones—and lit a cigarette. 'I need you to turn up, as if nothing has changed,' Marlena continued. 'The slightest thing could make him suspicious enough to blow this. We can't risk him changing anything about his operations; it would make my knowledge worthless and jeopardise the chance of his conviction. My life depends on it and suddenly I want to live, very much.' She exhaled a stream of smoke into the desert sky.

'Anyway,' she continued, shaking her head, 'the drama will

centre around the fact that Krok plans to announce my engagement to Aristo and Skorpios knows nothing about it. He will be furious with Krok when he finds out his partner is hosting a celebration for his son, and the woman he forbade his son to marry.' She flashed a smile. 'He won't be thinking that the bride-to-be is out to snare him.'

Stevie wondered if any other woman had used her engagement party to sting a mercenary and doubted it. Marlena was one of a kind.

'Doesn't he wonder what happened to the Medusa we borrowed?' she asked, remembering her flight from Sardinia.

Marlena waved her hand. 'I told him the engines were being repaired in a closed dry dock by a friendly boat mechanic. They are not difficult to replace. Krok's more concerned with finding out who tried to kill him. He thinks it might have been Skorpios. I think his insistence on announcing the engagement in this way is his method of provoking Skorpios into trying again—revealing himself. It would fit with the twisted way Vaughan's mind works.'

Stevie wanted Marlena's plan to work; she wanted the man rendered powerless, crushed, but there was a flaw in her thinking.

'I'm the problem, Marlena. I think Krok is already suspicious of me. If I turn up, it might put him on his guard.'

'What makes you think he suspects you?'

'He may have tried to kill me.'

Marlena raised a narrow eyebrow.

'Twice,' added Stevie, 'although I'm not sure that it was Krok . . .'

Marlena looked out at the distant hills. There was no sound, not even birds. 'The diving accident,' she said finally. 'The cliffs at Bonifacio.'

Stevie nodded. It was amazingly quiet out here, she thought, like the world was on pause.

Marlena kicked a clod of dried mud into the little volcano and watched it sink. 'That was me,' she said, looking up at Stevie. 'I tried to kill you. I thought you were a plant of some kind. I've had that before.'

'What?' Stevie recoiled.

'It wasn't Krok. I filled your tank with the exhaust from the compressor. I thought it was rather neat. Krok found out it was me, of course. He didn't believe you were an agent or anything else—"too vain, too stupid" were his words,' Marlena added, with her old smile of cruel satisfaction. 'He told me to leave you alone. But I saw you snooping about—checking maps, ringing phones, sneaking around outside locked doors. I knew you were up to something—and I was right. When I saw you standing like a little fool at the edge of the cliff, I couldn't resist giving you a little push.' She shrugged resignedly. 'We all have our time to go. I suppose it just wasn't yours.'

Stevie didn't know what to say. She was out in the middle of a desert with a woman who had tried to murder her. Twice. She glanced at the car. It wasn't far, but Marlena had the keys. She felt for her knife, strapped to her calf, and prepared to use it.

'Relax,' Marlena said, noticing Stevie's hand creeping towards the hidden blade. 'If I wanted you dead, I would have already tried.'

Stevie was not convinced. 'That's the point,' she reminded her cautiously. 'You did try.'

'You're no threat to me.' Marlena crushed out her cigarette. 'I need your silence now.' She looked up. 'And your help. I'm going to need friends after this, Stevie, and I won't have many left that I can trust.'

Stevie nodded slowly.

Marlena looked at her watch. A cloud of dust appeared above the dirt track: someone was driving towards the volcanos. Stevie followed the cloud but her eyes couldn't make out the vehicle. It was still too far away. She felt a shiver of fear. 'Company, Marlena?' she asked casually.

Marlena watched the eddy of grey dust and did not reply. As the vehicle drew closer, Stevie realised it was a dirt bike, the figure on it unrecognisable in a silver helmet and sand-coloured jacket as it roared to a stop by the four-wheel drive. The driver jumped off—a tall man, Stevie noted. She felt her mouth go dry with fear. What was Marlena planning?

She stood up, ready to face this new danger head on.

Marlena, who must have sensed her terror, laughed. 'Think of it as reparations, Stevie. Something to say, "I'm sorry I tried to kill you, *chérie*."'

The man lifted off his helmet and grinned. Stevie's blood rushed back to her face—she walked and then began to run towards Henning.

With her feet lifted off the ground, she clung to Henning, enveloped in his tight embrace, hoping he would feel the remorse in her body. Stevie did not know what to say. Fortunately Henning did: 'I see it takes a murderer to bring us together.'

Stevie smiled as he lowered her gently to the ground. 'Well, it's one way to answer the old "how did you two meet" question.'

They stared at each other, dusty faces, silly smiles, out in the desert plains of Central Asia, and time stood still. So still, in fact, that they did not notice the helicopter until it was hovering right above them.

It landed sending up blinding plumes of grey dust. Stevie and Henning covered their mouths and noses. She could just make out Marlena's violet wrap and a glint of gold sunglasses climbing nimbly aboard. As it lifted off the ground, Stevie noticed the golden scorpion painted on the tail.

'Skorpios!' she cried in alarm, expecting the strafing sound of gunfire—it was a trap for both of them.

Henning put his arm on her shoulder and shook his head. 'Aristo,' he said.

They watched the helicopter carry off the husband- and wife-to-be until it was nothing more than a fly-speck in the sky.

'I want to show you something,' Henning said unexpectedly, handing her the bike helmet.

They roared off into the scrubby desert, up towards the cliffs that towered above the plain. Below them now stretched the moon-scape, all dry mud and tussock; a prison, several pipelines and, smudged on the horizon, the oil rigs. Henning headed for a large boulder. 'Watch out for snakes,' he called back with a smile as Stevie made to follow him.

She made a face.

'Look.' He was pointing to some carvings on the back of the rock. 'What do you think they are?'

Stevie peered at them for a moment. 'They look like long-boats, but—'

'Exactly! Vikings.'

'Vikings? Here?' Stevie looked around the arid plain. It seemed unlikely.

'These cliffs were once the coastline. The Caspian was much larger thousands of years ago. Why not?' He shrugged. 'Thor Hey-erdahl told me about them once. He said when he saw them, he actually wept.'

Stevie looked at Henning, his face lit up with passion. There was nothing false about his love of ancient writings and history. That was something true she knew about Henning. Maybe it was enough.

He turned to her and wrapped his arms around her, then took

her hand and led her to another stone. 'This one is very special,' he said. 'It's graffiti.'

'In Latin.'

Henning nodded. 'It was left by a Roman legionnaire. This is the easternmost Latin inscription ever discovered.'

Stevie stopped and looked about her. 'What a strange place this is.' In the distance, the Caspian was a pale, milky blue, and tiny prehistoric-looking lizards ran about the boulders. They found a sliver of shade by a large boulder and sat, enjoying the breeze that blew in from the south. Henning had brought lunch: cold roast chicken and a bottle of white wine wrapped in aluminium foil, two tiny tin cups.

'There's a theory,' began Henning, pouring wine for each of them, 'that the Garden of Eden was not just a metaphor, and that it was in the Aji Chai valley, here in Azerbaijan.'

'Is there evidence?'

'There is some—and if you think about it, these lands have been inhabited for thousands of years. Cave-dwellers occupied the Caspian coast right here from the early Stone Age until deep into the Iron Age. Then Vikings made an appearance at some point—'

'The longboats,' said Stevie with a smile. She loved seeing Henning in full steam.

'Yes, and don't forget Zoroastrianism—one of the first great monotheistic religions—grew here in the sixth century BC, where Zarathustra was quite possibly inspired by the mysterious burning water at Qäsämänli.' He took another sip of wine and lit a Turkish cigarette. Stevie inhaled the smoke and the particular smell of that tobacco triggered memories of Moscow, of danger, and of love.

'Alexander the Great makes an appearance,' Henning was saying, oblivious to the shudders breaking through Stevie, 'followed by an Arab conquest in the eighth century. Islam had arrived, bringing the beautiful stone minarets and caravanserais, all still standing in old Baku. Azerbaijan went on to be devastated by the Mongols and Turkmens—several times, starting in 1225, and was then dragged into the Great Game with the arrival of the Russians in 1795.'

'And who would have thought we would end up here—'

'Playing at Adam and Eve . . .' Henning finished her sentence with a smile.

Stevie looked over and grinned into the dear face. Her heart felt full and she had never known that before. As Henning kissed her deeply, a tiny part of her wondered if it would last, but, for that moment, in the hills outside Baku, deep in Central Asia, with Henning at her side, Stevie was at peace.

# 18

Malaga airport is not the most charming introduction to Spain. Stevie weaved past the English club promoters—fake tans and tits—waving fliers for the next dance party and took her shoulder bag from the carousel. She had arrived alone, dressed in yellow Capri pants and a peach silk shirt, a Pucci scarf around her neck and large pink coral earrings swinging. Krok's drivers were picking up the party guests from the airport and she had to look the part. Her muddy boots from Gobustan would hardly be appropriate.

Clémence had invited Henning to the party but his flight had already been booked and they had to arrive separately. Stevie felt dishonest, concealing what she knew from him, yet there was no conceivable way that Henning could be let in on the operation. She slid over the subjects of Clémence and Marlena and Krok like a drop of water on oil. Henning knew only that her mission to investigate the Kroks was over and that this was, for all intents and purposes, a farewell.

By the luggage carousel, she saw Stéphane struggling with a large Vuitton suitcase and sashayed over. 'Yoohoo, Stéph,' she called, giving him a big smile and ostentatiously not helping him with his bag. Stevie decided she would attach herself to Stéphane. He would be perfect cover.

A fleet of cars was waiting, gathering guests as they arrived and driving them out through the mad, dusty roads, past the mangy chickens and scavenging dogs, the ugly buildings and oily seashore of Malaga itself, and out into the countryside. Stevie rode with Stéphane. From what he had to say about the preparations—he had been hours on the phone with Clémence—the occasion was to be a real extravaganza, a three-day blow-out of serious proportions.

'Is it a birthday?' she asked lightly, holding her fingernails to the light and examining her (hastily self-applied) nail polish. She wondered what the official reason for the party was.

Stéph pursed his lips and shook his head. 'I think it's a comeback.' Stéph was perceptive and canny; he had to be, living life by his wits. 'A sort of "they tried to kill me but I'm back and bigger than ever" party.'

'To reassure the clients,' Stevie said, nodding.

'Exactly.'

'Isn't it a bit risky for all those arms dealers and buyers and whatever to gather in one place for a party?' She kept her tone disinterested, but she did very much wonder.

'Oh, I think the law and other forces have been after Krok's friends for years. They haven't managed to get them before, and nothing's changed.' He changed tone, joking now. 'They are gathering for a private party, nothing more sinister than that, Officer.'

Stevie remembered the Costa and her realisation: evil likes to enjoy itself too.

'I suppose it is just a party.' She shrugged. 'It's not as if they are going to be actually buying missiles by the pool.'

Stéphane raised his eyebrows. 'Don't be so sure about that. I think—' he lowered his voice, but the driver's eyes were on the road and it was unlikely he could hear much '—Krok has something special planned. Clémence was very hush-hush on the phone, but when I saw her in Paris, we had champagne and macaroons at Ladurée and the combination always makes her chatty. She mentioned an exhibition of sorts, and an auction. Krok thinks it will generate more excitement, more notoriety for STORM, and drive the prices of his hardware up. He's probably right too. You don't get many more competitive super-egos in one place than with Krok's pals. They're quite an impressive bunch.'

'Oooh,' said Stevie. 'How exciting, Stéph.' That was not what she really wanted to say.

**Krok's villa was the modestly** named Palacio de las Maravillas (the palace of wonders), a white marble extravaganza overlooking Malaga and the sea. The convoy of cars drove through huge wrought-iron gates set in a wall three metres high. Stevie lowered her window a few inches and breathed in the atmosphere. Inside the compound, the lush grounds and water sprinklers turned the air cool and moist. As they passed the guard house, Stevie counted three mastiffs on patrol, massive creatures with jaws as big as her head, and shuddered. Clémence had invited her to stay at the house for the duration of the festivities; the woman now saw Stevie as the agent of her freedom and was keen to keep her close by. But, as the iron gates swung closed, Stevie couldn't help feeling like the doors of a cage were shutting behind her.

Cocktails were waiting by a pool shaped like a four-leaf clover and tiled with a picture of a gold AK-47 that shimmered every time a finger of wind stroked the surface of the water. A butler in uniform was handing around cigars. 'They're hand-rolled Cubans,' Stevie heard Krok bark over the chatter of the crowd as she and Stéphane joined the festivities. She turned and found her host, massive in a lemon polo shirt, a flesh-coloured bandage covering most of the right side of his face. A white eye-patch hid his right eye and the right hand too was bandaged. Apart from these obvious signs of violence, Krok appeared unharmed. Possibly the changes were an improvement on the original . . .

The butler approached and offered Stéphane a cigar; as he took one, Stevie noticed that the band on them read KROK, and was decorated with a tiny photo of Emile.

Stevie fixed a large smile on her face and drifted towards what she could see of Clémence: a large white hat. She accepted a glass of champagne from a waiter and used the moment to look around, her keen eyes hidden behind large sunglasses purchased especially for the occasion.

The guests were a mixed bunch. The women all heavily bejewelled; most of the men wore pale suits and sunglasses, though there were a few Africans in their national dress, a few Arabs in dishdasha and a small moon-faced man who looked a lot like Kim Jong Il. Stevie's gaze stopped, startled. A man with shoulder-length black hair, silver aviator sunglasses and full military dress uniform with medals stood a little apart from the main group. If she didn't know better, she might have mistaken him for Michael Jackson, but Colonel Muammar Gaddafi of Libya was a very different sort of man. He was surrounded by his infamous female bodyguard, a phalanx of twelve Amazons, all stunning to behold. Stevie allowed herself to stare at the famous grouping a moment longer, then cautiously continued her examination of the party.

She noticed Dado and Lisa Falcone, both as elegant as ever, and Skorpios, his immaculately cut, shark-grey suit, tortoiseshell glasses and powerful head noticeable among the others. Angelina, somewhat incongruously dressed in black, stood beside him, listening intently to the compliments of a small tanned man in cream velvet slippers. Al-Nassar was there with Lamia and his right hand. Marlena was already in place, the life of the party in purple palazzo pyjamas that would have been impossible on anyone else but on Marlena looked spectacular. Aristo was at her side, magnetic in his dark glasses, his brooding frown. Marlena glanced at Stevie and then away. The Pirate Queen had never paid Stevie much attention, and she would not start now. Everything was riding on Marlena's poise.

Stevie felt a cold claw on her arm; Clémence's red lips were mouthing words of welcome. Stevie automatically kissed her cheeks and smiled in return, murmuring, 'Darling, lovely party, oh, but the heat . . .'

The party moved inside as the heat of the day grew fiercer. A huge marble staircase descended to the middle of the foyer; the guests milled at its foot. Stevie was standing with Clémence; Marlena and Krok were nearby. She heard Marlena's ceramic tones reply to Krok's question: 'We're ready when you are, Vaughan. Everyone is on stand-by.' She was holding a large satellite phone that did not go with her delicate silk costume and fuchsia nails.

'Get everyone inside,' Krok barked at her. Guests were gently herded through the house and into a ballroom that quite took Stevie's breath away. It was dazzling white, with elaborately carved cornices in gold. Panels of mother-of-pearl made the walls shimmer, and an enormous white crystal chandelier hung above them from the domed ceiling. It was, Stevie reflected, an unlikely room for such a collection of guests. Possibly she could have imagined the glorious Dame Barbara Cartland, or Imelda Marcos, or even Liberace . . . Last to enter the room, walking by Krok's side, was Colonel Gaddafi.

A fresh glass of champagne appeared before her, hovering under Henning's charming, grinning face. How did he do that— just appear? He had a magician's lightness of movement. The other

thing, thought Stevie as she accepted the offering, was that he
always seemed to manifest at loci where the tension was strongest,
where the magnet had drawn the dark forces and collected them,
where things were about to happen. She wondered whether it was
subconscious . . . There were still so many things that remained
unexplained about Henning but, as he stood there with the sky
in his eyes, she decided that she might quite enjoy finding out the
answers. She was not the sort of woman who could bear a mystery for long; the unknown was risk. However, she did like that he
almost never wore sunglasses.

Her thoughts were interrupted: 'How is Rice?' Henning still
couldn't say the name without a certain hardness creeping into his
voice, but the concern was genuine.

'Out of the coma, thankfully,' said Stevie with a smile, though
her heart still worried for her boss. 'And he is speaking, which is a
great relief. They think there might be some paralysis in his bad leg
but it's a bit early to tell.' She took a quick sip of champagne to stop
the faintest prick of a tear in its tracks. She felt her nose turn pink
and knew Henning would notice. She was not a woman who cried
prettily. 'He was lucky,' she said simply.

'Yes, he was.' Henning's voice was tender, his eyes on her face,
missing nothing of her distress.

Stevie was suddenly and violently so sure of her love that it
startled her. She pulled back. 'I suppose you should flirt with me,'
she said lightly, 'for the benefit of the party guests.'

'Of course.' Henning nodded, amused. 'For the benefit of the
guests.'

Alas for Stevie, before he could begin his work, metal shutters
slid soundlessly down the long windows, shutting off the outside
light. As one the guests turned and looked about. Most were not at
ease with surprises, or the sudden blocking of potential exits. Krok

stepped smiling onto the bandstand—not unaware of the frisson that had run through the crowd—and addressed his guests.

'Welcome to the Palacio de las Maravillas. We are here because we are all men of blood.' Krok paused an instant too long after the word *blood*, and Stevie's heart leapt into her mouth.

*Steady on, Stevie.*

'Valued customers,' he went on, 'and loyal friends. First, I want to announce a piece of news that gladdens my heart.' That pause again, the joyless voice at odds with the words. 'Marlena and Aristotle Skorpios are getting married.' He grinned rather cruelly and Stevie saw his gaze seek Socrates'. The father of the groom didn't move; his face showed no emotion but his skin changed colour, became darker, his rage palpable despite the dark glasses as applause burst forth around him.

'But there is something more important to announce here today,' Krok went on. 'Someone tried to kill me a month ago. Obviously, I am immortal.' There was some appreciative laughter but Krok ignored it. It occurred to Stevie that he probably believed he was. 'What you will see tonight, ladies and gentlemen, will excite and reassure you of the capabilities of STORM to deliver anything, anywhere, no matter the odds stacked against us.'

The lights in the ballroom dimmed and there was a shudder of excitement in the vast room. A massive screen lowered from the ceiling. The STORM logo, a lightning bolt splitting the earth in two, spun into view then disappeared, leaving in its place the image of an ocean at sunset, a huge cargo ship carving white foam through it.

'This is the *Molotov Rostok*, a heavily armed nuclear-waste carrier. For those of you who are interested, she's two thousand, six hundred deadweight tonnage, length seventy-eight point six metres, breadth fifteen point eight, with a cruising speed of twelve knots. She's carrying a thousand drums of high-level radioactive waste. It is guarded by the UEAC troops—some of you will know them from personal experience—' and here Krok smirked '—reputed to be some of the toughest in the world.'

There was a murmur in the crowd again. Stevie tried to find Gaddafi in the dim light but instead caught the eyes of a female bodyguard, shining like a fox's, and quickly turned away. The Colonel was smart to use them; the girls missed nothing.

Krok's voice interrupted her thoughts. 'This, ladies and gentlemen, is happening in real time. Right now, the *Molotov* is transiting Yemeni waters and is on full pirate alert.'

Stevie could guess what was coming but it did not stop the feeling of horror flush up her spine when she saw them: three speedboats zooming out from the left-hand side of the screen, travelling at a furious pace. Even from this distance, Stevie could see that they were Medusas, monster Zodiacs, like the one she herself had driven. The *Molotov* did not stand a chance of outrunning them. The cargo ship noticed the vessels and began to zigzag, a classic anti-piracy manoeuvre that Stevie knew—and so did the men on board probably—was going to be useless.

The guests in the ballroom stood expectantly and watched, drinking champagne, as the men on the *Molotov* prepared to fight— possibly for their lives. Stevie's mouth went dry and she felt weak. There was something so horribly wrong in all of this and she suddenly wanted to be very, very far away. She was only grateful Rice wasn't here to watch it with her. She forced herself to focus on the screen: the image there grew suddenly close—a zoom.

'We have a satellite drone filming this,' went on Krok. 'Marlena calls it in.'

The sun was setting out on that dangerous ocean, glowing a deep red, as if in preparation for the violence to come. The boats fell neatly into line along the port side of the *Molotov*; a figure on the prow of the first boat raised a rocket-propelled grenade and fired into the bridge. There was an explosion, smoke pouring out. The *Molotov* slowed. The vessels zipped in and attached, as quick and light as water skimmers.

Water was pouring furiously from fire hoses, crew rushing about, but in the Palacio de las Maravillas, there was no sound. Stevie remembered the fear she had felt during her own experience with the pirates and pitied the crew. She had been right to assume it had only been a practice run, a warning. Back on the screen, the jets of water seemed to have little effect: the men in the Zodiacs, fitted with masks and amphibious apparatus, rappelled up the vertical walls of the massive ship with suction cups. There was a murmur of appreciation from the crowd. Indeed it was quite something to see.

'We have been training men in maritime assaults and we are providing this as a new service,' Krok intoned. 'The grenades you see on their belts are filled with CS gas—tear gas. Our men, of course, will retain the rebreathers they are wearing. We provide weaponry like the SAM you just saw—also very good for disabling helicopters—and the gas grenades, also available as small bombs, or with sarin.' This caused a stir in the crowd. Chemical weapons were in total contravention to the laws of conventional warfare.

*If that didn't implicate the man . . .*

'I have also developed something I like to call "Greek Fire" . . .' Here he paused, making sure he had the undivided attention of everyone in the room. 'Greek Fire is a chemical spray that can be diffused on water in the case of pursuit by other craft. It has the benefit of burning on water and clinging to anything that comes into contact with it. It's a kind of napalm of the sea. The early trials have been very promising.'

There was a muted round of applause.

'The Medusa speedboats,' Krok continued, 'are a new addition which some of you have already seen in action. Marlena will be taking orders today.' The crowd shifted—probably reaching for their cheque books, thought Stevie. In fact, how *did* one pay for things like SAMs and Medusas? She looked up at Henning; his eyes were fixed on the screen. He would probably know.

By the podium, Marlena's phone rang. She answered, listened for a moment, then: 'I will relay that.' She whispered to Krok, who announced in his ugly booming voice: 'The *Molotov Rostok* has been taken.'

Stevie's heart jumped into her mouth. There were some congratulatory noises for the skill of Krok's assault team, a smattering of applause that sounded to Stevie like so many birds trapped against glass.

Krok clapped his great paws together. 'And now, ladies and gentlemen . . . the auction of the *Molotov Rostok*.'

The idea of a room full of warlords and criminals and dictators and privateers—any of them—getting their hands on a shipload of nuclear waste and a full crew was appalling.

'What do they want with nuclear waste?' Henning whispered, his eyes narrowed. 'They can't make bombs with it can they?'

Stevie shook her head. 'Not nuclear bombs. But they can make dirty bombs, contaminate the area, food and water supplies, terrify the population—like the ones the Chechens threatened to set off in Moscow a few years back.'

Henning nodded. 'I remember.'

The bidding began. Thirty, fifty, seventy million dollars—the bids climbed hard and fast.

Krok, obviously not satisfied with the millions yet, gave a nod. Sacheverel appeared, his shining white head standing out in the crowd. He climbed onto the podium and offered his services as a broker in the negotiations for the hostages, and for the waste—the same services, he reminded the audience, that served Krok so well. If Stevie's stare could kill, the man would have dropped dead on the spot. It took all her self-control to keep calm.

'One hundred million in ransoms alone last year,' broke in Krok with a sly grin. Hands shot up around the room. Krok's grin widened even further.

Stevie prayed that Marlena's device was catching everything, that she would keep her cool, that she would go through with it; that they would not get caught.

In the end, the *Molotov Rostok* went to the moon-faced man for one hundred and seventy-five million dollars.

'Do you think that's Kim Jong Il?' Stevie whispered.

'He has many doubles,' murmured Henning, casting a glance at the new owner of a nuclear-waste carrier, one thousand barrels of waste, and twenty-five hostages. He was beaming. 'But it could be him,' he said finally. 'It's the sort of thing I imagine he would be tempted to buy; the North Koreans are so desperate to be taken seriously and to build their own nuclear bomb. It is not a lovely idea.'

No, thought Stevie to herself, the whole situation was terrifying. And even if they stopped Krok, the other men in this room—most of them—would continue their business as before. And as before, the world would be powerless to stop them.

**A feast had been organised**—a celebration for the newly engaged couple and, of course, for the new owner of the tanker—to be followed, Krok announced, by a *corrida*. Long white tables covered in silver cutlery and crystal glasses were set out under a marquee along one side of the house. A band had struck up a rather improvised version of the wedding march—designed, Stevie knew in her bones, to provoke Skorpios—and the guests and their assorted protection drifted out to lunch. Henning sat on one side of her, Stéphane on the other. Stevie noted with admiration that Marlena had managed to seat herself between the Colonel and Krok. She was on the opposite side of the table, a few seats up from Stevie.

It was too hot to eat; Stevie sipped water and champagne and looked languidly about as a prawn mousse was deposited by white gloves on the plate in front of her. It was served in a massive crystal goblet and looked like sorbet. She tinkled the goblet lightly with her spoon then set it down and turned to Stéphane. 'Darling, what's a *corrida*?'

Stéphane turned to her, slightly annoyed at having been disturbed from a close examination of the jewels of the African warlord's wife seated beside him. 'A bullfight, Stevie, men in boleros, red capes. Lots of *olé*.'

The warlord's wife turned to him and in a slow deep voice asked, 'Will there be blood?'

Stéphane nodded vigorously. 'Lots of it. Both man and beast's, if it is a good fight.'

This comment caught the attention of the men opposite and Stevie found herself drawn into conversation with Krok and the Korean guest. 'Explain, please,' he said, his eyes sharp and focused behind the tea-dark lenses of his large glasses.

Stéphane glanced quickly at Krok to make sure he had permission to take the floor. 'It is a supreme test of skill. The Spaniards are mad for it—it's in their blood. The bulls are bred especially for the fights by families who have been doing it for generations. The matadors also usually come from a long line of bullfighters and they are passionate to the point of obsession about their bulls.'

'A dynastic pursuit,' observed the Korean with growing interest.

Stéphane nodded deferentially. 'Quite. The greater the skill of the matador, the more exciting the fight, the more dangerous it is. And then, of course, the kill must be perfect.'

'The kill?' boomed the warlord's wife, licking her lips.

Inside, Stevie shrank from her and those carnivorous lips that looked as if they might strip the very flesh from her bones.

Stéphane nodded again. 'The matador has a slim sword called an *estoque*. When the timing is right—and the *corrida* is all about timing—the matador must plunge the sword between the shoulder blades and through the heart, hoping for a clean, swift kill. It's called *estocada*.'

After a short pause, the Korean asked, 'And is it ever the other way around? Does the bull ever kill the man, or is it all just for spectacle?'

'The bull does on occasion gore the matador. There are many injuries and occasionally—rarely, but it happens—the bull kills the killer.'

The Korean sat back with a satisfied sigh and smiled. He spread his short fingers and turned to Krok. 'This I would very much like to see,' he said quietly.

Krok smiled. 'Perhaps you will be lucky enough this afternoon.'

'I would consider it a very good omen for our future business if this were to transpire.'

Stevie's mouth went dry; she was quick to read between the lines of conversation and knew exactly what the man was really saying. He was asking Krok to arrange for the matador to die in the ring. That wasn't in Krok's power, Stevie knew, but the cruel desire of the Korean shocked her. It shouldn't have, but even now, after all she had lived through in her line of work, she was not yet immune to certain human responses.

The main course was served, whole quails with detached, feathered heads resting on the plate where once the live head had been. The effect was very odd and quite unappetising. She saw that Stéphane didn't touch his meat; Henning leant in and whispered, 'The heads don't match.'

'Pardon?'

'The heads of the birds don't belong to the bodies. The meat is quail—the heads belong to woodcocks. The heads and bodies don't match!'

Stevie had forgotten Henning's keen interest in ornithology. For some reason the mismatch bothered her as much as it seemed to bother him. She supposed that all was not as it seemed in the Palacio de las Maravillas, and that was true of the lunch as well. She swallowed and picked up her fork.

# 19

They were all issued grand commemorative tickets for the *corrida*, stiff gold-embossed card with a painting of a matador passing a huge black bull. Stevie wasn't sure how she would feel about the bullfight; she had never attended one, never wanted to see a mad bull pitted against a matador, but there was no escaping this one. Krok had taken all the '*sombra*' tickets for the guests, the shaded seats being far more comfortable in the heat than the cheaper '*sol*' ones. The round, whitewashed arena was filled with smooth sand and a tier of wooden seating rose up steeply, affording everyone a good view.

Their seats were ringside, elevated above the action—above the picadors and trainers—but right at the front. The heavy wooden doors of the arena were right beside them and Henning took his place at the railing. Next to him, the theatre was cut away and he had a perfect view of the sand and the action below.

'Amazing seats.' Stevie raised an eyebrow, feeling more nervous than she cared to admit. She glanced around at the crowd. The regular spectators had brought their own hampers and cushions, the women had fans. Everyone was dressed for a party, Krok's guests and the locals alike. The matador was very famous and the fight would be epic, historic, something they could tell their children and grandchildren about.

As they sat waiting for the picadors, Stevie looked about. All the women spectators opposite her in the *sol* seats were fanning themselves with their lace and paper fans. It looked like a thousand butterflies were resting there, fluttering delicately. Circe slid into her seat—Marlena could only be Circe—in a black lace dress that clung to her like skin to a snake. Aristo was at her side, a figure of devotion and ferocity, the maleness of his defiance and desire matching that of the bullring and the macho matadors. Everyone facing death in the ring; men of blood, every one, just as Krok had said; she was surrounded by them. Well, perhaps not Henning. He was not a man of blood. It was not as straightforward as that.

There was a ripple of fans and voices as the huge wooden gates opened and the picadors on their horses rode slowly into the ring. The picadors wore black hats and carried lances decorated with paper garlands. Their horses were covered in heavy mattress-like quilted material. Stevie whispered to Henning, 'Why are the horses wearing blankets?'

Henning leant in—possibly closer than strictly necessary. 'It's to save their bellies from the horns of the bulls.'

'I thought it was the matador who dealt with the bull?'

'Ultimately. But the horses are there to warm up the bull, give him a taste for goring and ramming. The picadors stab the bull a few times, to rouse him even more.'

This was a true blood sport. Stevie's sensibility recoiled but she would reserve her judgement until she had witnessed the whole spectacle.

A smaller door giving onto the ring opened and there was a hush. Suddenly, like a locomotive from a tunnel, rushed the black bull. '*Toro! Toro! Toro!*' shouted the crowd as the beast stormed into the ring, clouds of sand flying up from its hooves. The bull caught sight of the horse and stopped. It lowered its head and charged, catching the horse under the belly with its horns and lifting the animal high into the air, knocking it and its rider into the side of the arena. The picador whirled and gave a stab at the bull with his spear, drawing first blood.

The bull drew back, changed direction, and charged around the ring angrily, looking for something else to charge. He found the second horse and it too was rammed. The picador stabbed the other side and the bull charged off, heading straight for the first horse and rider, barely recovered from the previous assault. The rider struggled to turn the horse side on, the bull gored, the horse and rider were knocked to the ground in a cloud of dust.

Like swallows, the other picadors darted from behind the wooden barriers armed with their stiff pink and yellow capes. They dashed about, trying to distract the bull, to draw him away from the fallen pair. The bull snorted and bucked, charging first one then the other. The spectators groaned as one picador fell and was almost trampled under the bull's thundering hooves. He rolled away, another picador jumping in to distract the bull. There was a murmuring in the crowd.

Henning muttered, 'The crowd is anxious. There's word the bull is mad—*loco*—the way he went for the horses and the picadors. The crowd want the fight stopped.'

'Can they do that?'

'The crowd carry the bullfighting tradition within them. If a bull is unacceptable to them—or a matador for that matter—they can stop the fight.'

The horses had left the ring and the picadors and trainers were in deep conversation by the side of the ring.

'They're saying this beast comes from a long line of dangerous bulls. His father gored seven *toreros*, one of whom died. It will ultimately be up to Jesulin, the matador, to decide. He is young, and passionate about his art.'

'I think you would have to be.'

Stevie watched as the bull raced around the arena, sand flying up around him, bucking and snorting. He was a terrifying sight, related more to the Minotaur than to any bovine creature she was familiar with. Finally, the bull was locked back into its pen. Indecision, and the crowd was growing restless. Stevie's eyes found Krok, sitting between Skorpios and the new owner of the *Molotov Rostok*. He beckoned to one of the trainers, who approached. Krok said something to him and the man shook his head. Krok spoke again, good eye bulging now. This time the man removed his hat and, after a pause, gave a single tiny nod, turned and descended to the ring.

The crowd, impatient now for a decision—this bull or another—began to stamp its feet. The whole wooden arena shuddered with every pulse, the angry heart of tradition beating in the stifling heat. And then Jesulin walked into the ring.

A cheer that became a scream broke loose from the crowd; even Stevie gasped. It was as if all the rock gods and macho fighters of history had combined in one lean, dark-haired man. His presence made the air around him quiver. He would have been five foot ten at the very most, and yet he was a giant. He was dressed all in white, the gold embroidery on his short jacket and toreador pants glinting in the afternoon sun. He wore a black hat and a cape, and carried the long thin sword of the *torero*. He bowed briefly to the mayor, then searched the audience for Krok, who had set himself up like a prince in his box. Jesulin nodded his head to him in acknowledgement.

The young matador's posture was erect, almost that of a dancer, and indeed on his feet he wore what looked like embroidered black ballet slippers.

Stevie's pulse raced and she felt a surge of adrenaline. She did not want to be excited by the bullfight—everything about it repulsed her—and yet there, that Spanish afternoon, with a thundering beast, the smell of smoke and sage, Jesulin in the ring, she couldn't help but be caught up in it.

His eyes roamed the ring, cap in hand now. Stevie watched his face transfixed, and, light as dust, his eyes came to rest on hers. They burnt as black as coal and Stevie caught her breath. Then the gaze was gone. Stevie felt curiously shaken. Had she imagined that strange exchange of energy?

Jesulin slowly removed his cape and hat, and prepared his red cape. He walked solemnly, confidently towards the bull's gate. About twenty metres from the gate he stopped and got down on one knee. The crowd rippled with awe. It was an extraordinarily dangerous move, especially with such a strong and unpredictable bull. Jesulin held his cape out, supported by his sword, and took a moment. Stevie could almost feel the fire of concentration from where she sat.

He gave a small, sharp nod and the gate swung open. Then the thunder of hooves and the rush of one tonne of beast, half obscured by an inferno of dust. Jesulin, on the ground in front of the bull, spun like a diamond on his knee and the bull passed within centimetres of his body. He arched his back, accentuating the peril for the crowd, real as it was. The crowd, in turn, went wild. The bull reared to a stop, turned like lightning and froze. Eyes on his tormentor, he lowered his head and pawed the earth. Time slowed to match the tempo of the heavy black hoof; the crowd was silent.

The matador rose and stood squarely in front of the bull, chest raised in defiance, his motionless body a challenge to the beast. Suddenly the bull charged. Still the matador did not move, held his ground as the locomotive steamed towards him, long sharp horns aimed for the man's guts. The bull was three feet away; the matador twisted like a dervish, whirling his cape out to the side. The bull thundered through, snorting in fury at his horns having found no flesh, only the rippling cape and air. Stevie suddenly didn't want to watch the rest of the fight; she did not want to be in that ring of blood on that hot afternoon watching a man and a bull dance with death. But there was no way out.

Henning glanced at her. 'You look pale,' he said quietly. 'Is it the fight?' Stevie nodded and Henning reached out and took her hand in his.

The man next to Stevie, a handsome older Spaniard in a flat cap, turned and offered her a beer and a *jamon* sandwich from his picnic hamper. Stevie gratefully accepted. Perhaps it would help. 'It's the *tercio de muerte*,' he said, opening a beer for Henning too. 'The third of death.'

Stevie noticed foam on one side of the bull's mouth and she pointed it out to her new friend. 'What is that?'

The man's eyes narrowed. 'That is a bad sign. *Es un toro loco* . . . or they have drugged him.' He nudged a fat man in a fedora whose face hardened as he too noticed the pinkish foam on the bull's mouth.

'That is not a tranquillised bull,' the man in the fedora said. 'He is no kitten. He is a mad one. If they drugged him, it wasn't to weaken him.'

Stevie's eyes widened. 'What are you saying?'

The man in the fedora looked away, disgust on his face.

The bull charged again, and this time the tip of his horn caught the matador's shoulder blade, ripping the brocade jacket and opening a weeping red gash on the man's shoulder. Jesulin flipped and fell. The bull thundered up to him—out ran the *banderilleros* with their pink capes, trying desperately to distract the beast, to draw his fury towards them and forget the matador.

The bull would not be swayed. He charged through the men, scattering them like flies and made straight for Jesulin. The matador jumped to his feet and held out his cape, passing the wild bull close to his body, spinning to meet him on his way back. The crowd was in an uproar: they had never seen a bull so aggressive, so strong.

The bull charged again and Jesulin skipped a step or two backwards, passing him again. The matador was right below Stevie; she could see the sweat on his face, the sheen of pain, the determination. She could not swallow.

The bull came again, and this time it found Jesulin, the right horn piercing him like butter as the beast tossed him into the air. Stevie cried out, jumping to her feet; Henning and the rest of the crowd leapt up too. The *banderilleros* rushed in but no one could get close to the bull. Jesulin lay limp on the sand. The bull picked him up again with his horns and once more tossed him into the air. Stevie's heart was in her mouth; it was a terrible spectacle. Her eyes roamed the crowd for help and found Krok and his horrid guests.

The look on the mad mercenary's face, the anticipation, the satisfaction, told her everything she needed to know. She turned away. 'Krok's done this,' she said to Henning. 'He's done something to the bull to make him crazy, to kill the matador, to please the Korean.'

She gave a cry as the bull rushed towards the wooden barrier with Jesulin on his horns, the broken man motionless now. 'He wants to crush Jesulin against the wall,' whispered Stevie, terror rising. There was nothing she could do—she could only watch this drawn-out murder.

The man in the fedora next to her turned. 'Do you know who has done this to the bull?' he asked.

Stevie nodded. '*Si*,' she said, turning her head towards the box. '*Es él*'.

The man in the hat followed her gaze. Skorpios was staring back at them and Stevie turned quickly away, frightened.

Her neighbour in the fedora pointed at Skorpios. 'Him?'

Stevie shook her head. She stood and went to the railing, pointing straight at Krok. '*Es él*,' she repeated quietly.

The man in the fedora began to yell at the crowd. 'He has drugged the bull, the one-eyed *pirata* has drugged the bull.'

The crowd stomped and roared in anger. Krok stood and made as if to exit but all eyes in the ring were on him now, and he sat back down and pretended to ignore the outrage. His white knight unbuttoned his jacket and rested a hand on his holster.

A slow, rhythmic stamping began in the crowd, growing heavier and faster until the whole place was shaking. The bull snorted and began his charge. Stevie turned to see the creature bear down on the wall. The spectators stood, eyes wide with horror, unable to interfere in the events unfolding before them. Stevie went to step away from the railing—she had noticed she was leaning on a simple bolted gate, and it made her nervous—when Skorpios appeared beside her. He offered his arm to help her move away, quickly, before the bull crashed into the barrier, then grabbed her elbow before she could refuse. To Stevie's horror, the little gate swung open. The grip held her a moment then thrust her sharply backwards and let go. Stevie tumbled into the bullring.

She hit the sand with her shoulder, whirled around still on her back and was faced with the thundering hoofs of the bull. It snorted in fury, and kept on coming. Stevie curled into a tight ball, closed her eyes and tried not to anticipate what it would feel like to be gored by the beast, to be torn apart, trampled—to have everything end here in a dusty ring in Spain. Inside her head there was nothing, only the heat, the smell of manure and sweat and dust, and a wild prickling on her skin as it waited to be pierced. Then she opened her eyes. She decided she wanted to see death coming. There would be time enough for endless black oblivion.

Like a cat, Henning landed on the sand right in front of her and drew himself up to his full six foot three. The bull saw him drop into the kill zone and this time he stopped, one wild eyeball on the new arrival, so much bigger than the first. Henning reached slowly to the side, ever so slowly, and picked up a pink and yellow cape dropped by a *banderillero*. Stevie wanted to scream his name, tell him to get back, flee—*Don't be a fool, Henning*—but she knew that any sound could provoke the bull, could put them both in even more danger. Her body produced sweat instead, rivulets that stung her eyes and blurred what was happening in front of her. Henning dashed to the left, away from her. She saw the bull, the dust, Jesulin's body now dropping to the ground, the bull snorting, charging at Henning now, his back to the wall . . .

The crowd screamed in one voice, a terrible roar. Like a gymnast on a vault, Henning flew upwards. For a moment, he was silhouetted against the cloudless blue of the afternoon sky and for Stevie, looking up from the dust, it was as if he was flying. Then his body fell, hitting the barrier with a crash before bumping down onto the sand next to her.

The bull smashed into the barrier and there was a gunshot, the sound ricocheting through the stadium, joining the rushing sound in Stevie's ears. The bull collapsed between them, crushing Stevie's arm. She saw a fountain of blood spout between its eyes, the blood staining the sand around them red. The bull's body hid Henning from view. Her arm was trapped under the animal, electric flashes of pain told her it was broken but she didn't care; she felt completely removed from her body. It was already a carcass. The blood was seeping around her too now, she felt it, sticky and warm. She couldn't move, although she was sure there was nothing wrong with the rest of her body.

Someone—was it Jesulin?—rolled the bull off her arm and drew her to her feet; the sound of sirens. She looked down. The bull and the red cloud around him had swallowed Henning, who was motionless beside the beast. He lay as if sleeping, on his stomach, his head turned to one side for breath. She watched in horror as flowers of blood bloomed on his back. She collapsed onto her knees, reaching for him with her good arm, reaching for his neck to find a pulse as if for a hand-hold on a Corsican cliff, but someone was holding her back. The paramedics arrived in a cloud of dust and moved her aside, sat her down. She watched, numb to everything, as they lifted Henning onto a stretcher and put an oxygen mask over his face. Her vision swam. The last thing she felt was a pair of strong hands grasping her under the arms and dragging her away from Henning and all the blood.

# 20

A sleek yacht with a gleaming ebony hull steamed out to sea under a charcoal-wash sky. Her sails were black and she cut towards the open sea with purpose despite the weather, despite the fact that she was the only boat going out that afternoon. The autumn storms had already begun to pound the coast of the Hebrides and there was a freezing wind. Aboard the boat, a party of people, all beautifully dressed, all in black. Some huddled around the wheel in their woollen overcoats, others had gone inside to the warm light. A sailor handed around a silver tray of whisky: short measures in simple pewter cups—the same colour as the sky. His feet were sure as the boat bucked. Nobody refused a glass.

His name was murmured by every drinker, whispered, mouthed, declared. Faces were pale but no one was seasick. It was Henning's funeral and Stevie found it hard to raise her eyes and look at the horizon. They stung from hours of weeping, the lids chafed red. She had lined them in black although she knew they would run to mud when the fresh tears began to fall.

Somewhere out at sea, the schooner slowed; the faraway cliffs loomed like monuments, like a magnificent tombstone. Henning would have liked the view. A requiem began to play, not competing with the howling wind, but almost dancing with it, using its power to soar higher into the air, to spread further its lament. The dear body was ashes now and Iris held them in a stone jar. She was as pale as milk and thin as a blade; it seemed even the wind might snap her. It was unnatural to survive your child and Stevie would not have wished that fate on anyone.

Iris wore a black fur collar on a black coat, floor-length, with a double breast of onyx buttons. On her left shoulder she wore a large jewelled panther. The black netting she wore over her eyes did not hide enough of the sorrow in them. She stood at the stern, downwind of the gale, cradling the jar in her left arm. She removed her glove and the wind took it, spinning it twice before dropping it into the sea. Henning's mother opened the jar and took out a hand-ful of ash. She lifted her fist to the sky and then released it. The wind caught the matter and lifted it, spread it like music, carried it far. Henning had returned to the universe, to God, to eternity, in handfuls of ash. His remains made a cloud in the sky darker than all the others, before the wind tore it to strips and set him free.

Stevie began to sob, this time uncontrollably. She kicked off her ballet slippers and half ran to the prow of the boat, her bare feet clinging to the wet wooden deck. She needed to be away from the other mourners. The tulle in her black ballgown billowed up around her and she fought it down with freezing hands. On top, she wore a cable-knit jumper that she had dyed black, her broken arm in a sling. The jumper did little to keep out the wind, but Stevie didn't feel a thing.

She sat at the prow, her arms on the railing, her bare feet hanging over the side. The tip of a wave caught them for a moment, then fell back. Alone and unseen, she opened her mouth in a silent scream of agony, tears pouring down her face. She thought she might die. *Henning.* There had been another boat—a ferry, a frozen lake, a rope of gold, a beginning . . . And now the end had come and it was on a boat again but everything was different. Too soon, too late. The chop and spray of the waves wet her through but she could not move. Nothing mattered anymore; the world for her was dead.

She looked back at Iris, still standing on the stern. She watched as Henning's mother reached up to her chignon and pulled out the comb that held it. Her hair tumbled down and blew out with the wind as she shook it free.

Stevie stared; she suddenly remembered the Sardinian tradition: *Sciogliere i capelli al cimitero significa vendetta*. When a woman lets her hair down by the fresh grave of her son or father or husband, she is asking for revenge. Someone at the funeral must undertake to carry it out. Did Iris know what she was asking when she took out her comb? The grieving woman turned and caught Stevie's gaze. She held it for a second before turning away—but a second was enough for Stevie to know what Iris wanted. It was what she wanted too.

With no words, someone placed a heavy black overcoat around her slim shoulders. It was David Rice. He sat down beside her on the tossing prow and encircled Stevie with his arms. He held her so tightly she could hardly breathe and she was grateful. She felt that David's arms were the only thing holding her together right now, the only thing stopping her from jumping into the sea, from evaporating like her lover into clouds of cinder. She put her exhausted head on David's shoulder and closed her eyes. Her face was streaked black, but the tears had dried.

Rice let her rest there a moment then reached into the pocket of the overcoat and drew out a small red leather box. 'This came for you this morning.'

Stevie sat up and opened her eyes. The box was from Cartier. 'Who . . .?'

Rice shook his head. 'It came by courier direct from the shop.'

Stevie took the box gingerly. In the risk assessment business, mystery gifts were to be treated with extreme caution. Inside was a jewelled brooch in the shape of an owl. Underneath the brooch was a small scrap of blue tissue paper in the shape of an H. Stevie picked it up with trembling fingers; it disintegrated with her touch. She looked up at Rice, her lungs so tight she could hardly breathe. 'It's from Henning,' she gulped, her head spinning now. 'It's a message.' She paused to take a slow breath. Could it be possible? She had lain next to the bleeding body, seen the screaming headlines about the fatal goring in the Spanish papers—but the owl . . . 'He's not dead, is he?' she whispered finally.

Rice put a heavy hand on her shoulder. 'Don't do this to yourself, Stevie. It will only hurt twice as much. Henning is dead. You have to grieve, then move on.'

But Stevie was no longer listening. The blood and the wind in her ears rushed out all coherent thoughts.

*If . . . Why? How?! When? Where? WHY?*

The boat was coming in to port now and darkness was falling around them. In the half-light, the black ship with its black sails was almost invisible. Did Iris know? She had to find her. Henning's mother was walking down the gangplank, a handsome older man with thick silver hair was supporting her with a hand under her elbow. Stevie called out to her. Iris turned and her veiled eyes met Stevie's, then she looked away and kept on walking. Stevie rushed to the stern of the boat, but Iris had disappeared into the night.

# 21

Stevie did not know what to do, and half the time she felt she was going mad. Had she imagined the pale blue H made of tissue? But there was the owl brooch, sitting in its box. David disagreed, but to her it was proof that Henning was not dead. Who else could have sent it? No one else had a reason to. He wanted her to know. Stevie couldn't bring herself to wear the jewelled bird; her mind was a mass of contradictions and confusion that drove her wild and would not let her sleep. She was bewildered—elated that Henning was alive, and angry that he was pretending to be dead; she was afraid of why he had to pretend, afraid of how bad his injuries were, guilty that he had been hurt trying to save her, and unsure if she would ever see him again . . .

David Rice had opened his London flat to her, and she was to stay there as long as she wanted. Stevie knew it was his sanctuary and the offer meant a lot to her. Unfortunately, David was in Herefordshire; minor health complications had him on a forced rest cure, uncertain of a return date. Stevie roamed the rooms of his flat—even a few months ago, she would have been fascinated by every object in them, little clues to the private life of her boss that he kept so well hidden. But now it only made her more melancholy, reminded her of how close she had come to losing David too. Her world was in turmoil and nothing felt as it should be. And so she mostly stayed inside and ate almost nothing, drank only camomile tea with honey, or whisky. She hunted down Iris' telephone numbers and called them at different times throughout the day, but none of them were ever answered. Mostly, she sat on the Persian rug and watched the rain, and the cars moving about on the street below. When she did leave the flat, Stevie wandered the streets for hours, aimlessly, most often drawn to the river with its flat grey face and slow-moving traffic.

One day, standing in a mist of cloud and drizzle, Stevie found herself in front of the decommissioned submarine that Lord Sacheverel used as his office. It was besieged with reporters, cameramen, vans with radar dishes from a dozen different news services. They were lying in wait, thought Stevie. She stood there, the drizzle now gentle rain seeping through her cotton jacket, trickling downher neck, waiting with them. She remembered the party at his *palazzo*, the terrible frescoes of Nessus and Deianeira and the burning Heracles. She thought she understood now how Deianeira must have felt when she realised what she had done to her husband . . .

The door to the submarine opened and Sacheverel's white head appeared. He surveyed the crowd without interest and opened a large black umbrella. The pack pounced on him, baying like beagles, but Stevie did not stay to watch. She turned and kept walking downriver.

The next morning the headlines screamed their outrage at Lord Sacheverel and the Somali pirate connection: investigations would be pursued, pulpits were pounded, politicians made statement after statement of condemnation, all signifying, to Stevie, nothing. None of it seemed to matter anymore. It was as if the events of the last month had happened to someone else. She read about the arrest of Vaughan Krok. Federal agents had swooped on him at his Spanish palace and taken him away to an undisclosed location of indeterminate jurisdiction. A picture of him from the Reuters stringer showed him with a pillowcase over his head, a hooded bird of prey stumbling in chains, freckled red forearms and pale polo shirt identifying him as clearly as wing markings. Stevie felt a tiny flare of satisfaction, but the feeling died as quickly as it had come.

Marlena's wedding invitation caught her eye. It was sitting on the mantelpiece, embossed gold on thick card. It had come by courier and Marlena had written in thick black letters across it *PLEASE COME, STEVIE*, and signed it with an M. Stevie stared at it for a long time, then put it aside. Marlena had wanted to postpone the wedding in deference to Henning's accident, but Stevie had begged her not to. Who knew what Skorpios could dream up to stop the union going ahead in that time? Marlena and Aristo had to marry as quickly as possible. The wedding was in two days' time, in Monaco, but Stevie knew she wouldn't go. She did not like to think about love right now, when her own heart was in such turmoil. Happy Marlena who was so sure of her affections, and happy Aristo who had found the love of his life.

On the day before their wedding, Stevie found herself walking through Hyde Park, trying to ignore the signs of an early autumn this year. If Henning was alive, she thought, he would be badly hurt. She had seen his injuries with her own eyes in the bullring. However, it seemed that he could communicate if he was able to arrange for the owl brooch to be sent to her. This was a good sign—unless the brooch was not from him at all, and it was all a horrible practical joke. Stevie shook her head. She had to stop torturing herself with these thoughts. She should focus on Marlena's wedding instead.

Her intention that morning had been to head over to Bond Street and see if she could find a wedding present—although she wasn't quite sure what one bought a pirate queen on such an occasion, the effort would distract her. In the end, she settled on a single earring, a large pearl hanging from a thin, golden chain. Stevie felt it was elegant, and yet piratical. She had it wrapped, and organised for it to be sent to Monte Carlo. It felt like the first step towards a recovery of some sort—life did indeed go on.

Her fragile equilibrium lasted until she arrived back at David's flat, poured herself a whisky and turned on the television. Some holidaymaker's footage, a little shaky, but perfectly clear: Marlena on the Riva, Aristo on the dock, the fireball, the waving scarf above the water. The bride-to-be incinerated on the eve of her wedding.

*The horror.*

For a second, Krok's face flashed in her mind.

*Could he have arranged an assassination from an interrogation cell?*

No. She knew in her bones it was not him. She remembered only too well Socrates Skorpios' threat to kill Marlena if Aristo did not leave her, and there was no doubt in Stevie's mind: Skorpios would not be defied, not even by his own son, and so he had murdered Aristo's fiancée. Icy rage and deep sorrow flushed through her body in equal measures. The man was a monster, a beautifully dressed, urbane, sophisticated monster. She turned from the television in disgust and began to cry.

Days later, Stevie's phone rang. A private number. 'Stevie Duveen,' she answered cautiously.

'Stevie.' It was Iris. 'I need to talk to you. Will you have lunch with me tomorrow?'

'Where?' Stevie's heart thudded with anticipation. Perhaps Iris would have news about Henning.

'Paris. In the Bar Vendôme at the Ritz. Let's make it noon.'

———

At exactly twelve o'clock, Stevie walked across Place Vendôme and into the Ritz. Over her shoulders she wore a black tweed Chanel jacket that had belonged to her grandmother. The skirt had gone up in flames long ago in an incident that had never been explained to Stevie's satisfaction by its former owner. So, instead of a matching skirt, she wore her leather trousers, the ones purchased in Zurich and made infamous when she chased down a would-be assassin at the ice polo in St Moritz. She wore the owl brooch pinned to her jacket. Her broken arm was in a white silk sling.

Iris was waiting for her at a round table by the window, half hidden by some indoor greenery and a gold window drape. She rose to kiss Stevie, sleek as a sword in a grey cashmere dress and enormous pearls.

'Thank you for coming, Stevie. I didn't think it was wise to say too much over the telephone.'

The waiter brought two plates of *oeuf en gelée* and a bottle of Sancerre. When he had gone, Stevie took a sip of the wine and looked up at Iris. 'He's not dead, is he?' she said softly.

Iris shook her head, her lips pursed.

'So . . .?' asked Stevie, the rest of her question dying on her lips under the weight of so many others.

'Henning is very badly hurt,' began Iris, her eyes shining with tears now. 'He's in a clinic where they are doing the best they can. He has a punctured lung, ruptured intestines and blood poisoning.'

Stevie listened, her eyes widening in horror.

'Even if he pulls through,' went on Henning's mother, 'he may never walk again.' The elegant woman's tears spilt down her cheeks, the pearls of sorrow, and Stevie felt her own eyes sting. 'Why didn't you tell me at the funeral?'

Iris reached into her purse and pulled out a silver cigarette case. 'People were watching. I couldn't take the risk.'

'What do you mean, Iris?' Stevie pressed her. 'What's going on? Why is Henning pretending to be dead?' Stevie refused a cigarette with a small shake of her head. She sat back into the wine-red chair, her mind teeming with wild thoughts. Outside the dark clouds had gathered and were rumbling, threatening rain. It felt like dusk already.

'There are reasons why it was a good opportunity for certain people to think Henning is dead.' Iris exhaled a stream of smoke and turned her dark eyes on Stevie. 'It's safer that way.'

'Who are these people, Iris? What do they want with Henning?'

'That is as much as I can say, Stevie. The rest is Henning's story and it is his to tell, not mine.' She added softly, 'I'm sorry, Stevie.'

Stevie turned away and stared out of the window. Outside the rain had begun to fall in fat, heavy drops and the sky was black. The waiter brought a copper burner and frypan.

'I ordered ahead . . . I thought a crepe suzette might help,' murmured Iris. They sat in silence as the waiter lit the burner and poured brandy into the pan.

*Clever Iris*, thought Stevie darkly, *stopping our conversation with a judicious choice of dessert.*

The flaming dish was finally served and the waiter retreated.

'Can I visit him at least?' Stevie asked, leaning forward.

Iris shook her head. 'No one is allowed to see him. He can barely speak.'

Stevie swallowed her frustration and asked her next question. 'Did he send me this brooch?'

Iris nodded. 'He asked me to arrange it . . . he didn't want you to suffer.'

'He didn't want me to suffer . . .' Stevie's anger was rising now. 'And Henning didn't think that believing he had died for me in a bullring, then finding out he had come back to life with terrible injuries, and then being told that I was not allowed to visit him or speak to him or even know where he is because people are after him wouldn't upset me?' She took a breath and a swallow of the brandy that the waiter had poured into a balloon glass. 'Iris, I don't know what to think. It's as if everything I ever knew about Henning was actually nothing.'

The truth of what she had just said hit Stevie. Henning had always been mysterious, and she had made up her mind that she could deal with that, and that he would reveal his secrets little by little. But she had never imagined that his secrets would be so dark or so frightening; the reality of it was far from the fantasy and it was all too much. Stevie put her glass down, tears welling in her eyes. She fought them back and said slowly, 'The Henning I knew died for me in that bullring in Spain. This other Henning, with his deep secrets and his lies, is a stranger to me. You can tell him that next time you see him.'

Iris reached out and took Stevie's hand. 'You can't mean that, Stevie. You know the real Henning like no one else. He is still the same man. He loves you.'

Stevie looked away, not wanting to cry. The rain outside would do it for her.

'What happened in that bullring?' Iris asked gently.

And it all flashed back to her in a blinding instant.

*How could she have forgotten?*

The thrust that made her lose her balance, the tiny movement that had shoved her world off its orbit. Skorpios had pushed her. She was sure of it. He had reached out as if to help her but he knew what he was doing. He had shoved the bolt to the gate open and pushed her into the bullring; Henning had leapt in to save her. Henning had been gored because of that push, that bad hand with the scorpion ring, that man.

Suddenly she did not know whom to trust. Until she discovered what and whom Henning was running from, she would keep all truths to herself. As Iris had said, it was safer that way. 'I fell,' she said simply. 'Thank you for lunch, Iris, but now I must go.'

She rose and left the rich panelled room, holding her shoulders back and her head high, bracing her body against the shock of what she had just learnt. As she stepped outside the front door, she realised she didn't know where she was going so she stood under the cover of one of the rounded awnings and breathed in the rainy air, trying to decide on her next move. Two men were walking across the slick square towards her, the man furthest from her holding a large black umbrella. They wore dark suits and the wrong shoes for this sort of weather. Stevie could not see their faces but as they passed her, the man closest to Stevie turned his face towards her. She started: Aristo. He stopped, also surprised to see her.

'*Bonjour*,' he said softly. He was holding a Gitane between his thumb and forefinger.

'*Bonjour*,' she replied. '*Même le ciel pleure*,' she added with a small shrug, not knowing how much she should say in front of his companion.

'Even the sky is weeping,' he agreed, still staring at her.

Aristo's companion glanced at his watch. '*Nous allors être en retard, Aristo*,' he grumbled.

'*Je vais te rejoinder plus tard, Armand*. I have unfinished business here.'

The man shrugged and left, taking his umbrella with him. Aristo made no move to step out of the rain and into the entrance where Stevie was sheltering. Searching his face, Stevie saw that pain had changed him. The sense of indestructibility that came with youth, and that had clothed the Aristo she had known aboard the *Hercules*, was gone.

'Why don't you come out of the rain?' she said gently.

Aristo stepped under cover and pulled out his phone. *'Je suis au Ritz, s'il vous plaît, Helena.'* Then he hung up and turned to Stevie. 'Will you come with me?'

Stevie nodded. Of course she would. It seemed like it was the only thing in the world she could do. They stared out at the rain and the darkening streets in silence. Two minutes later, a navy blue Mercedes pulled up. A rather beautiful female chauffeur in a cap got out with an umbrella and opened the back door.

They crossed the streets of the city in the heavy car, Stevie cracking the window to catch the smell of soot and bread and newsprint and electricity—now mixed with rain—that was the scent of Paris. Aristo was silent and Stevie felt no need to talk. As they drove up the Champs-Élysées, she wondered what he wanted . . . They took a left turn just before the Arc de Triomphe, and stopped in front of a classic honey-stone Parisian building with a glossy black door. They got out and walked up three deserted flights of marble stairs to double doors. Aristo opened the doors and let Stevie pass into the flat without a word.

Inside was an *enfilade* of rooms, parquet floors, moulded ceilings, white-panelled walls, gathering dust. Stevie caught a glimpse of her reflection in a vast gilded mirror as they entered the sitting room, her face terribly pale, her eyes, lined with kohl, somehow too large. On the floor sat about twenty cardboard boxes, most still sealed, piled one upon the other. Aristo gestured to Stevie to sit on a pile and did the same himself.

'I'm so sorry, Aristo,' she murmured.

He did not reply but made a gesture with his hand. 'We were to live here,' he said finally. 'She was to have had anything she wanted, and we would have been happy.' He disappeared into the kitchen and came back with a champagne bottle, Roederer. From an open box full of tissue paper, Aristo fished out a beautiful silver fish knife and slit open another box beside him. All the boxes were full of china and silver, Stevie realised, exquisite objects that had now become the detritus of lives unlived. The pile of cardboard was a monument.

From the second box, Aristo took two perfect crystal flutes, delicately etched with flowers. 'If you don't object,' he murmured, removing the wire basket from the cork. 'An uncle of mine used to say, "When you drink champagne, you drink the tears of the world." I think it is appropriate, don't you?'

Stevie nodded. 'I do,' she replied quietly.

Aristo's eyes locked onto hers as he handed her a full glass. 'You lost your lover too,' he said simply, placing the beading bottle on the floor.

Stevie felt her whole body tremble, then settle. It was true. She nodded and accepted a cigarette, inclining her head slightly towards the flame burning on Aristo's silver lighter.

'Then we understand each other.'

He slipped the lighter back into his pocket and looked at her again, as if trying to make up his mind about something. Stevie was taken aback by the power of his stare. She had to remind herself that Aristo was only twenty-one . . . But then, Marlena had not been an ordinary woman either and she had chosen this boy. His strength should not have surprised her. Stevie surrendered and let him look, not repelling the attention but rather letting it move over her, see through her. As she sat, she found anger growing to replace the tree of sorrow and confusion. Anger first—irrationally?—at Henning, then fury at Skorpios, who had made everything die.

'Are you sure it was your father?' she asked carefully.

'I know it was my father.' Aristo drew sharply on his cigarette. 'There is no doubt in anyone's mind. And now all that is left for me is to do what is just.'

His words chilled her, but she could not fault him. For a father to do that to his son was to flout the laws of nature, of basic humanity. And both of them knew it was a wrong that would never be addressed in any court of law. In Aristo's eyes, the murder of his bride was a crime beyond law.

'He pushed me,' Stevie said, staring at the unused fireplace with its ornate marble frame. 'That afternoon at the *corrida*—you were there.'

'I thought the gate broke, you lost your balance.'

Stevie shook her head. 'Your father reached out his hand. I thought he wanted to help me, but he shoved the gate open and pressed me backwards. He wanted to kill me too.'

Aristo stubbed out his cigarette on the corner of a cardboard box and looked at Stevie. For a long time he said nothing. When he spoke, his eyes were on the window. The raindrops lashing against the pane sounded like a snare drum.

'I don't think it was you he was trying to kill,' he said finally. 'He had no reason to.'

'What do you mean?' Stevie's mind raced, and then in a flash of clarity she saw it. 'He wanted to kill Henning, didn't he?' she asked.

Aristo reached for another cigarette.

'He knew,' Stevie cried. 'He knew Henning would jump into the ring to save me, knew the bull would go for him. And I gave him the perfect opportunity, leaning against that little gate like a fool.' She stared wildly at Aristo. 'But why? Why would he want to do that?'

Aristo studied her for a moment. 'You don't know, Stevie?'

'Know what?' she replied quickly, her heart in her mouth.

'Henning was a spy.'

Outside, an angry driver leant on his horn; the rain kept

coming. Stevie suddenly felt sick. She had always known there was something mysterious about Henning, that there was more to the man than his job as a cataloguer of rare books—but Aristo's revelation cast a shadow far blacker than she had ever expected. Her broken arm was aching and she rubbed her shoulder. It made perfect sense, of course. Men like Henning—with access, contacts and legitimate reasons for asking all sorts of questions—were often recruited to the secret service . . . Stevie assumed British, but it could have been any of them, and it didn't really matter which . . . It explained his sudden appearances and disappearances, his encyclopaedic knowledge of guns, his seemingly endless and unorthodox list of 'friends', his evasiveness. But how had she, Stevie Duveen—experienced troubleshooter, assessor of risks, possessor of an unerring instinct—not seen it? She could never bind her life to that of a spy. The world of espionage was too full of darkness and deception. She had met too many spies to trust their kind. They were shifting waters and unknowable quantities and flashes of sunlight on glass. Not the sort of men you let into your heart.

Stevie turned away. Skorpios had obviously found out Henning's secret; most likely he himself had been one of Henning's targets. Men of his kind attracted that sort of attention, and governments always needed information on individuals of influence.

Leaning forward, Aristo said softly, 'I want revenge and I want you to help me.'

Stevie examined the young man. 'Why would you ask me?'

'You have motive. And—' he sought her eyes now '—Angelina told me about you, and what you did on the cruise ship. She said it was a secret, but that you do things . . . discreetly. She would never have told me, she said, if not for Marlena's murder; it shifted the paradigm of promises. That's how she put it to me.'

Stevie did not reply. Could she trust Aristo? Was *he* what he appeared to be? She had just learnt that she could no longer trust herself to know . . . Doubts swirled in her mind and the floor felt like it was falling away.

She took a deep, slow breath to steady herself then looked up: '*Sangue lava sangue*,' she said softly. She had meant it as a question but her voice failed to find the motivation to rise at the end and it came out as a statement: *Blood washes blood.*

There was a long pause as the words hung in the air, irrevocable now that they had been spoken—set free—forcing the two of them to acknowledge what they were really saying.

It was Aristo who broke the silence. 'I don't want to kill my father, Stevie.' He said it simply, lightly, as if it were the polite refusal of a small dessert. 'When I was a boy, he used to call me into his study and read me passages from Machiavelli—and he always came back to the passage that asked: is it better to be loved or feared?' Aristo shrugged and almost smiled. 'Perhaps he was trying to explain why he couldn't love me more.'

Stevie shut her eyes briefly in acknowledgment; she knew the passage.

Aristo went on. 'You know, of course, Machiavelli's answer: one would like to be both the one and the other, etcetera etcetera, but it is far safer to be feared than loved. To this end, my father is ruthless in his business deals, and prizes the reputation he has cultivated because of this. People fear him and this is the most important thing in the world to him. Isn't that why he killed Marlena?' Aristo's foot, rubbing against the side of the cardboard box, was the only thing that gave away the tension burning inside the young man. 'Stevie, the thing my father fears beyond anything in the world— and I include death here—is to be made ridiculous. This he could not bear. I want you to help me make his worst nightmare come true.'

Stevie noticed that, even when he stopped frowning, the furrow in Aristo's brow left a permanent shadow across his forehead. Her heart suddenly leapt for him, the wounded boy, the mirror of her own sorrow. She could believe in that.

Stevie did not know who she was crying for anymore when she downed the last of the champagne: for Aristo and Marlena and their obliterated future; for Henning and his bravery and his terrible injuries; for Henning and his betrayal and the end of their love; for herself and the death of the hope which had grown in her foolish heart. She decided then that Skorpios would pay for what he had done. Whatever she might feel about Henning now, she owed him that much.

## ACKNOWLEDGEMENTS

**I am grateful to Sophie** Edelstein, Rosie Garthwaite and Sam Swire for sharing their expertise with me. My brothers, Jason and Daniel, are always an inspiration, as are my parents, Michael and Manuela, who provide support, encouragement, and ideas—*grazie*! Fran Moore at Curtis Brown deserves another great big thankyou, as do Jane Palfreyman, Ann Lennox, Ali Lavau and the rest of the team at Allen & Unwin. Finally, a massive thankyou to my husband Nick, who always believes.